TRAUMA AND TRUTH

TEACHING RUSSIAN LITERATURE ON THE CHECHEN WARS

TRAUMA AND TRUTH

TEACHING RUSSIAN LITERATURE ON THE CHECHEN WARS

ELENA PEDIGO CLARK

BOSTON
2023

Library of Congress Cataloging-in-Publication Data

Names: Clark, Elena Pedigo, 1979- author.
Title: Trauma and truth : teaching Russian literature on the Chechen wars / Elena Pedigo Clark.
Other titles: Teaching Russian literature on the Chechen wars
Description: Boston : Academic Studies Press, [2023] | Includes bibliographical references.
Identifiers: LCCN 2022027886 (print) | LCCN 2022027887 (ebook) | ISBN 9781644694268 (hardback) | ISBN 9781644694275 (adobe pdf) | ISBN 9781644694282 (epub)
Subjects: LCSH: Chechni͡a (Russia)--History--Civil War, 1994---Study and teaching (Higher) | Chechni͡a (Russia)--History--Civil War, 1994---Literature and the war. | Psychic trauma in literature.
Classification: LCC DK511.C37 C63 2023 (print) | LCC DK511.C37 (ebook) | DDC 947.5/208600711--dc23/eng/20220616
LC record available at https://lccn.loc.gov/2022027886
LC ebook record available at https://lccn.loc.gov/2022027887

ISBN 9781644694268 (hardback)
ISBN 9781644694275 (adobe pdf)
ISBN 9781644694282 (epub)

Book design by Lapiz Digital Services.

Cover design by Ivan Grave.
On the cover: a still from Alexei Uchitel's 2008 film *Captive* (Plennyi).

Published by Academic Studies Press.
1577 Beacon Street
Brookline, MA 02446, USA
press@academicstudiespress.com
www.academicstudiespress.com

Contents

The war was the main thing we had to do in our life and we did it. The brightest, best thing in my life was the war and there won't be anything better. And the blackest, lousiest thing in my life was also the war, and there won't be anything worse. So my life has been lived.

—Arkady Babchenko, *One Soldier's War*

Introduction

> The first and second Chechen wars murdered Russian democracy in its cradle, for when the cannons sing the people thirst for blood and opponents of government become traitors to the nation; elections lose their meaning and parliament ceases to be a place for discussion. Everything that has happened since then and all that is happening today is but a consequence of this war.
>
> —Dmitry Muratov, "The Chechen Wars Murdered Russian Democracy in Its Cradle"

"Chechnya? Is that, like, Czechoslovakia?"

It is easy to laugh when students, and not just students, say things like that, but it was not so funny when social media was flooded with a wave of anti-Czech sentiment following the 2013 Boston Marathon bombing, as reported in *TIME* magazine.[1] And it is not so funny when people are caught flat-footed by the popularity of the Donbass separatist movement amongst Russians, especially Chechen veterans, on the one hand, and the popularity of groups such as ISIS with fighters from Chechnya and other parts of the Caucasus, on the other.[2] The world ignores Chechnya and the experiences of those who participated in both sides of the war, at its peril.

This book is designed to serve two purposes. Firstly, to provide an overview of some of the most significant writing by Russian-language writers on the Chechen Wars, and give suggestions for incorporating it into a university

---

1 Charlie Campbell, "Czech Republic Forced to Remind the Internet that Chechnya Is in Different Country After Boston Bombing," *Time*, April 23, 2013, http://newsfeed.time.com/2013/04/23/czech-republic-forced-to-remind-the-internet-that-chechnya-is-a-different-country-after-boston-bombing/.

2 Neil MacFarquhar, "For Russia, Links Between Caucasus and ISIS Provoke Anxiety," *New York Times*, November 20, 2015, https://www.nytimes.com/2015/11/21/world/europe/for-russia-links-between-caucasus-and-isis-provoke-anxiety.html.

curriculum. The initial impetus for this project came from my students' requests for more information on Chechen War literature. When I discovered that there was almost no scholarship available on the subject, I decided that someone needed to step up and fill that gap, and that that someone should be me. I would like to offer my sincere thanks here to all my students for their questions, encouragement, and support for this project. Their involvement in our discussions of contemporary Russian culture and Russian war literature have made this book immeasurably richer. I should particularly thank Russian Honors student Logan Stinson for his help, including co-writing an article on Chechen War literature with me, as well as our numerous discussions of the situation of veterans and the repercussions in Russia and the West of the Global War on Terror.

This project has taken a number of twists and turns over the past four years, as have the fates of the authors included here. The four writers I settled on for this book, Anna Politkovskaya, Mikail Eldin, Arkady Babchenko, and Zakhar Prilepin, are all, while very different, award-winning authors of books that deal explicitly about the Chechen Wars and that draw on their direct experiences of those conflicts. Despite their differences in style, temperament, and political convictions, all four of them share an underlying preoccupation with bearing witness to these wars and sharing the truth. This overarching interest in the truth, despite their differing methods of presenting it and different representations of it, is the thread that ties these four writers together in my analysis.

When making my choice of what works to include, I by necessity had to discard a number of extremely worthy authors. Those who wish to read more literature on the contemporary Chechen Wars should not limit themselves to these works and writers discussed here: they are only the tip of the iceberg. A major work translated into English not included here is German Sadulaev's *I Am A Chechen!*,[3] a novel made up of a series of semi-autographical stories about being a Chechen civilian during the wars. Meanwhile, Russian-speakers can enjoy Aleksandr Karasyov's *Chechen Tales*,[4] a collection of stories about Russian soldiers during the wars; Vladislav Shurygin's *Letters of a Dead Captain*,[5] another collection of short stories; or Vladimir Makanin's novel *Asan*[6] or his *Caucasian*

---

3 *Я—чеченец!* in the original Russian. First published in 2006. English translation first published in 2010.
4 *Чеченские рассказы* in the original Russian. First published in 2008.
5 *Письма мёртвого капитана* in the original Russian. First published in 2005.
6 *Асан* in the original Russian. First published in 2008.

Captive,[7] a novella that was made into the film *Captive*[8] by Aleksey Uchitel in 2008. Karasëv's stories may be particularly well suited for advanced students of Russian language wishing to read works of contemporary war literature and build their military vocabulary, as they are compact, while also containing extensive military jargon.

There are also numerous works by veterans, mainly in Russian but occasionally in translation as well, available at Lib.ru's section on the Chechen Wars.[9] These stories may also be useful for advanced Russian students wishing to familiarize themselves with contemporary war writing and contemporary military vocabulary. I am sorry not to be able to write about all of them here, but for reasons of space I had to limit myself to the four authors I considered most important and representative.

When making my selections for this book, I chose to include works only by those who participated actively in the wars, and who are on some level writing the "literature of trauma." This consideration was motivated by the idea that one of the main reasons contemporary Chechen War literature is important resides in how it reflects the trauma of the post-Soviet experience, something that will be discussed in greater length in the analysis of each of the four authors, and in the conclusion.

Of the four authors I focus on here, Politkovskaya spent a considerable amount of time reporting from the war zone, and Eldin, Prilepin, and Babchenko all fought for their respective sides. In keeping with my focus on the depiction of trauma, I have elected to accept Kalí Tal's proposal that the literature of trauma is "defined by the identity of its author."[10] The question of whether only someone who has experienced war firsthand can understand what it is like and write about it appropriately is something that the authors discuss directly, and I will let them speak for themselves in their respective chapters. Although I believe that those of us in the rear can also contribute important insights, autobiographical writing about lived experience is one of the hallmarks of the current trend of war writing.[11] Furthermore, at a time when "fake news"

---

7 *Кавказский пленный* in the original Russian. First published in 1995. Available in English translation in the anthology *Captives: Contemporary Russian Stories*.

8 *Пленный* in the original Russian.

9 Lib.ru, *Chechenskaia voina*, http://www.lib.ru/MEMUARY/CHECHNYA/.

10 Kalí Tal, *Worlds of Hurt* (Cambridge: Cambridge University Press, 1996), 17.

11 For an argument against "combat gnosticism," or the belief that only those with direct experience of combat have the insider knowledge and moral authority to write about war, see James Campbell's "Combat Gnosticism: The Ideology of First World War Poetry Criticism" and David A. Buchanan's *Going Scapegoat: Post-9/11 War Literature, Language and Culture*. One should also bear in mind Dominick La Capra's warnings of the risk of either over- or

and misinformation have become a widespread scourge in public discourse, works grounded in real-world, personal experience provide a refreshing dose of realism, not to mention reality. This is particularly the case in Russia, where official accounts of these wars often do not line up with the observations of eyewitnesses. While eyewitness accounts are problematic in their own way, in this case they may be the most reliable thing we have in our search for the truth.

The second purpose of this book, as I touched on briefly above, is to present what I believe to be an illuminating perspective on contemporary Russian culture and society. I frequently teach First Year Seminars on that very topic, and I always include a lengthy section on the Chechen Wars, because without understanding them, as I explain to my students, it is impossible to understand what is going on today in Russia, as well as in Ukraine and Syria. At the time of writing Syria is still racked with strife and Russia has recently invaded Ukraine following an eight-year civil war in the Donbass. In each of these cases, veterans from both sides of the Chechen Wars have acted as key agents in perpetuating the conflict. Put simply: the last war in Chechnya may have ended officially in 2009, but it is still being fought over and over again, just on other battlegrounds, some of which are inside their victims' heads.

The personal trauma that the authors depict here is, I believe, mirrored on a grand scale in current Russian culture and politics. At the same time, the Chechen Wars can also be seen as a symptom of the overall trauma of the dissolution of the Soviet Union, and the trauma their participants experienced as a stand-in for the trauma of the Soviet people as a whole. So while I do not want to undermine or make light of the specific traumas of these authors and of the victims of the Chechen Wars, and nor do I want to overgeneralize, I do suggest that the Chechen Wars were not an aberration, but simply a very visible example of the broader destruction and trauma of the late 1990s and early 2000s. And while they were very much the result of specifically Russian and Soviet history, they were also part of the Global War on Terror. These authors, and the experiences they depict, therefore, also share much with the writers of works about the long-running wars in Iraq and Afghanistan.

In both cases, it may be tempting for civilians to blame combatants and veterans for their participation in these violent conflicts, and to see them as the bearers and creators of violence within their own societies. Instead, I would argue that combatants are simply the most visible symptoms of a sickness we all

---

under-identifying with trauma survivors, and of accepting survivor stories uncritically (*Writing History, Writing Trauma*, preface 2014). With those caveats in mind, however, I decided to focus on works that fell into the category of eyewitness accounts and the literature of trauma.

share: the sickness of war. Rather than fencing them off from the rest of society, I encourage readers to consider how veterans are an integral part of their society and a reflection of its good and evil sides, often in magnified form. As Elliot Ackerman remarks in a recent opinion piece in the *New York Times* about the film *Cherry* and the involvement of veterans in the January 6, 2021 storming of the US Capitol building, "right now America could use a work of art that tells us something about ourselves."[12] The former Soviet Union, I contend here, has numerous works of art that tell it a lot about itself. By studying literature about the Chechen Wars, we can learn a great deal about the former USSR and its successor countries, military and civilian aspects alike.

Politics loom large in this book. All the authors surveyed are or (prior to their untimely demise) were latter-day revolutionaries and actively involved in the current anti-Putin opposition movement. This is, I readily admit, problematic, since this book, like much Western writing on contemporary Russia, has a distinctly pro-opposition, anti-Putin bias, which may not capture the actual situation on the ground on Russia. However, it is also representative of the work available to the English-language reader and of an important trend in current Russian society.

Still, despite all predictions by Western academics, journalists, and politicians of its imminent demise, Vladimir Putin's rule of Russia is now entering its twenty-second year. This is intriguing, even if, for Putin's critics, alarming. But an even more alarming question might be: What would happen if the opposition succeeds in its aim of overthrowing Putin? What is the Russian political opposition like, what is Russian society like, and, after sowing this violent wind, what kind of whirlwind might be reaped? And most importantly, what can be done about it?

I don't have any easy answers to these questions, especially the last one, but I do believe that understanding is the first step on the journey. Western intellectual tastes might find most of the authors surveyed here unpalatable, with their devotion to Islam (Eldin), their outspoken support of libertarianism and militarism (Babchenko), or their hard left turn to a socialist nationalism that looks worryingly fascist (Prilepin). Nevertheless, empathy and understanding may be the best thing those of us on the outside have to offer them; at the very least, their stories can help us get inside their minds a little better. I discuss them here without political judgment, although I do argue that in these writers the grand tradition of Russian literature lives on. After all, Tolstoy and Dostoevsky

---

12 Elliot Ackerman, "My Veteran Problem," *New York Times*, February 12, 2021, https://www.nytimes.com/2021/02/12/opinion/veterans-Capitol-Cherry-film.html.

were fairly outspoken themselves. Russian literature that wasn't out on the edge wouldn't be Russian literature, and, if nothing else, it is heartening to see that tradition continue.

The subtitle of this book implicitly asks what, exactly, Russian literature is. Soviet literature is fairly easy to pin down, but how much of Soviet literature should count as "Russian"? And what about post-Soviet literature, when many of its authors may or may not be ethnically Russian, may or may not hold a Russian passport, but are heirs to the Russian literary tradition and write in Russian nonetheless?

This is an especially vexing question for this particular study. While all the texts included here were originally written in Russian, not all of them have been published in Russian. *The Sky Wept Fire* is available only in an English version, while *One Soldier's War* is different in each of its translations. Furthermore, one of the authors included here is from a breakaway republic that was willing to go to war in order to gain its independence from Russia, and the author even took up arms in service of that cause.

It is both ironic and tragic that Eldin, the Chechen author included here, does not live in Chechnya and writes in Russian. Indeed, he is perhaps the most consciously aware that he is writing in the Russian and Soviet literary tradition, and peppers his works with references to "the Russians" such as Tolstoy. The question of why he might do this, and what effect it produces, will be explored in greater detail in the relevant chapter. For now, I will simply say that, despite their tortured and complex relationships with Russia—and all the authors discussed here have a complicated, contradictory, painful relationship with Russia—I consider all these authors to be, if not always "Russian," writers of Russian literature.[13]

This book also addresses the question of what literature itself is. Multiple forms are reviewed here. Anna Politkovskaya was a journalist who wrote newspaper articles and nonfiction essays, Mikail Eldin and Arkady Babchenko are also journalists who wrote impressionistic memoirs about their experiences in the wars, while Zakhar Prilepin is a former journalist who writes fiction based on his own life experiences.

The difficulty of defining literature is compounded when we come to contemporary writing. We have to decide on the fly what is "important" and what is not. When studying older literature—say, from the Soviet and pre-Soviet

13 For an in-depth examination of Caucasus literature about the resistance to Russian colonialism over the last two hundred years, see Rebecca Gould's *Writers and Rebels: The Literature of Insurgency in the Caucasus*.

periods—it is easy to pick out the important authors. New, previously ignored authors may be discovered, but the canon is pretty well set. But when we come to the present, we are tasked with creating the canon ourselves, which proves to be no easy task. On top of traditional print publishing, there is a dizzying quantity of online journalism, blogging, and self-publishing, all of which can blend together into an amorphous mass, much of it low quality but, particularly in an increasingly censored society such as Russia's, also an outlet for creative, unique, and oppositional voices.

A significant advantage to studying contemporary writing, however, is our unmediated access to the authors themselves. In fact, the seed of what would become this book was planted from meeting Babchenko when he came to give a reading at the University of North Carolina–Chapel Hill while I was working on my PhD there. Whenever possible, I have interviewed the authors themselves, as well as their translators. All of the living authors (Babchenko, Eldin, and Prilepin) were gracious in answering my questions and contributing to my understanding of the material. I offer a special thanks to Eldin, who Skyped into my classes to answer questions and also worked individually with students who chose to do their final projects on his book. Anna Gunin, Eldin's translator, also provided some very enlightening observations about the process of translating his book. Nick Allen, Babchenko's translator and a war correspondent himself, was also very helpful, answering my questions as well as Skyping into one of my classes and discussing his translation with students, as well as journalism and war more broadly. Finally, John Crowfoot, the translator of Politkovskaya's *A Dirty War*, obligingly answered all my questions about the work and its publication.

Studying living authors gives us the opportunity to see their work and political positions develop in real time. This is especially the case for Prilepin and Babchenko, who are active on social media. They use it as a platform to express their thoughts and ideas, many of which are not welcomed either by the Russian authorities or the West. Prilepin, in particular, has been involved in the current conflict in Eastern Ukraine in a way that may make many Westerners squeamish and want to throw him out of the potential canon immediately, even though he is the most popular and well regarded of these writers within Russia and Russian literary culture itself. This leads to more questions. Do we in the West canonize someone who was a member of the National Bolshevik Party before taking up arms in support of the Donetsk People's Republic? What about someone who was a member of the Chechen resistance, such as Eldin? And if we refuse to consider authors meritorious because of their political convictions and actions, how are we any different than the Russian authorities, which many of these authors speak out against?

Indeed, none of the authors is excessively friendly to any power structure, and all of them, both directly through their words and indirectly through their actions, challenge the reader to consider what is "right" and what is not. There are no easy answers here, no clear-cut divisions between right and wrong. The Chechen Wars were a moral quagmire, and everyone who got sucked into them got their hands dirty. The only one of these writers to emerge with a reasonably clean conscience was Politkovskaya, who is the closest we have to a heroic figure and canonical writer amongst the bunch.

However, she was certainly not in the business of providing her readers with easy answers, instead demanding that they rise to the occasion; and she was critical of all the actors involved, including Western NGOs, whom she accused of anti-Russian bias, self-serving aggrandizement, and plain old incompetence. No one gets away scot-free in Politkovskaya's writing; no wrongdoer is safe from criticism. Her articles will shake up anyone who reads them, and enrage anyone trying to get away with what they shouldn't.

And this is another one of the reasons why I chose these particular authors to include in *Trauma and Truth*. They all come to the Chechen Wars from different directions and treat their subject matter in different ways; they are all have a truth to tell and they are all determined to tell that truth no matter what, and hopefully shake up a few readers in the process. None of the works included here are "light reading"; none of them will leave the reader indifferent. The reader may turn away in horror or rail against the author, the wars, or fate itself, in response to the stories told here, but they are unlikely to forget what they've read. All these authors' works are shocking, and deliberately so, but they are more than mere "shock-fiction," designed to elicit an immediate response and nothing more. All these authors knew that they had important stories to tell, and they were determined to tell them and share their experience and their truth with the world, whatever the world thought about that. To do so, they borrowed from their own lives and from the formidable arsenal of literary technique that an education in Russian literature had given them.

The results are stories that are brutal yet vulnerable, heartfelt yet detached, outraged yet accepting, and beautiful in their unflinching portrayal of the most horrifying of human actions: all-out war. Taken together, these works suggest an emerging genre, or a new twist on a genre Russian writers have been writing for a century or more: the war confessional, the hybrid war memoir/novel, war reporting that is really anti-war reporting. Reminiscent, sometimes more consciously, sometimes less, of earlier Russian war stories and tales of the Caucasus such as *A Hero of Our Time*, *Hadji Murat*, and *Red Cavalry Tales*, these works nonetheless provide their own take on war. War is not just a senseless waste of time or the outcome of the untraceable workings of history, as Tolstoy would have it: war is Evil with a capital E, and modern warfare is the mass destruction of human lives with weapons that wreak havoc on an unimaginable scale, and all to no purpose. The apocalypse has arrived, and it has arrived in the form of tanks, mines, machine guns, and aerial bombardments, all unleashed to no particular purpose or benefit other than to terrorize people and put money in the pockets of those standing far off on the sidelines. Even those who maintain their physical integrity—read: who are not blown to pieces—in the face of this superhuman horror, struggle to maintain their psychic integrity. The result is that months or years later, these surviving witnesses struggle to put together coherent accounts of what they witnessed, producing instead disjointed fragments as they sweep together their shattered memories and attempt to reassemble them into something can be shared with an audience.

Perhaps one day the Chechen Wars will have their massive, sweeping epics, comparable to Tolstoy's *War and Peace* about the Napoleonic Wars, Mikhail Sholokhov's *And Quiet Flows the Don* about World War I and the Russian Civil War, or Vasily Grossman's duology *Stalingrad* and *Life and Fate* about World War II, but that day has not yet arrived. Instead, we are still trying to pick up the pieces and put together something that looks even vaguely like sense. The wars still seem more like a bad dream, one that can't be shaken off upon waking, than historical facts, and the literature on them presents them as such. The result is a truth that is deeply felt and deeply personal for each author here, even as they try to share their experiences with the rest of us.

A Note on Transliteration and Citation

In general, I have used the Library of Congress transliteration system for all Russian names here. The exception are names and titles that are already commonly used in English. I have chosen to follow common English usage for the place names Chechnya, Grozny, and Khasavyurt. Anna Politkovskaya, Arkady Babchenko, Alexei Navalny, Aleksey Uchitel, and *Novaya Gazeta* have already been published in English under those spellings, and so I have chosen to retain those spellings in this book to avoid confusion.

The geopolitical tensions resulting in and from the Russian invasion of Ukraine in February 2022 meant that, as this book was going to press, a number of the websites and videos I used as sources during the original research phase were either taken down or blocked to visitors from within the United States. It is my hope that the situation will ameliorate soon and that future readers will be able to access these useful resources again.

The Structure of This Book

This book begins with a brief historical background to the Chechen Wars and a short overview of the theory of the "literature of trauma" and some of its key works. That is followed by the four main chapters, each dedicated to a different author and a key text by them. I have chosen to begin with a chapter on Politkovskaya, followed by Eldin, then Babchenko, and then Prilepin. This sequence follows the increase in what I believe is the relative difficulty of the texts. Because each text is highly fragmented and nonlinear, which I argue is representative of the trauma the authors and/or the nation they represent has experienced, I include detailed analyses of the central texts in order to reconstruct the narratives and show how this seeming disconnected, fragmentary style serves the author's overall purpose. And although I do tie the works in this book to the theoretical approaches I use, primarily those regarding the literature of trauma but also theories of gender where appropriate, I always attempt to make the text itself central, and allow it to speak for itself.

Politkovskaya's journalistic articles are written in a straightforward style and are easy to understand, although readers may find it challenging to reconcile the sometimes seemingly contradictory positions she takes. I have taught a variety of Politkovskaya's works in several courses, and students generally find them the most approachable of the texts I use about the Chechen Wars. In the chapter dedicated to her I give a close reading of *A Dirty War,* her first collection of articles on Chechnya published in English, and provide some suggestions for how to interpret the apparent contradictions of her work. I reference in particular the concept of a feminine "ethics of care" as an alternative philosophical, moral, and political stance to the more standard masculine "ethics of rights" or "ethics of logic."

Eldin's background as both a journalist and a poet comes through in his impressionistic memoir. It contains strongly journalistic elements, especially at the beginning, and presents the events he describes largely in chronological order. However, it focuses more on his subjective experiences and internal states than it does on objective facts, and becomes increasingly figurative and poetic. It is also markedly influenced by Sufism and presents a non-Western, non-Christian worldview. This can make it somewhat difficult but also rewarding for English-language readers more used to reading Western literature. I have taught it myself in courses on contemporary war literature; and learned that students find it simultaneously engaging and challenging. In the chapter here, I provide what I believe is an illuminating interpretation of the text by discussing how the psychological states Eldin describes can be seen as representative of severe trauma. Because his memoir is often impressionistic and nonlinear, I provide an overview of what happens in the text and give in-depth analyses of his use of pronouns, different points of view, and metaphors and figurative language to portray his psychological experiences and ethical ideas.

Babchenko is also a journalist, and his memoir includes a number of articles he has written. Although his writing style is in some ways more straightforward than Eldin's, the actual structure of the book is complex and can be very challenging for readers. I provide an analysis of the structure and tie its fragmented nature to the effects of trauma and PTSD, something Babchenko has been outspoken about throughout his career. I also discuss his subversion of gender roles and the conventions of the war memoir, and show how mythology appears in this seemingly hyperrealist, gritty book. I have used *One Soldier's War* several times for introductory courses on Russian war literature and on contemporary Russian culture and society, and highly recommend it as an engaging and thought-provoking work.

I end with Prilepin. While he has also worked as a journalist, Prilepin's most significant writing is his fiction, albeit of a heavily autobiographical kind. Although some of his works have been translated into English, I focus mainly on his debut novel, *Pathologies* (*Патологии* [*Patologii*]), which has yet to be made available in English. I therefore finish with a work that would be suitable for graduate-level seminars with readings in Russian, in order to give both a fuller picture of the literature on the Chechen Wars, and to present possible reading ideas for teaching the topic on various levels. In my discussion of *Pathologies*, I provide an analysis of its narrative structure, with its circular pattern and extensive use of flashbacks and flash-forwards. I also make use of both the theory of trauma and questions of gender, which brings the analysis of *Pathologies* back full circle to that of Politkovskaya.

Finally, I conclude with some possible takeaways from these works for understanding contemporary Russian culture, politics, and society. These takeaways are deliberately broad and provocative, designed to stimulate discussion and debate.

1

A Brief Historical Background

> The roots of the conflict dig deep. Long before they came to fight a guerrilla war with Russia at the end of the twentieth century, the Chechens were the most rebellious people in the Russian empire.
>
> —Gall and de Waal, *Chechnya: Calamity in the Caucasus*

Officially, the first of the two Chechen Wars that racked Russia during the 1990s and early 2000s started in the dying days of 1994. But their origins stretch back much farther than that.

In the eighteenth and nineteenth centuries, the Russian Empire was eagerly expanding in every direction it could. An especially prized commodity was a warm-water port, a need which sent generations of autocrats and generals questing south, towards the Black Sea. Inconveniently, the people of the Caucasus stood in the way.

The Caucasus is a mountainous region between the Black Sea and the Caspian, populated by a diverse group of non-Slavic peoples, all of whom needed to be subjugated in the name of Russian expansion and progress. The Chechens were the largest and most warlike of the nations that fell under the sights of Russia's army. Furthermore, by the time they came into conflict with Russia, they had converted to Sufism, which they had melded with their own native traditions to create a unique but still Muslim culture. All the elements were set up for a clash of civilizations, especially once the charismatic Imam Shamil began preaching resistance to the Russians and a strict adherence to Sharia law. His resistance was successful for a time; his attempts to make Chechens more mainstream and observant Muslims, less so. And eventually he was forced to surrender and

Chechnya became another province in imperial Russia, although Chechens always chafed under their forced unification with their conqueror.

With the advent of the Soviet Union, there was a brief period of hope for increased Chechen independence, as Lenin promoted a policy of comparative autonomy and ethnic pride amongst the non-Russian territories. Stalin, despite, or maybe because of, being Georgian himself, took a much harder line against ethnic minorities in general and Chechens in particular, culminating in the 1944 deportation of half a million Chechens to Kazakhstan, including Red Army soldiers serving on the front against the Nazis.

This action, as well as decimating the populace—more than one hundred thousand Chechens died of hunger, cold, and illness during and immediately after the deportation—served to further harden Chechen hearts against Russia and the Soviet Union. When the USSR began to break up and the non-Russian republics declared their independence, Chechnya did the same, despite being a region of Russia, not a separate republic. This led to a peculiar situation that lasted for three years, from 1991 to 1994, when Chechnya styled itself as an independent country, under the leadership of former Soviet general Dzhokhar Dudaev, while its citizens still used the ruble and their old Soviet passports. Consumed with other, bigger, problems, Moscow largely ignored this problem, perhaps hoping it would go away on its own.

Instead, it escalated. By 1994 Dudaev was unpopular in Grozny, and Boris Yeltsin, Russia's first post-Soviet president, was no less unpopular in Moscow. Both were strong and flamboyant personalities, and the two men were on a collision course. In November of 1994 the Armed Opposition, an anti-Dudaev resistance group funded and armed by Moscow, attempted to stage a coup in Grozny. They failed, but the following month Russia itself decided to take Grozny.

The invasion and first battle of Grozny was a shambles from the Russian perspective, as was the entire conflict. Some generals refused to participate in the campaign, instead resigning or being forcibly retired. Others fought more or less willingly, but the assault was unplanned and uncoordinated, and instead of capturing Grozny in a few hours and stamping out Chechen pretensions to independence, as was expected, large numbers of Russian troops were killed by a handful of lightly armed Chechen irregulars, and a protracted and bloody civil war was on.

The de facto loss of the war by one of the largest armies in the world to a small number of guerrilla fighters is impossible to understand without understanding just what a mess Russia was in the mid-1990s. Yeltsin was only tenuously holding onto power, many workers were not being paid regularly, and basic social services were spotty at best, with people who had once believed they belonged to the greatest nation on earth being forced to beg on street corners for crusts of bread. The Russian troops, especially the teenage conscripts, were poorly equipped, poorly trained, and often hungry. The practice of *dedovshchina*, an especially brutal form of hazing, was destroying not just morale but lives, as new recruits died or committed suicide as a result of it. And the war in Chechnya was deeply unpopular, and triggered a level of lawlessness within the Russian military that Westerners often have a hard time even comprehending: desertion, often on a large scale; mothers going down to the front, which, after all, was inside their own country, and dragging their sons home; Russians taking up arms for the Chechens, out of either political or mercenary motives; and Russian soldiers selling their own weaponry to Chechen rebels, even though those very bullets might be shot back at them the next day. When Chechen forces recaptured Grozny in August 1996 and essentially forced Russia to sue for peace, it seemed like Russia's military star had set once and for all, and Chechnya had finally achieved its longed-for independence.

Unfortunately for Chechnya, that was not the case. The Khasavyurt Accords, which officially ended the war, left Chechnya's exact situation vis-à-vis Russia up in the air. It was still a semi-rogue state that was neither fully independent nor a real part of Russia. Worse than that, instead of rebuilding after the war, Chechnya collapsed into corruption and crime. Following the ill-fated invasion of Dagestan by Chechen warlord Shamil Basaev in the summer of 1999, and a series of terrorist bombings within Russia in the fall that were blamed on Chechen terrorists (the actual identity of those responsible remains in question), Russians were much more supportive of a second war, a situation compounded by the eagerness of veterans of the first war to return to the one place they felt truly at home: the front line.

The second war, which began in the fall of 1999 and stretched on for the next decade, was in some ways even worse than the first. Having learnt from their earlier failure, and taking a page out of US military tactics used against their fellow Orthodox Slavs, the Serbs, during the NATO bombing of Belgrade in the spring and summer of 1999, Russian forces were much more ruthless this time around, aggressively bombing populated areas with planes and artillery before sending in ground troops. This effectively ended the most active aspect of the war by the summer of 2000, but did not stop the killing. Chechen forces responded with a series of terrorist attacks and suicide bombings, the most infamous being the 2002 hostage crisis at the Dubrovka theater,[1] and the 2004

1 On October 23, 2002, a group of approximately fifty Chechen separatists, led by Movsar Baraev, took the performers and audience of the popular musical *Nord-Ost* hostage. The

hostage crisis at the school in Beslan.[2] Both caused high numbers of civilian casualties, including large numbers of children, and although Russian forces themselves bear a considerable amount of the blame for the high casualties, the actions of the hostage-takers and suicide bombers turned popular opinion both in Russia and in a post-9/11 West against the Chechens. The second war disintegrated into a series of terrorist incidents on the Chechen side, and brutal cleansing operations on the Russian side, which dragged on for years. Matthew Evangelista's description, delivered back in 2002, of a Chechnya plagued with a "motley mix of warlords and criminal gangs," while the Russian side was characterized by an "undisciplined array of police, army, and interior ministry units, responsible for looting and terrorizing the civilian population,"[3] continued and in many ways continues to hold true, over a decade after the war has technically ended.

Officially the war is generally considered to have been over by 2008-9, but the region remains plagued with violence, and Chechen citizens have been convicted of a series of high-profile contract killings, including that of opposition politician Boris Nemtsov and Anna Politkovskaya herself. And the dictatorship of Ramzan Kadyrov,[4] the pro-Kremlin current president of Chechnya, has squandered whatever shreds of goodwill the West may have harbored towards Chechnya as a beleaguered and oppressed nation with his numerous alleged human rights abuses, one of the most recent and alarming being the campaign that began in 2017 and continued until at least 2019 to detain and torture men

---

hostage crisis lasted fifty-seven hours, after which the theater was stormed by Russian special forces who used a powerful sleeping gas to render everyone in the theater unconscious. Tragically, they did not provide adequate supplies of the antidote or proper medical treatment to those affected; as a result, not only were all the hostage-takers killed during the storming operation, but over one hundred hostages were as well.

2 On September 1, 2004, Chechen separatists under the control of Shamil Basaev (although he did not participate in the action directly) seized a school in Beslan, North Ossetia, during the "First Bell" ceremony celebrating the beginning of the school year. Nearly twelve hundred people were taken hostage, the majority of them children and even babies. After three days, Russian troops stormed the school. 331 hostages were killed during the storming, more than half of them children.

3 Matthew Evangelista, *The Chechen Wars: Will Russia Go the Way of the Soviet Union?* (Washington, DC: Brookings Institution Press, 2002), 198.

4 The Kadyrov family fought against the Russians during the first war, but then changed sides during the second war. Ramzan's father, Akhmat-Hadji, who was also a target of Politkovskaya's criticism, was president until he was assassinated on May 9, 2004. Ramzan essentially inherited the post, although he did not officially become president until 2007, and has become one of the most powerful and influential figures in the Putin administration.

suspected of being gay.[5] Grozny has been rebuilt from the ruins to which it was reduced in the early 2000s, but what is happening there gives most observers little reason for hope that there will be a genuine renaissance of Chechen culture, or a flourishing of Chechnya as a unique Islamic, and yet European, nation.

These are pessimistic conclusions, but that does not mean we can shy away from them. The Chechen Wars and their aftermath are anything but pretty. And yet, even terrible events can lead to good things. While what happened and continues to happen in Chechnya was a tragedy that nothing can justify, it also led to many examples of courage, heroism, and human goodness, and it pushed some of its witnesses to produce significant works of literature. We owe it to them and to ourselves to examine them without flinching, and appreciate them for what they are.

---

5 Human Rights Watch, "Russia: New Anti-Gay Crackdown in Chechnya," May 8, 2019, https://www.hrw.org/news/2019/05/08/russia-new-anti-gay-crackdown-chechnya.

2

The Literature of Trauma

> Literature of trauma is written from the need to tell and retell the story of the traumatic experience, to make it "real" both to the victim and to the community. Such writing serves both as validation and cathartic vehicle for the traumatized author.
>
> —Kalí Tal, *The Literature of Trauma*

Given the highly traumatic nature of the twentieth and now twenty-first centuries, it is perhaps surprising how little the literature of trauma has been studied, especially the Russian literature of trauma. Perhaps the extreme pain of the experiences it chronicles, and the fact that they are still within living memory, pushes people away. However, there are several excellent studies of trauma and the literature around it, and I have used them, combined with close readings of the works I discuss, as my theoretical basis for much of this book. A short description of some of the key works on the literature of trauma and their points is below.

A foundational work in the modern study of trauma is Judith Herman's *Trauma and Recovery: The Aftermath of Violence—From Domestic Abuse to Political Terror*, first published in 1992. In it Herman outlines key features of trauma and post-traumatic stress disorder, and describes parallels between the experiences and behaviors of domestic violence victims and combat veterans.

Drawing on both interviews with trauma survivors and literary accounts of trauma, particularly the writing of Vietnam veteran Tim O'Brien, Herman describes three basic expressions of PTSD: "'hyperarousal,' 'intrusion,' and 'constriction.' Hyperarousal reflects the persistent expectation of danger; intrusion reflects the indelible imprint of the traumatic moment; constriction reflects the numbing response of surrender."[1] She also discusses the effects of trauma on memory, saying that traumatic memories "are not encoded like the ordinary memories of adults in a verbal, linear narrative that is assimilated into an ongoing life story,"[2] and that "[t]raumatic memories lack verbal narrative and context; rather, they are encoded in the form of vivid sensations and images."[3] As I will demonstrate, these states of hyperarousal, intrusion, and constriction, narrated in fragmented, vivid scenes, are a significant feature of several of the works I analyze in this book.

Another key feature of traumatic response that Herman describes is the approach-avoidance dance many trauma survivors conduct in their relationships with others. As she puts it, "Trauma impels people both to withdraw from close relationships and to seek them desperately. [. . .] The traumatized person therefore frequently alternates between isolation and anxious clinging to others."[4] This back-and-forth can also be seen in the writing of the authors surveyed here, as they reach out to the reader only to draw back and insist that no one can understand what they have been through.

Herman drew on war writers such as Tim O'Brien when constructing her theories, and in the epilogue to the 2015 edition she references Phil Klay's *Redeployment,* a collection of short stories about the recent US invasion of Iraq, as she affirms the continuing relevance of her descriptions of trauma. Modern scholars of war and trauma literature have found equal resonance in Herman's theories in their own work. Mark A. Heberle's *A Trauma Artist: Tim O'Brien and the Fiction of Vietnam,* draws heavily on Herman's concepts in its analysis of O'Brien's writings. Heberle argues that O'Brien's work "mimics traumatization through style, organization of narrative, and point of view," and says that "[a]mong the characteristic devices of such enactments are repetition; fragmentation; violation of temporal sequence; lack of affect, understatement, irony, and other markers of emotional constriction; and images and actions resonant of unspeakable violence."[5] As I will show, the literature of the modern Chechen Wars also contains similar mimicry of the experience of trauma and PTSD.

---

1 Judith Herman, *Trauma and Recovery: The Aftermath of Violence—From Domestic Abuse to Political Terror* (New York: Basic Books, 2015), 35.

2 Ibid., 37.

3 Ibid., 38.

4 Ibid., 56.

5 Mark A Heberle, *A Trauma Artist: Tim O'Brien and the Fiction of Vietnam* (Iowa City: University of Iowa Press, 2001), chapter 1, "Posttraumatic Stress Disorder and Vietnam."

Another contemporary scholar who discusses the relationship between trauma and artistic representation is Harriet E. H. Earle, in *Comics, Trauma, and the New Art of War*. Earle goes farther than Heberle, arguing that

> [i]t is not enough simply to mimic the symptoms of trauma in order to create "traumatic art" not only because it is reductionist and incorrect to suggest that there is only one goal in the representation of trauma—traumatic art is also about emancipation, relief, revenge, and the need to tell—but also because traumatic events are almost always impossible to recreate with any degree of accuracy due to the nature of traumatic memory.[6]

This idea that traumatic events are impossible to recreate or share is another thing that will come up in the literature on the Chechen Wars. As we will see, the authors surveyed here repeatedly express the impossibility of conveying the true experience that they are intent on sharing. How much of this is due to the fragmentation of memory that occurs when the psyche is subjected to trauma, how much is due to what Herman describes as "the grandiose feeling of specialness sometimes found in victimized people,"[7] and how much is due to the inability to fully share one individual's experience with another, is a question worth exploring in more detail while reading such works.

Another foundational work in the field of trauma studies is Kalí Tal's *Worlds of Hurt: Reading the Literatures of Trauma*. In it Tal compares works by three different groups of trauma survivors: Holocaust survivors, Vietnam veterans, and rape and incest survivors. As well as arguing that the distinguishing feature of the literature of trauma is the identity of the author, Tal makes another crucial distinction that is often elided by other authors on the subject: the difference between the combat veteran and other trauma survivors. As well as arguing that works on war by veteran-authors should be approached differently by the critic than works on war by non-veterans, drawing on psychology and sociology as well as literary theory,[8] Tal also points out that:

---

6 Harriet E. H. Earle, *Comics, Trauma, and the New Art of War* (Jackson, Mississippi: University Press of Mississippi, 2017), 9.

7 Herman, *Trauma and Recovery*, 204.

8 Tal, *Worlds of Hurt*, 116-17.

> combat soldiers, though subordinate to their military superiors and frequently at the mercy of their enemies, still possess a life-or-death power over other people. [. . .] The soldier in combat is both victim and victimizer; dealing death as well as risking it. These soldiers carry guns; they point them at people and shoot to kill. Members of oppressed groups, by contrast, almost never control the tools of violence.[9]

The question whether the authors under consideration in this book, particularly the two Russian soldiers Babchenko and Prilepin, are victims or victimizers, is one that should be borne in mind while reading their stories.

To sum up, the key theoretical points from the field of trauma studies and the literature of trauma that I will use in my own analysis is the understanding that exposure to trauma causes memory to fragment and become nonlinear. Trauma survivors often feel compelled to bear witness and "to tell and retell the story of the traumatic experience, to make it 'real' to both the victim and the community."[10] However, trauma survivors tend to feel as if their stories fail in their prime objective of describing the trauma and allowing others to experience it, both because of the inherently nonlinear, nonverbal nature of traumatic experience, and because of the sense many trauma survivors have of being set apart and made special because of what they have undergone.

The result is a literature of fragments and flashbacks, one that constantly strains to reach the reader, even as it declares the impossibility of achieving that desperately desired goal. The three male authors under consideration here are particularly frustrated by their inability tell the truth that they are set on telling. It is therefore fitting to start with the one female author I discuss, whose truth-telling was hampered largely by external forces—external forces that would ultimately prove fatal.

---

9 Ibid., 10.
10 Ibid., 21.

3

Anna Politkovskaya: The Martyr of Russian Journalism

> Grozny today is a living hell. It is another world, some dreadful Hades you can only reach through the Looking Glass.
>
> —Anna Politkovskaya, *A Dirty War*

It is impossible to start any discussion of Russian writing on Chechnya without beginning with Anna Politkovskaya. Anyone who has any familiarity at all with Chechnya, Russian journalism, or contemporary Russia knows the name Politkovskaya. A furious truth-teller, Politkovskaya always had the courage of her convictions, descending into chaos, corruption, and the hell of the Second Chechen War in order to shine the light of her reporting on the deserving and undeserving alike. It is our loss that she paid the ultimate price for her beliefs.

Politkovskaya was born Anna Stepanovna Mazepa in 1958 in New York, where her parents, Ukrainian Soviet diplomats, were then stationed. The family later moved to Moscow, where she spent much of her childhood and adolescence. While a student at Moscow State University's school of journalism, she and fellow student Alexander Politkovsky married in 1978; she graduated in 1980, defending a thesis on the Silver Age poet Marina Tsvetaeva, despite having already given birth to two children, Ilya and Vera. She worked as journalist, first at *Izvestia,* then at *Obshchaya Gazeta,* throughout the 1980s and 1990s, before taking the job that would make her a figure of international fame and national infamy: as an investigative journalist for *Novaya Gazeta,* one of the few independent newspapers in what was becoming the increasingly censored and state-controlled Russian mass media.

Politkovskaya covered the Second Chechen War extensively for *Novaya Gazeta*, making repeated journeys into the war zone, where she spoke with Russian and Chechen soldiers alike. She also interviewed refugees in camps, civilian aid workers, politicians, bureaucrats, technicians, soldiers' families, and ordinary Chechens trying to survive back in Moscow, which had suddenly become a hostile foreign country for these people previously considered its citizens. Many of these interviews and essays were later translated into English and published in *A Dirty War* (2001) and *A Small Corner of Hell: Dispatches from Chechnya* (2003), as well as in *Putin's Russia: Life in a Failing Democracy* (2004), *A Russian Diary: A Journalist's Final Account of Life, Corruption, and Death in Putin's Russia* (2009), and *Is Journalism Worth Dying For?: Final Dispatches* (2011).[1]

The extensive translation of Politkovskaya's articles into English means that there is a wide variety of potential teaching materials to choose from. *A Dirty War* and *A Small Corner of Hell* both concentrate almost entirely on the Second Chechen War, making them particularly suitable for courses dealing with the Chechen Wars or on contemporary war literature, while the later books are more broadly focused. *Putin's Russia* is also an excellent resource for courses on post-Soviet Russian culture, politics, and society. The organization of these books into separate and self-contained essays and articles means that it is not necessary to assign the entire book, which can be a real benefit when trying to give an overview of the grand sweep of the post-Soviet condition in a single term or semester.

Advanced students of Russian may also benefit from reading Politkovskaya's articles in the original as a good introduction to standard journalistic Russian. Furthermore, her spoken Russian was clear and eloquent, and I have found that interviews with her are a useful resource when exposing advanced students to the Russian of the modern *intelligentsia*. The "Anna Politkovskaya Raw in War" interview,"[2] which has been freely available on YouTube for the past several years, is a three-minute video that can be used for both language and culture classes to give the students a taste of Politkovskaya's speaking style. There is also a 2011 documentary about her, *A Bitter Taste of Freedom*,[3] written and directed by Marina Goldovskaya, that is well worth watching.

---

1 Originally published in 2007 in Russian as *За что?*

2 RAWinWAR, "Anna Politkovskaya Raw in War Interview," YouTube video, 3:38, n.d., https://www.youtube.com/watch?v=HHfu5vXSbzk.

3 *Горький вкус свободы* in the original Russian.

While Politkovskaya herself comes across as mild-mannered and soft-spoken, her journalistic activities were anything but. Taken together, Politkovskaya's work is not so much a slap in the face as it is a stunning blow to the back of the head: American readers, used to the careful hewing of mainstream American news to the middle of the road, may be taken aback by Politkovskaya's overt presence within the text. She had no fear of taking a position and making it clear, even if it meant contradicting herself. For Politkovskaya, the truth was "out there," and she chased after it with the tenacity of a bloodhound, spurning her own initial conclusions with the same fearlessness with which she treats the mendacity of cowardly politicians and slogan-spouting officers.

She quickly gained a reputation both at home and abroad, receiving multiple awards. A partial list includes the Golden Prize of the Russian Union of Journalists, the "Journalists Against Corruption" Prize, the Artyom Borovik Prize for Investigative Journalism, the Global Award for Human Rights Journalism, the Most Courageous Defence of Free Expression Prize, the Courage in Journalism Award of the International Women's Media Foundation, the Andrey Sakharov Prize for Journalism as Action, the Prize for Journalism and Democracy of the Organization for Security and Co-operation in Europe, the Olof Palme Prize, and the Civil Courage Prize of the Northcote Parkinson Fund. Respect for her on the Chechen side was so high that during the *Nord-Ost* hostage crisis, she was brought in as a negotiator; she personally carried bottles of water and juice (paid for by journalists covering the crisis, since no official funds were forthcoming) into the theater to give to the hostages.

These actions inspired tributes from colleagues and admirers. Oksana Chelysheva, journalist and deputy chair of the Russian-Chechen Friendship society, wrote that "Anna never hesitated to hurl words of truth that often echoed painfully, but she was not rigid. This simply was her personal method of work—if she felt she could help, she didn't hesitate to act"[4] and "Anna Politkovskaya's name has become an international symbol of genuine journalism, a rare commodity in contemporary Russia."[5] Mariana Katzarova, a researcher on Russia and Chechnya for Amnesty International, said of her: "Anya was a truth-seeker with every fiber of her being. She just could not remain silent; she could not play it safe. She was a fierce spirit, a whistle-blower, a caring and loyal friend, a deeply loving woman, who stood up for humanity."[6]

---

4 Oksana Chelysheva, "Anna Politkovskaya. One Voice Amid Silence," *Problems of Post-Communism* 54, no. 5 (September/October 2007): 41.

5 Ibid.

6 Marina Katzarova, "Ten Years with Politkovskaya. Lessons in Truth, Courage and Humanity," *Problems of Post-Communism* 54, no. 5 (September/October 2007): 51.

She also gained enemies. While in Chechnya investigating abuses by Russian troops, she herself was detained by Russian officers, interrogated, threatened with rape and attacks on her children, put through a mock execution, and poisoned.[7] During her investigation into acts of torture and murder committed by Sergei Lapin (code name The Cadet), an officer in the Khanty-Mansiysk Combined Militia Unit, *Novaya Gazeta* received death threats addressed to Politkovskaya, and demands that her articles be retracted.[8] When she attempted to fly to Beslan during the hostage crisis there, she was first denied a flight, and then, once she finally got on board a plane, was poisoned en route and fell into a coma.[9]

Most fatally of all, her harsh criticism of the Kadyrov regime garnered the enmity of Ramzan Kadyrov, who, in an interview she conducted with him on June 10-11, 2004, and which was published in *Novaya Gazeta* on June 21, 2004, said to her: "You've[10] gotten between the Chechens. You are an enemy. You are worse than Basaev."[11] Later during the same interview, one member of Kadyrov's retinue told Politkovskaya: "you are an enemy of the Chechen people" and "you must answer for this," while another declared "You should have been shot back in Moscow, on the street, like they shoot people over there in Moscow. You should have been shot."[12] Ramzan's response to this threat uttered in his presence to a guest and a woman old enough to be his mother? He echoed his henchman's statements: "You are an enemy . . . Shot . . . You are an enemy . . ."[13]

In the fall of 2006, she was working on an article about torture, something she announced on Radio Liberty on October 5, 2006.[14] She had also acquired a video showing what appeared to be torture victims. Voices from off screen can be heard making threats and insults in Chechen and appear to belong to members of the Chechen security services.[15] Two days later, on October 7, 2006 (Putin's birthday), she was shot and killed in the entrance of her apartment building.

---

7 Anna Politkovskaya, *A Dirty War: A Russian Reporter in Chechnya,* trans. John Crowfoot (London: The Harvill Press, 2001), 51-3.

8 Anna Politkovskaya, *Is Journalism Worth Dying For? Final Dispatches,* trans. Arch Tait (Brooklyn: Melville House, 2011), 180-1.

9 Ibid., 252.

10 Throughout the interview Politkovskaya used the formal "vy" form with Kadyrov and his retinue, while Kadyrov and his followers, most much younger than Politkovskaya, used the informal "ty" form.

11 Anna Politkovskaya, "Tsentrovoi iz Tsentoroia. Interv'iu s Ramzanom Kadyrovym," *Novaya Gazeta,* June 21, 2004, http://politkovskaya.novayagazeta.ru/pub/2004/2004-051.shtml.

12 Ibid.

13 Ibid.

14 Politkovskaya, *Journalism,* 382.

15 Ibid., 385.

Her death caused a furor internationally—but less so at home. While Condoleezza Rice, then US Secretary of State, and heads of state all over Europe expressed their condolences, and German Chancellor Angela Merkel pressed Putin to solve the murder during their meeting just a few days later, on October 10, 2006,[16] Putin was conspicuously silent in the immediate aftermath of her death. He only broke his silence during that meeting with Merkel on October 10, when he promised that the crime would be punished but insisted that Politkovskaya's "influence on political life in Russia was minimal."[17] Ramzan Kadyrov, meanwhile, claimed that "I was not bothered in the slightest by what Politkovskaya wrote [. . .]. She was a woman, and I have never lowered myself to trying to settle scores with women."[18]

Politkovskaya's interview with Kadyrov in June 2004, however, suggests otherwise: not only did he give multiple examples of his personal dislike for her, but his unchivalrous, to put it mildly, attitude towards her and towards women in general was on full display. Politkovskaya, who was no stranger to threats, intimidation, and personal danger, eventually got up and left, and "sobbed all the way to Grozny"[19] from the intense psychological stress of her 36-hour ordeal. While this does not directly implicate Kadyrov, it does put a lie to his words after her death. Meanwhile, "the indifference, instead of outrage, with which the Russian public at large reacted to the murder"[20] was notable, with "the majority of journalists conflicted,"[21] rather than openly outraged, over Politkovskaya's assassination.

The official investigation of the murder was even muddier than the initial reaction. The first official suspect was Boris Berezovsky, a Russian oligarch who had taken up residence in London to avoid persecution.[22] It was not until 2008 that anyone was brought to trial, and after a three-month-long trial fraught with complications—the trial was first opened to the public, then closed; there was a move, later denied, to replace the judge—all three of the defendants, none

---

16 Andrei Kolesnikov, "Vladimir Putin and Angela Merkel Work Together," *Kommersantъ*. October 11, 2006, https://web.archive.org/web/20070930184736/http://www.kommersant.com/p712110/r_527/Putin_visit_Germany/.

17 Politkovskaya, *Journalism*, 405.

18 Ibid., 397.

19 Politkovskaya, "Tsentrovoi iz Tsentoroia."

20 Natalia Roudakova, "Journalism as "Prostitution": Understanding Russia's Reactions to Anna Politkovskaya's Murder," *Political Communication* 26, no. 4 (2009): 413.

21 Ibid.

22 Sergei Sokolov, "Ne smeite govorit', chto ubiistvo raskryto," *Novaya Gazeta*, October 7, 2016, https://www.novayagazeta.ru/articles/2016/10/06/70089-ne-smeyte-govorit-chto-ubiystvo-raskryto-video

of whom were the actual gunman, were acquitted in early 2009. The judge immediately reopened the case, but the second trial did not conclude until June 2014. This time there were five defendants, including the original three defendants as well as Rustam Makhmudov, the man accused of being the actual gunman, and Lom-Ali Gaitukaev, who organized the hit. All five of them were convicted. However, the contractor behind what was clearly a contract killing has never been named. The hopes of those who wish to uncover the whole truth may have received another blow when Gaitukaev, who received a life sentence for his part in the murder, died in prison of cirrhosis of the liver on June 10, 2017.[23]

Of course, suspicion falls heavily on two suspects: Vladimir Putin and Ramzan Kadyrov. Whether either or both of them were involved directly has yet to be proven, but in any case their hostility towards journalists in general and towards her in particular created an environment in which killing her must have seemed like a safe thing to do. Certainly, when her words against them and against the power structures in Russia and Chechnya—and not just a few words, but thousands upon thousands—are taken into consideration, the surprise is not that Politkovskaya was assassinated, but that she survived for so long. And while her death was a tragedy, it may not have been completely in vain. Resistance movements have long known the power of the martyr. Anna Politkovskaya lived for the truth, and very likely died for it, too. It is fitting, therefore, that her death brought an intense focus on the truth behind it and on the political corruption and atmosphere of violence that led it. The truth may not have set her free, but she may very well have set the truth free, for those who have ears to hear it.

---

23 "Ubiitsu Politkovskoi podvela pechen'," *Novaya Gazeta*, June 13, 2017, https://www.gazeta.ru/social/2017/06/13/10719695.shtml

A Dirty War

A Dirty War, the first of Politkovskaya's books on Chechnya, is a collection of her articles written for *Novaya Gazeta*. Her articles had gained the attention of her first English-language translator, John Crowfoot, who advocated strongly for them to be published, and she eventually went on to become one of the "star authors" of Harvill Press.[24]

While *A Dirty War* demonstrates the fragmented style of all the works under review here, I argue that this is less an expression of personal trauma, as it is in the works by male authors, but an expression of the national trauma Politkovskaya was trying to represent, combined with a deliberately feminine "ethics of care." As I show, Politkovskaya favors what Western feminist critics would consider a gender essentialist approach to her work and her presentation of the stories she gathers. She does so, I contend, in order to tap into the power of feminine social roles and to challenge a rights- and theory-based understanding of society and the social contract. She is presenting a truth that is multifaceted and interdependent, while also remaining true to her core values.

A Dirty War is an eclectic mix, designed not to give a "balanced" view in the American style, where each side is presented as having its own merit, but to elicit sympathy for those who deserve it, rage against those who have earned it, and spur the readers of *Novaya Gazeta* to action, something Politkovskaya considered to be critical if Russia was to pull itself out of the mire of cruelty and incompetence in which it had found itself. "By tolerating such things on our own doorstep and allowing the State's officials to perform these acts of violence against us," she warns, "we shall very soon have our own Pinochet. We shall be so relieved, in fact, when he comes that we'll throw ourselves at his feet, and beg him to save us."[25]

The articles in *A Dirty War* are arranged in chronological order, which gives them a certain level of coherence, but they also appear to be carefully chosen not just by date, but in order to provoke a particular reaction, and drive home Politkovskaya's main point of government corruption and callousness, something which she sees aimed indiscriminately at everyone who falls under the government's purview, and something to which she returns again and again.

The book opens with two articles she wrote in the summer of 1999, before the Second Chechen War had even started, about the struggles the families of

24 Email interview with John Crowfoot, August 3, 2017.
25 Politkovskaya, *Dirty War*, 93.

soldiers who had been killed in the first war were going through to have the bodies returned to them. On various occasions, the bodies of Russian soldiers killed in action were "held hostage" by the Chechens, so that "Again we are forced to bargain, and this time it is the most outrageous of all the trades known to mankind, when the goods up for sale are a pile of decomposing human remains."[26] Why, Politkovskaya demands, do the Chechens feel able to hold the bodies of soldiers hostage? Because, she argues, the return of the bodies has on the Russian side gotten caught up in red tape and plain extortion, and so "The Chechens look at us, and they see a demonstration of the most fantastic cynicism at the highest level. We were the first to trade and barter human remains. We are no worse and no better than they are: the Chechens are merely playing along with the Ministry of Defense."[27] Already in this first article Politkovskaya emphasizes the shared responsibility between both sides for the atrocities to follow, and places the blame ultimately back on the Russian government. An inhuman interest in procedure, along with plain greed, has corrupted the organizations involved, and the larger the organization, the greater the corruption. The Russian government, as the largest and most powerful of the organized players in the problem, is the fundamental root of the evil.

Politkovskaya does not wallow only in hopelessness, however. She finishes the article by saying:

> I have a suggestion. All involved in the division of budget funds should, for the good of their souls, meet one of these mothers [of soldiers killed in action] at least once a week. If they were obliged to look them in the eye, answer their questions, and say something in their own justification, that would be a great help. They would stop imagining that they could avoid having to answer for themselves.[28]

This opening article of the collection thus lays out Politkovskaya's main argument: dehumanized organizations are not only unforgivably callous towards real human suffering, but they are, motivated as they are by inhuman concerns, inherently inefficient and ineffective. What is needed is to return to real human connections, cutting through all the bureaucracy, red tape, and protocol that shields government actors from facing their fears and their duties.

---

26 Ibid., 6.
27 Ibid., 13.
28 Ibid., 14.

If you intend to do someone wrong, or even intend not to do right by them, you must look them in the eye, which may make you reconsider your actions.

A maxim which Politkovskaya uses on herself in the next article, in which she visits the laboratory morgue responsible for identifying the bodies of missing soldiers, and speaks with Colonel Shcherbakov, the head of the morgue and who, in the previous article, was accused of "cynical time-wasting"[29] and "career-building."[30] What she presents instead upon interviewing him is a person struggling to do even the bare minimum while caught up in bungling, incompetence, and other people's careerism. He is, she concludes after meeting with him, "a unique specialist whose knowledge is now desperately needed [...] that Moscow has driven to its limit and will soon finish off."[31]

The abrupt switch between the two back-to-back articles, from villainizing Shcherbakov to sympathizing with him, only seems inconsistent if viewed from a protocol-based perspective rooted in impersonal rules, which is the very thing Politkovskaya is attacking. By creating a person-to-person connection with each of her interviewees, and presenting their stories, not with impersonal, unbiased detachment, but with a living empathy for each of them, she is able to give the reader all sides of the story while still supporting her central belief, that the personal and practical should trump all considerations of the impersonal and theoretical. And by starting off the book with these two articles, she frames the problem as one that precedes and supersedes the bare facts of the Second Chechen War, which is merely symptomatic of a deeper problem, rather than an underlying cause. Politkovskaya's use of the short, disconnected form thus serves to support her overall story arc in a way that a more connected narrative may not have been able to.

The next article, "A Dirty War," continues to follow the organizational principle of jumping around in order to uphold the greater point. In it, Politkovskaya interviews Dagestani refugees who have been displaced following the invasion of Dagestan by the Islamic International Brigade, led by Shamil Basaev and Ibn al-Khattab, in August 1999.

What is most striking about this piece is Politkovskaya's repeated emphasis on the refugees' wisdom, good sense, and status as financially sound property owners. Rather than painting a picture of miserable indigents, she is at pains to show these Dagestani villagers as essentially middle-class homeowners whose

---

29 Ibid., 10.
30 Ibid., 12.
31 Ibid., 22.

"sturdy massive-walled houses"[32] have suddenly been bombed into oblivion. These people may be Caucasian villagers and now refugees, Politkovskaya shows the reader, but they are, or were before tragedy struck, prosperous, proud, and hardworking, at first unwilling to abandon their homes, since "too many generations had toiled to build [them]."[33] But when faced with the necessity of leaving their family homes, "None of the women shed a tear [...]. They are strong-spirited women who are used to surviving."[34] In contrast to the "various media commentators" from Moscow who call the Dagestanis "savages from the hills,"[35] Politkovskaya says that these people are not a drag on Russia but "infinitely wiser and more principled than all of our Moscow politicians put together."[36] Again and again in this article, Politkovskaya contrasts the Dagestani villagers with representatives of the Moscow elite, always in the Dagestanis' favor. Even their simplicity and naivety is a plus, since it gives them "a decisiveness and clarity that we have long forgotten."[37] Rather than being bogged down in theoretical considerations and abstract concerns, these simple (but not poor!) villagers are able to cut right to the heart of the matter, laying bare all the foolishness and prevarication coming from Moscow.

It is also not coincidental that many of the people featured in this and other articles are women. Politkovskaya herself was in some ways an example of a liberated woman and a feminist figure, traveling into war zones and fearlessly taking on authority figures. However, Politkovskaya's writing is not entirely "feminist" as it is generally understood in the West. Like the women in the Soldiers' Mothers' Committees interviewed by Maya Eichler in *Militarizing Men: Gender, Conscription, and War in Post-Soviet Russia,* she often upholds gender stereotypes about feminine nurturance vs. masculine violence. And also like the soldiers' mothers, she bases a lot of her power in her status as a woman upholding traditional ideas of femininity. As Eichler notes, "Their [the soldiers' mothers] ability to act publicly was linked to a motherist approach that emphasizes women's responsibilities for their children."[38] Politkovskaya in many ways did a similar thing, presenting herself as acting selflessly, for the good of others, and therefore able to speak out in a way that other, more self-centered

---

32 Ibid., 26.
33 Ibid., 27.
34 Ibid.
35 Ibid., 30.
36 Ibid.
37 Ibid.
38 Maya Eichler, *Militarizing Men: Gender, Conscription, and War in Post-Soviet Russia* (Stanford: Stanford University Press, 2012), 86.

actors, could not. Her power as a speaker comes precisely from her self-effacing femininity.

Be that as it may, she also demonstrates a pro-woman slant, both in her tendency to feature women's stories, and in her clearly stated belief in the courage and common sense of women. These "simple" Dagestani women may hold beliefs that an educated Muscovite could find laughable, but they nonetheless possess a wisdom that the (male) politicians and generals cannot access.

And Politkovskaya's belief in personal, practical action is itself a markedly "feminine" tendency. When she praises individuals for stepping in to help the refugees, and says that "The present catastrophe in Dagestan has once again shown that ordinary people are a hundred times better and purer than our authorities. At best our clumsy and unresponsive regime thinks only of itself and does nothing,"[39] this is not just an attack on government corruption and incompetence, but, it could be argued, an attack on a stereotypically "masculine" mode of thinking and behavior, one that values rules and abstractions over empathy and person-to-person contact. Politkovskaya does not explicitly describe it as such, but her whole approach to problem-solving is a protest against the largely masculine world of ranks, rules, and regulations. In this way she demonstrates what authors such as Juliann Emmons Allison call "an ethics of care," which "privileges our human, emotional connectedness and social interdependence rather than [. . .] the rights-based ethic on which the democratic peace is conventionally premised."[40] Indeed, Politkovskaya's entire ethics is an ethics of care, interdependence, and practical rather than theoretical help, one that puts her in direct contrast with the largely masculine world she is confronting.

Her "ethics of care" is also related to her emphasis on personal experience rather than theoretical knowledge; as Allison notes, a care-based perspective "notably distinguishes care epistemologically from a rights-based perspective. Care as a foundation for moral choice is obviously grounded in experience rather than pure reason as a source of knowing or validating behavior."[41] Eichler, citing Sergei Oushakine, also notes the emphasis in narratives about the Chechen War on personal experience rather than official reports.[42] One reason for this emphasis is undoubtedly the widespread censorship and misinformation in

---

39 Politkovskaya, *Dirty War*, 33.

40 Juliann Emmons Allison, "Peace Among Friends: A Feminist Interpretation of the 'Democratic Peace,'" *Peace & Change* 26, no. 2 (April 2001): 207.

41 Ibid., 210.

42 Eichler, *Militarizing Men*, 39.

official reports about the wars. However, in Politkovskaya's case it also seems tied to her "ethics of care" and her focus on a feminine, experiential worldview.

This explicitly feminine approach to reporting does not prevent her from taking a sympathetic and supporting role vis-à-vis people fulfilling stereotypically "masculine" duties. In the next article, "Tainted Tins: How the Soldiers are Fed," she interviews OMON[43] troops stationed on the Chechen border, exposing the horrifying living conditions they are experiencing, despite the fact that they "recently performed an act of heroism,"[44] breaking through enemy lines when they were surrounded by bandits. Never shy of using vivid language, Politkovskaya, like the war reporter she is at heart, describes how, "Guided by their senses, they crawled out at night, stealthily and silently, tracing a great arc across Chechen territory, beyond the surrounding fighters, where death waited behind every hill."[45] The drama and the action are evident in this passage, but it is included not so much to valorize the Lipetsk OMON unit and tickle the reader's senses, as to contrast the troops' heroism with the treatment they receive from an indifferent and uncaring Moscow. The Lipetsk OMON unit's courageous act, made more commendable in Politkovskaya's eyes because they were doing it in order to save their wounded comrades, is not presented so much as an example of soldierly valor and Russian patriotism, as it is an example of caring for others.

And not only does Politkovskaya present it as a caring action, she uses it to further her own agenda of caring for others. As she demands in the next paragraph, "How could people who have shown such bravery in impossible circumstances and, weeks later, continue to face mortal danger every day, now be living like stray dogs that no one cares for? Is this how the Motherland repays their valor?"[46] The Motherland, this passage suggests, should be a concerned and loving mother, but Russia is currently failing in the most basic duty of a mother towards her sons: feeding and clothing them. The OMON troops were not given new uniforms to replace the ones destroyed in their escape, and

43 ОМОН (OMON): Отряд мобильный особого назначения, or "Mobile Special Purpose Unit," were essentially riot police attached to the Ministry of Internal Affairs. In theory they were merged, along with SOBR and MVD troops, into the new National Guard of the Russian Federation in 2016, but as of January 2021 OMON officers still sometimes operate under the old insignia, as can be seen in the photographs of the January 2021 protests in support of opposition activist Alexei Navalny (see, for example, Alan Taylor, "Photos: A Second Weekend of Protests in Russia," *The Atlantic*, February 1, 2021).

44 Politkovskaya, *Dirty War*, 35.

45 Ibid., 36.

46 Ibid.

instead "had to rely on their well-disposed comrades to cover their nakedness."[47] Even worse, they are given tins of rotten meat, although "if were not for the tins from Semikarakorsk then the Motherland would be offering its heroes nothing more than gruel."[48] The Motherland's neglect is contrasted with the behavior of the locals: "When the local women notice how thin the soldiers defending them are, they bring them food out of the kindness of their hearts."[49] The difference is explicit: the Motherland, an abstract entity run largely by men, is a failure as a mother, while individual women are able, through their person-to-person connection, to take care of their "sons" when the Motherland fails.

Which is not to say that Politkovskaya sees the personal actions of women to be the panacea to Russia's problems. Although she repeatedly praises individuals, particularly women, who step up to protect and rescue those who can't stand up for themselves; saying, for example, of a Russian woman protecting her Chechen fiancé that "His Muscovite fiancée in Yeltsin's declining years in power has to hide Arslan from the Moscow police, just as simple Russian women once concealed their Jewish neighbors from the Gestapo,"[50] thus drawing a direct line between the (heavily female) unofficial resistance against the actions of the current Russian regime, and the Resistance to Nazi occupation during World War II, she does not suggest that simply turning all responsibilities over to private charity is the appropriate response. Politkovskaya is not an anarchist or a libertarian: she is merely aware of the failings of the government to fulfill its responsibilities to its citizens.

This is apparent both in her warnings of the consequences of the mistreatment of Russian soldiers by their superiors, and her interviews with mothers who "kidnapped" their sons serving on the front and tricked or dragged them home, often against their will. On her visit to the OMON troops at the border, the ones who have neither new uniforms nor edible food, she remarks:

> the soldiers point their weapons at everyone who isn't in uniform or riding in an army vehicle. No one trusts anyone else here and they're all afraid of each other.
>
> That's how we now behave, yet the land around is part of our country, it's not a fascist, gangster-run republic. We created

47 Ibid.
48 Ibid., 37.
49 Ibid.
50 Ibid., 52.

> this situation. Only officers who are daily shown how little they count could behave in this way.[51]

The rank-and-file soldiers and police officers, she implies, may be behaving inappropriately and even carrying out atrocities, but they are not at fault, or at least, the fault is not entirely theirs. The rot comes from the top, and soldiers who feel abused or abandoned by their government and their superior officers are going to perpetuate the cycle of abuse by taking out their frustration and trauma on those who can't defend themselves: that is, ordinary Chechens and Dagestanis. While caring individuals, particularly women, can and should counteract this systemic abuse and neglect on the personal level, their interventions are only somewhat effective, since they themselves are caught up in the same destructive system as those they are trying to save.

This is made clear in "Criminal Mothers: Hundreds Break the Law," about the aforementioned mothers who "kidnap" their sons and take them home from the front, often against their sons' will. This means that their sons are now deserters, with their mothers accomplices to their crime, but the mothers whom Politkovskaya interviews consider the sacrifice worth it, saying, for example, "I brought my sons up myself. The State gave me nothing, not a kopeck. But when they needed someone to die for them, then they were there at the door, in a flash [. . .]. So now they want my next son? Not for anything in the world."[52] Having a live deserter as a son was better than a dead or permanently disabled war hero.

The problem is not just that the soldiers are being asked to fight an unjust war, but that the injustice affects those who honestly and valiantly serve their country, believing themselves to be doing the right thing. Their good will is exploited by a state that takes without giving, and because the decay and corruption are systemic, it is impossible to fight on a person-by-person basis, even though Politkovskaya presents that as the only way at the present moment to get anything done at all. The issue is not a lack of goodhearted and well-intentioned individuals, but an impersonal and selfish state structure that limits the good that these individuals can do, leaving the fortunes of disabled soldiers and their families up to the vagaries of fate.

That individual action is not enough, and that people will have to take matters into their own hands, even if that means going outside the law, is stressed in the interview with Maria Fedulova, from the Committees of Soldiers' Mothers, after which Politkovskaya warns:

---

51 Ibid., 40-1.
52 Ibid., 45-6.

> This is the first thing parents must know: those who return from the fighting will enjoy no allowances or privileges; not for re-training, artificial limbs, medicine, jobs, or, least likely of all, accommodation. Everything will depend on whether they can find some kindly helper where they live: if the head of the local administration feels so inclined, he will pay for an artificial leg, but nothing can force him to do so. If the lad can find a sponsor to support this job training then all is well; if he can't, there's no hope. The regime stresses that it has taken a decision to begin the war, but accepts no responsibility for the consequences.[53]

The fundamental problem, as Politkovskaya makes clear here, with the direct person-to-person approach to dealing with things is that it relies on luck, chance, and the favorable disposition of people in positions of power. Disabled veterans are not going to receive the aid that they need without coming across "some kindly helper"; they are dependent on winning the favor of local politicians, doctors, and other gatekeepers to the benefits they have supposedly earned. Politkovskaya concludes this article by arguing that, not only did the "kidnapper" mothers do the right thing by spiriting their sons away from the front, but that "the most effective antidote to war as in any primitive society is the maternal instinct."[54]

However, she implies, the underlying issue is the existence of a "primitive society." In a more civilized society, the maternal instinct would not be criminalized and driven to antisocial acts of desperation, but would be integrated into the laws and systems so that they worked in harmony with maternal cares and concerns, rather than against them. Russia, according to Politkovskaya, does not need anarchy or some kind of hyper-capitalist or libertarian everyone-out-for-themselves free-for-all; what it needs, in fact, is a state with rules and regulations and systems, but ones that are humane, serving the people instead of subjugating the people to their service. Russia, Politkovskaya seems to be implying, needs something more like a matriarchy.

It is not just the Russian government that draws her fire. She is highly critical of both sensationalist journalism and Western aid organizations. When she attempted to organize an evacuation of disabled pensioners from Grozny, chronicled in the article "Kalashnikov and the Old People's Home," she remarked with outrage that her colleagues' "only interest in our operation

---

53 Ibid., 47.
54 Ibid., 50.

was to capture some dramatic events [. . .]. Not once did we hear an offer of help,"[55] and that Western human rights organizations are "mainly engaged in the theoretical defense of human rights. The practical side of things does not greatly worry them."[56] Although these organizations were, according to Politkovskaya, active in gathering information about human rights abuses committed by the Russian side against the Chechens, "When it became clear that the elderly were being held in Grozny by Chechen fighters, people representing a powerful and influential organisation such as Human Rights Watch did not show the faintest desire to help."[57] Such side-choosing is anathema to Politkovskaya, who demands that suffering be alleviated, no matter who causes it.

This indifference to on-the-ground suffering by Moscow-based and Western aid and human rights agencies is noted not just in connection with the evacuation attempt of a small number of disabled pensioners from Grozny, but in the treatment of all the refugees in Chechnya and Dagestan. *A Dirty War* contains multiple articles about the situation of those in refugee camps, which Politkovskaya compares repeatedly to the Gulag system and to Nazi concentration camps, saying explicitly at the end of "Camp Guards: Using the Jailers' Long Experience," about the use of prison guards to run the refugee camps: "The name for it is a concentration camp. All they need now is to start designing gas chambers. And for as long as one set of gangsters faces another we can feel nothing but doomed."[58]

Treating refugees as criminals and prisoners is, Politkovskaya believes, not only inhumane but a recipe for disaster, either by creating a second Nazi/Stalinist regime, or making the Chechen conflict unresolvable, or both. Therefore, it is in everyone's best interests to reduce people's suffering as quickly and efficiently as possible, but there are few who have that as their primary goal: the Russian government and its actors are primarily interested in maintaining short-term power, Western agencies are mainly focused on exposing Russian abuses in order to advance their own anti-Russian agendas, and journalists are just there to get an exciting scoop. This, as in the case of the disabled veterans who cannot rely on the government that has taken everything from them, leaves refugees at the mercy of individual acts of kindness.

---

55 Ibid., 92.
56 Ibid., 92.
57 Ibid., 92-3.
58 Ibid., 75.

And while individual acts of kindness can be effective, they are by their nature sporadic and disconnected. In "The Basic Instinct of Empire: Two Faces of the Russian Army," Politkovskaya says that:

> The lives of thousands of civilians become dependent not on the will of those who write the orders in Moscow and Mozdok but of the man who actually carries out the order. Everything depends on his intellectual level and moral qualities. Anyone can shoot where they like in this war. Survival now depends on a whim.
>
> [. . .]
>
> We know of instances when air-force pilots jettisoned their bombs into the river on the outskirts of villages so as not to commit the sin of bombing their peaceful inhabitants.
>
> We know of cases of quite the opposite kind. The pilots deliberately fired on the Rostov-Baku Highway when refugees were fleeing along it from the war zone, and then flew past a second, third and even a fourth time when they saw that someone below was still moving. The war is rapidly acquiring two faces and each potential victim hopes and prays that they will be lucky and meet the "kind" face of this war.[59]

Even as she praises those individuals who do show the "kind" face of the war, Politkovskaya, either directly or in the words of her interviewees, criticizes the necessity of relying on this individual kindness, both because it is unjust and because it is unreliable. Returning to the camps, Politkovskaya says in despair after seeing people in particularly desperate circumstances: "If people survive in the Karabulak camps it is down to chance and miracles. It only happens *in spite of* the now-established system where everyone expects payment for helping the refugees."[60] Politkovskaya herself records multiple instances in which she was able, through her personal intervention, to ameliorate someone's individual situation, but, as she says, "I don't want things to be done 'just for me.'"[61] The refugees should not be thrown into such chaos, dependent on people largely interested only in fleecing them while they are desperate, but should be able

---

59 Ibid., 83-4.

60 Ibid., 102. Politkovskaya's ambivalent attitude towards individual rather than collective action is expressed even more strongly in *A Russian Diary*, where, regarding individual efforts to investigate vote-rigging, she says, "People only react when something affects them personally [. . .]. We have emerged from socialism as thoroughly self-centered people" (125).

61 Politkovskaya, *Dirty War*, 98.

to count on an organized and effective system of aid, one that has not been forthcoming.

Politkovskaya does seem to believe that creating something better is possible, and argues that this is essential not just on humanitarian grounds, but for the very survival of Russia. In the section titled "What Can We Do?" of the article "Ingushlag: A New Concentration Camp," Politkovskaya provides her pager number for those interested in providing concrete aid, and exhorts her fellow citizens, "We must get the better of this appalling misfortune. And we must do so together. The last consideration is the most important of all, because we will only remain united in future if we act together now. Otherwise we shall become so many wild and hunted wolves each retreating to hide in its lair."[62] By combining individual acts of kindness, she seems to imply, a new, more humane and effective, system can be created, but that system must be founded on a genuine desire to help fellow humans, and must put their needs above that of the system, rather than subordinate their needs to that of the system itself.

Which may be why Politkovskaya takes care to present the struggles of those who are failing to provide the aid needed by the refugees, and even those widely believed to be responsible for the atrocities committed, with more stories of the victims sandwiched in between. In "Concentration Camp Village: A New Russian Type of Settlement," she interviews Isa Madayev, local administrator and military commandant of Chiri-Yurt, a village that was first bombed, and then, while still in a state of ruins, received several thousand refugees from other, even more destroyed, places. Her interview with him underscores the extreme difficulty administrators faced when trying to acquire even basic goods such as flour for the people in their care: Madayev finally gave up on the regional authorities and went directly to Moscow in the hopes of finding someone who would do something there for the people under his care. Such a trip is the kind of thing that in a different article Politkovskaya might present as frivolous travel, just the kind of time- and money-wasting that authorities engage in while their people shiver and starve, but in the interview with Madayev, just as in the interview with Colonel Shcherbakov, the head of the group that was painstakingly—and, allegedly, incompetently—identifying soldiers' remains at the beginning of the book, she shows us why what appears from the outside to be administrative incompetence is often necessitated by circumstances. Those circumstances are often the cowardice and incompetence of others. Still, in her description of the fiasco that was the refugee camps, something she covers at length in *A Dirty War*, Politkovskaya shows us both the incredible suffering of

---

62 Ibid., 67.

the refugees, and the superhuman, but often ineffective, struggles of the people in charge, many of whom, despite appearances to the contrary, did in fact want to do right by those in their care, but were unable to provide even basic services such as food, water, and heat.

The articles are juxtaposed to achieve a maximum effective of multiple perspectives. Following the interview with Madayev are two more pieces about refugees, the second of which, "My Homeland," is a collection of essays written by refugee children. Politkovskaya presents the circumstances of their composition (third-graders attending "school" in a tent in a refugee camp), and notes that even small children have turned away from a "Russian" identity to a Chechen one, and see their country as separate from Russia. Then the children are allowed to speak in their own voices, with their essays reprinted in Politkovskaya's article.

Politkovskaya's goal in including these essays is manifold: to demonstrate the depth of feeling of these refugee children; to show their opposition to the Russian operation in Chechnya, which has taken on the state of an armed occupation of hostile territory; and yet also to underscore the similarities between these Chechen refugees and the Russians back home in Moscow and the rest of the Russian heartland. These essays are written in Russian, on a familiar topic, and Politkovskaya stresses that the teacher, Jamila Djamilkhanova, "speaks a faultless literary Russian."[63] These refugees thus possess key elements of "Russianness"—their education in the Russian literary language, as well as a love of the homeland—something that, most likely, Politkovskaya wished to emphasize in order to lend authority to their anti-Russian sentiments. By allowing these children to speak (in Russian) in their own words, in these separate but thematically linked essays, Politkovskaya increases the polyphonic effect of her work, while underlining the main theme tying the book together, that of the atrocity of the Second Chechen War, even further.

"My Homeland" is followed by "The Decisive Battle," the last article of part two ("War") of *A Dirty War*. In it Politkovskaya, for the first time, presents an interview with two Chechen fighters, Lema and Ruslan. Once again, she allows people who might be considered "the enemy" speak for themselves, after prefacing the interview with the words "Try as we might, we cannot square events in Chechnya today with what the authorities say. It is not just that reality is more complicated. Quite simply it does not correspond with the propaganda."[64] This idea, that while official proclamations lie, there is a truth that can be reached by

63 Ibid., 156.
64 Ibid., 163.

speaking to "the people" directly (even if those people are the same ones who issue lying official proclamations), underpins Politkovskaya's writing, and can be seen very clearly in "The Decisive Battle."

It begins with the above-quoted statement about the disconnect between reality and the officially spouted propaganda, then allows the Chechen fighters to speak with their own words, which are simultaneously admirable and alarming: "That's why this war will never end," says Lema, after proclaiming that he expects the war to end and Chechnya to be liberated, at which point he will settle down peaceably. However, "Even if the troops leave," he tells Politkovskaya, "they won't escape our vengeance."[65] The piece finishes with "An Essential Postscript," in which Politkovskaya says, "Both sides support the same ideology: neither one nor the other has any pity for the civilian population as it is driven and harried across Chechnya [. . .]. This kind of fighting can go on without end and always provide serious arguments on both sides of the barricades."[66] In other words, both sides can make both logical and emotional appeals to their respective peoples, but these logical and emotional arguments serve, not to end the war, but to continue it. This is why the new, multifaceted yet coherent, truth that Politkovskaya presents is so important: because what is needed to end the war is such a new truth, not a return to the same tired half-truths that both sides keep spouting.

The third and final part of *A Dirty War*, entitled "Restoring Order: May 2000-January 2001," is somewhat misleading, since, as Politkovskaya stresses, the war is not in fact over. Instead, it would drag on for several more years, and Chechnya is still experiencing serious problems with lawlessness, violence, and a mass exodus of refugees.

The section begins with "A Reduced City: Plans to Rebuild Grozny," which chronicles the difficulties facing the engineers and planners attempting to make Grozny habitable again. As with the running of the refugee camps, the problem as Politkovskaya presents it is not that there is no one willing to do the work, but those who are willing to do it are hampered by sabotage from below (Politkovskaya recounts how, as she was touring one of the city reservoirs, their party came across raiders destroying generators in order to strip them of copper) and indifference from above, along with a lack of central planning. Grozny could be restored fairly quickly, but because so many people are looking out for themselves and their short-term interests rather than the long-term interests of the entire population, the city will probably remain in ruins for some time.

---

65 Ibid., 168.
66 Ibid., 169.

Interestingly, and tellingly, that article is immediately followed by "The Name's Shamanov: Russia's Youngest General." In it, Politkovskaya interviews General Shamanov, who, she points out to him directly, was known as "Cruel Shamanov" for his harsh and aggressive actions. It is apparent at the beginning of the article that Politkovskaya is not kindly disposed towards Shamanov. Nonetheless, she allows him to tell his side of the story, and what comes out is that, despite being a general and a "Hero of Russia," Shamanov's story is similar to that of other Russian soldiers, although with a longer list of indignities, since he has a longer record of service than most. Politkovskaya sets up the problem generally at the start of the article:

> Thousands of men, from privates to generals, are quietly returning home but do not find the long-desired peace in our company. It's difficult for them, away from the fighting. They have altered dramatically and are now strangers to friends and family. People shrink from them and fear them. Some are even openly reproachful: "What can you do, apart from kill?" Those who survived the fighting, it seems, must not show their faces anywhere.[67]

Shamanov outlines the extreme poverty of the officer corps in the 1990s, so that senior officers were forced to become taxi drivers on the side in order to make ends meet. Shamanov himself retained his patriotic convictions and committed multiple acts of heroism while on the front, despite his general's rank that could have allowed him to sit back in safety and lead from the rear. But, following his return from the war, he says that "People just don't understand. I don't feel happy in Moscow."[68] He describes at length the psychological and physiological stresses soldiers undergo on the front, and the lack of resources (something Politkovskaya had already discussed in "Criminal Mothers," at the beginning of the book) for their rehabilitation upon their return to civilian life. The final picture Politkovskaya presents of him is how, at an event for former paratroopers, "Shamanov's sturdy, powerful figure expressed nothing but his total and irreversible loneliness. It was painful to look at him."[69] The image she gives of him is of a man who has, rightly or wrongly, devoted his life to his

---

67 Ibid., 179.
68 Ibid., 187.
69 Ibid., 191.

Motherland, only to end up so broken and cut off from everyone that he cannot find company even amongst his own brothers-in-arms.

The point of the article about Shamanov is not to defend his actions, but to cause the reader to sympathize with him *in spite of* his actions. Shamanov may have done a number of unpleasant (to put it mildly) things, but he, like the Chechen fighters interviewed in the previous section of the book, was acting out of sincere conviction, and the result has been the near-total destruction of his life and his personality. Although on the surface he has many things going for him, much more so than the average veteran of Chechnya, the fact of his "total and irreversible loneliness" is highly sinister, especially against the backdrop of Politkovskaya's calls to work together. How, she seems to be asking, can a man like Shamanov work together with others? The war has left him utterly isolated, internally if not externally. The information given at the end of the interview, that he had just achieved political office, is thus less a congratulatory postscript on how things were going right for him, and more a warning. This, Politkovskaya is saying, is the kind of people we are electing to public office.[70] No wonder, the reader might be inclined to think, so many of our officials don't have much fellow feeling for us, if they believe that we have no fellow feeling for them. Worse than the damage to the territorial integrity of Russia done by the war is the damage it has done to Russia's social and psychological integrity, if the best, brightest, and most highly ranked of its warriors end up like this.

The interview with Shamanov is immediately followed by "The Ordinary Man Does Not Need Freedom: Chechnya's New Leader," an interview with Akhmat-Hadji Kadyrov, whom Putin had just appointed head of the provisional government of Chechnya. As can be guessed by the title, Kadyrov says a number of alarming things, from the point of view of a believer in freedom and/or liberal democracy, including the statement that "Freedom, in fact, is something the

---

70 In *A Russian Diary* Politkovskaya describes Shamanov's subsequent political activities thusly: "The province [Ulyanovsk] is one of the poorest, turned into a mere source of raw materials for big companies based elsewhere and, worse, into a rubbish tip for waste materials. This is thanks to the efforts of the governor, effectively imposed on the voters by the presidential administration, that great hero of Chechnya, Gen. Vladimir Shamanov. Under him the crime bosses of Ulianovsk came out of the underground. Shamanov openly depended on them and was surrounded by ex-soldiers who had retrained as gangsters, a minor sideways movement in Russia. Shamanov himself was thoroughly stupid and incapable of managing civilians" (295). Politkovskaya's sympathy for him was short-lived, disappearing as soon as more evidence of his misdeeds came to light. She also describes once again the army-to-crime pipeline that was significantly enlarged by the widespread criminal and human rights offenses committed by both sides during the Chechen Wars. Shamanov may indeed be a victim of circumstances, but so are his victims, in a vicious circle that no one seems to be able to pull out of.

ordinary man [. . .] does not need."[71] In response to Politkovskaya's argument that "You can't destroy a single idea in someone's head, except by decapitating him,"[72] he says, "Anyone who will not admit that he is wrong and will not turn back, will meet such an end."[73]

At the same time, he speaks out against suicide bombings and pledges a commitment to restoring peace, order, and jobs to Chechnya, all things that were sorely needed. He says, and Politkovskaya allows him to say, that he is the one committed to ending the violence and making Chechnya a peaceful and prosperous country again, making him, it would seem, the best of the not very good choices for the post of head of Chechnya.

Nonetheless, Politkovskaya concludes the interview with a postscript in which she says, "This interview left a strange feeling. On the one hand, it all made sense: Kadyrov is on the side of the truth and ordinary people. On the other, literally every word was tinged with petty untruths."[74] Kadyrov may, possibly, be a better choice to oversee the rebuilding of Chechnya than any of the other candidates, but even so, by Politkovskaya's reckoning, he is inherently tainted by these "petty untruths."

Unlike Shamanov, who in Politkovskaya's depiction is shown as someone who spouts jingoist propaganda but is also unafraid to face up to unpleasant truths on occasion, and whose tragedy is that he cannot get others to listen to and believe these unpleasant truths, Kadyrov is shown as someone who is fundamentally disconnected from what goes on around him, and is afraid even to leave his guards and his compound in Gudermes in order to walk the streets, mingle with the people, and find out what is going on in the country he is supposed to be governing. Shamanov's moniker of "cruel" is, Politkovskaya implies, justly earned, but he, for all his aggression and ostentatious heroism, does have the courage of his convictions, and he has paid the price for them in (comparative) poverty and personal loneliness. The impression given by the interview with Shamanov is that he might be an occasional blowhard and a borderline war criminal, but he is not a liar; indeed, his main problem, now that he has returned to civilian life, is that he insists on living life according to his own moral rules and telling what he sees as the truth, which isolates him from everyone around him. Kadyrov, however, who switched allegiances between the first and second wars, can come out with fine words upon occasion, but he is

---

71 Politkovskaya, *Dirty War*, 194.
72 Ibid., 197.
73 Ibid.
74 Ibid., 200.

depicted as having a moral center of doubtful stability, claiming to act for peace while threatening his enemies with decapitation. Almost as bad, as not worse, is his apparent cowardice, seen in his unwillingness to leave Gudermes. Shamanov seems to earn Politkovskaya's grudging respect and even sympathy; Kadyrov receives neither.

One might be tempted to see this as some kind of hidden chauvinism on Politkovskaya's part, seeing the Russian as heroic and the Chechen as cowardly and two-faced, but the rest of the book is filled with more than enough stories of cowardly, incompetent, and dishonest Russians, and heroic Chechens, to dispel that notion. The issue is not one of ethnicity, but of truth-telling or the lack thereof. Politkovskaya's own commitment to telling her version of the truth, no matter what the cost, inclines her to sympathy to others with the same commitment, even if they disagree about what those truths are. It is those who don't know what the truth is, and who fall into "petty untruths," consciously or not, who receive the full force of her disapproval. The juxtaposition of these two interviews, with Shamanov and Kadyrov, allows this to be seen clearly. Putting these two interviews back to back does not simply tell two different sides of the story, giving a Russian a voice and then a Chechen, it contrasts two different approaches to the truth, and reveals, in case the reader was in any doubt, which one Politkovskaya favors.

It also sets up the next section of the book, as untruths, petty or otherwise, feature heavily in the next several articles on the rebuilding of Chechnya and the supposed peace process. The two interviews are followed by a series of short pieces about the plight of the elderly in Grozny, and the struggles of mothers to have their sons' remains returned to them. These were themes from the first part of the book, and now Politkovskaya returns to them again, as if to show that nothing has been fixed, and the same problems that plagued people in 1999 continue to remain stubbornly unaddressed in 2000-2001, despite the fine promises of the officials she had spoken to the year before. She dwells at length on the chaos, lawlessness, and incompetence that rules in supposedly pacified Grozny, finally concluding:

> To begin with I thought how senseless everything happening here was. If you look at it from the State's point of view, why scatter a vast number of mines around the city and receive in return an astronomic growth in the number of disabled people, who require tons of medicine, artificial limbs and so on? And then scatter more mines. And again ferry in medicine, etc. Now

> it's clear what the State is up to. Its concern for the situation is purely virtual; the only reality is the scattering of mines.[75]

The State is conducting an elaborate charade, operating, like Kadyrov, with a tremendous disconnect between its words and its actions. This is hammered home in "We're Disposable: For the Attention of the Prosecutor-General's Office," a short piece about casualties among Russian troops, that begins, "Millions of my fellow citizens stubbornly refuse to understand what is going on today in Chechnya. It bears no relation to the propaganda in Moscow,"[76] and is concluded by tales of brutal hazing, sometimes ending in death, of Russian soldiers by each other.

It is followed by "Elections in a Battle Zone," a longer article about the difficulty, not to mention ludicrousness, of holding supposedly free and fair elections, or any sort of elections at all, in what is still an active battle zone. In it, Politkovskaya, as is her custom, allows her interviewees to speak their own words, and then adds her own musings, concluding with "This mockery of human liberty cannot continue indefinitely. No matter how much they try to disguise the battle zone as an area controlled by the Constitution there will never be enough camouflage to hide everything."[77]

Taken together, the point of these two pieces is clear: all talk of a constitutional democracy, or even basic human decency, by the Russian state is at best obfuscation, and at worse a deliberate and cynical sham, designed to distract citizens—voters—in both Moscow and Chechnya from the atrocities taking place in the Caucasus. It is a form of bread and circuses, Politkovskaya seems to be saying, except there's no actual bread—the lack of food for all parties involved, including the Russian troops themselves, is something to which Politkovskaya returns again and again in *A Dirty War*—and the circuses aren't very funny, since everyone involved is forced to be a gladiator or a sacrifice. This is the kind of "truth" that everyone has to discover, not the more rational-seeming, convenient truth peddled by the government and, Politkovskaya maintains, other, more servile, journalists.

Indeed, by the end of the book the impression Politkovskaya gives of Grozny and of all of Chechnya is of a topsy-turvy, Looking Glass country, where not only the infrastructure, but the very concepts of truth, justice, freedom, and basic social rules have been utterly upended. As she says in "Guns in the Night:

---

75 Ibid., 218.
76 Ibid., 244.
77 Ibid., 253.

Making Enemies": "While you're in Chechnya you do gradually get used to the idea that anything might happen, and that no one will be called into account. The republic is a symbol of contemporary servitude."[78] The complete lawlessness and anarchy that has permeated every level of civil and not-so-civil society has led, not to greater freedom, but to a terrorist state, one in which it is impossible to perform basic actions such as walking around town or even going to the bathroom without hiding from snipers and considering the placement of mines. Soldiers live in terror of their own comrades, and refugees and wounded veterans are dependent on the individual whims of administrators for the procurement of basic necessities such as food and medical treatment. Rules, regulations, and fine sentiments are used, not to help people and make things run more smoothly, but to justify mistreatment, abuse, and corruption by covering them up with a camouflage of nice-sounding lies.

A close reading of *A Dirty War* suggests that it is these lies, and this misappropriation of the truth, that is the ultimate, fundamental problem that Politkovskaya attacks. She begins the book by attacking the waste, corruption, and heartlessness she sees behind the delay in identifying soldiers' remains, moves on from there to the problem of refugees, then the mistreatment of Russian troops by their own government, and then allows representatives of the state, including those with whom she disagrees, to speak with their own words, before finishing with a series of pieces on the failed rebuilding of Grozny and Chechnya following what was supposed to be the conclusion of the war, even though, as she shows, the war was still actively going on.

Indeed, the final two pieces in *A Dirty War* show just how much chaos Chechnya was still in at the end of 2000. They are also highly fragmented. One of the last articles of the book, "Two Weeks: A Chronicle of Violence," is not an article per se, but a list of events that took place in Chechnya in two weeks in fall of 2000 while Politkovskaya was covering corruption in Yekaterinburg rather than Chechnya. It provides a grim litany of combat actions, exploding landmines, arrests, and murders. The effect, placed at it is near the end of the book, is of a country that is literally exploding into fragments that may not be possible to put back together. This is the truth that the authorities in Grozny and Gudermes don't know how to deal with, and that the authorities in Moscow don't want you to know about: a fragmented, violent, chaotic truth of death and dissolution.

The penultimate article in the book, "Treatment Deferred: Until After a Political Settlement," continues the theme of death and dissolution by examining

78 Ibid., 270.

what is happening at Grozny City Hospital No. 9, which Politkovskaya calls "the most accurate mirror of all that is going on in this blockaded city at the end of the twentieth century."[79] In it Politkovskaya describes the heroic lengths to which the few remaining doctors in the one remaining hospital in Grozny go to in order to save what patients they can, but what is also revealed in the article is the madness that was engulfing Grozny in the second winter of the war. As the war dragged on and the worst of the fighting was in theory already over, Politkovskaya shows that, rather than getting better, things were getting worse. The devastation of the war left Grozny in ruins—Politkovskaya calls it "this appalling contemporary Stalingrad"[80]—and destroyed much of the medical infrastructure, along with everything else. According to Salman Yandarov, head of the traumatology and orthopedics department, the situation was "absolutely surreal."[81]

The surreal nature of the situation in which they found themselves included both the conditions under which the doctors were treating patients—anesthetics brought in as humanitarian aid were being sold on the black market instead of brought directly to the hospital, for example, so that patients' relatives and hospital staff would have to go out and barter for them with drug dealers before an operation could take place—and the causes of the injuries themselves. Although the official line was that the fighting was over, and, somewhat contradictorily, that those who were injured were combatants, according to Yandarov, the vast majority of his patients were civilians injured by mines. Worst of all, some of these mines were planted not with the intention of wounding rebel fighters, but specifically with the intent of injuring civilians: Grozny was struck by a wave of apartment minings that winter, with the purpose of preventing people from returning to their old apartments now that peace has supposedly come to the city, thus allowing their neighbors to take over the apartments themselves. Of this, Politkovskaya says, "Such atrocious cruelty did not occur the previous winter in Grozny, nor this summer or autumn. Mined apartments typify the present winter. There may be some logic behind it, but it is the thinking of humans who have lost all decency."[82] Grozny has been transformed into a place that is not only structurally ruined, but where the people themselves have degraded from civilized beings into bandits who will blow up their neighbors and steal anesthetics from the gravely injured.

79 Ibid., 300.
80 Ibid., 301.
81 Ibid., 304.
82 Ibid., 301.

This degradation of morality is simultaneous with, and related to, the degradation of truth that occurred as the war progressed. The war brought out both the best and the worst in people, so that black-market drug dealers profiting off the misery of the wounded were operating side by side with doctors motivated by their commitment to the Hippocratic Oath. "The only remaining question," Politkovskaya says, "is which of them will win?"[83] But the problem is that the distorted, palatable half-truths are more easily lapped up by the people in Moscow. "Everyone is tired of this war. Even of talking about it. At least, in my native Moscow,"[84] Politkovskaya laments. The situation in Grozny was by then so surreal that the lies seemed more plausible, and so those not directly affected by the tragedy would turn away and distract themselves with other, more frivolous thoughts. This only added more twists to the knot in which the residents of Grozny were caught up in, as not only were they trapped in such a hellish situation, but few would believe them and their Cassandra-like pronouncements.

It is against that background that Politkovskaya sees herself as, if not the sole truthteller, then a member of a small group of those dedicated to telling the truth and thereby inspiring their fellow citizens to action. This is not an "elite" group, as Politkovskaya makes clear: those with access to the truth include people from all strata of society, both Russian and Chechen; but it is a "selective" group, in that it is for those with ears who can hear, and the strength of will to look upon the atrocities being committed in Chechnya and not look away or accept pleasant lies in lieu of an unpleasant truth. Politkovskaya gives many people voice in her articles and interviews, and shows that the truth of the situation is complex and multifaceted, but she is not in doubt that there *is* a truth, and one that can be revealed and understood. What is necessary is not an advanced intellect or education—those seem to stand in the way of understanding—but a willingness to accept the truth when it is spoken. Indeed, it is the simple folk who often have the best ability to grasp the truth, since they are living directly in it and don't have the luxury of telling themselves and others lies.

The final article in *A Dirty War*, "Murder Or Execution? One Year On and Still No Investigation," provides the final frame for the theme of truth versus lies. Written in January 2001, it tells the story of the massacre in Novye Aldy, a suburb of Grozny, which took place in February 2000 and in which dozens of civilians were murdered by Russian troops during a *zachistka* (sweep, cleansing, or mopping-up operation), multiple rapes were committed, and homes were

83 Ibid., 306.
84 Ibid., 307.

burned down. As of the time of writing, no one has yet to be held accountable for this by a Russian court;[85] when Politkovskaya covered the story, in 2000-2001, the victims and their families were still attempting to convince the authorities to begin an investigation of the matter, but with no success. Furthermore, their attempts to do so only fueled more cover-ups and lies on the part of the authorities. For example, although the relatives of the victims, in contravention of Muslim customs, delayed burial of the bodies in the hopes that an investigation would take place, and later, according to Politkovskaya, requested exhumations of the bodies, the officials "offer the shameless lie that the Chechens, faithful to their customs, refuse to allow the bodies to be exhumed and therefore the investigation is prevented from going ahead."[86] The surviving residents of Novye Aldy thus had to deal with official foot-dragging and outright prevarication as well as their original trauma.

Politkovskaya presents the actions of Russian forces as irrational and deceptive throughout her description of the affair, starting with the initiating, and ostensibly legitimate, military action. Although, she says, there were never any fighters or fighting in Novye Aldy, the settlement was subjected to heavy fire for all of December and January. Then:

> On 30 January [. . .] a special military operation to lure Chechen fighters out of Grozny—Shamanov's little trick. The Chechen field commanders were deliberately misinformed that, if they were prepared to pay, then the Feds were ready to create a corridor for their organised retreat from the city. The money was handed over, but the fighters soon found they had been led into a minefield.[87]

In another writer's hands, this episode could have been depicted as an example of the kind of overt firepower combined with clever strategizing that led to the Russian victory—"victory"—of the second war. Politkovskaya, however, depicts it as yet another example of the Russian military heartlessly targeting civilians for no reason, and as the abandonment of the rules of war—the same kind of moral degradation and collapse of civilized behavior that causes people to mine their neighbors' apartments in Grozny. Once again,

---

85 Russia was found guilty in 2006 and 2007 by the European Court of Human Rights in cases brought by families of some of the victims.

86 Ibid., 314.

87 Ibid., 310.

we see that, while Politkovskaya disapproves, to put it mildly, of putting rules and regulations above human welfare, she does believe in there being rules that are obeyed—they just must be rules that prioritize human welfare above other considerations, including military prowess and success.

Those who break these, largely unwritten, rules of conduct, become the focus of her disapprobation, even if she previously sympathized with them. General Shamanov received semi-sympathetic treatment in her interview with him, but that was because there he was a truthteller and a figure of pity. Now, though, his (by some measures, successful) military operation is described as "Shamanov's little trick," involving the use of "deliberate" misinformation—a grave sin in Politkovskaya's book. Her changing attitude towards him is not a manifestation of instability, but part of her own commitment to an overarching set of beliefs and behaviors, against which individuals are repeatedly measured. Just as Colonel Shcherbakov is originally villainized, and then later defended, in the first two articles of the book, as his true motives and behaviors are uncovered, revealing the false accusations of his detractors, so is General Shamanov alternately pitied and attacked, depending on his relationship to the truth.

Although Politkovskaya does not draw any straight lines directly from the "trick" that lured the Chechen fighters out of Grozny under false pretenses to the abuses committed by Russian troops during the mopping-up operation, she does present them as all being part and parcel of the same mindset, one that is fundamentally devoid of rationality and human decency. When a deputation largely composed of elderly men set out on February 3 to ask the Russian soldiers not to fire on Novye Aldy, they were shot at, and one of them, an ethnic Russian, was killed. The actual *zachistka* of February 5 is described as "an irrational and bloody settling of scores,"[88] an interesting combination of words, including as it does irrationality + violence + justice. The perpetrators of the atrocities in Novye Aldy, called "animals"[89] by other Russian soldiers, are ostensibly upholding the basic principles of justice and the rule of law, while in fact subverting, or more accurately, utterly destroying, them.

That justice has been subverted, even destroyed, is made clear by the subsequent inability of the victims' families to convince the authorities even to begin an investigation into the matter. Politkovskaya then details how staff in the Prosecutor-General's office have been trying to get out of investigating the affair, or even speaking about it on the record, since, they claim, they have received

88 Ibid., 311.
89 Ibid.

threats from on high, and also from military officers who were involved in it or similar atrocities. Her response to this is:

> That's a little hard to believe, of course. Only time will tell. Meanwhile, we must accept the fact that among the majors, colonels and generals that the country is praising, defending and decorating with awards there are also war criminals. Among the heroes are a percentage of unspeakable scum. And we all live together, side by side.[90]

This passage defines what for Politkovskaya seems to be both the ultimate problem, and its ultimate solution. Russia is praising, defending, and decorating war criminals and scum along with, or in many cases in lieu of, actual heroes and defenders of the motherland. And the two are all mixed up together—in fact, although Politkovskaya does not come out and say it, some of them even inhabit the same body, as in General Shamanov, whom she presents as both a hero and a villain. This is problematic for Politkovskaya, for whom, despite her willingness to tell everyone's side of the story, there is really only one truth and one moral code, against whom everyone is measured. Unsurprisingly, given Politkovskaya's own courage and the strength of her convictions, many people fall short, and she considers it her task to reveal the deeds of evildoers, and exhort her fellow citizens to shrug off their sloth and indifference and join her helping the helpless and standing strong against untruth and injustice.

At the same time, the fact that "we all live together, side by side" seems to be the path she considers most helpful for breaking down the barriers that allow people to wall themselves up in sloth and indifference, not to mention outright untruth. Both her words and her deeds demonstrate that for her, the personal connection and individual interactions with her fellow humans are the route to true understanding and the "truest" form of the truth, as well as morality and decency in their most basic forms. For Politkovskaya, the truth is perhaps not so much "out there" as within us, and each person must search within their heart for the compassion and human feeling that is guaranteed to be there, if they can dispel the greed, cowardice, and the hardened carapace of bureaucracy and officialese that is holding them back.

Politkovskaya's chosen medium for her work, individual newspaper articles, is thus the best medium in which for her to pursue her aims. It allows her to interact one-on-one with a variety of people, telling their stories and using

---

90 Ibid., 315.

them to touch the hearts of her readers, spurring them to action. Out of these fragmented little truths, she is able to build one big truth, one that says war and violence are wrong, and the most important thing is not victory, but compassion.

Politkovskaya is the only female writer featured here, although she was far from the only female reporter covering the Chechen War—indeed, as Thomas de Waal notes in his introduction to *A Dirty War*, "It is an interesting phenomenon that many of the best journalists in Chechnya have been women."[91] To this illustrious group could also be added Nobel Prize winner Svetlana Alexievich, whose *Zinky Boys* is a similar piece of war coverage, although of the war in Afghanistan rather than Chechnya. These female writers are marked by their courage, both in visiting war zones and in covering "taboo" and "unfeminine" subjects; indeed, all of them are known for their outspokenness, and some of them, most notably Politkovskaya herself, have paid the ultimate price for it.

At the same time, it may not be coincidental that the only female writer surveyed here is a journalist rather than a novelist or memoirist. While Politkovskaya, like Alexievich, has a distinct voice and uses it to voice her opinion loudly, she is always peripheral to her own story. Indeed, these pieces are not "her story" at all—they're all somebody else's story, which she is presenting to the world. She uses her own experiences as a way to give other people voice and introduce other people's lives to her readers, rather putting herself front and center. The flip side of her connection with others is that, while there certainly is an "I" in Politkovskaya's writing, most of the writing is not about her "I." This is not a criticism, but a remark that in contemporary Russian writing, it is perhaps more acceptable for women to be journalists than novelists. One of the reasons why Politkovskaya is writing in short forms rather than longer epics, and about other people than about herself, may be because that is what women are supposed to be doing.

I would also argue that by writing other people's stories, she is writing the literature of trauma, although in her own way. As Tal notes, she is driven to bear witness to the trauma she sees, to "tell and retell" it in order to make it real for her audience. By presenting fragments of many different people's stories, Politkovskaya shows, not the trauma of an individual personality, but the trauma of the nation as a whole. Her short, disconnected vignettes of other people's lives demonstrate a kind of national PTSD, even as she uses these brief flashes of other peoples' memories and experiences to reconstruct the story overall. Unlike actual trauma victims, however, she does believe in her ability to reach others and share her story with them—at least when she is telling the

---

91 Ibid., xxx.

story of her nation, not the story of herself; she is generally reserved in her accounts of her own personal traumatic experiences. In her articles she presents the experience of a nation traumatized by corruption, cruelty, and war, without the sense of special apartness and oscillation between closeness and withdrawal that can mark the actual victims of trauma. While she often expresses frustration with the people back in Moscow who close their eyes and ears to the truth she wants to tell, she always has faith that that truth can be conveyed.

Politkovskaya began as a newspaper journalist, and it is not surprising that her work is in short, discrete pieces. This tendency is most noticeable in her first book, *A Dirty War*; by *Putin's Russia*, the essays are longer and form a more coherent whole. This structure is, though, not just a result of Politkovskaya's journalistic training: by giving us short vignettes, she is able to present the multifaceted nature of the Chechen Wars without sacrificing her own unifying perspective. In all her essays and articles on Chechnya, she seeks to drive home the incompetence, the brutality, and the sheer stupidity of the war. Rather than saying, as American journalists might, that each side has merit and each side's perspective must be taken into consideration, she seems to be saying that each side has some shred of humanity to which it is still clinging, but that all the sides are drowning in pointless, meaningless bungling and short-sighted adherence to their own short-term interests. We are invited to empathize with all the participants in the war, even those most responsible for its cruelty, but this empathy is not supposed to allow readers to wring their hands and give up; it is designed to jolt the reader into action. A smoother, more linear narrative account would not have the same impact. The very nonlinear, unconnected nature of the stories both puts the reader into Politkovskaya's own shoes as she is there on the ground, jolting from place to place and interviewing such disparate figures as Chechen fighters, OMON troops, and teachers at refugee camps, and also, like a kaleidoscope, allows the reader to reorganize the stories in multiple ways, each time seeing a new pattern emerge. The main thing holding the stories together is Politkovskaya's driving will and rock-hard righteousness. Despite the fact that these stories are not about her, it is her personality that comes through as the unifying force throughout these works.

Her unified and unifying personality stands in contrast to the personalities revealed in the next works covered, all written by participants in the combat itself. For them, the war was fragmenting not because there were so many points of view that needed to be considered, but because of the intense psychological and physical suffering they underwent. Politkovskaya in her works appears as a whole person turning her lens to others in an attempt to piece together the truth; these other writers are fractured people, turning their lenses on themselves in attempts to piece back together their psyches and their very lives.

4

Mikail Eldin: Rebel With a Cause

It is only possible to write beautifully about war if you have never witnessed it from within.

—Mikail Eldin, *The Sky Wept Fire*

Chechen Writers

A story of Russian literature about the Chechen War is necessarily Russo-centric. But what about the other side? The Chechens who participated, including those who fought against the Russian federal forces, were also Russian speakers and Russian citizens, even as they took up arms against their country of citizenship in defense of their country of nationality. This awareness of their dual, split situation is reflected in the writings of Chechen authors in general, including the one featured here, Mikail Eldin.

Although their situation and their identity is not so much split in half as it is pulled in three different directions at once.[1] As well as their Chechen patriotism and their Russian education, Chechen writers were also products of the Soviet

1 Early Soviet-era Chechen authors whose work features the tension and relationships between Chechen, Russian, and Soviet culture include Magomet Mamakaev, Arbi Mamakaev (no relation), Magomed-Salakh Gadaev, and Abuzar Aidamirov. Still-living Chechen authors who touch on the theme of Chechen self-identification include Apti Bisultanov, Lechi Abdulaev, and Musa Beksultanov. All these authors had complex relationships with Soviet power, often working for Soviet newspapers and engaging in translation work that was part of the Russification of Chechen culture, while also writing in Chechen and agitating for Chechen literature and increased Chechen independence.

Union, and may harken back to the Soviet past as least as much as they do to Chechen history and the Russian present. Indeed, German Sadulaev, perhaps the most well known of the contemporary Chechen writers, is even a member of the Communist party, and his Communist ideals (or is it Soviet nostalgia?) are something he shares with Zakhar Prilepin, a Russian author who fought for the federal forces in Chechnya and then volunteered to fight with pro-Russian forces in the Donbass.

One of the underlying themes/issues/problems for all the writers surveyed here, but felt particularly acutely by the Chechen ones, is their connections and their shared culture with the other side. Commentators on the conflict like to speak of the radicalization of this generation of Chechens, and their growing ties with Islamist groups, and there is some truth to this, but in fact Chechen writers are products of the same Soviet system as their opponents, and there is surprisingly little room for Islam there, just as there is little room for Orthodoxy amongst the ethnically Russian writers. Even Eldin, who is writing with the goal of explaining and justifying the point of view of the Chechen opposition, and who explicitly discusses his faith on multiple occasions in his book, grounds many of his descriptions with Soviet cultural touchstones such as the heroic war movie, something he shares with Arkady Babchenko, who fought on the opposite side.

Chechen works, then, shed a somewhat unexpected light on the Chechen experience: those who considered themselves patriotic Chechens, and who even took up arms against the Russian federal forces, were operating at least as much from a worldview shaped by Soviet ideals of fairness, equality, valor, and honor as they were out of national identity or religious conviction.

Needless to say, this makes their situation even more complicated. For Chechen writers, the conflict is much less black and white than it is for the Russians. While those of the Russians who served in combat against the Chechens become quite successful over the course of the conflicts in "othering" the Chechens, calling them bandits, using racial slurs to define them, or reducing them to a handful of features, normally their beards, Eldin, who made the conscious decision to take up arms against the Russian forces, sees himself as having much in common with the Russians who are occupying their country by force. Indeed, Eldin, who believes in the code of the warrior, repeatedly praises the Russians for their courage in battle.

The reasons for this sympathy are no doubt legion, but it seems likely that a major factor is their shared language. For non-Russians of the former USSR, Russian is both a blessing and a curse. It is the language of the oppressor, and in some cases was used to wipe out indigenous languages, but it is also the lingua franca of an enormous country, and allows people from small, insular regions such as Chechnya to communicate with the wider world.

Not only to communicate, but, as can be seen in these books, to empathize, even with those who seemed bent on destruction of these people's homeland. This leads us to a sticky question, one that these works here imply, even if they do not ask directly, and which they do not, and perhaps cannot, answer. Namely, is it a good thing for an oppressed group to be able to understand and empathize with its oppressors? Especially when the oppressing group has such a hard time finding any empathy in their own hearts? Politkovskaya's writing was largely aimed at "setting fire to the hearts of men," as Pushkin put it, and awakening sympathy for the plight of the Chechens amongst her fellow Russian citizens. She was also appalled by the heartless violence of a few representatives of the Chechen side, notably Shamil Basaev, the Kadyrovs, and those who led the attacks on the Dubrovka theater and the school in Beslan. Chechen writers such as Eldin also seek to awaken sympathy for their people and their cause amongst their readers, but it is interesting to note how much sympathy, even if at times it seems unwilling, they have for their Russian enemies. While the Russian writers featured here are shattered or pulled apart by the violence of war, Chechen writers were already fragmented before the conflict ever began, torn between their Chechen and their Russian sides, as well as their hoped-for independent future and their Soviet past.

Although the Russians were also, of course, shattered. The collapse of the Soviet Union, which led directly to the conflict in Chechnya, was, for all its seemingly nonviolent nature, one of the most shattering events of the twentieth century. Millions of people woke up one day with passports for a country that no longer existed. Chechen writers may feel the problem more acutely than their Russian comrades, but it is, at its heart, similar for all of them. The breakup of the USSR was a cataclysm that was played out in miniature in Chechnya, and inside the psyche of every person who was touched by its violence. Small wonder that the artistic productions of the people affected are made up of shards and splinters.

Mikail Eldin and *The Sky Wept Fire*

For most readers, Mikail Eldin may be the most mysterious and elusive figure featured here. Unlike the Russian authors profiled in this book, he is not a celebrity in either Russia or the West. Although he, like the other authors I discuss, also began his career as a journalist, he reported for the arts and culture section of the local Chechen-language paper *Vast* (*Image*) in Grozny,[2] which drew considerably less notoriety than Politkovskaya's or Babchenko's deliberately provocative work, not to mention Prilepin's active PR campaigns for his literary and political activities.

After being forced to seek political asylum in Norway, Eldin has continued to speak out against the Russian conquest and oppression of Chechnya, but in a low-key fashion. When I began this project, it was impossible to find out anything about him through normal research channels, and I am indebted to his translator Anna Gunin for putting me directly in touch with him. In January 2021, however, he gave a series of in-depth interviews in Russian to the Czech-based opposition Russian media project *NEP Prague*.[3] These interviews provide considerable interest to educators and scholars on multiple fronts. In them, Eldin gives a direct account of his background, his activities for the Chechen cause, and his experiences of detention and torture by Russian forces. This is interesting in and of itself, and could be used for Russian-speaking students wishing to engage in research on the topic. The interviews could also be used in advanced Russian classes in order to expose students to the Russian spoken in the North Caucasus—Eldin's Russian is fluent and correct but spoken with a marked Chechen accent.

Furthermore, Eldin provides an interesting corrective to the widespread admiration of opposition blogger and politician Alexei Navalny. When the interviews were given mass protests had just broken out across Russia in response to Navalny's recent arrest. In the interviews, Eldin and the interviewers discuss Navalny's troubling statements vis-à-vis the Caucasus, and his position as a populist, nationalist politician. Although an in-depth discussion and critique of Navalny's platform is beyond the scope of this work, it is worth noting that one

---

2 Mikail Eldin, phone interview, February 3, 2021.

3 NEP Prague, "Ia real'no khotel umeret'," YouTube video, 40:59, January 29, 2021, https://youtu.be/D2bLQCws60g; and NEP Prague, "Russkie ne dolzhny molchat'," YouTube video, 36:05, January 30, 2021, https://youtu.be/-88FM2DjwWw.

of the benefits of studying lesser-known writers from marginalized communities is their fresh take on the political and social issues of the day.

Eldin's position as someone on the margins of the mainstream Russian opposition and of mainstream Western anti-Russian sentiment is reflected in his publisher's presentation of him and his book. As someone who fought for a cause that was only somewhat accepted in the West, he is a tough sell to a mainstream Western audience, and the fine line his publisher has had to walk can be seen in the official publicity materials surrounding his book. According to his author's bio blurb from the *Granta* website, "When the First Chechen War began in 1994 Mikail Eldin was a young arts journalist hunting for a story. By the time of the second Russian invasion five years later, he was a battle-scarred reporter who had survived firefights and brutal torture at the hands of Russian troops."[4] However, the title of his book, *The Sky Wept Fire: My Life as a Chechen Freedom Fighter*, suggests that he did more than merely report on the war, and the front matter of the book itself states that "Mikail Eldin worked as a journalist before taking up arms in the conflict with Russia. He eventually left Chechnya in fear for his life and secured political asylum in Norway, where he now lives," while the back cover says "On the eve of the First Chechen War, Mikail Eldin was a young, naive arts journalist. By the end of the second war, he had become a battle-hardened reporter and mountain partisan who had endured torture and imprisonment."[5]

This coyness about what, precisely, role Eldin played in the wars reflects the ambiguity of his position and the West's attitude towards the Chechen side of the wars. No one (outside of Russia) denies that the Russian forces committed terrible atrocities, and especially during the first war, Western organizations and media sources tended to support the Chechen side. But the Chechen forces were not always good guys in white hats either, and worse than that from the point of view of Westerners, they became increasingly associated with terrorists. Quite aside from the current Western preoccupation with Islamist groups such as Al-Qaeda, ISIS, and the Taliban, for Westerners to support the Chechen fighters also opens up several other nasty cans of worms: does supporting Chechen separatism mean they are also morally obliged to support Basque separatists, the Provisional IRA in Northern Ireland, and American right-wing militias, all of whom have claimed the title of "freedom fighter"? And what about

4 Mikail Eldin, "The Second Night is Ending," *Granta*, accessed May 5, 2022, https://granta.com/the-second-night-is-ending/.

5 Mikail Eldin, *The Sky Wept Fire: My Life as a Chechen Freedom Fighter*, trans. Anna Gunin. (London: Portobello Books, 2013).

the Donbass separatists? Is the American alleged support of self-determination really support of an anti-Russian agenda, which falls apart in the face of pro-Russian demands for autonomy and self-determination. And, perhaps most pressingly of all, can English-language readers in a post-9/11 world handle the concept of nationalism with a Muslim face?

The presentation of Eldin's book to the English-language reader flirts with these issues of language and definition: he is a "partisan" and a "freedom fighter," and certainly, in no way, related to al-Qaeda (which is true: he does not mention any such ties in the book, and also told me during a personal interview that the wars were not about religion but about national self-determination, an opinion also expressed by a number of experts on the subject).[6] The word "jihad" is strenuously avoided. The English-language reader is told, soothingly, at the beginning and end of the book that Eldin is not unlike American Revolutionaries or other "good guys" in the history of Western civilization. Eldin's journalistic activities are stressed, aligning him with Politkovskaya and other heroes of the Russia-focused Western intelligentsia.

Which is not to say that any of that is false. On the contrary, the persona he presents in his book is indeed that of a naive but idealistic young journalist who finds himself caught up in a struggle to defend his homeland from foreign invaders. While his military activities are touched upon, the main focus of much of his stories about himself is journalism, and while he professes a sincere and passionate Islamic faith, which he credits with saving him from madness or suicide during and after the torture he experienced at the hands of Russian forces, he shows zero affinity for any kind of international Islamist movement. His Islam is the religion of Sufi mystics, whom he quotes at the beginning of each section of the book, not that of al-Qaeda and its offspring. So while *The Sky Wept Fire* has a definite political agenda, that of giving the Chechen side of the story and justifying the actions of the Chechen anti-Russian opposition, Eldin's story is as much that of one man's life-changing experience of warfare as it is a presentation of the Chechen point of view. That being said, the Chechen point of view is stressed throughout the book: Eldin is acutely aware that he, unlike his Russian counterparts, is one of the few mouthpieces his people have, and strives to speak as loudly as possible in response.

Although Eldin's native language is Chechen, *The Sky Wept Fire* was originally written in Russian, and then edited and translated into English before being published by Portobello Books in 2013. It won a PEN award, and received critical acclaim in the West, hailed as a "powerful, lyrical and disturbing

6 Eldin, Skype interview with author, July 29, 2017.

memoir."[7] It has not, however, been published in Russia or in Russian, and thus brings up the question of what, exactly, is "Russian" literature. Does anything written in Russian count, even if the author is not only not Russian, but has a strong opposition to being part of Russia, and the final form of the text is not published in Russian? In our first Skype conversation, Eldin and I discussed this issue, and the fact that, while Chechens of his generation received the same Soviet education as their Russian counterparts, and are influenced by classical Russian literature—he spoke particularly warmly of Tolstoy's *Hadji-Murat* and *The Cossacks* as being examples of vivid war writing based on first-person experiences—they must orient themselves to an international audience if they want to tell their story to the broader world, and that he considers himself an international writer as much as anything.[8]

Like the other works discussed here, *The Sky Wept Fire* is composed of short, semi-connected scenes. It also has few concrete references to specific individuals: Eldin warns the reader in the preface that, although he has attempted to make his account as accurate as possible, he has omitted names and other identifying information, because of his "strange memory, which has blotted the names from my mind, leaving only the faces and their actions."[9] He presents this decision as one resulting from his understanding of the historical process. His story is thus pitched to the reader as both historically accurate, and an ahistorical tale of universal significance, while hinting at the psychological disintegration of the narrator that will appear as the book progresses.

The book begins with a short background of the start of the first war from the Chechen perspective. Like Politkovskaya, Eldin sees Russia's actions in the war as cynical, dishonest, and self-serving, but Eldin ascribes to them much more competence and forward planning than Politkovskaya does. Throughout the book, Eldin emphasizes the supposed conspiracy amongst the Russian high command to exploit the Chechens' legitimate grievances for their own, anti-Chechen ends, even as he lauds the courage of many of the low-level Russian soldiers. How true these widely spread rumors of conspiracy are is a matter of much debate: while some members of the Russian high command were no

---

7 Arifa Akbar, "The Sky Wept Fire: My Life as a Chechen Freedom Fighter by Mikail Eldin, trans by Anna Gunin—Book Review," *Independent*, December 12, 2013, http://www.independent.co.uk/arts-entertainment/books/reviews/the-sky-wept-fire-my-life-as-a-chechen-freedom-fighter-by-mikail-eldin-trans-by-anna-gunin-book-8998790.html.

8 Eldin, Skype interview with author, July 29, 2017.

9 Eldin, *Sky Wept Fire*, xi-xii. In our first Skype conversation, Eldin explicitly told me that the torture that he underwent has damaged his memory, making it occasionally difficult to remember names or dates, even as he cannot forget the interrogations themselves (Eldin, Skype interview, July 29, 2017).

doubt cynical and self-serving in the extreme, and there are allegations that they deliberately provoked the 1999 invasion of Dagestan led by Basaev and Khattab, and may have masterminded at least some of the apartment bombings in the fall of 1999 that served as a pretext for the second war and a major reason for its popularity amongst ordinary Russian citizens,[10] there were also others who protested against the decision to go to war, especially at the beginning of the first war. Furthermore, Russian governmental and military actions, most notably in the first war but also the second, were marked by such stunning levels of incoordination and incompetence that it is hard to credit them with the ability to carry out a complex and far-reaching conspiracy. Although perhaps conspiracies flourish amongst the manure of corruption and incompetence.

Be that as it may, Eldin starts off the book with an us-them dichotomy, which is both a Chechen-Russian dichotomy and one that separates those who are pure of heart from those who are not. Those who would cynically exploit the war and their people's misery, who are mostly but not entirely Russian, are the "them," and those who bravely fight for their homeland, whether Chechen or Russian, are accorded the status of "us," even if they were fighting for the other side. Eldin's division of the world into two sides is less one of pure ethnicity and more one of ideals, behavior, and an appropriate code of honor. Although he is more partisan than Politkovskaya, Eldin is nonetheless a journalist before he is a fighter, and even after undergoing the shattering experiences that lead him to take up arms for the Chechen side, he still writes with a journalist's eye for the bigger picture.

The first several chapters, none of which are more than a few pages, of the book's first section, entitled "Ragnarok," are, despite depicting the early action of the first war in short bursts and snippets, the most linear and clearly journalistic. After the opening chapter explaining the entrance of the Armed Opposition, anti-Dudaev forces bankrolled by Russia, into Grozny in November 1994, Eldin describes his own first encounter with military action, as he and his fellow residents of Grozny run around the city, gawping at the tanks that are rolling down their streets and wondering what in the world is happening.

Two things stand out in this section of the narrative: the emphasis on the naivety of Eldin and everyone else in Grozny, and the difference between the cinematic treatment of war everyone had grown up with and the actual reality of war. Both of these things come together to form the underlying impression of a narrator who is, while coherent on the surface, split internally between

---

10 See for example Matthew Evangelista's discussion of the events in the chapter "Putin's War" from *The Chechen Wars: Will Russia Go the Way of the Soviet Union?*

unrealistic expectations and his experience of reality. Like Politkovskaya, Eldin here is a truth-seeker, but he starts out by thinking that he knows the truth, only to discover that what he knows is actually fiction. He has to set aside his expectations, created by a lifetime of Soviet films and Soviet propaganda, in order to grasp what is actually happening around him.

The naivety of Eldin and many of the other people he encounters in the early days of the first war is stressed repeatedly. During the initial action in November 1994 Eldin considers it his duty as a journalist to cover the conflict, and heads blithely out into the battle zone, with little comprehension of what that actually means. On the first day that tanks of the Armed Opposition roll into Grozny, everyone assumes that those who had joined the Armed Opposition had done so merely as a way to get weapons funded with Russian money. "Seeing this naive faith of ordinary Chechens in the Chechen sense of national consciousness and comradeship made me well up with a feeling of pride and pity for them,"[11] Eldin says.

Eldin depicts the Chechen people as being, on the eve of the first war, naive and overly trusting in their own good nature. During this time:

> we stubbornly refused to believe that the Chechen spiritual world had imploded at the moment when [. . .] ordinary Chechens took up weapons against their fellow Chechens. And when we finally accepted the blunt truth, we ended up losing countless lives, and many of the living would lose what was most precious of all: their Chechen spirit.[12]

This passage is intriguing, especially coming from someone who is writing as a "Chechen freedom fighter." The Chechens are not depicted here as wily, hardened fighters, as they tend to be in works written by ethnic Russians, but rather, as people with an almost childlike belief in the goodness of their fellow citizens and Chechens. But this goodness is an illusion, belief in which allowed the Chechen spiritual world and national consciousness to be destroyed. And yet accepting the truth of the situation was also destructive to the "Chechen spirit." Truth here for Eldin is not the healing, illuminating force it is Politkovskaya, but a double-edged sword, one that can destroy the fictions that bind a people together even as it reveals wrongdoing.

---

11 Eldin, *Sky Wept Fire*, 8.
12 Ibid., 8-9.

Eldin himself partakes in the same naivety at the beginning of his story. That day, November 26, 1994, his response to the sound of shelling is to take off in search of the action, seeking a good story. A journalist ostensibly out seeking the truth, he needs to give himself comforting fictions in order to be able to do his job, and he does not even realize how woefully unprepared, practically and psychologically, he is for what he is about to experience. When he and a group of other young people are fired on by a squadron of Russian planes, they avoid being hit through sheer luck, since "In our naivety, it simply hadn't occurred to us to disperse when the planes had appeared."[13]

Afterwards, congratulating himself on his successful tour of what had become a war zone, he thinks, "So now I had witnessed war: I had seen its blood and its corpses, I had heard small-arms fire and had even been fired at myself—or so it had seemed, at any rate. I was naive, and didn't have the vaguest notion of what lay in store for me."[14] Eldin thinks at this point that he knows the truth, but in fact, his understanding of the truth is so colored by his misapprehension of what war is like that he struggles to recognize the truth when it appears to him as attack planes coming out of the sky. His naivety gives him and his fellow Chechens a certain purity of heart, but it leaves them defenseless, figuratively and literally, when they are faced with attack.

This naivety and misunderstanding of what is happening around them is at least partially a result, Eldin suggests, the result of expectations formed by watching Soviet war films. When on that first day he walks around the combat zone, he says "it all felt like one of those war games we used to play as kids at Pioneer camp [. . .] it felt like we'd stumbled on to the set of some Soviet war film. Everyone here felt the same elated thrill and privilege to be witnessing this."[15] The first day of fighting, when the Armed Opposition brought their tanks into Grozny and were repelled by pro-Dudaev government forces, was comparatively bloodless, and everyone involved, according to Eldin, felt the same sensation of playing a game or being part of a movie. As he walks away from his first encounter with tanks, he even congratulates himself on having had such a marvelous adventure.

But on the way home he stumbles into the aftermath of another battle, and this time, he sees the corpses of soldiers killed when their tank was hit by enemy rounds. The sight is horrific, and Eldin can only make sense of it by seeing it as a kind of gruesome fairy-tale moment: "The scene looked like a giant cannibal

---

13 Ibid., 19.
14 Ibid.
15 Ibid., 14.

had decided to make lunch and had been chopping up plenty of meat."[16] Prior to witnessing real combat and its results, Eldin's sense of "reality" had been formed by Soviet war movies and Pioneer games, and encountering an actual war zone and real death and destruction shoves him out of this cinematic "reality" into a state of semi-hallucinatory fantasy, which is the only way he can make sense of the horrific, real reality before him. The sight of those mangled human corpses shocks him out of his optimistic complacency and forces him to conclude:

> So all those Soviet war films had been nothing but lies. The hero had always died beautifully with a smile on his face and with time to bid farewell to his comrades. And the enemy had died ugly deaths, falling face down, arms and legs sprawled out like spiders. The soldiers here on both sides had been raised on the same films as I had. They too had believed in these beautiful wartime deaths.[17]

Eldin stresses that everyone on both sides saw themselves as taking part in a noble, uplifting game, without real consequences. If a hero (and of course everyone saw themselves as the heroes) were to die, he would do so nobly, elegantly, with time to say a few inspiring words of farewell to his comrades before striking an attractive pose and passing peacefully into death. The true horror of death in combat, especially when caused by modern weapons of war, is so appalling that the humans who witness it have difficulty comprehending it, and often end up retreating into fantasy, madness, or mindless panic in response to it.[18] This is something that soldiers on both sides of the conflict, as well as civilians who have been caught up in in it randomly, describe: when faced with the truth of war, the human mind retreats into hiding, or, if that is impossible, makes up metaphors and stories in order to make sense of it: it is not humans and their machines who have done this, but a "giant cannibal" making lunch.

---

16 Ibid., 18.

17 Ibid.

18 When asked directly whether he thought modern warfare was more horrific than war in the past, Eldin stated, however, that "there is no difference—war is a terrible thing" (Skype interview, July 29, 2017), a sentiment also echoed by Babchenko. However, all the writers featured here specifically mention the destructive effects of high-powered weaponry and the damage it can do to the human body.

This is in accordance with Herman's description of the response to traumatic events. As she says:

> Traumatic reactions occur when action is of no avail. When neither resistance nor escape is possible, the human system of self-defense becomes overwhelmed and disorganized. Each component of the ordinary response to danger, having lost its utility, tends to persist in an altered and exaggerated state long after the actual danger is over. Traumatic events produce profound and lasting changes in physiological arousal, emotion, cognition, and memory.[19]

When exposed to trauma, the human mind stops making sense of what is happening. Physiological perceptions may become distorted, and memory may fragment and become separated from both intellect and emotion.[20] As Eldin depicts it, the unwillingness of the human mind to grasp the horror of that most human of actions, war, leads people to dress it up in pretty clothes and turn it into something that is both morally acceptable and aesthetically pleasing.

Furthermore, like the Muscovites and Westerners whom Politkovskaya is trying to shock out of their complacent fictions, the ones who can't bear to look the war in the face and who therefore tell themselves that Russia is a great and benevolent nation, that all Chechens are terrorists, or there's nothing that anyone can do about the atrocities taking place, the Chechens as Eldin describes them are at the beginning of the war caught up in happy fictions about the nobility of war. Everyone, both opposition and government soldiers, as well as the civilians witnessing the fighting, saw what was taking place as either a minor thing that would soon be over with few consequences, or a grand adventure that would be sure to end happily.

In these opening chapters of *The Sky Wept Fire*, Eldin is writing both as an individual and as a representative of the Chechen nation. In his depiction of the beginning of the first war, both he and the Chechen people in general were naive, full of romantic notions about themselves and about what war was like. He and his people were living in an illusion of nobility and romance, fueled by both the "Chechen spirit" and by a lifetime of imbibing Soviet ideology and Soviet war films. They therefore, despite the breakup of the Soviet Union and Chechnya's precarious position as a region, did not expect the outbreak of

---

19 Herman, *Trauma and Recovery*, 34.
20 Ibid.

total war, and if they did think about it, they thought of war more as a grand adventure in which they would get to prove their nobility and heroism, than as a destructive holocaust that would endanger their nation and snuff out tens of thousands of lives.

When Eldin's, and by extension his people's, sense of reality is shattered by the actual experience of the war, the initial reaction is to retreat or make up stories as an explanation of, and shield from, the brutal realities of the situation. The two realities—imagined and real—thus clash. The result, for Eldin-as-narrator, and, he suggests, for his people as well, is a kind of dissociative break. In the following chapters, Eldin switches in places from a first-person to a second-person narration. This allows him to generalize his experiences, while also distancing himself from them.

The first place in which the second-person narration appears is chapter 7. In the first six chapters, Eldin describes the events of November and December 1994, leading to the storming of Grozny by Russian federal troops on December 31, 1994. This, Eldin says, left Grozny looking like "the set of an apocalyptic horror film."[21] His perception of events has already switched genres, from heroic Soviet war film, to horror, a switch in genre that is accompanied by a switch in narrative point of view.

This change in point of view allows Eldin to generalize his and Grozny's experiences during the early days of the first war, connecting them to the human experience overall. He begins by exposing some of the delusions of modern civilization, delusions that get stripped away when faced by a kill-or-be-killed situation such as war:

> Modern man, raised on the ideals of goodness and compassion to all beings, aware of the sanctity of life, naively assumes that he's frightened of blood and the sight of it will make him queasy. **Yet he is deluding himself**. It is only when you find yourself in a situation where death and blood are as natural as life itself that you realize that anyone can cope with the sight of blood—and if you can't, then something is wrong with you. What's more, the sight of fresh blood awakens man's primordial instincts, boosting his chances of surviving in extreme circumstances.[22]

---

21 Eldin, *Sky Wept Fire*, 38.
22 Ibid., 34, emphasis my own.

In the first six chapters, Eldin identifies primarily as a journalist, and attempts to give a journalistic account of the events of the first days of the war. Yet, as he emphasizes, his ability, and that of everyone else involved, was hampered by his naivety, his illusions about the nature of war, and his belief in the inherent nobility of the Chechen people, as well as his leftover Soviet ideology, which, although he had ostensibly repudiated it, still formed his core expectations for human behavior. The behavior of both sides in the conflict, which was marked so egregiously by a mixture of cynicism and incompetence, destroyed much of his faith in civilized behavior according to Soviet ideals, while the nature of war itself stripped him of his outer layer of civilization, revealing a more primitive underlayer. Modern civilization is shown to be a shared fiction, and once that fiction is pierced by the reality of death and violence, humans discover their animal instincts coming to the fore, ready to save them from destruction.[23]

This discovery of the animal nature lurking within the civilized human does, or can, trigger a crisis of identity and faith. Without the trappings of modern civilization, what makes a human, human? In this chapter, Eldin describes, using the second person and thus distancing himself from his own transformation, while broadening the reach of his conclusions, his return to an older, pre-Soviet warrior morality, as well as a deepening of religious faith:

> Obeying an ancient instinct, he tries to survive by killing his own kind. The only difference is that the warrior—a sacred class—will kill only warriors, whereas a coward will try to wipe out everyone, anything that breathes, life itself, because the worm of a tremendous fear is gnawing his heart, making him wantonly cruel. Once you have cultivated a calm, philosophical approach to death, you start to view blood and corpses as mundane, humdrum even. And when that happens, the only thing that can save you is a deep, sincere faith in God—and it doesn't matter which God, or even whether it is God at all you believe in, so long as your belief is sincere and is not a belief in Evil, otherwise you'll become a slave to instinct. It is instinct that helps you survive, but faith is what keeps you from turning into a beast, what helps you stay human. If you give yourself up to instinct without faith, you'll soon turn into an animal, while if

23 In our first conversation about this aspect of war and its effects on the human psyche, Eldin stated, "In war, a person can only be what they are. In war, a person's essence is revealed in five minutes" (Eldin, Skype interview, July 29, 2017).

> you nurture only faith without instinct, you'll end up a crazed fanatic.[24]

Here Eldin describes a regression to a prehistoric state, and an attempt, on the part of the individual, but presented as on the part of a society, to retrace the steps of civilization and recreate within oneself the progress of civilization, rediscovering and making anew rules that prevent humans, who carry the seeds of a violence much more deadly than that of any other creature that walks the earth, from destroying themselves and their world.[25]

However, the attempt is only partially successful, hence the transformation of Grozny from a modern city into the set of an apocalyptic horror film. Eldin describes the battle that took place in similarly apocalyptic terms, turning the first storming of Grozny into a semi-supernatural battle between good and evil that could easily be imagined as the climax of an action movie:

> And so, in this city, the finest warriors of this once-united great country came together in lethal battle. A battle from which no one could emerge as victors or vanquished; merely as survivors or corpses. A battle where to survive meant victory: victory not over the adversary, but over death. [. . .] The Russians were fighting for the right to stay alive, while the Chechens were fighting for all the former generations who had fallen in combat against this Empire; they were fighting for all those who had been unable to retaliate during the period from 1944 to 1949; they were battling with Death for Life itself. And the battle was brutal and majestic; it was a hymn to human courage and valour.[26]

Here in this pivotal chapter Eldin moves away from chronicling the day-to-day events of the opening gambits in the First Chechen War, and ascribes to it a greater significance, as both a civil war within a former superpower, and as a battle between the forces of Death and the forces of Life. Mere politics and

---

24 Eldin, *Sky Wept Fire*, 34-5.

25 This is similar to Sergei Bodrov Jr.'s description of his character, the disaffected Chechen War veteran Danila Bagrov, in the film *Brother* (Брат): "I imagine people in the original chaos, who are sitting by a fire in their cave and understand nothing in life other than the need to eat and procreate. And suddenly one of them stands up and pronounces some very simple words about how it is necessary to defend one's own people, to defend women, to defend one's brother . . ." (Bodrov, *Sviaznoi*, Amphora, 2007, 303).

26 Eldin, *Sky Wept Fire*, 37.

considerations of troop positions and the like are dismissed as secondary: for both sides, this was a struggle for survival, not just physical survival, but cultural, moral, and spiritual survival as well.

Which side Eldin believes to have the spiritual upper hand is obvious: it is here in this chapter that he first makes explicit his belief in the importance of faith. As Eldin's belief in civilization, Soviet ideology, and the country that was once his crumbles, he turns to religion instead, and transforms the war from a minor regional conflict over territory and oil rights, run by people on both sides who are largely concerned with holding onto power and lining their pockets, to a grand battle between Good and Evil, with himself firmly on the side of Good. This belief would sustain him throughout the war, and lead him to see it in very different terms from those of his fellow Russian citizens fighting on the other side.

Eldin's discussion in the very next chapter of the treatment of Russian troops by their own officers, and his comparison of the actions of the Russian fighters versus the Chechen fighters, underscores his "conversion" and his fundamentally different understanding of the conflict from that of the Russian writers here. Chapter 8 opens with this passage:

> It was staggering to see the attitude of the Russian command towards the corpses of their own soldiers. These were young men who had fulfilled their duty to the homeland honourably, and they were hardly to blame if their country had been taken over by a band of traitors and misanthropes. The Chechens appealed to the Russians many times, proposing a few days' truce for the sole purpose of clearing the soldiers' corpses from the streets of the city. The Russian generals, though, in their infinite wisdom, decided that this was a ploy by Dudaev to buy time to reposition and they rejected the offer. Yet the dead, whatever their nationality or faith, no matter what they were fighting for, by virtue of their death had fully exonerated themselves before the living. A man who has beheld God's great mystery ahead of you cannot be guilty before you. Only a coward who doesn't have it in him to face his fate in open combat could dishonour an enemy corpse. Yet the Russian authorities dishonoured the corpses of their own soldiers. Rest in peace, boys! You fell on the

> battlefield and you are free of blame. This battle has reconciled its fallen fighters with the world and with one another.[27]

This passage contains a number of interesting and contradictory moments. The issue of the disposal of the bodies of the soldiers killed in combat was a key issue for Politkovskaya as well—*A Dirty War* begins with two articles on precisely that topic, and it comes up several more times in the book. The search by mothers for their sons' remains is a recurring theme in accounts of the Chechen Wars, as is the accusation that the Russian authorities had little interest in finding their soldiers who were missing or killed in action, or providing closure to their families.

Both Politkovskaya and Eldin are horrified by the cavalier attitude of the Russian authorities towards the bodies of the fallen, although from different perspectives: Politkovskaya sees it as an abdication of Russia's duty to provide maternal care to her citizens/sons, while Eldin sees it as a contravention of the code of the warrior. It is easy, and probably correct, to see this as a gendered approach to the issue, as well as representative of different cultural understandings, but both writers come to the same conclusion: that, symptomatically of their irresponsible and exploitative attitude towards their people in life, the Russian authorities had little concern for the proper treatment of their people's bodies in death, and this lack of concern had wide-reaching consequences—in Politkovskaya's view, the suffering of the families of those fallen in battle; in Eldin's, the displeasure of spiritual forces with the Russian cause.

Where their account and their opinions differ is in the actions of the Chechens: Politkovskaya says that the Chechens engaged in corpse-trading, holding soldiers' bodies hostage and extorting money from their families for their return. Although sympathetic to individual Chechens caught up in the violence, and understanding of why they might wish to rebel against Russian rule, Politkovskaya had little patience with the Chechen authorities, and was as quick to comment on crimes and atrocities committed by the Chechen side as the Russian; indeed, she was frustrated with Western human rights organizations who lionized the Chechen fighters while attacking Russia and minimizing Russian suffering. For Politkovskaya the two pillars of her moral scaffolding were telling the truth and alleviating suffering. Eldin is also primarily concerned with telling the truth—in his first conversation with me he said his main concern was to "be truthful"—but he is telling a more personal truth than

27 Ibid., 39.

Politkovskaya, and giving his eyewitness account of what he saw, which did not include corpse-trading.[28]

And just as Politkovskaya could recognize and honor compassion regardless of who produced it, Eldin admires honor and fighting spirit, whether it is demonstrated by Chechens or Russians. The passage quoted above is not the only place he praises the courage of ordinary Russian troops, whom he judges separately from their commanders. He does not deny that individual Russians are capable of acting rightly. In one telling episode, he recounts the story of a Chechen drug addict who witnesses abuses committed by Russian OMON troops. The addict later slips into the OMON barracks and knifes several of the OMON troops sleeping there. He is captured alive and threatened with torture, but then: "a seasoned colonel walked up and shot him once in the heart, quickly and painlessly. He handed the corpse over to the Chechen women: 'Bury him decently. He may have lived like a bum. But he died like a man.'"[29] Eldin distinguishes between those who are cowardly—for example, fully armed OMON troops tormenting unarmed civilians and torturing captives—and those who are able to recognize and honor the code of the warrior. The colonel here is not compassionate, but he recognizes the warrior spirit of the nameless drug addict and gives him a quick, honorable (and manly) death and returns his body to his people for proper burial. He therefore, despite being on the enemy side, proves himself to be a brother in honor, or at least to share the same code of the warrior, as the Chechens.

This sharp division of the world into "us" and "them" is something that all the writers surveyed here share, although they place the division differently. Politkovskaya distinguishes between those who share her values of truth and compassion; those who do, regardless of nationality, are treated as "one of us," while those who do not are called out for their bad behavior and treated with scorn and derision. However, these borders are permeable, as people who change their behavior, or whose behavior is revealed to be good rather than bad, as in the case of Colonel Shcherbakov, are brought into the fold of the "good." There are also a few people who seem to straddle both worlds, and whom Politkovskaya treats ambiguously, most notably General Shamanov,

---

28 Eldin also discussed what he saw of the treatment of Russian prisoners during our first interview, and said that during the first war prisoners (and presumably, their bodies) were returned to their mothers with no strings attached if their mothers came and asked for them. He saw a contrast between Chechnya under Dzhokhar Dudaev, whom he considered to be an honorable and visionary leader, and post-Dudaev Chechnya, in which less honorable behavior became more common (Eldin, Skype interview, July 29, 2017).

29 Eldin, *Sky Wept Fire*, 42.

who manages to be jingoistic, honest, deceptive, courageous, and cruel in turn. Although Politkovskaya's worldview is somewhat black-and-white, she is able to see that not everyone acts in black-and-white ways all the time, and she is able to take up their point of view when it suits her purposes. Eldin also sees the world in black-and-white; while he acknowledges that there were Chechens who acted in less than honorable ways during the conflict, his own understanding of what is the right way to act is straightforward: a drug addict could redeem himself by dying bravely while attacking cowards and defending the honor of his people, but a good person couldn't be a coward or a drug addict.

Eldin's commitment to the code of the warrior means that he can recognize those fighting on the other side as being one of "us," as, paradoxically, does his conception of the conflict as a battle between the forces of good and evil. The evil is done by cynical or self-serving authorities off in Moscow, who force their warriors to fight against the Chechens; or by cowards, but a person can fight for the other side and still be a man of honor. Although his morality as expressed in the book is clear-cut, it can also make him sympathetic and understanding towards the Russians whom the Chechens are fighting against: they are united both by a shared Soviet culture, and a shared warrior mentality/morality.

This is in contrast to the Russian combat veterans whose works are featured here, whose bonds are of shared experience rather than shared morality. While able to sympathize with those who transgress morally, providing that person has a similar shared experience, they are unable to feel any connection with those who do not share their experiences, thus isolating them from both the Chechens and their own fellow Russians upon their return to civilian life. Eldin's in some ways more rigid morality, however, allows him to acknowledge anyone who shares it as a brother-in-arms.

After the break in the narrative provided by chapters 7 and 8, Eldin returns to a largely first-person account of his actions and experiences during and after the first siege of Grozny. Although these chapters are narrated in a fairly conventional manner, Eldin once again emphasizes the surreal nature of what was taking place, and how disturbing an effect it had on the minds of everyone who experienced it. Of his time hiding out in the city during the siege, Eldin says:

> Everything that existed beyond the boundaries of this small piece of land seemed like an inane television show where people merely acted out their roles till the day they dropped dead. Real life existed only on this patch of the planet, because here you were vividly aware of each second of life granted to you by fate.

> Here, each breath might be your last and for that reason each breath was bursting with life. Here, each moment lived was filled with the most profound sense of purpose. Life here was real.[30]

Eldin contrasts the falsity of life away from the war with the "real life" of living in the war zone, which has transformed in his conception of it. Earlier, combat zones struck him as the set of an apocalyptic war film; now it is the outside, nonwarring areas that are like a television show. True reality was the war zone and the business of getting through day-to-day actions such as bathing and washing his clothes without access to modern conveniences, and while in constant danger of death.

Eldin, like the other authors featured here, has a tri-faceted experience of war: it is a horrifying, end-of-days apocalypse in which not just death, but a death of unimaginable, superhuman violence, can strike at any moment; it is also "normal life," in which people go about their ordinary daily activities such as eating, sleeping, washing, and playing; finally, because of the combination of those two factors, it leads to a heightened, "more alive" life: since death can come raining down out of the sky at any moment, those living under its threat are living life to its fullest. The "more alive" life may be a result of what Herman identifies as hyperarousal, which can continue long after the original traumatic event is past. This tripartite perception, in which those in the war zone are not only split between their old and new lives, but between their old and new perceptions of what life is like and what reality is, is very likely one of the factors behind the psychological distress of those touched by war: not only have they been traumatized by its violence, but it has altered their very perception of reality.

Eldin contrasts his own, "true" perception of the events of the first siege of Grozny with the false perceptions of those on the Russian side, and in doing so, sets up a dichotomy between surface perception and a deeper apprehension of the true meaning of events. The first siege of Grozny ostensibly ended in a Russian victory, as Russian federal forces occupied the city, while the Chechen resistance was forced to retreat from the city. Despite this:

> It was the Russian Army, with General Grachev at the helm, that had conclusively lost the battle for Grozny, just as Marshal Zhukov in his time had lost the battle of Berlin. The victor on the battlefield is not the side that wins control of a particular

---

30 Ibid., 48.

> territory [. . .] but the side that inflicts the greatest damage on their opponent while sustaining the fewest losses themselves. In the battle for Grozny, the losses on the Russian side simply bore no comparison with those on the Chechen side.[31]

Just as he linked the behavior of the fighters during the early days of the battle with that of warriors in pagan Chechen culture, thus putting the events of the first siege of Grozny in a broader historical and cultural context, so does he link the outcome of the siege with events in World War II, giving a larger, and for citizens of the former USSR, highly resonant, context to the events in the First Chechen War. This is part of his overall strategy of viewing the Chechen Wars not as a petty regional conflict, but as part of the grand scheme of history, with implications for the grand battle between Good and Evil.

In this Eldin is, paradoxically enough, perhaps the most "Russian" of the writers surveyed here. Indeed, his technique here is highly reminiscent on one level of Tolstoy's in *War and Peace*: both seek to situate the war they are describing in its place in the course of human history, and both contrast surface events with the deeper truths these events signify. In the case of the first siege of Grozny, Eldin says, "the only people not to understand this [the Russian defeat] were the Russian soldiers hoisting their flag over the ruins of the Presidential Palace and taking their pictures against its backdrop."[32] The Russians, Eldin implies, were mistaking surface ripples for the current, perhaps because their eyes had not yet been sufficiently opened by life in the war zone. They still thought they were living in a movie, a movie in which they were the heroes, and had not yet learned to understand the real truth of situation, or see it in its historical significance. Eldin and his fellow Chechens, however, had already achieved a state of heightened awareness that enabled them to perceive the underlying reality of the situation, and had not yet been broken by trauma. In Eldin's case, that break would happen soon.

After the first storming of Grozny, Eldin escapes the city and makes his way to the village of Urus-Martan, which was still relatively untouched by the war. Now, safe from the war zone, Eldin senses the psychological split that exposure to it caused even more acutely, something that is exacerbated by the split between his chosen outer persona and his inner convictions. He is still presenting himself as an impartial journalist, even though internally he had already sided with the Chechen resistance.

---

31 Ibid.
32 Ibid., 48-49.

The result of the tension between his inner convictions and outer persona was intense psychological pressure, something manifested in the text by the switch from the first-person narration of the rest of the chapter to the second-person generalizations with which it ends: "At least there you were free to respond to people's actions, be they friends or enemies. Here all you could do was grit your teeth and keep quiet."[33] By physically leaving the war zone behind, Eldin and the others who had experienced it had not left it behind psychologically, but rather carried it with them to relatively peaceful Urus-Martan. The mental strain, and the split between inner and outer selves, is represented by the change from a first- to a second-person or general, impersonal, narrative voice, something that Eldin will use with greater frequency as his tale becomes more traumatic.[34]

From Urus-Martan, Eldin travels first to Shatoi, and then to Vedeno, the headquarters for the Chechen resistance. There he embeds himself within the Chechen forces, becoming ever more entwined with their efforts as he covers their actions as a journalist. There are several chapters, told in a straightforward first-person style, in which he describes some of the operations he witnesses, and his increasing involvement with the resistance movement.

This is interrupted in chapter 13, which describes a bombardment by Russian forces. The entire chapter, in which Eldin's position is subject to aerial bombardment and he himself is lightly wounded, is told in the second person/general narrative voice, highlighting the dissociation Eldin feels from the events, and his altered perceptions during it.

The entire chapter is full of this kind of dream-sense, in which the narrator seems to be watching it from the outside while simultaneous experiencing it, and in which fantastic, impossible events take place, violating the laws of physics and ordinary perception of space and time. The "you" of the chapter feels both very close to events, certain that he is able to predict where bombs will hit and falling objects will land, and completely separated from them, with black-out moments which he cannot remember, even though he apparently did not lose consciousness, since when he "comes to" he is on his feet and moving.

In the opening chapters, when Eldin first witnesses combat and the effects of modern weapons of war on the human body, he can make sense of it only as a film or a fairy tale. Here, when he is actually caught up in it, he cannot understand

---

33 Ibid., 53.

34 Anna Gunin, the translator of *The Sky Wept Fire,* has confirmed that the English-language translation of the pronouns "entirely mirrors the original," and expresses the belief that "the use of the second person was a spontaneous dissociation process on the part of Mikail" in response to the trauma of reliving his experiences in the filtration camp (Gunin, email interview, July 29, 2017).

it even as something unreal: the situation is both supremely real, and supremely surreal, demanding a new narrative voice in order to convey the disorienting horror of the experience. Afterwards, Eldin is stricken with a strange, inexplicable terror, which goes away, but, as he says, "it will come back . . . Later it will return with more clarity . . . But you are a fatalist."[35] Faced with the incomprehensible destructive power of an aerial bombardment, Eldin turns to fatalism as the only way to deal with something beyond human comprehension. As he continues to be put under unbearable psychological pressure, the fatalism will morph into a transcendent religious faith, the only thing that enables him to withstand what happens to him.

Following the description of the bombardment, the first section of the book returns to a largely linear, first-person account of Eldin's official transformation from journalist to member of the Chechen resistance. This, he tells us, ends badly for him, as he maintains some of his journalistic enthusiasm and naivety, failing to be adequately cautious and observant. The first section of the book ends with a warning that such carelessness, or merely holding to peace-time levels of observation and perception, can in a war end in disaster:

> In war you need to use not just your five senses: you have to know how to listen to your heart, your sixth sense, your intuition, or whatever you want to call it. Failure to listen to your heart can lead to the direst of consequences. One of the many transformations that you undergo in war is the sharpening of your intuition, the ability to scent danger. And you must learn to exploit this truly priceless gift if you wish to survive the abnormal situation that is war.[36]

By leaving behind the trappings of modern, civilized humanity and returning to their primitive roots, humans in combat conditions gain an extra sense, or a whole host of extra senses, something that Babchenko describes as well. As Herman notes, trauma causes perceptions to alter, and focus on particularly intense images, something that "gives the traumatic memory a heightened reality."[37] As Eldin experiences it, under these extreme conditions, human perception sharpens, and humans merge with their environment, not only becoming hyper-aware of it, but feeling as if they and it are one. This is something

35 Eldin, *The Sky Wept Fire*, 64.
36 Ibid., 69.
37 Herman, *Trauma and Recovery*, 38.

that Eldin describes in greater detail in the next section of the book, in which his communion with the natural world forms a contrast to the appalling brutality he experiences at the hands of Russian federal forces.

Section two of *The Sky Wept Fire* is titled "From the Wheel of Time into the Circle of Pain," and has as its epigraph an excerpt from a Sufi parable about the need to feel the pain of others in order to achieve true enlightenment. And so while on one level section two is the story of Eldin's capture and torture by Russian forces, on another level it is a discussion of connection with others, and empathy or the lack thereof.

The first two chapters of section two are meditations on the nature of the forest, into which the Chechen resistance forces have retreated. This theme is continued in the next chapter, which begins:

> In the forest you have to become a shadow. You must melt away, merge with the forest. Particularly if there is a war on and you are a participant in that war. You must move without snapping one dry twig underfoot, without rustling last year's leaf fall, without disturbing the branches or grass. You need to be able to become any tree, bush, hollow or hill, you need to know how to stop smelling like a human if you are to trick the enemy. Your enemy is strong and wily. He too knows how to melt into the forest.[38]

This passage sets up the communion with, and transformation into, the natural world that is an essential part of becoming a warrior. At this point it appears that the narrator, who is currently speaking in second-person generalizations, has achieved the transformation into a semi-human, semi-animal warrior who can speak with nature and become part of the natural world. This belief in a nonhuman identity is listed by Herman as a symptom of PTSD,[39] although the authors surveyed here do not describe it explicitly as such. Here, Eldin describes the warrior as connected to the natural world, and through it, with his enemy, who is also connected to the natural world through his status as a warrior. The two are thus in communion with each other and the world at large, which shelters and provides for them even as they seek to destroy each other.

The narrator's apparently successful merger with the natural world, and therefore his success as a warrior, is further underlined a few sentences later, when Eldin writes, "After spending many hours merging into the shadows of the

38 Eldin, *The Sky Wept Fire*, 75.
39 Herman, *Trauma and Recovery*, 121.

bushes and gazing through the remaining eyepiece of your binoculars, you've discovered the presence and location of two cleverly concealed Hurricane multiple rocket launchers."[40] The natural, human, and mechanical worlds have all been transformed into a single whole; the enemies have also undergone their own transformation, but slightly less successfully than the narrator. The narrator is thus confident—overly confident.

Still writing in second-person and general structures, Eldin recounts how he comes up with a plan to take out the Hurricanes and sets off to bring the information to headquarters. In a hurry, and believing the path to be safe, he disobeys his orders to travel only under guard. And at first everything seems safe. But:

> Suddenly you are overcome by a burning wave of inexplicable fear, just like before the bombing in Shatoy. Your foreboding is so powerful that for a while you cannot take a step, while your friend walks on several metres ahead. You realize your intuition is alerting you to danger; you also know that you should trust your intuition—it has never let you down. Right now the most logical action would be to drop to the ground, keep low, and crawl ahead on all fours to find out the source of this sudden foreboding. But, overcoming your fear, you shut out your intuition through an effort of will and switch on your cold reason. And according to your reason there cannot be any danger; the enemy could not have come so close unobserved.[41]

And indeed, when, a few paces later, Eldin encounters a group of armed fighters on the path, he takes them for members of his own side—until they arrest him at gunpoint.

This whole section is about the nature and danger of perception. Eldin believes he has managed to merge with the forest, to learn to read its signs and rely on it for protection. This leads him, he says, to become overconfident and, when his intuition does warn him of approaching danger, he ignores it and relies, fatally, on reason instead. The application of reason renders him doubly vulnerable, causing him to shut down his "true" senses, disregarding the warnings they give him, while making him believe that his surface-level perceptions are correct. Like the Russian soldiers he criticizes in the previous section for misapprehending

40 Eldin, *The Sky Wept Fire*, 75.
41 Ibid., 77.

the true nature of events and therefore believing that they had won the battle of Grozny, Eldin himself has failed to sense the deeper currents and, wrapped up in his own hubris and self-satisfaction, falls into fatal error.

Once captured, Eldin realizes he must try to protect his companion, who is unarmed and was acting as a guide to Eldin out of friendship. Therefore, he decides not to fight back. His warrior-senses having failed him, Eldin stops trying to merge with the forest, and attempts to merge with destiny and fate instead. He is aware of what happens to captured Chechens, and has some inkling of what awaits him.

Still, he is not completely cut off from those around him: one of the soldiers who searched him finds the codes he was carrying and, instead of turning them in, tears them up and throws them away. For this, Eldin says, "You are grateful to your enemy for having understood you. For understanding that you are doomed. And as one warrior to another, he shows you respect in your ill fortune."[42] The code of the warrior and the bonds of combat still connect (some) people even in situations such as these.

Eldin's descriptions of the torture he undergoes are both hyperrealistic and hyper-surreal. The narrative, which throughout the book is done in bursts and pieces, loses even more of its linearity, so that it is difficult to follow the outer, objective progression of events. What is foregrounded instead is the narrator's mental state and the breakdown and transformation caused by the experience of torture.

Eldin is first given some "light" roughing-up, which includes being shot, shortly after his capture. His captors threaten to kill him if he doesn't tell them what they want to know, and when he refuses, he is promised even more torture later. He is aware that this is not an empty threat, and tries to prepare himself for what is to come, attempting to summon up the necessary courage and to find greater meaning in the suffering that he knows he will undergo:

> You realize that what's happening to you now is just a gentle limbering-up for what is to come. You know that you will die. And you'll die slowly and painfully. Nobody will be compassionate enough to release you with a blessed bullet. Everything you've done up till now ostensibly to save your own skin—denying that you were a combatant, agreeing to keep quiet about the weapons—was done in pursuit of the one goal that matters to you: bringing closer the moment of death, so the torture will

42 Ibid., 79.

> end quicker. Yet you also know the torture you'll undergo will purify you of all sins and you'll stand before God with a shining face. Perhaps the torture will even purify your torturers of their sins. You are a fatalist. You will have to travel through hell for an eternity in order to reach your paradise, your peace, that is so near at hand. That's what you are hoping. You are so tired. God is merciful, after all. He does not sentence people to serve their time in hell twice. So what now? Now there's nothing for it but to wait. Wait for the helicopters to come for you, bringing . . . Not just your death. No, something more horrible still.[43]

After this, he is transferred from the local base in Shatoi to the main Russian base in Khankala, although that is not made clear at the time: the story of his torture is even more devoid of specifics than the rest of the narrative. Eldin's transfer from Shatoi to Khankala is recounted, not as a matter-of-fact journey, but as both the pinnacle of his achievement as a warrior, and the first step on his path to a higher state of purification and enlightenment:

> You may be lying wounded and beaten, face down on the dirty floor of a helicopter, but never in all your brief life has anybody shown you such honour as this. And what counts most of all: it is your oldest mortal foe showing you this honour. The Russians consider this tiny person so dangerous to their vast country that they have brought two helicopters especially for you. The reality is that helicopters always fly in pairs, but that does not matter, for this is the last mark of respect you will get in your life. So you cling to this false belief. In just twenty minutes or so, perhaps sooner, you will have to answer before God for all the sins of your ancestors. Meanwhile, you try to remember anything that might be of help in the battle to come. You feel the helicopter descending—it is over. You've arrived. This is your final stop. From here on you will start on a different journey, known but unknown, and thus terrifying. From here you will depart for eternity. This is a journey you'll have to make, one way or another. But how you make it is up to you.[44]

43 Ibid., 82-83.
44 Ibid., 85.

The physical, mental, and spiritual transformation that Eldin will undergo are already signaled here, as is the truth/falsehood dichotomy that appears throughout the book. Semi-delirious with pain and terror—he had already been beaten and shot at this point, as well as left to suffer from thirst, and was aware that worse things awaited him at his destination—Eldin enters into a delusion of grandeur, believing that the Russians have ordered two helicopters just to transport him to Khankala, a "false belief" that he uses to comfort himself. This is in line with Herman's descriptions of the mental state of victims of captivity. According to her, "People in captivity become adept practitioners of the arts of altered consciousness. Through the practice of dissociation, voluntary thought suppression, minimization, and sometimes outright denial, they learn to alter an unbearable reality."[45]

In Eldin's case, this semi-delirious state allows him to access a higher knowledge, a transcendent truth beyond the mundane truth of the rather grubby and horrid reality that he is just a low-level soldier who stumbled into a Russian patrol through bad luck and carelessness, and is about to be subjected to some rather meaningless torture in an attempt to extract some fairly meaningless information out of him. One truth of the whole situation is that his silence would not save the Chechen cause, and if the Russians managed to break him and extract every last crumb of knowledge from him, it would not advance their cause very far at all either. So even though this is war and he, an enemy combatant, has indeed been captured by the Russians, his torture at their hands is essentially a pointless exercise. Another writer—Politkovskaya, for example—might have dwelt on the pointlessness and the inhumanity of what he is put through. But Eldin conceives of the torture, just as he does the entire war, not as a horrifyingly ridiculous exercise in futility, but as a grand battle between good and evil. Therefore, the fact that he is transported from Shatoi to Khankala is not mentioned explicitly, but rather left for the reader to piece out after the fact, because the precise location of where all this took place is irrelevant. The true site of his torture is not a military base in Khankala, but Hell. And not just a "small corner of Hell," as one of Politkovskaya's books on Chechnya is titled in English, but Hell as a vast, omnipresent concept that can be accessed anywhere and everywhere there is suffering and torture.

Eldin's attitude towards torture, as towards war in general, is ambivalent. Although at several points in the book he speaks out against people, mainly Russians, whose behavior he considers cowardly for tormenting nonwarriors, and he certainly bears no love for his torturers, he does not condemn it outright,

45 Herman, *Trauma and Recovery*, 87.

just as he does not condemn war outright. While both have unpleasant aspects, and should be conducted according to rules of honor, he seems to imply that under the right circumstances both torture and war are acceptable, or at least, war is sometimes necessary, and torture is an inevitable facet of war, just as death is. His primary concern as he tries to prepare himself for what he knows is coming is not to avoid it, or to rail against the brutality and clear transgression of civilized behavior of his captors, but to find the strength to undergo this necessary and unavoidable test with honor. The rules of civilized behavior no longer apply here, and he does not waste any time lamenting that fact, but instead focuses on survival and not betraying his code of the warrior.

Accordingly, his attitude towards the torture he himself undergoes is ambivalent as well. Both waiting for it and actually undergoing it cause hideous physical and mental suffering—he is not only beaten extensively, but also hung up from his arms in various excruciating "stress positions," burned with cigarettes, subjected repeatedly to electric shocks, and has needles jammed under his fingernails—but at the same time, the suffering is not without its "benefits." Or not so much benefits, as enlightenment: the torture, which breaks both his physical and mental integrity, also lifts up to a higher state of understanding, and, in its own peculiar way, opens him up to a new kind of love, also of a very peculiar sort.

During a particularly dreadful torture session, when he is being shocked with electricity and burned with cigarettes, Eldin thinks, "What can you do with this hatred devouring you from within, like a sudden horrific affliction? You can oppose it with a weapon that is even stronger: love. You can love this pain. Understand that this is cathartic. Become a masochist for a while."[46] Although he does not in fact learn to love the pain, he is able to keep himself from breaking completely and betraying his comrades, and he is able to experience a higher level of consciousness because of this suffering. While his exposure to combat and warfare allowed him to develop his intuition and become one with the physical world around him, as well as developing a sense of brotherhood with others who also hold to the code of the warrior, even if they are on the opposite side, his experience of torture puts him in touch with his religious faith and gives him access to heaven and hell on what feels like a very real plane, even as it, once again, brings him closer to his enemies.

After a day of horrific torture, Eldin's injuries are treated and he is led away to a cell and reunited with his friend who was also captured. This respite from

46 Eldin, *The Sky Wept Fire*, 91.

active torture, however, only allows Eldin to think about the possibility, which he considers highly likely, that he is going to be executed that very night.

The expectation of immediate death, on top of the torture he has already undergone, puts Eldin in a transcendent state in which he converses directly with God. After being forced to conceal and prevaricate under extremely difficult conditions, and being cajoled, wheedled, and lied to in turn, Eldin now has immediate access to a higher truth—not just the truth of what he was actually doing, and what his captors actually know, but divine Truth. He is able to communicate directly with the Divine, which he expects to join soon physically as well as mentally. This causes him to seek to shed himself of all hatred and sin:

> You begin your conversation by forgiving all your friends and enemies. You forgive everyone who at some point might have harboured bad thoughts towards you, and in doing so has sinned. You even forgive your torturers and executioners. No, not out of neighbourly love, but in the name of God, who created each one of us. You beg the Creator to forgive them too, lest a single one of His creatures remain guilty before Him on account of you. You've thrown off the heavy weight of all worldly affairs and worries, all thoughts of life, and with a light soul, purified of love and hate, of joy and grief, you are ready for your meeting with God. There is only sadness, an endless, vast sadness. You slowly drift into a twilight zone between the two worlds.[47]

In what he thinks are his pre-death meditations, Eldin feels an intense sense of connection with the Divine and everything that it has created, including his enemies and torturers, who, like him, are children of God. Physical and mental suffering has purged him of all worldly emotions, both positive and negative, and, having been purified, he does not want others to remain impure because of him, since they are all one. In this "twilight zone between the worlds" Eldin feels himself to be both alive and dead, able to connect with either world, even as he is detached from both of them. In this limbo state, he even yearns for death, but then he realizes that "You still have a little further to go. You still have to crawl your way through hell,"[48] and he regains consciousness, returning to the cell in which he is imprisoned.

---

47 Ibid., 96.
48 Ibid.

The return to reality severs the connection he feels with his enemies and with the Divine. Or rather, he still feels connected to them, but knows that the connection is only one way. He has become vulnerable, physically and emotionally, and, while he has achieved a level of enlightenment that his torturers have not, that only makes them more dangerous to him:

> For the first time in your life you are frightened of the dawn. You know they won't shoot you straightaway. You realized that during the night. You wait. Afraid. Afraid of not being able to take it. You don't trust your willpower and you don't trust your tongue. You're frightened of ceasing to be their enemy. You may have forgiven them, they may have stopped being the enemy to you, but you must be the enemy to them. They do not know how to forgive. They're revelling in their physical dominion over you. They are not free of hatred, and that is their curse.[49]

Eldin divides the Russian soldiers he encounters during his imprisonment and torture into three groups: those who beat him indiscriminately and with no real art; those who torture him methodically and deliberately; and those who try to help him, either out of compassion, as in the case of the doctor who treats his injuries, or from brotherly solidarity, one warrior to another, as in the case of the unknown soldier who throws away the codes Eldin was carrying prior to his capture, and who shields him from harassment and beating by the other soldiers immediately following his capture.

Those in the last group have some kind of an overarching moral code and sense of awareness of others, and are thus capable of forming a connection with others, even the "enemy." Those in the first group are also capable of sensing and forming a connection with others, although in their case the connection is largely unconscious, a matter of subconscious projection:

> The soldiers beating you are unleashing all their fury, their dread of death, their sleep terrors and nightmares. They are blaming you personally for their grim, tented existence, for the cold and the hunger. To them the one person guilty of all their woes is you. And in any case, you are the enemy. All their hatred centres

---

49 Ibid., 97.

> solely on you—because you are right here in front of them. They beat you because they're afraid; of you, of combat, of death."[50]

Such people have had their civilized exterior stripped away by the fear and horror of war, and have not (yet) been able to replace it with anything else, but instead are prey to every passing terror and whim that passes through their heads. Although they are susceptible to influence from others, which is why they react so strongly to their circumstances and their prisoners, they are largely unaware of their susceptibility, and are incapable of feeling a connection with others on a conscious level.

The second group, the professional torturers, are detached on both levels, incapable of feeling either the conscious compassion of those with an overarching ethical code, or the unconscious responsiveness of those who have lost their ethical code. Lacking both animal responses and human awareness, these are the people who are the most dangerous, the most inimical. Enlightenment and an awareness of the Divine will serve as little shield against them: only fate and good luck will.

Eldin's fear of the professional torturers is justified, as he is taken for another interrogation, even more brutal than before, although he still does not break and confess. When he is shown his reflection, though, it brings home just how damaged he has become, leading to a sense of doubling: "From the mirror someone stares back at you. But it is clearly not a human. And it is certainly not you . . . No, this freak does indeed have your eyes. Rather, the expression in the eyes is yours."[51] After the trials he has undergone—successfully, by some measures—he has become both human and nonhuman, self and nonself.

In his new state, he provokes a different reaction from his captors. Those who are capable of feeling compassion for him, such as the doctor who treats his wounds, make a point not only of ministering to him physically as much as possible, but of trying to help him mentally as well: "His [the doctor's] officer friends come in. And seeing your condition, they try to cheer you up with jokes and demonstrations of hand-to-hand combat moves."[52] This paints a bizarre picture of life in the detention center: while some of the officers there are focused on destroying Eldin and the other prisoners in every way possible, subjecting them to horrific physical torture and also threatening to raze their home villages to the ground, end their family line, and desecrate their bodies

---

50 Ibid., 88.
51 Ibid., 101.
52 Ibid., 103.

after death, others not only attempt to treat the wounds inflicted by their colleagues, but go out of their way to tell the prisoners jokes and cheer them up.

This underscores both the schizophrenic split within the Russian forces themselves, and the importance of good luck, rather than policy, when dealing with them. As Politkovskaya also chronicles at length, whether a prisoner or refugee lives or dies depends largely on how well disposed the individuals they encounter are to them. Official policy is either hostile or indifferent, and there are plenty of individuals who have little interest in doing even the basic tasks of their duty, or who are taking the opportunity the war provides to feather their nests and perhaps indulge in their sadistic proclivities. But serving right alongside them are people who are motivated by concepts of duty, conscience, and/or fellow human feeling. Although Eldin understand the problem differently than Politkovskaya, and responds to it differently, seeking to develop detachment and a fatalistic acceptance of it as one of the trials he must undergo as part of his struggle against the forces of evil and Empire, rather than sharpening his outrage precisely against the inhumanity and illogic, it is the same issue.

Eldin's account of the torture he undergoes is delivered in a general, second-person almost stream-of-consciousness style, focused mainly on his inner state, with few concrete details.[53] Even the actual torture he undergoes is described more as he experiences it than what actually happens to his body: "an insane pain shoots up like lightning from your fingertips . . . Shattering your brain into smithereens, it surges back down . . . And finding no escape route, it thrashes through your nerves, ripping and searing them . . . After the first wave, a second one strikes, still more raging."[54] It is only later that he realizes that the pain is caused by needles being driven under his fingernails; at the time he cannot process what is happening. During this period he has two states: an almost mystic detachment, and suffering so intense he cannot grasp what is happening around him, and the writing reflects that, showing his contradictory mood swings and surreal perceptions.

Concrete details that connect with regular, external reality begin to reappear in chapter 9, when the torture is stopped in order to avoid killing him. It is then that he mentions that he has been at the base in Khankala for five days; before that, linear conceptions of time and place had little meaning. As he explained in

53 In his first conversation with me he said, "It was extremely difficult to talk about the torture in the first person. I found myself writing in the second person, and that was easier. It was as if I were seeing myself from far away. I could still feel and empathize with myself, so young and foolish, but I understood myself better from a distance" (Eldin, Skype interview, July 29, 2017).

54 Eldin, *Sky Wept Fire*, 107.

an interview, while he was being tortured, time seem to stretch out into infinity, so that he could not believe that his first torture session lasted a mere ten hours, or that he survived the entire ten hours of torture, while the "rest" periods between interrogation sessions felt extremely compressed,[55] something that is reflected in the structure of his descriptions of his time there. But in chapter 9, when he is no longer being tortured, a sense of reality and normalcy slowly returns.

Even so, chapter 9 is still narrated in the general/second person, and includes details about the negotiations that are going on between the Russians and the Chechens over him—the Chechens have offered to trade two captured Russian soldiers for Eldin—and Eldin's transfer to a filtration camp, something he awaits with dread, having heard the horrifying stories of the abuses perpetrated in these filtration camps.

However, luck is with Eldin at this particular moment, as the investigator assigned to him treats him comparatively humanely. Eldin's encounter with this comparatively humane investigator triggers a return to a first-person narrative:

> Here the most important work was done by the intelligence operative assigned to you. He decided how you lived, when you underwent torture and beatings and so forth. And thus he played an essential role in the prisoner's life. The operative assigned to **me** wasn't too bad. **I** met him around fifteen minutes after arriving in the cell. **I'd** been summoned for interrogation.[56]

The return to a first-person narrative, ten chapters into the section of the book on Eldin's capture and torture, is followed by a scene in which Eldin, for the first time in this section, is able to connect with one of his captors on the level of truth. While the kind doctor and his similarly humane colleagues at the base in Khankala treated Eldin like a sick child or wounded dog, the interrogator demonstrates an interest in Eldin as a journalist and writer:

> "The number of times I've tried to explain. You wouldn't understand it, anyway," I said wearily.
>
> "I will understand. Try to explain it to me."
>
> And here I broke down and began speaking with enormous emotion about my desire 'to see everything with my own eyes

55 Eldin, Skype interview, March 19, 2018.
56 Eldin, *Sky Wept Fire*, 113, emphasis my own.

> and write a book about it'. The whole time he looked me intently in the eye. The other officer jumped to his feet and said, 'We're not interested in your fantasies. Just tell us the truth!' delivering a blow to my head. But the officer who asked the question stopped him from planting a second one.
>
> "What do you want to hear from me? This is the only truth I know," I told him.
>
> "I believe you. You're a man burning with belief. My name's Nikolay," he introduced himself.[57]

At this moment, Eldin and his interrogator are able to connect on an intellectual level, and recognize each other's essential truthfulness and shared belief. Although they can never wholly trust each other—Eldin suspects that Nikolay is using the "good cop" technique on him—they do discover a number of shared interests, especially literature, and hold a number of animated, and apparently genuine, conversations on the topic. Significantly, Nikolay is one of the few people who is mentioned by name in Eldin's story. His recognition of Eldin's truthfulness—a truthfulness that is only partly a matter of facts, since Eldin never does give up all the information they want to know from him, but is much more a matter of inner conviction—breaks the hallucinatory nature of Eldin's thinking and returns him to a more mundane, coherent plane, one in which proper names have meaning.

Eldin no longer feels merged with the natural world, as he did in the forest, or as if he has access to the Divine and a higher plane of knowledge, as he did when he was first being tortured. Instead, he is once again able to communicate with another human being using the ordinary means of human communication: words and ideas that are grounded in day-to-day experience. Although his existence in the filtration camp still had a large element of the absurd to it—he describes it as "more like an aberration than a logical consequence"[58]—his return to a shared, human conception of truth enables him to regain a coherent sense of self and differentiate himself from other individuals and the world around him. He has, essentially, returned from a primeval state of consciousness to a modern one.

The remaining chapters in section two are narrated in alternating first- and second-person form. Eldin discusses the torture techniques used in the filtration camp, although, since he himself does not undergo any physical

---

57 Ibid., 114.
58 Ibid., 117.

torture while there, he discusses it a straightforward, factual manner, claiming that tales of the tortures inflicted on detainees in the camps, especially the stories of mass rape of the men held there, were exaggerated for propaganda purposes. This is an interesting claim, particularly in light of the fact that in *One Soldier's War,* discussed later, the one form of hazing that Babchenko claims to resist successfully is gang-rape. For both these writers, physical abuse, especially beating, is, while unpleasant, not especially shameful; in fact, it can lead to mental toughness and/or spiritual enlightenment. Psychological torment and terror are in some ways more shattering. Sexual violation, however, is beyond the pale, and both writers skirt around the subject, suggesting that it can happen, but denying its frequency or its threat to them.

After dismissing the danger of sexual assault as greatly over-exaggerated and only affecting "certain men,"[59] those for whom their captors felt not hatred but "contempt,"[60] Eldin describes the effects of the psychological pressure he experienced at the filtration camp. Of it he says, "Psychological torture is one of the most brutal and barbaric forms of torment, because it assaults your most vulnerable point: your mind."[61] The loss of mental integrity, something that Eldin has been experiencing in various forms since the beginning of the war, now appears to him in all its horror, and the next chapter, describing the effects of depression, switches once again to the second person:

> There is one more aspect to the filter camp that poses a very real danger. Something more dreadful than any torture or beating. It is depression. Grim and gloomy, consuming you from within slowly and steadily like a venomous man-eating worm, the depression is horrific. It surrounds you on all sides like some stinking green swamp sludge, seeping into your being, into your heart and soul, eating you up.[62]

This section of the book began with chapters on the merging of the human and natural worlds caused by the heightened perceptions necessary to survive in a war zone. While undergoing torture and fear of imminent death, Eldin's perceptions become unmoored from mundane reality, and he is able to transcend his physical body and access the Divine. Depression, however, is depicted not as

59 Ibid., 125.
60 Ibid., 123.
61 Ibid., 126.
62 Ibid., 128.

a merger with the natural and divine worlds but as being consumed, making the sufferer an inert mass, separate from the surrounding world and yet at its mercy: "From now on you'll experience nothing at all. Neither life nor death. You'll have no soul, no body. Time will cease to exist; its endlessness and its fast flight are gone. All that exists is you. Like some vegetable life form."[63] This is the true horror; earlier, while undergoing physical torture, Eldin had reconciled himself to the possibility of death, but now he actively contemplates suicide, stopping himself only by turning to his faith, which forbids suicide as the worst of sins, and by reminding himself that he is a warrior. This also reminds him that "You're just like plenty of other men—even among the enemy there are plenty just like you. Yet at the same time you are unique."[64] This reminder of both his shared humanity and his individuality help pull him out of the swamp of depression and set him back on the path to coherent, first-person thinking.

The last few chapters of section two cover Eldin's release from the filtration camp in exchange for Russian prisoners held by the Chechens, and the end of the first war. The last year of the war is covered in a scant two chapters, with few concrete events mentioned. The important thing for Eldin is not the external events of the war, but his own internal struggles, which reached their peak during his detention and interrogation. It was then that he overcame the forces of disintegration within his own psyche and successfully combatted depression and isolation, recognizing his shared connection with others around him, as well as his own individual humanity. The composition of the section makes his own personal victory a precursor or harbinger of the victory of the Chechen independence forces, thus heightening both the implication of the interconnectedness of all things that he had discovered as part of his transformation from journalist to warrior, and the emphasis on the personal, individual nature of this war for him.

For Eldin, the split between the personal and the political was largely nonexistent: just as the struggle for Chechen independence was representative of a larger battle between good and evil, his personal struggle to avoid breaking or going insane while under interrogation was representative of the Chechen struggle as a whole. In Eldin's writing, the story is not so much fragmented as it is a form of pointillism: smaller episodes represent, and make up, the greater whole. There is no need for him to write a grand epic narrative, since all that is important can be contained in a short episode of only a few paragraphs. This is similar to how traumatic memories can be recalled, when "one particular set

63 Ibid.
64 Ibid., 129-30.

of images crystalizes the experience [. . .]. The intense focus on fragmentary sensation, on image without context, gives the traumatic memory a heightened reality."[65] In Eldin's case, the disconnected and fragmented nature of his writing here is actually representative of a kind of wholeness: because everything is a reflection of, and a part of, something larger, it already forms a grand whole and does not need to be epic in scale in order to be epic in meaning.

Section three, titled "Autumn Shot Dead," covers the second war and is nearly as long as the first two sections put together. Structurally, it is similar to the first two sections: chapters or passages of descriptive narrative, explaining the action of the second war, alternating with chapters or passages written either in general statements, if the passage is designed to draw together the various themes discussed into one general statement, or in the second person, if something particularly traumatic is being described. A notable change, however, is the addition of multiple passages told in the first person plural—stories of a collective "We." The theme of the smaller or the individual being part of, or standing in for, the greater or the group thus comes into even sharper focus in the final section of the book.

The virtue of communal or abstract thinking over an individualistic mindset is suggested subtly in the opening paragraph of the first chapter, which is about the most beautiful time of year in Chechnya. Spring, the chapter starts off by asserting, is not the most beautiful season, because in spring "life's egotism comes to the fore."[66] Instead, "The most beautiful time of year in Chechnya is autumn. Autumn heralds a brief period of harmony between life and death, between light and dark, between the mind and the soul. Autumn is a time of placidity, where every living thing cannot but help get a little closer to the God that created it."[67] The emerging life-force of spring actually prevents living beings from comprehending their interconnectedness with each other and with God; it is the more peaceful time of autumn that allows communion between humanity, nature, and the Divine.

Accordingly, nature in the autumn of 1999 is aware of the impending catastrophe, even if the humans are not. While in section two, upon merging with the forest, the warrior was able to sense what was going on in the natural world, here the natural world is able to sense what is about to happen in the human world, and attempts to communicate with humans and warn them of the approaching disaster, which, again, is depicted not as a provincial war, but a

65 Herman, *Trauma and Recovery*, 38.
66 Eldin, *The Sky Wept Fire*, 147.
67 Ibid., 148.

titanic struggle between good and evil, understood in religious and mythological terms:

> They [migrating cranes] knew. They could sense it. They are angels of the earth, after all. Calamity was closing in on Chechnya. A brutal calamity, terrifying in its barbarism. A huge dragon with many heads had departed from the snowy northern steppes for our warm, fertile land. It was heading south again, with its glittering scales of steel. And the whole world, which declared its highest values to be human life and liberty, was to watch the latest murder of a small nation and secretly rejoice. Rejoice that the dragon thirsting for human blood had gone to a small nation somewhere down south, and not to them.[68]

Chechnya here is both the sacrificial virgin, being fed to the dragon in order to keep it from devouring the entire village (an interesting gender reversal, given the markedly masculine terms in which Eldin routinely identifies Chechenness), and, ironically, a kind of St. George (the patron saint of Russia), called upon to defeat the dragon and save the world. This concept of a tiny band of the chosen who are called upon to save the world is the stuff of myth and modern fantasy, and in the next paragraph Eldin continues the theme of a small band of chosen martyrs/courageous warriors: "they [the ones who will die] are the chosen ones. Their chosenness will bring them hell on earth and martyrdom, and through their suffering they'll purify all of their nation's generations of sin. To them befalls the cruel honour of burning in the flame of forgiveness."[69] This, it is implied, is the lot not just of the Chechen resistance fighters to die in the upcoming fighting, but of Chechnya itself, which is taking upon itself, Christ-like ("the autumn is to be crucified and shot dead"),[70] the burden of dying for the world's sins.

Chechnya is thus a, or perhaps the, central figure in both the post-Soviet world, and the new Age of Terror—central to both because it serves as a focus for anxieties within post-Soviet Russia about the collapse of the Russian Empire, and Western fears of Islamist radicalism. The writers surveyed here all discuss the contradictory and confounding nature of Chechnya, the Chechen Wars, and outsiders' reactions to it. Are Chechens the enemy, or ordinary,

---

68 Ibid., 149.
69 Ibid., 149-50.
70 Ibid., 150.

Russian-speaking, Soviet-educated guys like us (Prilepin)? Is the country a beautiful paradise or a hellish war zone (Babchenko)? Are Chechens and the Chechen resistance fighters victims of human rights abuses or perpetrators of them (Politkovskaya)? How should Chechnya be conceptualized, by Chechens and non-Chechens alike? This struggle to conceptualize one tiny—but outsized in its impact—corner of Russia is emblematic of the struggle to conceptualize the entire country, now that it is neither Tsarist Russia nor the USSR, while still bearing the history and scars of both those empires.

Eldin is careful to paint a picture of Chechnya as the true heir to Soviet ideology, modern democracy, and the concept of religious tolerance and pluralism, even as he makes his Muslim faith central to his own experience of the war. As he explained in an interview with one of my classes, although he had been raised as a Muslim, it was not until he experienced combat and particularly torture that he turned to religion in a conscious attempt to avoid a psychological breakdown.[71] At the same time, he sees the rise of imported Islamist radicalism in some sectors of Chechen culture to be an erasure of Chechen heritage rather than a welcome resurgence of piety.[72] As a Chechen nationalist, he is equally opposed to all forms of foreign interference or cultural assimilation.

Accordingly, in chapter 4 of section three, he discusses the increased brutality of the Russian troops during the second war and their alienation from their Chechen counterparts, in contrast to their shared culture and ideals of the first war:

> In the first war the Russian soldiers and officers had retained a certain spirit of romance, a respect for the right of the Chechens to be masters of their own destiny. After all, both sides had emerged from the same school of patriotic rhetoric, believing the Soviet Army to be the "defender of peace and friend of liberty". At that time the principles of democracy weren't just an empty phrase.[73]

Like Politkovskaya, in many ways Eldin is an idealist who believes in a just and humane society guided by the concepts of democracy and the observance of human rights, and his writing reflects those ideals.

---

71 Eldin, Skype interview, March 19, 2018.
72 Ibid.
73 Eldin, *The Sky Wept Fire*, 159.

By the time the second war began, however, Russian soldiers and the Russian people had undergone several years of anti-Chechen propaganda (it should be noted that the Chechen resistance and Chechen government were not entirely innocent of the crimes of which they were accused; no one came out of either of the wars with clean hands), and the treatment of Chechen civilians and prisoners was even more brutal than before. In response, according to Eldin, the Chechen resistance fighters became even more determined, but not, he is careful to stress, out of religious fanaticism.

As an example he gives an interview with a unit commander he conducted while working as an embedded journalist amongst the Chechen troops. The commander he interviews emphasizes that the fight is to remove the Russian Army from Chechnya, and that faith is a separate issue. Eldin then comments that amongst the Chechen troops were many Russian Christian volunteers who were fighting not out of hatred for Russia, but in order to drive Federal troops out of Chechnya. The fight was not, according to Eldin, a matter of local, unshareable bonds such as blood or regional origin, but nor was the bond that held the Chechen fighters together a matter of religion. They were not tied to the worldwide Islamist movement, but to the ideals of democracy and self-determination. Therefore, non-Chechens and non-Muslims were welcome to join their ranks. The important thing was a shared belief, not in any particular religion, but in the right of Chechnya to be an independent nation.

The use of "we" to describe Chechen actions in section three is therefore a reflection of the communal spirit Eldin ascribes to the Chechen forces, as well as a description of his participation in group actions. The "we" he uses is, like the "you" that features so prominently in his accounts of traumatic events, both personal and general. It appears at certain points in his descriptions of the Chechen retreat from Grozny (the same one which Politkovskaya described as "Shamanov's little trick," when Chechen forces were lured out of Grozny believing they had safe conduct, only to discover the exit was mined and Russian troops were waiting for them), which is narrated in a mix of "I," "you," and "we." The "we" passages are largely about the decision of the first column exiting Grozny not to fire back if fired upon by Russian forces, in order to give those behind them a better chance of breaking out. This "we" thus seems to be a claim to collective solidarity and to the need to sacrifice, not the fighters' lives, but their honor and their reputations as warriors:

> And from the right the enemy are firing on us. They're firing randomly, it's true. But why are we silent, Commander, when we're clutching weapons in our hands? Let us off the leash,

> Commander, and we'll silence them. We'll silence plenty of them for good. All their tanks and artillery, aircraft and hardware are powerless against us in the night. Night is for warriors whose spirit is stronger. Our enemy isn't cowardly or weak. But we are angrier. We'll fight with no regard for losses. Not for our country, not for freedom. Not for our religion, not for some lofty cause. We will fight for the silence. For our painful, bitter silence on this frosty, burning night! But we cannot reply. We cannot condemn to death our comrades who will break out tomorrow.[74]

The egotistical desire to respond to insults to their honor is thus held in check by the sense of collective responsibility. The connection between collective thinking and collective responsible is made explicit during a later episode, when Eldin, observing fellow fighters who are acting inappropriately due to tension and fear, thinks, "You wonder, *Why exactly should we tolerate them?* This use of the collective 'we' helps you position yourself mentally as upholder of the common interest."[75] The collective, impersonal "we" is thus a check on selfish, hasty, or thoughtless behavior, restraining the thinker from acting out on his first, animal-like or instinctive impulses. The "we" makes him feel part of something larger, turning him from a totally instinctive, and thus dangerous, unthinking creature, into a conscious being who is capable of thinking beyond the moment and the self.

Drawing together the multiple passages in which Eldin describes the ideal or essential qualities of the true warrior, we see that he considers both a primitive state of communion with nature, and an enlightened state of contact with the Divine, as well as the rational ability to control immediate, self-centered reactions and impulses in order to act for the greater good of the community, to be necessary. The true warrior must be able to balance these three, often conflicting, mental states in order to be effective and not to fall prey to either physical destruction, by falling into the hands of the enemy through carelessness, or to spiritual destruction due to cowardice. It is here in section three, in which he chronicles the retreat from Grozny and a number of months spent hiding out in the mountain forests, that he particularly emphasizes the necessity of strength of spirit and the need to balance out the physical, mental, and spiritual, something he himself does with greater or lesser success during various forced marches and other difficult situations.

---

74 Ibid., 193.
75 Ibid., 266.

But to return to the retreat from Grozny, it is narrated in dream-like tones, over several chapters. During his account of it, Eldin does not use "I" at all, and the events are jumbled up and lacking in concrete detail, so that it is difficult to know exactly what is happening as far as distances traveled, stopping places, and so on. Those are treated as inconsequential, or possibly unknowable: the narrator appears to be in a mental fog or on the edge of a mental breakdown.

In the chapter prior to the retreat from Grozny, Eldin meditates on the nature of memory and the self, as well as the subjective, uncatchable nature of time. His mind's eye travels to a park in the city, where he remembers throwing snowballs with a girlfriend, and he thinks:

> Wait . . . Did that happen to you? Was that really you? No, it can't have been you. It was that other guy, whom you persist in identifying as you. But does it matter? Surely he won't mind if you return for a moment and become him? If you become, for an instant, as happy as he was back then? No, of course not. He'll understand. After all, he is your reflection in the unshattered mirror of the past. Now he is gone. He's dead. Or rather, you're dead, and he is alive.[76]

This transformation/psychic split between the prewar and postwar self, which is given a particularly striking treatment here, is a recurring theme throughout the book—indeed, it features on the blurb on the back—and is both personal and general: throughout the book Eldin explicitly describes his own transformation and that of his fellow fighters, and implies that Chechnya and the entire former USSR underwent a similar transformation, from "romantics" who naively but charmingly believed in the ideals they had been taught as Pioneers, and who thought war was just a really, really big game like the ones they had played together at Pioneer camps, to either hardened professional soldiers, or self-serving cynics.

At the same time, the pre- and postwar selves, both personal and national, are not completely divorced from each other: the individual humans still remember their pasts, and the nations are still shaped by theirs. Even later on in the second war, when Chechnya and Russia have both changed almost beyond recognition from their Soviet and Imperial selves, and Grozny has been all but razed to the ground, the fundamental forces behind the war are still the same they

76 Ibid., 191.

have always been between the two nations: Russia's desire to colonize versus Chechnya's desire to be independent.

These opposing desires put the two countries on a collision course that, Eldin and his interviewees state repeatedly in the book, can only end when Russia withdraws from Chechnya and recognizes it as an independent nation. Still, the two countries have so much shared history, and the people have so much shared culture, that Eldin is able understand the Russians. While on some occasions this understanding is conscious and consciously chosen, as in an episode later in the book when he interviews some Russian contract soldiers he meets in the market, and thinks afterwards, "I realize that they are the enemy—only yesterday we might have met on the battlefield—but after all, the enemy are human too; they have feelings and thoughts,"[77] in the chapters on the retreat from Grozny, the connection between the narrator and the Russian forces appears to be on a psychic plane, in which the narrator, who is attempting to film the retreat rather than participate directly in the fighting, seems to know what the Russian forces are thinking, just as he knows what the soldiers on his own side are thinking. Not only that, but their thoughts and actions are so intertwined it can be difficult to tell them apart, as in this passage, describing how some of the Chechen fighters leaving Grozny try to take a village in order to get some cover from the Russian forces firing on them:

> The enemy know that now they'll be coming under fire from light machine guns, powerful flamethrowers and grenade launchers, their fire will be met with a storm of fire, and they cease their attack on the column. The enemy know all too well how adept their opponents are at shooting. And they have no desire to become their targets. While their comrades are covering them, the fighters take the village.[78]

The narrator confidently states what the enemy are thinking, not as a supposition but as certain knowledge, as if he can read their minds, and then, in the same paragraph, jumps back to the actions of the fighters on his own side. While this could just be taken as carelessness, if it is a slip of the pen, it seems like a Freudian one, suggesting that in the heat of battle, during this extremely stressful and traumatic moment, the narrator (who is filming everything on camera) is experiencing a supra-rational state in which he feels a connection

---

77 Ibid., 220.
78 Ibid., 194.

with the other fighters and the other side, and that they have all merged into one. While in the preceding chapter he described the psychic split between his past and present self, occasioned by his experiences in the war, in this chapter everything and everyone are one, brought together by the stress of combat, which enables him to sense beyond his own self and his own limited perceptions. His ordinary consciousness has disintegrated, but rather than being shattered, it can now reach out and commune directly with other consciousnesses.

This state lasts only as long as the hellish retreat from Grozny, during which many of the fighters, including Eldin, suffer from hallucinations brought on by hunger and cold. Chapter 15, the final chapter about the retreat from Grozny, ends with the words "Your soul is troubled. You feel people are tired of the war. And that is the most disastrous thing that could happen. That is bad."[79] Here the narrator is still able to sense the thoughts and feelings of others, but rather than helping him understand the enemy, or bringing him closer to his comrades, this sense gives him a premonition of doom, telling him that the people are tired of war and their spirit is in danger of breaking. This revelation breaks off the dream-like story of the retreat from Grozny and returns the narrative to a more factual, matter-of-fact account of the situation following the retreat, which was grim.

The remaining chapters of the book recount Eldin's in-between state following the retreat, during which he spends part of his time hiding out in the mountains with rebel forces, and part of his time down amongst civilians, even "going legal" at one point. However, the war inexorably winds down, and not in the Chechen forces' favor, leaving Eldin to deal with his dashed hopes and survivor's guilt. In keeping with the overall trend of the book to interpret events through a larger lens, one that shows the hidden truth behind the mundane truth, this loss is presented not as a loss, but as a victory: "The people, whose finest sons had sacrificed themselves, managed once again to preserve their Chechen spirit,"[80] while "All your fallen brothers-in-arms had won their battle. They'd departed this world as victors. Those who fall in battle have lost; it's only the survivors who lose battles."[81]

This interpretation of events may seem sophistic or overly convoluted, but it is in keeping with the theme of the book at large, in which the main battle is spiritual rather than physical. In the face of such overwhelming odds, it is indeed astonishing that the Chechen forces managed any sort of victory at all. In works written by Russian authors, who experienced the Russian side of the war,

79 Ibid., 208.
80 Ibid., 274.
81 Ibid., 275.

much of the Russian comparative lack of success is ascribed to incompetence and poor planning, and the effectiveness of the Chechen forces is given little weight, while the low morale of Russian soldiers is dwelt on at length. In contrast, Eldin emphasizes the high morale of the Chechen forces, and their success and maintaining their fighting spirit, their faith, their Chechen ways, and their humanity, despite all the pressure they experienced to break. While Eldin admits that certain Chechens did disgrace themselves by acting in cowardly, selfish, cynical, or un-Chechen ways, the people as a whole showed themselves to be stronger in spirit than their Russian colonizers—and managed a number of military successes as well.

The war as Eldin recounts it, while following the same basic timeline and course of events, was a very different thing than it was for the other, Russian, authors featured here. It was not a breakdown of common sense and human decency, which must be set right as soon as possible, as Politkovskaya depicts it, nor is it an exercise in pointless, soul-destroying torture and terror, as Russian combat veterans Babchenko and Prilepin depict it. While Eldin openly acknowledges how scarring the war was to him, transforming him from an idealistic romantic to a hardened soldier and in the process leaving him with traumatic memories, which keep returning to him in random order ("My memories refuse to follow the rules of chronology")[82] and forcing him to relive painful moments again and again ("Now you have to continue running across the blade of the knife and dying every day in your memories"),[83] it also allowed him, and by extension, his nation, to rise to the occasion and demonstrate, not heroism, but the true bedrock of their nature. Eldin is skeptical of heroes, writing with barely concealed patience of young men in the second war who dream of glory and, during the retreat from Grozny, sacrifice themselves pointlessly by running into a minefield, but he does believe in the potentially purifying nature of war. In war, he says:

> a man becomes the person he truly is. War, this hell incarnate, mercilessly reveals the essence of each person who finds himself there. That is why war is terrible and wonderful at the same time. It is only there that you can see with your own eyes the depths of man's fall and the heights of his nobility both at once. War is the concentration of all man's animal passions and all his noble yearnings. Those who dream of being a hero don't last long in a

---

82 Ibid., 278.
83 Ibid., 275.

> real war . . . And this flawed story is not about heroic war, or high-flown war, but real war. War seen through the eyes of an ordinary civilian. It is a fragment from my never-ending conversations with the ghosts of my memories.[84]

War, according to Eldin, is the best gateway to truth. It forces humans, individually and as a group, to integrate within themselves their animal and divine sides, and understand who they really are. The ultimate truth serum, war can lead those who are able to be led to a higher consciousness, a higher understanding of reality and the essence of being. Unfortunately, the price is high, even for those able to pay it. Knowledge of this truth has left Eldin permanently scarred psychically (and physically too, after what he underwent during his interrogation by Russian forces, although he does not dwell on that as much). Eldin does not claim that war is "worth it." But he does claim that war can have value, and can even act to elevate the warrior to a higher state of consciousness and understanding. While trauma led to a nonlinear fragmentation of his memory, it also led to enlightenment. And although he emphasizes that only those who have experienced war can truly understand it, his memoir shows him overcoming the sense of special apartment and oscillation between clinging and withdrawal that so often marks PTSD victims. Instead, *The Sky Wept Fire* is full of scenes of connection with other humans, with the natural world, and with the divine. The need of the trauma victim to share their story with the world, in order to bear witness and make it real for others, appears to be fulfilled at least partially here, hinting at the possibility of catharsis and healing.

His Russian counterparts, however, while undergoing much of the same suffering, came away with a very different understanding of war. For them, as we will see, there was little that was elevating about it. It could reveal truth and show those who experienced it who they really were, yes, but who they really were was not necessarily a good thing. For Eldin, war was a purifying, sacrificial flame. For the Russian soldiers, that flame was often the flame used by an addict to prepare their next dose. War was not so much a spiritual experience as the strongest narcotic in the world, one they found themselves drawn to again and again, even as it destroyed them, inside and out.

---

84 Ibid., 279.

5

Arkady Babchenko: "The Motherland Will Abandon You, Son. Always"

It's not true what the song says, that birds don't sing and trees don't grow in war. In fact, people get killed in the midst of such vivid color, among the green foliage of the trees, under the clear blue sky. And life hums on all around. The birds brim with song, the grass blooms with brightly colored flowers. Dead people lie in the grass, and they are not a bit scary in appearance as part of this multicolored world. You can laugh and chat alongside them—humanity doesn't freeze and go crazy at the sight of a body. It's only frightening when people shoot at you.

And it's very frightening that the war is in color.

—Arkady Babchenko, *One Soldier's War*

Of the writers covered here, the one who gets the most controversial press is undoubtedly Arkady Babchenko. In fact, his Facebook post about the plane crash on December 25, 2016 that killed members of the Alexandrov Choir raised such a furor in Russia that members of the Duma called for his deportation and a petition was created to that effect; within twenty-four hours it had gotten 130,000 signatures.[1] Although used to accusations and abuse, Babchenko found the level of vitriol, not to mention the number of death threats, to be so concerning this time that in 2017 he fled Russia for the safety of himself and

1 Arkady Babchenko, "The 'Unpatriotic' Post on Facebook that Meant I Finally Had to Flee Russia," *Guardian*, February 24, 2017, https://www.theguardian.com/world/2017/feb/24/unpatriotic-post-facebook-finally-flee-russia.

his family. He relocated to Ukraine, only to leave it following the election of Volodymyr Zelensky to the presidency. At the time of writing, his residence is unknown.

His dramatic "death" and resurrection in May 2018, which were revealed to be part of a sting operation conducted by Ukrainian security services in order to reveal an alleged Russian plot to assassinate Babchenko and other prominent activists, cemented his reputation as a trickster and agent of chaos in politics and journalism in the post-Soviet world. While international outcry against the incident was vociferous, Babchenko has maintained an unrepentant attitude, and has only grown in notoriety as a result of it.

The bare outlines of Babchenko's early life have little to suggest the firebrand he would become. Born in 1977, he grew up in Moscow and after high school entered university, intending to study law. However, he was drafted in 1995 and ended up serving part of his two-year term of service in the North Caucasus, including in Chechnya during the first war. He finished his first term of service in 1997 and returned to university, receiving a degree in international law. By all appearances, he could have settled down and lived a "normal life" as a lawyer.

But when the second war broke out in 1999, Babchenko volunteered for it. Why he did so, even he finds hard to explain. In an interview with the *Guardian*, he says that he had developed an "adrenaline dependency" and that "The way it drew me back was unbearable. Only my body had come back from the first war. My mind stayed there. My body walked around and looked at this world without understanding it. And seeing as the world didn't accept my body, it returned to where my mind was."[2] In the preface to *One Soldier's War*, his memoir about his experiences in the two wars, he writes that "war is the strongest narcotic in the world."[3] In an interview on the Crimean Tatar TV channel ATR he says that he volunteered for the Second Chechen War not to go to Chechnya, but to go to war as such, and had the war in the Donbass broken out then, he most likely would have taken part in it along with all the other Russian volunteers.[4] Certainly he is not alone in this: all the writers surveyed here, along with many others, found themselves magnetically drawn back to war zones again and again, no matter how much they hated war, and how much they wished to be back home again once they arrived.

---

2 Meg Clothier, "No Quiet on the Chechen Front," *Guardian*, November 21, 2007, https://www.theguardian.com/books/2007/nov/21/biography.

3 Arkady Babchenko, *One Soldier's War*, trans. Nick Allen (New York: Grove Press, 2007), x.

4 Facebook post, September 9, 2017.

While the compulsion to return to war zones may seem bizarre to outsiders and even to the people experiencing the compulsion themselves, this is a common response to trauma. As Herman notes, trauma survivors "often feel impelled to recreate the moment of terror, either in literal or in disguised form."[5] Furthermore, "There is something uncanny about reenactments. Even when they are consciously chosen, they have a feeling of involuntariness. Even when they are not dangerous, they have a driven, tenacious quality."[6] In Babchenko's writing we see both the need to recreate the "moment of terror," and the sense that the narrator has little or no control over his actions, including his compulsive need to return to war zones.

He was demobilized for the second time in 2000. Then began a checkered career as a journalist, blogger, political activist, and, he claims somewhat accidentally, writer. "I did not mean to write a book," he says in the preface to *One Soldier's War*, "I just couldn't carry war within myself any longer. I needed to speak my mind, to squeeze the war out of my system."[7] The result was a series of stories based on his experiences in Chechnya, for which he won the Debut Prize for Courage in Literature in 2001. A number of his stories were collected together and organized into a book, titled *Война* (War) in the original. In 2007 it was translated into English and published in Britain as *One Soldier's War in Chechnya* and in the United States as *One Soldier's War*, receiving rave reviews by English-language war writers and reviewers.[8] Con Coughlin in a review for the *Telegraph* compares it to *Jarhead*, and Henrik Bering called it "Perhaps the most haunting and ruthlessly honest among recent small-war memoirs."[9] Fred Doucette, in his review for the *Globe and Mail*, said of it, "This is a great book. From cover to cover, it is filled with the realities and horrors of a war that barely touched the West. To read it is to have a soldier's-eye view of what some called the Russian Vietnam."[10] Virginia Rounding said in her review of it that

---

5 Herman, *Trauma and Recovery*, 39.

6 Ibid., 41.

7 Babchenko, *One Soldier's War*, xi.

8 It is hard to say that there is a "canonical" version of the book, as it is slightly different in each language. Babchenko originally wrote a number of stories in Russian, but different stories were chosen for different editions. According to English translator Nick Allen, the finished English-language product left out a few of the stories that were presented in the original Russian-language manuscript (Allen, email correspondence, August 8, 2017), and Babchenko confirms that the Russian, German, and English versions all have slightly different collections of stories (Babchenko, Facebook correspondence, September 6, 2017). For the purposes of this book I am using the English-language version as the core text.

9 Henrik Bering, "Fightin' and Writing," *Policy Review* 163 (October/November 2010): 83.

10 Fred Doucette, "In Any Language and In Any Place, War Is Hell" (review of *One Soldier's War*, by Arkady Babchenko), *Globe and Mail*, March 15, 2008, https://www.theglobeandmail.com/arts/books-and-media/in-any-language-and-in-any-place-war-is-hell/article1201584/.

"Babchenko has transcended reportage, and succeeded in turning his terrible war experiences into art,"[11] and Jo Glanville chose it as one of the top books of 2007, calling it "a devastating testimony from an extremely talented young writer."[12] The dust jacket of the US edition is covered in accolades from Kirkus Reviews and writers such as Mark Bowden, author of *Black Hawk Down*. Abroad, *One Soldier's War* has been published in twenty-two countries, and translated into sixteen different languages.[13]

Back in Russia, however, Babchenko's reception was decidedly mixed. Although he was named one of the founding writers of the new genre of Chechen War prose, along with Prilepin and Karasyov,[14] and Debut Prize notwithstanding, some questioned the literary and aesthetic value of his work. When "Alkhan-Yurt," a long short story/short novella about his experiences in the second war, was published in *Novyi mir* in 2002, critic Andrei Nemzer said of it that, while he could take the "Afghan" prose of Oleg Ermakov seriously, and it was possible that such prose would one day be written about Chechnya, "'Alkhan-Yurt' was not that story."[15] Valeriia Pustovaia, while acknowledging that Babchenko was the first to write, and write so searingly, stories about a war that was happening in real time, complains of "Alkhan-Yurt" that

> [i]ts value lay in its reality, not in its images or style or anything else. That text, significant as it was as an eyewitness testimony, that text lying there on the table, an intact chunk of a war zone, that text that cried aloud—how could it possibly be analyzed without that analysis turning into an undisguised stream of invective over the pain that was displayed in it?[16]

While she admits that the text is "effective," she dislikes the fact that the tone of the story is "one of grievance and complaint,"[17] forcing readers sitting comfortably back in Moscow to feel bad about what is happening to Russian

---

11 Virginia Rounding, quoted in "Power and the Proper Soldier," *Guardian*, November 17, 2007, https://www.theguardian.com/books/2007/nov/17/featuresreviews.guardianreview.

12 Jo Glanville, "Books of the Year 2007," *New Stateman*, November 22, 2007, http://www.newstatesman.com/books/2007/11/faber-novel-review-press.

13 Arkady Babchenko, "Voina ot pervogo litsa. Interv'iu v 'Trude,'" LiveJournal post May 11, 2012, http://starshinazapasa.livejournal.com/396147.html.

14 Rudalyov, "Obyknovennaia voina."

15 Andrei Nemzer, "Fleita v rasstroennom orkestre," http://www.ruthenia.ru/nemzer/jurnaly12_02.html.

16 Pustovaia, "Guy with a Gun," 76.

17 Ibid., 77.

citizens in a faraway—but not actually that far—part of Russia. Ekaterina Kozlova, meanwhile, was even more critical, arguing that Babchenko was "interesting not as an author, but as a personality," that his writing was "Primitive. At the absolute lowest level. A school essay,"[18] and that he would never write anything else.

These criticisms of Babchenko's early work, while dressed as critiques of literary incompetence, seem to be more a response to the discomfort his writing elicits in his readers—I routinely assign *One Soldier's War* in my own classes, and it always provokes a strong reaction, not always positive, from my students—and to his vigorously expressed political convictions, rather than to actual defects in Babchenko's prose style. His writing is indeed "primitive" while also exhibiting noticeable elements of literary technique, something Pustovaia finds fault with, saying that the construction of "Alkhan-Yurt" "reeks of literariness"[19] even as she warns other war writers not to follow in his footsteps.[20] Like Politkovskaya, reading Babchenko is often an experience akin to being hit repeatedly in the head with a hammer. Hammers, though, are highly effective tools—and weapons.

It is not just his official prose and traditionally published pieces that Babchenko uses to make an impression. He was involved in organizing the massive 2012 political protests on Bolotnaia and Manezhka in Moscow; unsurprisingly, for those acquainted with him and his writing, he did not get along well with the other organizers.[21] Even less surprisingly, he was arrested during the protests and later fined. Since then he has become an outspoken critic of the Russian opposition movement, while also criticizing the Putin regime and Russian society in vitriolic terms, particularly the annexation of the Crimea and Russian involvement in the war in Eastern Ukraine. While he continues to be a lightning rod for controversy, he also reflects a strain of embittered cynicism in contemporary Russian culture; his phrase "The motherland will abandon you, son. Always," which forms part of the title of this chapter, became a popular internet meme about the treatment of Russian soldiers by their government.

In recent years he has moved to publishing much of his work independently, through the project "Journalism without Middlemen,"[22] in which he makes

---

18 Ekaterina Kozlova, "O literaturnoi storone boevoi medali," *NG Ex Libris*, October 23, 2003, http://www.ng.ru/ng_exlibris/2003-10-23/5_babchenko.html.

19 Pustovaia, "Guy with a Gun," 79.

20 Ibid.

21 Arkady Babchenko, "Bolotnaia. 5 let," *Ekho Moskvy*, May 7, 2017, http://echo.msk.ru/blog/ababchenko/1976598-echo/. *Ekho Moskvy* was shut down and its website removed in March 2022.

22 «Журналистика без посредников» in the original Russian.

his essays and articles freely available and readers are invited to contribute as much as they want to support his work. As part of this, he is very active on social media, writing frequently on sites such as LiveJournal, where he posts at http://starshinazapasa.livejournal.com as Starshinazapasa, which translates as "reserve Sergeant Major"; Twitter at @StarshinaZapasa, where at the time of writing he has over 142,000 followers; and Facebook, where at the time of writing he has over to 262,000 followers. He also blogs actively for sites such as Ekho Moskvy and Kasparov.ru. Aside from the political content of his social media posts, they are potentially also of interest to language teachers: Babchenko's writing style is pithy, witty, and often full of barracks *mat* (Russian obscenities), making his short posts a useful tool to introduce students to contemporary vernacular Russian. His extensive use of Twitter means he has hundreds of readily available posts that are less than 280 characters, as well as longer Facebook and LiveJournal posts. Although the compressed nature of Babchenko's style in general, especially when expressed on social media, can make it a challenge to readers unfamiliar with current Russian culture and politics, his use of simple grammatical forms makes it ideal for students just starting to dip their toes into contemporary journalistic prose. I personally have used his Facebook posts to teach *mat*, to good effect.

On and off social media, his writing and his public persona contain certain contradictions, contradictions that also appear in *One Soldier's War* and that he seems to embrace openly: namely, that he hates war and violence, but presents himself as a "Soldier, Veteran, War Correspondent" (from his Twitter profile); his profile picture on LiveJournal is of him standing in front of a burnt-out tank; he often calls for armed or military intervention as the only effective response against political opponents; and, of course, until 2014 he continued to visit war zones and write about war. Although a particularly unpleasant incident with the Ukrainian army, which at the time of writing he has not yet revealed in full, calling it "my exclusive,"[23] has turned him off from spending time on the front lines, he continues to speak out actively against the current Russian regime, arguing that his "adrenaline dependency" is still, it seems, affecting him.

---

23 Arkady Babchenko, Facebook post, July 6, 2017.

One Soldier's War

That war is a sickness is one of the most prominent themes of *One Soldier's War*. Prilepin named his novel about Chechnya *Pathologies*, but it is Babchenko who brings out the true pathology of the experience. A blazing indictment of war and the Russian army from first page to last, his memoir also conveys the "good" sides of war: the heightened senses, the adrenaline rush, the sensation of living through a "peak experience," the close bonds formed between comrades in arms. Indeed, this brotherhood of the damned, and the (often unwilling) ties holding together those who served together is something that makes its appearance repeatedly throughout the book. Unlike Eldin's concept of a code of honor that unites those of the warrior caste, for Babchenko these bonds are formed through mutual experience. Again and again in the book he stresses that only those who have lived through war can understand it and be part of the group—only to attempt to convey to the civilian reader just what the experience was like.

This emphasis on mutual experience, and contradictory relationship with civilians, is in line with Herman's description of the specific difficulty combat veterans have with processing PTSD and reintegrating into civilian society. As a way of dealing with both physical threat and psychological trauma, military units form particularly tight-knit units, which they believe will keep them safe. As Herman says:

> In fighting men, the sense of safety is invested in the small combat group. Clinging together under prolonged conditions of danger, the combat group develops a shared fantasy that their mutual loyalty and devotion can protect them from harm. They come to fear separation from one another more than they fear death.[24]

Babchenko goes back and forth between emphasizing the brotherhood of combat experience and trying to share that experience with the reader. This is also in line with Herman's observations about the relationship between trauma survivors and others:

> Trauma impels people both to withdraw from close relationships and to seek them desperately. The profound disruption in basic

24 Herman, *Trauma and Recovery*, 62.

> trust, the common feelings of shame, guilt, and inferiority, and the need to avoid reminders of the trauma that might be found in social life, all foster withdrawal from close relationships. But the terror of the traumatic events intensifies the need for protective attachments. The traumatized person frequently alternates between isolation and anxious clinging to others.[25]

One Soldier's War can in a way be seen as the author's attempt to connect with others, even as he withdraws from his readers whenever he feels that the relation is growing too close. Although seeing it in "merely" those terms is overly reductive, it is one way to understand the sharp swings back and forth between intense intimacy with the reader and the insistence that no one can understand the war experience who hasn't been there.

The book is divided into three sections of unequal lengths. Structurally, it is in some ways the most complex of the books covered here, despite or perhaps because of its apparent naivety and nonliterary writing style, and so I provide a detailed description and analysis of it in this chapter.

The first, and shortest, section, is a series of one-to-three-page vignettes, arranged in nonchronological order and with few concrete details about place and time. It is only by comparing them to the later sections that it becomes evident that these stories contain the same characters as the later, longer, stories about Babchenko's service in the second war. The second, and by far the longest, section, is in approximate chronological order and chronicles Babchenko's actual service, from his first arrival in the North Caucasus in 1995 during the first war, to his return to civilian life following his second tour of duty. The third section, also fairly short and made up of fairly short stories, contains Babchenko's journalistic, postwar writings on other soldiers, both in the combat zone and afterwards, as they struggle (and fail) to assimilate back into civilian life.[26]

Although the text is full of details, they are in the main not historical details—it is often difficult to place exactly when and where, in the greater scheme of the war, the stories are taking place. This is most likely in part due to the fact that, Babchenko tells us in the preface, while the book is for the most part autobiographical, and everything in it is true, "A few stories have been

---

25 Ibid., 56.

26 When asked about the organization of the book, Babchenko said that he and the editor worked together on the order of the stories, but did not provide concrete details of the organizational process (Babchenko, Facebook correspondence, September 6, 2017). The impression he gives when speaking of the book and its structure is that it arose organically, without much deliberate planning.

compiled from several real episodes that have been compressed into a single period and shifted in time. Some events I did not witness personally but I can vouch for their veracity."[27] The stories are thus "true" in the sense that they are based on real events, but they represent an emotional, psychological truth as much or more than they do a list of external events. Like *The Sky Wept Fire*, the book is aimed at telling internal, rather than external, truths, and in service of that, it uses the author's autobiographical experiences, and the autobiographical form, as a jumping-off point, a way of grounding the text and giving it a level of authority that nonautobiographical fiction cannot claim.

In this it is working in a rich vein of Russian literature, particularly war and camp literature: Tolstoy, Babel, Solzhenitsyn, and Shalamov all did the same in their quest to expose the horrors of war or of the Soviet gulags. It is also part of Babchenko's personal belief in the importance of direct experience and direct action: in a Facebook post on June 20, 2017, he criticizes those who pat themselves on the back for expressing their pity and outrage on social media and then forgetting about it. Feeling sympathy for someone means helping them, he says, so either do something, or be quiet. For Babchenko, deeds count far more than words.

Writing and publishing his stories, however, was as much a deed as it was words. Not only did he find the act of writing to be a necessary catharsis, but it enabled him to do two important things: maintain (mental) contact with those he had left behind when he returned alive from the front, and create a memorial that would make sure that the war and its victims would not disappear completely. He mentions in the preface the problem, also discussed by Politkovskaya, of even pinning down the number of casualties to the nearest thousand, let alone finding out what had happened to individual soldiers who were killed or missing in action. With the Russian authorities obfuscating the events in Chechnya, and so many of Russia's citizens outside of the war zone more than willing to turn a blind eye to what was happening down there, it is Babchenko's mission to force them to pay attention. "Let the war remain in people's memories. It must not be forgotten"[28] are the final words of the preface. Babchenko's writing on it is so aggressively striking that it is unlikely that anyone who reads it will forget it any time soon.

---

27 Babchenko, *One Soldier's War*, xi.
28 Ibid., xxi.

Section One

The ten stories of section one are the original ten stories that were published in 2001 as "Ten Episodes About War,"[29] for which Babchenko won the Debut Prize. They are the first works that Babchenko wrote, immediately after his return from the war, and are the most stripped-down of the stories in the books, each one only a few pages or even a few paragraphs in length. This makes them ideal for introducing Russian students to contemporary military prose. "Mountain Brigade,"[30] the first story in the collection, is perhaps best suited for this purpose, as it is only three-and-a-half paragraphs long, with simple sentences and extensive use of military jargon and acronyms. At the time of writing it and a number of the other stories are freely available online in Russian.[31]

Chronologically the stories of section one fit in the middle of the events described in the book as a whole, and the stories themselves, as can be discovered by careful comparison, are not presented in chronological order. They are by far the most fragmented and impressionistic of the stories included in the book; although rich in certain details, and not lacking in the internal states and philosophical musings on war that mark the later, longer stories in the book, their primary effect is to give snapshot impressions to the reader. They truly are sketches, with none of the characters, including Babchenko/the narrator, developed beyond the simplest degree.

That does not mean that they are "primitive." Or rather, they are, but in their primitiveness and their careful choice of significant details, they achieve an effect that lusher, more ornamental prose would struggle to produce. The notable lack of emotional outbursts on the part of the narrator and other soldiers highlights the horror they are experiencing, rather than flattening it. As with Prilepin's Egor Tashevsky, as will be discussed in the next chapter, Babchenko's narrator appears to be suffering from constriction, one of the hallmarks symptoms of PTSD as categorized by Herman. However, that also serves an artistic purpose. There's no need for the narrator to wax on about how terrible things are, because the circumstances speak for themselves.

The first story, "Mountain Brigade," opens with a challenge: "Only those who have spent time in the mountains can imagine what it's like."[32] This introduces a

---

29 «Десять серий о войне» in the original Russian.

30 «Горная бригада» in the original Russian.

31 For example, at https://magazines.gorky.media/october/2001/12/desyat-serij-o-vojne.html through the online service *Журнальный зал* (Journal Reading Room).

32 Babchenko, *One Soldier's War*, 3.

regular refrain in *One Soldier's War*: it is necessary to experience all this in person to understand it, and having experienced it, you will be forever changed by it and separated from those who have not experienced it. Except that Babchenko is determined to make the reader come as close to experiencing it as is possible via the medium of text.

Writing in the second person—one of the few places he does so in the book—he lists all the things someone setting off on a mission into the mountains has to load onto their body. This listing of things soldiers have to carry seems strongly reminiscent of Tim O'Brien's landmark work of American war literature, the short story "The Things They Carried," which opens a book of the same name, but Babchenko's own story is similar to O'Brien's only very superficially. It is unlikely that Babchenko was directly influenced by O'Brien's story, as Babchenko's English is limited and "The Things They Carried" was published in Russian in 2018, a decade after *One Soldier's War* came out. And in any case, "Mountain Brigade" has a different focus than O'Brien's story. While O'Brien is interested in memory, in his own story, Babchenko emphasizes the physical suffering of the soldiers on the march and the further physical and emotional suffering this presages. He describes loading up with food, supplies, and ammunition of various kinds, which "get in the way when you walk, rasping on your groin and hips,"[33] your own grenade launcher and that of a comrade, clothes, tent . . . It all adds up to such a tremendous weight that "when you take your first step uphill you realize there's no way you'll make it to the top, even if they put a gun to your head."[34] Somehow, the narrator—the point of view switches from the second to the first person once the platoon sets off—does manage to haul his own bodyweight in weapons and survival gear up to the hut where they are to camp out, replacing the Buinaksk mountain assault brigade. The hut strikes the narrator, who had been camping out in apartments in Grozny before then, as pathetic, but he and the others in his platoon realize, as they talk to the brigade they are relieving, that things are only going to get worse: "We watched as they left and each one of us felt scared, because soon we would have to follow them. Our heights were already waiting for us."[35]

This sets up the rest of the stories in this section, as well as the rest of the book. The reader has been duly warned: this is going to be a rough scramble, and it will get worse before it gets better. And it's not clear what we—the readers or the protagonists—are going to get out of it. The platoon's trek up to the hut

---

33 Ibid.
34 Ibid.
35 Ibid., 5.

is presented as essential in order to support the infantry units already up there. But in fact, the platoon does not appear to offer any immediate good to anyone: there's no heroic battle, no tears of welcome as they arrive at just the right moment to save their comrades pinned down by enemy fire. Instead, the brigade they're relieving views them "with malice in their eyes,"[36] since they now have to head out on "a nine-hour march and then the storming of some strategically important hill."[37] The narrator's tone is ever-so-slightly dry here: is the hill really so strategically important? Probably not, it is implied. In fact, while the narrator does not come out and say so explicitly, there is a suggestion that the whole thing is an exercise in futility—a very brutal, very grueling, exercise in futility. And the worst part of it is not the fighting itself, but the rest of it: the march up the mountain under all that gear, so difficult it makes grown men cry; camping out in the middle of nowhere; the complaints and hostility of the other, equally miserable, soldiers . . . for Babchenko, the true hell of war is not so much the battles but everything else. It is that "everything else" that will serve as the focus for his stories.

The second story, "The River Argun," continues the theme of the day-to-day horrors of the war. They are camped next to the River Argun, which they use for water and bathing. It even seems almost idyllic until two rebel jeeps fall into the river upstream, polluting the water with dead bodies that the soldiers cannot remove. They have no other water source, though, so they continue drinking the corpse-flavored water.

In these first two stories, combat action is notably absent. In stories three and four, titled "Chechens" and "Chechens II," the narrative moves to Grozny, and, it can be assumed, back in time, since in "Mountain Brigade" the narrator mentions leaving behind the plush apartments of Grozny. Now, though, the soldiers are camped out in these plush apartments, abandoned by their lawful owners. They realize that their chosen building is next to a building occupied by Chechen rebels, but, "Spitting on the war and ignoring security regulations as we hankered after comfort, we had chosen a mousetrap that afforded us no escape route."[38] They are not shot, however—not because their Chechen counterparts didn't try, but because their Fly rocket launcher jammed when they attempted to fire it. The reader is teased with the possibility of exciting scenes of military valor, but in "Chechens" it all comes to naught: the expected attack never happens due to equipment malfunction.

---

36 Ibid., 4.
37 Ibid., 5.
38 Ibid., 8.

It is not until "Chechens II" that any actual shooting takes place. The narrator hears a shot just as he enters "his" apartment. Terrified, he gets into an undignified struggle with his boots, and then into an equally undignified argument with his partner, Shishigin, who was "on the can" when the shot happened. To their dismay, they now have to go downstairs and investigate the shot. Bold, devil-may-care warriors they are not: for the first—but not the last—time Babchenko's vivid imagination manifests itself in the text, turning a short walk into an epic journey: "Each step lasts forever, and in the time it takes to move down the ten-foot-long eternity of the hall it seems a thousand generations have been born and died on earth and the sun burned out and was born anew."[39] Throughout the trip to the neighboring apartment, the narrator keeps telling himself "Arkasha, don't go, don't go";[40] he goes anyway, only to discover . . . an empty apartment. Open battle has once again been avoided; in fact, there is no sign of the enemy at all.

The first four stories are, while explicit about many of the unpleasantness of war—the dirt, the dead bodies, the fear, the heavy manual labor—almost comic in their treatment of it. The narrator and his comrades are dirty and frightened and exhausted, but the violence is always either averted, or off-screen, so to speak. In the fifth, and shortest, story, "Yakovlev," the violence suddenly jumps, horrifyingly, onto the page. A soldier from the company, Yakovlev, goes missing during the storming of Grozny. No one can be bothered to look for him and he is assumed to have deserted, a common occurrence. But when OMON troops are engaged in a mopping-up operation, "In one cottage cellar they found a mutilated body. Yakovlev. The rebels had slit him open like a tin of meat, pulled out his intestines and used them to strangle him while he was still alive. On the neatly whitewashed walls above him, written in his blood, were the words *Allahu akbar*—God is great."[41] Those are the closing words to the story. There is no expression of shock at his death, horror and outrage at the torture he had undergone, or remorse for not searching for him earlier. There is no need, this extremely compressed three-paragraph piece implies by its structure, for any of that: what good would it do? The narrator's—and there is no real central narrator here, just the occasional "we" or "they" as required by the development of the events—emotional reactions would be utterly superfluous, even self-indulgent, just as Babchenko argues in his Facebook post referenced above. And anyway, everyone, the spare prose style suggests, is too physically, mentally, and

39 Ibid., 11.
40 Ibid.
41 Ibid., 13.

emotionally drained by their own part in the fighting to display, or even feel, any kind of reaction to Yakovlev's gruesome death. It is just another dreadful thing among all the dreadful things that they are undergoing, until they have become completely numb. Babchenko is putting the reader into the soldiers' minds not through extravagant displays of emotion and pleas to understand how terrible this all really was, but by the exact opposite: through a laconic delivery that strips away everything that might distract the reader from the true horror of the events being described.

Story six, "The Cow," jumps ahead in time and returns to the mountains: the platoon has gotten a wounded cow from the Buinaksk brigade they relieved. At first, this seems like it might be a heart-warming story: they feed her hay, bringing her back from the brink of starvation, and in return she starts producing milk, which they drink "like God's nectar."[42] But then she starts to get worse again. They decide to put her out of her misery, which turns into a tragically farcical scene: the cow is so weak she can barely walk, making them curse her "For dragging out her own execution"[43] as they haul her to the ravine where they have planned to do the deed. For the first time, the Russian soldiers are actually shown as shooting at something: one of them shoots the cow but only hits her nose, and cannot bring himself to take a second shot. The narrator is the one who eventually manages to kill the cow, although this is in no way depicted as a heroic act. Afterwards, they seem to mourn her, standing and looking at her dead body for a long time. This opening act of military violence by the narrator and his comrades is in fact not very military at all: they shoot, not the enemy, but a wounded cow, and even that they can't get right and find upsetting. The way it is set up is almost funny, except that it isn't: the cow both provided for them, and provoked genuine affection, until they had to destroy her and she became just another corpse.

In "To Mozdok," the next story, there is once again a turn away from anything stereotypically heroic: the platoon is camped out in the mud and the rain, the miserable conditions turning them into animals, when the narrator is suddenly summoned and told to go to Mozdok to visit his mother, who has come down to see him. "These words," he says, "instantly separated me from the others";[44] now all he can think about is the warmth and cleanliness waiting for him, and the worry that he might get shot on the ride there.

---

42 Ibid., 14.
43 Ibid.
44 Ibid., 17.

"To Mozdok" might seem like a throwaway story, and compared with some of the others it has less impact, but it is part of a recurring theme throughout the book: the alternating state of estrangement and closeness that the narrator feels for his comrades and for the world around him. In "Chechens," when he and Shishigin successfully liberate a stove from the apartment their Chechen counterparts have abandoned, he feels like "there was no one closer or dearer to me on earth"[45] than his partner. But in "To Mozdok," the cold, rain, and mud drive the soldiers apart, causing them to break out into frequent, pointless arguments, something that only ceases for the narrator when he is called away. The influence of events and physical circumstances on the mood of the soldiers is something that Babchenko stresses, in part because it accurately reflects the reality of the soldiers' lives, and in part because it is one of the main points he wants to make in the book: the suffering and trauma experienced by Russian troops, and the abuses and atrocities they commit, are a result at least as much of the specific, unpleasant, circumstances they find themselves in as they are of the nature of war in the abstract. It is not that there is no abstract for Babchenko, but the details of daily life trump all considerations of concepts such as duty and honor. Russian troops appropriate civilian apartments, steal food, kill animals, and attack noncombatants not because they are inherently evil and want to bring harm to the Chechen people, but because they are miserable and desperate and often literally starving to death. And this seemingly trivial suffering—dirt and hunger—is worse, and drives people to do worse things, than the actual violence of war.

This is driven home in the next two stories, "The Ninth Neighborhood" (titled «1-й микрорайон», or "First Neighborhood," in Russian) and "Sharik." In "The Ninth Neighborhood," the protagonists are back in Grozny, fighting alongside pro-Russian Chechen troops. Several of them are severely wounded, and, as the other soldiers are helping with the evacuation, one of them, Sigai, picks up a blown-off leg and carries it to the transport vehicle. When he returns, he says to the narrator, "When I went off to war, this was what I feared most, blown-off legs, human flesh. I thought it would be horrific. But then it turns out there's nothing horrific about it."[46] This is a point that Babchenko will return to repeatedly throughout the text: dead and damaged bodies are a "normal" occurrence, and it is easy to get used to them. Unlike Eldin, who finds his first sight of human bodies destroyed by modern weapons of war to be almost unbearable, and who cannot process what he sees at first, Babchenko has the

45 Ibid., 9.
46 Ibid., 21.

opposite experience: he expects it to be much worse than it is. But at long as the dead body is not yours, it is of little importance.

While the humans in Babchenko's text are often cut off from each other, he, like the other soldiers in these works, can feel himself at one with nature and fate. This theme first appears in "Sharik," which, like "The Cow" starts off almost hopefully. The platoon has adopted a stray dog, whom they have named Sharik (the Russian equivalent of Rover or Fido), and with whom they feel extremely close: "We talked to him like a person and he understood everything. Here, at war, everyone and everything seems to be at one with their surroundings, be it a person, a dog, a tree, a stone, a river. It seems everything has a spirit."[47] This charming sentiment, however, holds behind it another, much less charming one. They know that it is dangerous for the dog to be around them, which they tell him explicitly, and tell themselves that he understands: "just one word and it was all clear. We warned him and off he went. But later he came back anyway, because he wanted to be with us. It was his choice, no one forced him."[48] A lovely picture of a faithful dog, adopted by a friendly Russian platoon, begins to emerge.

"Then," the next paragraph begins, "our food started to run out."[49] Within a day, they decide to kill Sharik and eat him. No one wants to do it, but after a very few hours of hunger they do it anyway. "Next morning," the story ends, "they brought us supplies of oats."[50] Killing and eating Sharik may have sated the soldiers' hunger for a few hours, but it was not necessary for their survival.

These two very disturbing (especially for dog lovers) pages are not just a throwaway story about the inhumanity that war drives its participants into, although that is a theme. Nor is it just a story about the harsh conditions and lack of provisions that the Russian troops suffered from, although that, too, is a major and recurring theme of the stories and of the book as a whole. Rather, it is part of slowly building wave of violence that washes through the stories, reaching its crescendo in the tenth, final story. Here, in the penultimate story, the protagonists of "Sharik" initially seem nonviolent, even kind. Their connection with the greater world of plants, animals, and the earth seems to place them on a higher spiritual plane, one in which they are like idealized Native American warriors, at one with the natural and spiritual worlds and humbly aware of their place in the greater scheme of things. When the narrator states that "they

47 Ibid., 22.
48 Ibid.
49 Ibid.
50 Ibid., 23.

[everyone and everything] are entitled to make their own decisions—where to grow, where to flow, where to die,"[51] this sounds like a statement of respect for all living things, a belief in noninterference and nonviolence.

The second half of the story explodes all that. Or perhaps it places the protagonists on the same level as acts of nature, part of the death-dealing fate that surrounds them and their environment. They have merged with their dangerous environment and are just as dangerous to their surroundings as their surroundings are to them; anyone or anything who crosses their path must do so knowingly, aware of the danger that they, the protagonists, pose. The human protagonists have no control over their actions and the death and destruction they wreak on those who have the misfortune to encounter them. Sharik, the dog, is the thinking, reasoning being here, the one with free will and the ability to tell the difference between safety and danger, good and evil. His decision to stay with the soldiers is thus made of in full knowledge of his likely fate at their hands, removing all responsibility for his death from those who carry it out.

This could be taken as a simple evasion of responsibility for evil deeds, a knee-jerk blaming of the victim for actions the actor is unwilling or unable to admit to or face, and there certainly is an aspect of that here. Something that Babchenko returns to over and over again in the book is the idea that he and everyone else in the war was caught up in physical and psychological forces beyond their control. Even seemingly rational, conscious choices such as whether or not to reenlist for the second war are neither rational nor conscious, and once hunger takes over, humans find themselves acting like animals, or worse. "Sharik" opens with a mention of the stray dogs of Grozny who fed on human corpses; it closes with humans feeding on a canine corpse. The difference is that the dogs are not the ones killing the humans, while the humans are the one who consciously and deliberately kill the dog who has come to them seeking shelter and companionship, and who trustingly "sat at our feet and listened to us discuss who would kill him."[52] The human protagonists are relatable and sympathetic as they go back and forth between their affection for Sharik and their desire for food. They are also revealed as the true monsters, different from the natural world with which they feel so close because they use their human powers of reason to rationalize a terrible and taboo act, the killing of a companion in order to feed themselves.

"Sharik" is also the first time in the opening cycle of stories in which the protagonists manage to plan and carry out a killing effectively. In the first five

---

51 Ibid., 22.
52 Ibid., 23.

stories they don't kill anyone at all—on the few occasions when they think they are going to engage with the enemy, the enemy has already disappeared by the time they arrive. It is not until "The Cow," story number six, that they are actually shown committing violence, when they decide to shoot the dying cow and put her out of her misery. They initially botch the operation, however, and mourn the cow's death afterwards. In "Sharik" they agonize over whether or not to kill him, then consciously make the decision and carry it out with brutal efficiency, before enjoying the fruits—meats—of their labors. Although these stories show the protagonists in a pitiful, at times even goofy, light, they also show them becoming increasingly hardened to death and destruction, able to kill first a cow, a creature humans routinely kill and eat, then handle human flesh with equanimity, and then kill and eat a dog, a creature Russians, like Westerners, generally consider to be a member of the family, not food.

This rising tide of casual violence reaches its apex in the tenth story, "The Apartment." On the surface it appears to be almost cloyingly sentimental. The protagonist, speaking in the first person, recounts how he finds and occupies an abandoned apartment in Grozny, going there when he could to rest and indulge in fantasies that he is just returning home from an ordinary workday. He is greeted by his fantasy wife, who "comes over to me, curls up on my lap and tenderly rests her little head on my chest. 'Darling, where have you been so long? I was waiting.'"[53] The protagonist imagines her kissing him, exclaiming over his dirt and his injuries, complaining about how scary the war is and how she wants to leave, and telling him she's afraid that his rocket launcher will go off accidentally as she feeds him borscht. When he has to leave to go back out into the city, he imagines her wishing him goodbye:

> She comes over and puts her arms around my neck and presses herself against me. 'Come home soon, I'll be waiting. And be careful, don't get shot.' She fastens the top clip of my harness and finds a small hole on the shoulder strap. 'I'll sew that up when you get back,' she says, and kisses me good-bye. 'Go on, off you go now or you'll be late. Take care . . . Love you!'[54]

Afterwards, the protagonists says, "I am seized with melancholy but I also feel good, as if it had all really happened."[55]

53 Ibid., 25.
54 Ibid., 26.
55 Ibid.

There are a couple of significant points about this story. First of all, after the straightforward unsentimentality of the previous nine stories, with their blunt presentation of the realities of war, "The Apartment" is a sudden departure into the realms of romantic fantasy, as the protagonist, like the most banal hero in the most generic war story, dreams of his girl waiting faithfully for him to return, waiting only for his arrival to jump selflessly into action, soothing his hurts both physical and mental. Against the backdrop of the previous stories, however, it *is* effective: what would have been intolerably treacle-y as a standalone work stands in sharp contrast to the other stories in the cycle, putting them all into perspective. This nonhero and casual dog-killer is capable of dreaming about idealized women, idealized romance, and idealized domestic scenes. It's not sex that he wants here: it's sympathy, served with a side of homemade soup. This fantasy was so powerful that, he tells us, he came every day to the apartment to indulge in it.

This all seems very sweet and rather harmless. As part of the imaginary dialogue between him and his imaginary wife, though, she asks him if he had a good day. "'Yes,'" he tells her, "'I killed two people.'"[56] This is the first time in the cycle that the protagonist admits to killing actual humans. It shows up as a seemingly meaningless line, just something he says to his "wife" as he's waiting for her to serve supper. She reacts not with horror, but with the words "'Well done, I'm so proud of you!'"[57] and then begins fussing over his hands, which are cracked and bleeding from the dirt and the cold. The fact that he took two human lives that day is treated as nothing more than another day at the office, something to remark over briefly and then move on to more important matters.

It is, however, the culmination of the violence that the cycle has been flirting with from the beginning, as the protagonist goes from failed attempts to confront the enemy, to killing a cow, to killing a dog, to killing two human beings. Each time he and his fellow soldiers are more blasé about it: they are terrified of his potential confrontation with the Chechens in the neighboring apartment, upset over the death of the cow, unhappy over their decision to kill Sharik (which in no way stops them from carrying it out), but here, in the final story of the cycle, killing two humans is nothing more than a good day at work.

This is a contravention of the "rules" of war writing, especially popular first-person memoirs about war, in which a protagonist's first kill is something

56 Ibid., 25.
57 Ibid.

to be feared, dreaded, anticipated, and celebrated.[58] In the conventions of a genre that American author Brian Van Reet has defined as "The War on Terror Kill Memoir,"[59] we are assured two things: "First, the claim to authenticity (autobiography, memoir, firsthand). And second, the assurance that the reader will learn the intimate details of taking human life."[60] In such books, the first kill is a defining moment in the protagonist's life, as he (it's normally a he) worries about it beforehand, feels tremendous relief and perhaps a rush of God-like power upon carrying it out, and goes on to rack up an impressive kill list for the rest of the book.

But there is none of that here. Although Babchenko's memoir relies heavily on point one of the formula Van Reet lays out (authenticity and autobiography), there is very little of point two (the intimate details of the taking of human life). In fact, it could almost be called an "anti-kill memoir." The main character's "first kill" scene is of a cow, whom he disposes of with an efficiency that suggests this is in fact far from his first kill. Here and in the rest of the book we rarely see him kill anything, especially humans, and there is nothing at all about that momentous first kill.

There are several possible reasons for this. It may be as simple as that, in a book that is largely autobiographical, and in which the main character also goes by the name "Arkady Babchenko," Babchenko may not have wanted to, or felt capable of, writing about something so personal and so emotionally wrenching as a first kill,[61] although he certainly shares many other intimate and emotionally intense moments. Equally possible, and more in keeping with the ethos of the book, is the fact that such a moment would have drawn attention away from the main thrust of the book, which is about the day-to-day, noncombat experiences of the ordinary Russian soldiers. Although Babchenko does not come out and say so explicitly, it is implied that the real war experience was not the fighting but everything that happened in between. Battle scenes happen quickly, in such a haze and at such a distance that most of the time, the soldiers have no idea if

58 For an example of more conventional war writing and the theme of the "first kill" from a Western perspective, see for instance *Sniper One* by Sgt. Dan Mills, about a British sniper in Iraq, or *American Sniper* by Chris Kyle, both of whom describe their first kills in detail and explicitly express no regrets afterwards.

59 Brian Van Reet, "A Problematic Genre, the 'Kill Memoir,'" *New York Times*, July 16, 2013, https://atwar.blogs.nytimes.com/2013/07/16/a-problematic-genre-the-war-on-terror-kill-memoir/.

60 Ibid.

61 In an interview on Ukrainian radio he said that he was "almost sure that there's no blood on my hands" (Babchenko, Facebook post, July 11, 2017), insisting that he almost certainly didn't kill anyone, a belief he echoes in the Foreword to *One Soldier's War*.

they've killed anyone or not. The most important thing is not the bullets they shoot at others, but the bullets that are being shot at them.

The ten-story cycle that makes up section one of *One Soldier's War* is less in-depth, less intense, and in some ways, less affecting than the following, longer stories, since it does not allow the reader to become as invested in the protagonists' development and fate. It is also more difficult to follow, with the stories jumping back and forth between Grozny and the mountains. It does, however, set the tone and the theme for the rest of the book, and ease the reader into the action: jumping straight into the next section, with its horrifying descriptions of terror and hazing, might be a little too much for many reader without some warm up and preparation. These first ten stories also describe the psychological arc the main character will take, from naive, frightened newbie to hardened killer who hates the war but can't go home. Had Babchenko ended his writing career just with them, it is unlikely that he would have the reputation he does today, but they signal the unique, abrasive, painfully raw war writing that is to come.

Section Two

Section two, by far the longest section of the book, is also the most coherent and chronological. And brutal. The violence hinted at in section one comes exploding off the page in section two.

It starts out innocuously enough. "The Runway," the first story of section two, begins with an eighteen-year-old Babchenko and his friends lying on their backs on the edge of a runway, basking in the sun, enjoying the warmth, and waiting to find out what is going to happen to them. It is 1996 and the war is winding down, or so they tell each other: even if they are sent to the front, they won't actually see any really dangerous action.

Each of the soldiers in their little group is named and given a brief biographical background, often with touching details about the lack of martial ability of each of them: one can't wrap his footcloths properly, one is always hungry despite his small stature, one is afraid of the older soldiers, and so on. These kids are the "little soldiers" (солдатики) that Egor and the other full-grown special forces soldiers in Prilepin's *Pathologies* look down on, as we will see in the next chapter. They are all enjoying getting a full meal for the first time in a while: they had not been fed for the entire train journey from Sverdlovsk to the Caucasus. Their hunger and the incompetence and indifference that led to fifteen hundred teenage boys being left without food for a multiday journey is narrated matter-of-factly, with flashes of humor, as the others tease the hungriest of the group for his obsession with food.

Child-like, the new conscripts trustingly accept their situation. It is the adults they encounter who understand what is going on, and their reactions appear, ominously, early on in the story. The narrator describes in brief flashbacks how they ended up on this runway on the edge of Chechnya: the major who was trying to convince them to volunteer to serve in the Caucasus told them that it would be warm and pleasant, but "His pupils were full of fear and his uniform stank of death";[62] at one stop on the train journey down, the women selling food on the platform "saw what sort of train it was standing on the line, started to wail and blessed us with crosses drawn in the air";[63] while when their train stops by the main entrance to another station, "people averted their eyes as they passed us."[64] These inexperienced conscripts, most still teenagers, have been marked for

---

62 Ibid., 33.
63 Ibid., 31.
64 Ibid., 38.

death, something that they only begin to understand as they sit by the runway, enjoying the sun, telling jokes, swapping song lyrics and ornamental pins, and dreaming about food and girls.

The reality of what they are facing dawns on them gradually, as they watch cargo helicopters being unloaded. Other soldiers are moving shiny, silver-colored sacks out of the helicopters and onto the ground, before later loading them up into trucks to be carried to refrigerated train cars waiting at the station. At first the boys think that this must be humanitarian aid. Only when they see that the sacks are full of something soft do they understand that they are not humanitarian aid but "dead Russian boys lying in the arid steppe in a strange southern town."[65] No one else pays them any attention, and the boys tear their attention away from the body bags and return story-telling and joking, but now with the knowledge that they are soon to be loaded up in those same cargo helicopters and transported to the same place that is producing those silver sacks.

The horror slowly grows in them as they see the refugees desperately trying to get on any type of transport away from there, the lightly wounded soldiers drinking and sobbing as they try to process what has just happened to them, and hear the screams coming from the field hospital nearby. Just as the people in the train station on their journey down couldn't look these young soldiers in the eye, the young soldiers can't bring themselves to look at the older soldiers who have just returned from the front, and whose fate, they realize, they are about to share. The story starts off with descriptions of the unique qualities of each of the boys in their little group of friends, but as they continue to sit there, their lack of uniqueness, and their bondage to the common fate of everyone else there, becomes clearer and clearer to them, and along with it, horrifying intimations of their own, very likely imminent, mortality:

> We aren't the first on this field. There were tens of thousands before us, awaiting their fate just like us, and the steppe has absorbed their fear like sweat. Now this fear oozes from the poisoned ground, flooding our bodies and squirming somewhere in the pit of our stomachs like a slimy worm, chilling us in spite of the burning sun. It hangs over the place like fog, and after the war they will have to purge this field of the fear, like they would radiation.[66]

---

65 Ibid., 36.
66 Ibid., 38.

Their comprehension of their shared fate with all the other soldiers who have sat on that field, awaiting transport just like them, elevates them—although the story is told in the first person singular, much of it is actually narrated in the plural, as the narrator links his experiences, his understandings, and his fate with those around him—for a moment above their personal concerns, letting them see the past and the future and things that concern, not just them, but everyone who has ever had anything to do with this beautiful, horrible field.

Still, they cannot yet truly comprehend what awaits them, and it is hard, especially for hungry teenagers, to keep focus on higher, abstract considerations of life, death, and fate for very long. They soon return to talking about girls—a subject they know more about by hearsay than by actual experience—food, music, and other prosaic, non-war-like things. But their attention keeps being pulled back to how terrible things really are, as the dead and wounded are carried past them, and more boys just like them are loaded up into cargo helicopters and flown off to the front, with everyone responsible for loading up the cannon fodder and unloading the maimed and the dead going about their business as if it's just another day at the office, which for them, it is.

"The Runway" comes immediately after "The Apartment," and in it, we see Babchenko looking at his future, even though he doesn't understand it at the time. He is afraid, and rightfully so, of ending up in one of those silver sacks; what he actually becomes is one of those people who shoot at other people, and handle dead and wounded bodies, with casual disinterest. In "The Apartment" killing two humans is nothing more than a good day at work, something to be mentioned casually, but here in "The Runway," where his journey begins, he can hardly bring himself to look at the more experienced soldiers who have witnessed, and dealt, death, and are now suffering the consequences.

The split between their current, almost idyllic, circumstances, and what is happening just on the other side of the ridge, the consequences—dead, wounded, and traumatized soldiers—of which they see before their eyes whenever they can't manage to look away fast enough, strikes the narrator with increasing strength, the more he witnesses on the runway and closer he comes to being loaded up and shipped off to the "meatgrinder" himself. As he's writing down the lyrics and chords to a song that one of his friends is dictating, he thinks:

> The sun is shining brightly, the birds are singing and the steppe overwhelms with the scent of lush grass and apricots. This is real life, bright, sunny, brimming with vitality, and everything should be just great, wonderful as we begin to wake. It's inconceivable

> that on this beautiful day those damned helicopters keep landing on the runway and people unload bodies and lay them out in a row in the sun. You just want this to be a place where people love, have families and don't butcher each other. War should happen in rotten places, not where it's good. War should happen inside the Arctic Circle where life is dark and gloomy and where there's no sun for half the year. We can't believe that they brought us to the edge of paradise, with its tang of apricots, only to wrap us in silver sacks.[67]

Immediately afterwards, the narrator is told by one of his friends that the major who is choosing, "like he is the very Lord of Fate,"[68] who will be loaded up next, has put down Babchenko's name for the next shipment of soldiers. He and his friends are upset, not only that he is about to be sent to the front, but that their group is going to be split up. They all go to the major together and the others ask to be sent with Babchenko to the front. But it turns out they've misread the situation: it's not Babchenko who's being sent to the front, but the others; he is being sent to Mozdok, in the rear.

This dramatic turn of events is the clearest example, in a story rife with them, of how Babchenko uses and then subverts the genre conventions of the war story. He is aware of how this is supposed to go: terrible wars take place in terrible places, the close-knit group of friends stays together, the hero goes off to prove himself in combat. But none of that happens here. Instead, they are in a semi-tropical paradise where the smell of ripening fruit almost overpowers the stench of diesel fuel and blood, the group is split up, their pleas to be kept together falling on deaf ears, and the hero of the story watches his friends get loaded up to be flown to the combat zone, while he himself is sent to the rear.

Furthermore, he is not disappointed to be deprived of this opportunity to demonstrate his courage and his manhood: instead, he is glad to be saved from the terrible events taking place just on the other side of the border, thinking "Now there's no more war. I have left it all behind and that is that. I feel sorry for Kisel and Vovka but it's more of an abstract sense of pity, like childhood memories, not really pity even."[69] His joy at his reprieve overpowers every consideration of friendship, even though a moment earlier he really had tried to be reassigned to stay with Kisel and Vovka, and thoughts of duty and honor do not even enter

---

67 Ibid., 43.
68 Ibid., 42.
69 Ibid., 47.

his head. He is still so naive that he does not understand how naive he really is, unquestioningly accepting what other people say or do to him, incapable of experiencing any kind of sustained feeling, even terror at his potential death or outrage at the position he and his friends have been put in. At this point in the story of his development, he truly does live in the moment, with flashbacks to the very near past and only a hazy conception of the future or of the separate existence of others. The two passages quoted above, when he envisions the field where they are waiting as poisoned with fear as if with radiation, and when he thinks that war should not take place somewhere so beautiful and full of life, are the two moments when he experiences a brief glimpse of a larger, abstract, shared fate and comprehension of what war means.

His passive, naive acceptance of his situation extends to his posting to Mozdok, which he assumes is a good thing, ignoring the ominous detail that they are being transported in the same Ural truck that earlier had been used to transport body bags from the runway to the train station. The final words of the story, as he is being driven off to Mozdok, are:

> I feel like a deserter but it's as if a weight has lifted from my shoulders. My God, I'm not going to be loaded onto that helicopter! The worst part is over and now the main thing is to get as far away as possible from that runway. I hold on to the metal canopy arch, trying not to fall to the floor where dead people have lain.[70]

The narrator of "The Runway" is naive, but the story itself is far from naively constructed. As mentioned above, here as in the previous stories Babchenko plays with the conventions of the war genre, teasing the reader by building expectations of some kind of grand battle sequence or heroic baptism by fire, only to turn things on their head: there's no "action" at all, nothing but carefully built tension as the narrator and his friends wait with mounting horror for their turn to get in the helicopter and be flown to the "meatgrinder" and likely death. And then the narrator gets a last-minute reprieve and isn't sent into the meatgrinder at all, but off to a safe zone, far away from the front.

The closing lines of the story, however, subvert the subversion. The narrator is not loaded up into the helicopter that is hauling live boys off to Chechnya, and coming back an hour later with their dead bodies, but he *is* loaded into the same Ural truck that was transporting those same dead bodies to the refrigerator cars

---

70 Ibid., 47-8.

on the siding, something the protagonist is acutely aware of. He thinks he has escaped death, and perhaps for the moment he has, but there is no real escape for him: even the rear is a place of death, something he is about to discover extremely painfully in the next story, "Mozdok-7."

"Mozdok-7" is the longest of the three stories about the first war, and, even though it takes place entirely in the rear, probably the most disturbing. It begins where "The Runway" leaves off, with the arrival of Babchenko and the others in the truck at the base in Mozdok.

Right away, the narrator inserts details that suggest this may not have been the reprieve they were hoping for. As soon as they get out of the truck, they see other soldiers shoveling gravel, "their faces stupefied and submissive as they work away steadily, like prisoners of war in a concentration camp. A pall of dust rises in the air and settles on their bare feet. Some of them have toes streaked in blood; clotted trickles run across their dusty skin and coagulate on the ground."[71] The protagonists—Babchenko and the other soldiers in the truck—are immediately unsettled by this scene, whispering to each other, wanting to know why the soldiers shoveling the gravel are barefoot and what kind of a place they've ended up in.

Their unease grows as they witness a badly shell-shocked officer stumbling around, shouting at passers-by, and see tanks with their treads and turrets blown off. They might not be in the actual combat zone, but the combat zone is emphatically making its presence felt here in Mozdok.

The scene becomes increasingly surreal that evening, as the six who arrived that afternoon sit, unfed, waiting for orders, watching planes take off for night missions. The sight is beautiful, but Babchenko finds himself thinking, "that's someone's death taking flight; all of these pilots must have killed at least one person and they will kill many more, maybe now, maybe tonight."[72] The new soldiers hang around, unsure what to do, until finally retreating to the barracks and bedding down for the night, still unfed. Babchenko dreams of being a silvery body bag that flutters like a butterfly; as his dream-consciousness is reassuring his mother that he is still alive and everything is fine, "someone kicks me off the bed and I land on the floor."[73]

What follows is a harrowing, and lengthy, description of *dedovshchina,* the hazing of younger recruits by soldiers nearing the end of their term of service. Literally "granddadism" or "rule of the granddads," the name refers to the practice

71 Ibid., 49.
72 Ibid., 52.
73 Ibid., 55.

of calling soldiers in their last six months of service "granddads" (*dedy*). The *dedy* had the unwritten but very much understood right to use and misuse the less experienced soldiers, particularly those in their first six months of service (*dukhy*, or spirits), as they saw fit. This culture of extreme hazing is believed to have started only in the 1960s, when the Soviet army began admitting recruits with criminal records, and soldiers were drafted in call-ups every six months, leading to defined cohorts of soldiers who were drafted at the same time. The results have been tragic. It is believed (official statistics are hard to come by) to have caused dozens if not hundreds of deaths by abuse or suicide, and left thousands of young recruits severely injured.[74] As part of its program of reforms, the Russian army has recently reduced its period of service from two years to one, it is thought in part to combat *dedovshchina*.

The focus on *dedovshchina* is one of the things that set Babchenko's writing apart from that of his peers: while Prilepin in *Pathologies* and Karasyov in *Chechen Tales* reference *dedovshchina* as something that does happen, they give it little weight, creating regiments for their fictional stories in which *dedovshchina* is only a minor problem. It's combat and bureaucratic incompetence that their protagonists fear. Babchenko's nonfiction work, however, places *dedovshchina* front and center, elevating it to something as bad, or even worse, because it was more frequent and more difficult to escape, than actual combat.

Like "The Runway," "Mozdok-7" is composed in rough chronological order, although there are few details about exactly how long a period it covers—it must have been several weeks, but no more than a season, since by late summer 1996, when the next story takes place, Babchenko has already left Mozdok and is in Chechnya. The important thing, though, is not external chronology, but the characters' internal chronology, which makes it feel as if their time in Mozdok is an eternal, inescapable, absurd Hell.

While Babchenko is not specific in terms of time, which has little meaning to him and the other young soldiers at Mozdok, he is specific about the kind of abuse they receive, which to them is much more meaningful. He describes how in theory, according to the rules of *dedovshchina*, the newer conscripts

---

74 See for example Rodric Braithwaite's "Dedovshchina: Bullying in the Russian Army," *Open Democracy*, March 9, 2010, https://www.opendemocracy.net/od-russia/rodric-braithwaite/dedovshchina-bullying-in-russian-army; Human Rights Watch's "Russia: The Wrongs of Passage," May 8, 2019, https://www.hrw.org/news/2019/05/08/russia-new-anti-gay-crackdown-chechnya; Viacheslav Izmailov's "V Genshtabe strashnaia dedovshchina," *Novaya gazeta*, July 10, 2006, http://2006.novayagazeta.ru/nomer/2006/51n/n51n-s11.shtml; and Steven Lee Myers's "Hazing Trial Bares a Dark Side of Russia's Military," *New York Times*, August 13, 2006, https://query.nytimes.com/gst/fullpage.html?res=9E06E7DF173EF930A2575BC0A9609C8B63&pagewanted=1.

("spirits"), have set rules of conduct to demonstrate their humility, and how each one "belongs" to an older recruit (the "granddads"), who can abuse his "spirit" and extort money and service from him, but is also supposed to protect him from the other "granddads."

"But there is none of this in our regiment," Babchenko says. "All that stuff [. . .] is just child's play. It's the big league here."[75] All the older soldiers beat the younger soldiers viciously and indiscriminately. In one of the many episodes recounted here, Babchenko describes how he is beaten for failing to bring Timokha, one of the older soldiers, six hundred thousand rubles, or more money than Babchenko would earn for his entire service period:

> He gets up and punches me in the nose, from below, hard. The bridge of my nose crunches and my lips become warm and sticky. I lick the blood from them and spit it out on the floor. The second blow hits me under the eye, then I take one in the teeth. [. . .]
>
> He makes me do push-ups and when I'm on the way up he kicks me in the teeth with a dirty boot. He catches me hard and my head snaps right back. I lose my bearings for a moment, my left arm collapses under me and I fall on my elbow. My split lip gushes onto the floor, and I spit out blood and the polish that I had scraped off Timokha's boot with my teeth.
>
> "Count!" he yells.[76]

Babchenko and one of his friends do end up raising the six hundred thousand rubles by stealing car radios, but by then Timokha has already gotten plenty of money by stealing and selling arms out of the armory, and Babchenko is able to keep the money for himself. It does him no good as protection, however, with scenes such as the one described above repeated on a nightly basis. Babchenko takes to hiding in the toilet or locking himself in the armory, but that also fails to protect him, and he learns that not only is fighting back counterproductive, but there is little point in avoidance: when the older soldiers call him to report for his beatings, he shows up promptly, hoping to get it over with as quickly as possible.

The only time he fights back is when, during one particularly vicious session in the toilets, the older soldiers contemplate gang-raping him. He tries to fight

75 Babchenko, *One Soldier's War*, 82.
76 Ibid., 58.

them off with a shard of glass, and they decide it isn't worth it. He pays for it later, however:

> That night they rough me up even worse, wreaking vengeance for that flash of resistance in the latrine, and the whole recon company piles on top of me to administer the beating, not even letting me get out of bed. This isn't even a beating—they are grinding me down to nothingness, like scum, and I am supposed to act accordingly, not try to wriggle out of it. They throw a blanket over me and force me from the bed, drag me into the corridor and beat me there. It carries on in the storeroom, where they lift me up by the arms and pin me to the wall so I don't fall. I start to lose consciousness. Someone delivers a fearsome punch to my right side and something bursts, piercing my very core with a burning pain. I gasp hoarsely and fall to my knees, and they carry on kicking me. I pass out.[77]

Hideous as this incident is, it ultimately saves Babchenko: the next day his sergeant-major notices his pitiful condition, and deals out retribution himself to the ringleaders of the attack on Babchenko, and spends the night with Babchenko in the barracks, setting up beds for them "behind the wall, so that no one can come and fire a burst through the door,"[78] in order to protect him from further vengeance.

Babchenko-the-character, and the other new conscripts, are horrified and outraged to the point of tears, desertion, and suicide attempts by their treatment. Looking back on it, Babchenko-the-author, while he does not condone the behavior of the older recruits, understands it. In a long passage halfway through the story, he provides a series of explanations for the extreme viciousness of the older soldiers' behavior, which exceeds all the bounds of ordinary hazing:

> Our older conscripts have already killed people and buried their comrades and they don't believe they'll survive this war themselves. So beatings here are just the norm. Everyone is going to die anyway, both those doing the beating and their victims. So what's the big deal? [. . .]

---

77 Ibid., 104.
78 Ibid., 106.

> Because our Motherland makes us kill people, our own people, who speak Russian, and we have to shoot them in the head and send their brains flying up the walls, crush them with tanks and tear them to pieces. Because these people want to kill you, because your soldiers arrived yesterday straight from training and today they are already lying on the airstrip as lumps of charred flesh [. . .].
>
> Everyone hates everyone else in this regiment—the hatred and madness hang over the square like a foul black cloud, and this cloud saturates the young boys with fear, just like pieces of barbecue meat being marinated in lemon juice, only they get stewed in fear and hatred before they get sent off to the meat grinder. It will be easier for us to die there.[79]

The presence of war, just over the ridgeline, and the constant fear of death, Babchenko argues forcefully, make the soldiers exceptionally violent. These young people, many of them not yet twenty, have already killed other human beings and narrowly escaped death themselves; instead of making them humble or thoughtful, it transforms many of them into crazed addicts to violence, terrified of the war but hooked on it, needing to get their fix by attacking their own comrades when they're not in the combat zone, which they love and hate in equal measure.

At this point in his career Babchenko-the-character cannot see, or can see only dimly, the love/addiction of the combat veterans for the thing that has destroyed them and stripped them of their civilized humanity, revealing the monsters who are worse than beasts underneath. Babchenko-the-author, who as the text progresses makes his presence more strongly felt with passages such as the one cited above, does understand: over the course of the book his character will become, if not quite as sadistically brutal as his tormentors in Mozdok in 1996, largely indifferent to violence and torture even worse than what he experiences here.

The tension between the two voices—that of Babchenko-the-character, a naive teenager who goofs around with his friends, decorates the envelopes of his letters home with silly notes and hand-drawn illustrations, and cries over a love note he finds in the pocket of somebody else's old uniform, and Babchenko-the-author, who has undergone the experiences that his younger self so anticipated and feared, and has emerged with much in common with the tormentors of

---

79 Ibid., 82-4.

his younger self, makes "Mozdok-7" particularly effective: Babchenko's almost affectless delivery of the beating scenes, as if he is narrating something that is happening to someone else, and has little interest in the outcome, draws the reader in, paradoxically, even more, and has even more shock effect, than a more emotionally extravagant style would. This affectless delivery is characteristic of Herman's description of a common response to the memory of trauma, in which "the traumatized person [. . .] may remember everything in detail but without emotion," as part of the experience of constriction.[80] However, it is also an effective artistic technique. The flat matter-of-factness of these scenes renders his occasional outbursts of emotion even more striking, making them stand out vividly against the backdrop of the author's almost casual acceptance of what has been done to him, hammering home not only the inhumanity, but the absurdity, of what is taking place in these barracks on the edge of the war zone.

Babchenko's near-rape and subsequent especially severe beating signal a shift in the narrative. Although he makes it clear that he does not consider this kind of hazing to serve any value as a rite of passage, instead destroying group morale and making the younger soldiers incapable of gaining any kind of useful combat skills, as they learn only to cower, lie, and steal rather than shoot straight, dig foxholes, or set and disable trip wires, the text itself is structured in such a way that that moment does indeed serve as a rite of initiation. His attempt to defend himself from his would-be rapists is the only time in the story that he successful evades any of the violence they inflict on him, and the only time they take him at all seriously as a fighter. Afterwards, the focus of the narrative shifts from the beating of the younger soldiers, to their work moving dead bodies.

In "The Runway," the sight of body bags jolts Babchenko and his friends out of their enjoyment of the sunny southern warmth and makes them realize just what is happening: they are sitting on the edge of a war zone, and boys just like them are being killed by the dozen, only a few miles away. When they are loaded into the same truck that earlier had been used to transport dead bodies, they react with squeamish horror and try to avoid touching the floor where the bodies had lain. But now, in August 1996 (one of the few exact time references in this and the other stories), one of the many battles of Grozny is taking place, and Babchenko and his friends are assigned to a burial detachment, a gruesome task that is handled with the same horrified distance as the beatings:

> The bodies keep coming, a steady stream of them, and it seems it will never end. There are no more of the pretty silver bags.

80 Herman, *Trauma and Recovery*, 34.

> Bodies torn to pieces, charred and swollen, are brought to us in any state, in heaps. Some bodies are more than half burned—we refer to these among ourselves as 'smoked goods,' to the zinc coffins as 'cans,' and to morgues as 'canning factories.' There is no mocking or black humor in these words, and we say them without smiling. These dead soldiers are still our comrades, our brothers. That's just what we call them, there's nothing more to it than that. We heal ourselves with cynicism, preserve our sanity this way so as not to go completely out of our minds.
>
> So we unload bodies, again and again. Our senses are already dulled, and we don't feel pity or compassion for the dead. We are so used to mutilated bodies by now that we don't even bother washing our hands before we have a smoke.[81]

Here and elsewhere in the book, the ease with which humans accept the death of others is emphasized. The young soldiers' first contact with death, in the form of the "pretty silver bags" being unloaded from the cargo helicopters and left on the edge of the runway, is so upsetting they can hardly process what they are seeing. A few months later, when they have to handle the corpses of their comrades themselves, they still can hardly process what they were doing, and very quickly became hardened to the horrors surrounding them. They never became quite as hardened to the pain they themselves suffered from the beating administered to them, but they became hardened enough to accept it more or less uncomplainingly, and to watch it with casual disinterest when it was happening to others.

At the same time, their suffering did forge a collective identity of sorts. While Babchenko and the other young soldiers feel nothing but terror and hatred for the soldiers who beat them, and quickly learn to treat the bodies of the soldiers they were processing as objects, they are nonetheless aware that these bodies belonged to "our comrades, our brothers." And in one of the angriest passages of the story, and of the book as a whole, Babchenko says, speaking in the first person plural:

> Shorn-headed boys, sometimes morose, sometimes laughing, beaten up in the barracks, with broken jaws and ruptured lungs, we were herded into this war and killed by the hundred. We didn't even know how to shoot; we couldn't kill anyone,

81 Babchenko, *One Soldier's War*, 107.

> we didn't know how. All that we were capable of was crying and dying. And die we did [. . .] We so wanted to live. Get that into your heads, you fat, smug generals who sent us off to this slaughter [. . .] We were betrayed by everyone and we died in a manner befitting real cannon fodder—silently and unfairly.[82]

While Babchenko-the-character feels largely alone, Babchenko-the-author, looking back on his experiences, expresses a strong sense of solidarity with a certain subset: those other young recruits who had undergone those same experiences. This sense of solidarity does not justify, in his opinion, what was done to him: quite the opposite, in fact. The injustice of what happened to him and his comrades forces them to draw together, or at least, forces him to act as their mouthpiece, to speak as "we" and give voice to all these boys who are incapable of speaking for themselves, often because they are no longer among the living.

"The Runway" ended by identifying Babchenko and the other young soldiers in his group with the dead: in the final scene in that story, they are loaded into the same Ural truck as the body bags. "Mozdok-7" ends in much the same way: their regiment is preparing to deploy to Chechnya proper, and the soldiers, after working the burial detail, put a lot of effort into making themselves identifiable if they are killed and mutilated, supplementing their official-issue dog tags with sturdier, homemade ones and tattoos on their chests. In the final lines of the story, Babchenko and his friends are speculating about how many soldiers have been deployed in the recent wars; the story ends with the words: "[H]ow many of them have died?"[83]

War stories lend themselves naturally to the archetypes of the heroic descent into the underworld and heroic return. Babchenko's nonfiction account of his own war experiences is, on the surface, highly subversive of the typical war story, stripping it of all its heroic trappings. At this point, more than a hundred pages into the tale of his first encounter with war, he has not actually encountered it at all: the expected deployment to the front is thwarted at the last minute, and he is sent instead to what should be a peaceful, safe assignment in the rear. Instead, though, these expectations are also subverted, and what should have been a safe haven for our protagonists turns out to be another dimension of the underworld, dropping him into Hell unexpectedly and leaving him even more defenseless than a more typical story arc might, since his attackers are not shooting at him

82 Ibid., 108-9.
83 Ibid., 121.

from a distance, but breaking into his bedroom and assaulting him in his sleep, while his friends look on helplessly and the officers whose duty it is to protect him turn a blind eye. And rather than becoming heroic warriors themselves in turn, Babchenko and his friends find themselves, Persephone-like, becoming not just denizens of the kingdom of the dead, but members of its ruling class, so to speak, as they spend their days processing dead bodies.

The comparison of Babchenko and his friends with Persephone may seem like a stretch, but, in a further subversion of the conventions of the war genre, Babchenko-the-character and his friends are all given subtly feminine characteristics, aligning them with Persephone just as their story aligns with hers. Draftees, they are essentially "kidnapped" by older male authority figures and dragged off against their will to this Land of the Dead; many of them send pleas to their mothers to bring them home, and in many cases, their mothers expend consider effort to rescue them from the war zone, but with limited success. The virginity of most of the boys, Babchenko included, is stressed repeatedly, as is Babchenko's sexual vulnerability to the older men who surround him: his act of defiance, when he prepares to fight back with a shard of broken glass when they discuss gang-raping him, is largely symbolic, and it is mainly good fortune that protects him, not his own fighting prowess.

This feminization of the new recruits is something Maya Eichler, in *Militarizing Men: Gender, Conscription, and War in Post-Soviet Russia* notes as an important trait of the hazing process, in which "the hierarchy among conscripts based on seniority is also a *gender* hierarchy, in which senior men feminize more junior men to establish their rule. [. . .] Enduring their feminization is a phase that conscripts must pass through on their way to achieving 'manhood.'"[84] Babchenko, however, refuses to accept the necessity of this process and remains stubbornly associated with feminine traits throughout the story. There is even a faint hint of the kind of love plot frequently seen in romance novels, which borrow heavily from the Persephone myth:[85] following the rape attempt and horrific beating, Savchenko, the one officer in the regiment who sticks up for the new conscripts, avenges the attack on Babchenko by viciously beating the attackers and asserting his authority over them, and then takes Babchenko under his personal protection, even sleeping side by side with him in the barracks. While there is nothing sexual or romantic about Savchenko's relationship with

---

84 Maya Eichler, *Militarizing Men: Gender, Conscription, and War in Post-Soviet Russia*, 66.

85 See for example Barlow and Krentz's essay "Beneath the Surface: The Hidden Codes of Romance," in *Dangerous Men and Adventurous Women*.

Babchenko, experienced readers of romance novels will immediately recognize the storyline and tropes used here.

So although the young soldiers here are clearly and unequivocally male, the mythological/archetypal underpinnings of the story are those of the female, not the male, heroic journey, in which the vulnerable, innocent young person is abducted and dragged down to the Land of the Dead, where she must then defend herself from sexual predation while learning to negotiate this dangerous new territory in which she finds herself, before finally being accepted as one of the rulers of the underworld herself and returning to the world of the living—but always with one foot back in the land of the dead, whose threshold she now permanently straddles.

While Babchenko says that he had no conscious intent to include myths or archetypes in the stories[86] I would argue that one of the reasons for the powerful effect of *One Soldier's War* is its (probably unconscious) gender subversions: like all war stories, it taps into deeply rooted archetypes, but it taps into archetypes for the opposite gender. Even the front cover of the American edition subtly underscores this: a group of young soldiers is shown lying close together in tight confinement at the bottom of the frame, with the picture fading to a misty blue background claustrophobically close above their heads; the focus is on a single figure in the foreground, staring fearfully at the camera with large, bright-blue eyes in a pale, smooth, hairless face.[87] While the figure in the picture is obviously male, he possesses a number of features that are normally troped as female in European writing: smooth skin and large eyes (which are indeed female features), as well as pale skin and blue eyes (also marked as feminine in European/Western writing, even though they are not linked with biological femaleness, as well as a signal of vulnerability and virtue). The young soldier in the foreground stands out from his darker, more obviously stubbly faced, comrades in the background, giving a subtle suggestion of a vulnerable young woman trapped down in the underworld amongst a group of men. The reader is thus set up to experience this as a "feminine" story from the moment of picking up the book. The whole thing—cover plus story—affects the reader on the subconscious plane, causing the reader to experience the narrative arc as being

86 Babchenko, Facebook correspondence, September 6, 2017.

87 Adding to the "abduction and imprisonment" theme is the fact that this is a photograph of conscript soldiers who had been taken prisoner during the first battle of Grozny and were being held in the bunker of the Presidential Palace in Grozny.

highly unusual, making the story both shockingly fresh on the conscious level, and deeply satisfying on the unconscious level.[88]

While "Mozdok-7" uses myth and archetype in subtle, nonobvious ways, the next story, "The Summer of 1996," borrows openly from myth, making the journey into the Underworld hinted at in the first two stories explicit. At the end of "Mozdok-7" the regiment is preparing for deployment to Chechnya proper; "The Summer of 1996" opens with their physical journey across the border and into the war zone.

The boys' youth and innocence is emphasized once again: in the opening passages, they are riding in trucks carrying humanitarian aid, passing the time by eating sweets and drinking lemonade. They do not appear to be in any immediate danger, but before they even reach Chechnya, there are signs that they are traveling to the Land of the Dead: the road they are on was built by German prisoners captured during World War II, and as they are driving along, they pass a cliff face painted with the words "ALL LIFE IS CROWNED WITH DEATH."[89] Shortly afterwards, they reach the border, which is not just a line on a map between two territories, but a psychological and spiritual borderline as well:

> A sergeant with a pockmarked face lifts the barrier and we cross the border into Chechnya. He eyes us from top to bottom, looking each one in the face as if he wants to remember us, all the boys he lets pass. Like Cerberus guarding the gates to Hades, he stays on this bank and the people go past him on their way to the underworld from where there is no return.[90]

---

88 Although what Babchenko does here is unusual, it is not without precedent. For example, Jon Snow, the beloved character from George R. R. Martin's wildly popular *A Song of Ice and Fire* series, shares similar characteristics of the Persephone character: he is young, vulnerable, and virginal, and is "kidnapped" and forced into a Land of the Dead where his physical safety is threatened, and he finds a protector who also initiates him into the world of sexuality. It should be stressed that in neither case is there any gender confusion: these explicitly male characters remain explicitly male, they simply undergo an archetypal journey more commonly associated with female characters. Readers wishing to explore the archetypes and tropes of the heroine's, rather than the hero's, journey may find Gail Carriger's book *The Heroine's Journey: For Writers, Readers, and Fans of Pop Culture* a useful resource. Aimed at a broad audience, *The Heroine's Journey* connects ancient myths with contemporary popular books and movies in an accessible style.

89 Babchenko, *One Soldier's War*, 123.

90 Ibid.

Once they pass the checkpoint at the entrance into Chechnya, the road itself becomes different, and is littered with the burnt-out vehicles, destroyed in earlier battles. The boys in the armored personnel carrier also become different, affected by the sights around them and the knowledge that other boys just like them have died on this very road:

> We have suddenly become different—Zyuzik, Andy, the commander, all of us—as if our places have been taken by mannequins, while our souls remain on the other side of that barrier at the checkpoint. It's as if we have aged a thousand years.
>
> In an instant the day becomes black too—no sun, no sky, no life, just a dead road, craters and burned-out vehicles. That barrier has separated us from the world that existed before as if with an invisible borderline.[91]

Shortly afterwards, the young soldiers receive their baptism by fire. Rather than covering himself in glory, Babchenko is mainly confused by the fighting: he does manage to loose a few rounds, but he cannot see his targets and has no idea if he is shooting in the right direction, if he has managed to hit anyone, or what is happening at all. His perceptions play tricks on him, causing him to lose most of his vision and hearing during the actual firefight; afterwards he thinks, probably incorrectly, that he can hear the Chechens (whom he never sees) running away through the bushes.

Babchenko's introduction to battle, and the first time we see him actually firing a gun at the enemy, happens a full third of the way through the book, and is anticlimactic. He himself has little idea what was happening, and he barely even has time to be frightened before the battle is over. Having entered the underworld, he has his first true brush with death, but it is given a scant two pages. The other battle scenes in the story are treated even more briefly, and are also strangely undramatic, with Babchenko describing his own active participation in his first real battle in a single short paragraph: "We open fire on the village, aiming at the source of the mortar shells. Our bullets disappear into the yards of houses, and once again everything is just the same, the roofs shine and the trees sway, and death and emptiness. It's just nonsense, some idiotic dream."[92] Fighting is in some ways so extraordinarily strange that he experiences it as a dream or an out-of-body experience, the only way he can maintain any

91 Ibid., 124.
92 Ibid., 133.

sort of sanity at all in the face of the death that threatens him, and with which he threatens others.

And yet in many ways, he discovers, war is "still just ordinary life, only taking place in very tough conditions with the constant knowledge that people are trying to kill you [. . .] We live the same life that people lived in the steppe a thousand and even ten thousand years ago, and death here is just another natural phenomenon like hunger, thirst or a beating."[93] Still having to deal with hunger, thirst, and hazing, the fighting itself is just one of the many things the young soldiers face on a daily basis, and it takes up much less of their time and attention than searching for food and water and trying to avoid particularly sadistic officers and older soldiers. Accordingly, in the text it is given short shrift, appearing almost incidental to the story.

The fighting may be incidental, and there are no grand battle scenes in "The Summer of 1996" or anywhere else in *One Soldier's War*, but the soldiers are still in Hell, still in the Land of the Dead. Babchenko devotes relatively few words to the nature of battle, instead discussing the difference between life and death, and how, even when they were not fighting, which was most of the time, the young soldiers were increasingly aware that death was stalking them, surrounding them on all sides. The true theme of "The Summer of 1996" is not fighting per se, but the super-fine line between life and death that exists in a war zone, and the soldiers' increasingly intense response to that knowledge.

The close proximity of death is brought home during that first journey, when they cross the border into Chechnya and find themselves under fire. The driver of the other truck in their convoy is killed right before Babchenko's eyes with the first shot of the battle; once the battle is over his body is loaded up on top of Babchenko's carrier, and keeps sliding down onto Babchenko as they drive down the road. "At first I am afraid to touch him," Babchenko recounts, "but later I put my hand on his knee and press him to the armor. His knee is warm."[94] The dead body of the man who happened to look Babchenko right in the eyes just before he was killed is now pressed up against Babchenko, who happened to have the good fortune to survive the firefight, but the body does not even feel dead, as it is still warm to the touch in the summer heat. And that is all the attention that Babchenko gives to him, consumed as he is by the physical needs of his own still-living body, which wants a drink and a cigarette.

The physicality of life and death, and the desire of living bodies to go on living, becomes a growing preoccupation of the story as the young soldiers become

---

93 Ibid., 134.
94 Ibid., 126.

more inured to death, and yet also more aware that it could happen to them. Babchenko also underscores, here as in "The Runway," the disconnect between the living, vibrant natural world, and the death that stalks the soldiers, and that they themselves are responsible for causing. A little later, when the regiment is in Grozny, the carrier Babchenko is riding on comes under fire. Babchenko and the other soldiers fire continuously into the windows of the apartment buildings they are driving past, and Babchenko finds himself noticing the brilliantly blue sky above him. "You can't kill people with such beauty around" he thinks—and then their carrier runs over a wounded soldier with an audible "crunching of bone."[95] The disconnect between the beauty of the natural surroundings, and the horror of the human actions set against that beautiful backdrop, helps underscore the psychological rift that is growing within the narrator, as he is no longer observing the war from the outside, as he was during "The Runway," but is now an active participant in it. Instead of describing this psychological rift as such, though, Babchenko uses well-chosen descriptive details to suggest it, and to suggest as well the narrator's lack of comprehension of what is happening to him. Babchenko-as-character is still more or less the same naive child he was in "The Runway" and "Mozdok-7," reacting instinctively to circumstances and looking for distraction from his concerns, rather than reflecting on them seriously, in part because of his youth, in part because the atrocities he not only witnessing, but committing, are too horrifying for the human psyche to process them.

Although by this point Babchenko has possibly killed someone, maybe several someones, he does not mention it, and does not know who his victims are, or even how many of them there are. He rarely sees the people shooting at him, and at whom he shoots in turn, instead firing blindly at the buildings in which the people shooting at him are hiding. Although to the people hiding out in the village huts and city apartment buildings on which he fires he and his comrades are angels of death, they do not see themselves that way, instead feeling dissociated from their actions, and rarely seeing their consequences. The deaths and dead bodies that they do see, hear, touch, and smell are those of other Russian soldiers, as their comrades are shot, burned, crushed, and sometimes brutally executed in front of them. Those are the bodies that Babchenko and the other young soldiers have to confront, and regular exposure to them makes them largely immune to the sight of death and destruction of others, and desperately anxious to preserve their own, equally fragile, lives. When one of them is injured and has to be taken to the hospital, the rest are envious of his good fortune.

---

95 Ibid., 136.

Babchenko takes this opportunity to attack a few more conventions of the war genre:

> Authors of lousy war books say that it's better to be dead than a legless cripple, but that's bullshit, of course. We know that the main thing is to live, and we are willing to live in whatever form that may be, even as a bluish trunk with no arms or legs on a beggar's trolley. We just want to live. To live, not die. That's all there is to it.[96]

The young soldiers are acutely aware that they are in the Land of the Dead, and that they themselves are halfway in the grip of death themselves. This makes them all the more eager to escape death's clutches, to live, even as they sit next to corpses and death-dealing weapons. For them, life is still very sweet: the war has aged them prematurely, but it has not completely stripped them of their youthfulness, instead intensifying it. When not on duty, "we stop being soldiers and become normal boys [. . .] We stop talking about death and killing, we shed any thoughts of all the terrible things that have happened to us the day before and we simply live. And for this reason every minute seems sharp and fresh."[97] Later, after the second war, the older Babchenko will contemplate thoughts of suicide, but the teenage Babchenko and his equally youthful friends are still overflowing with life here in this place of death.

This leads them, like Eldin's idealized warrior in *The Sky Wept Fire,* to develop superhuman senses that help keep them out of danger, as civilization is stripped away from them by the war. For all their love of goofing about, they are quickly being turned into killing machines, not out of sadism—although Babchenko admits that they can be sadistic, something that their youth exacerbates—but out of an intense, instinctive desire to survive. They are not the battle-hardened veterans that they would be later, but they are well on their way: "Pincha and Murky aren't even nineteen but they have already killed people. We have no hobbies or interests. We are turning into animals, honing our hearing like a cat's while our eyes detect the slightest movement [. . .] All we can do is survive."[98] When they are under bombardment, they learn to rely on these extra senses, these instinctive responses to danger, that they have developed, since "If we were to rely on our sense and judgment we'd have been dead long ago. Instinct

---

96 Ibid., 140.
97 Ibid., 148.
98 Ibid., 149.

works faster. This is life itself talking inside us, making us fall and look for a deep enough hollow in the ground while it turns over inside us like a slippery cold worm. It's the only thing that saves us."[99] Probably by developing hyperarousal as Herman defines it, they have become one with the world around them, like Eldin's true warrior is supposed to in *The Sky Wept Fire*, and Egor wishes he could, and occasionally manages to do so, in *Pathologies*, thus achieving what might be called "enlightenment" as fighters. Their "enlightenment," however, is not very enlightening, as it serves only to keep them temporarily, physically alive, with no concomitant mental or spiritual awakening. That, for Babchenko, will come later.

While Babchenko-as-author inserts a number of these semi-philosophical passages in "The Summer of 1996," the bulk of the text is devoted to detailed physical descriptions of how the soldiers live, the food they eat, the water they drink, the air they breathe and smell, the glorious natural world around them and its contrast with the manmade destruction of the war, in which they are now directly complicit. This helps give the reader an inkling of what, Babchenko claims, no one who has never been in a war can truly know: namely, what war is like. It also conveys the psychological state of the characters, who were almost entirely focused on the minutiae of day-to-day survival and their intense connection with the world of the living, here in this Land of the Dead.

"The Summer of 1996" opens with the regiment's physical journey into Chechnya, and their metaphorical journey into Hell. It closes with the reverse: a cease-fire is declared and Russian forces withdraw from Grozny. That this is dangerous journey out of the Land of the Dead is made just as clear as the original descent is in the beginning of the story. Despite the cease-fire, death still stalks them: as they pull out of Grozny, "The Chechens laugh behind us and make throat-slitting motions."[100] They drive past a checkpoint manned by officers from the pro-Russian Chechen militia, who are being left behind by the Russian troops to face almost certain death at the hands of their own people; afterwards, Babchenko says, "I see them before my eyes for a long time after, these ghosts on the roadside at Achkhoi-Martan."[101]

The column comes to a bridge where they are held up at a checkpoint run by Chechen forces, and the Russian soldiers are acutely aware that they are surrounded by armed, hostile Chechens. Babchenko catches the attention of one of the Chechens, who is "laughing as if he's killed me and I'm his trophy. He

99 Ibid., 150.
100 Ibid., 152.
101 Ibid., 153.

doesn't see me as a living person, all he sees is my severed head."[102] Babchenko responds by threatening the laughing Chechen with his rifle, nearly setting off a conflict that could have destroyed the entire column. They manage to make it across the bridge and out of Chechnya without loss of life, but it is a near thing, and it is at that moment that we see Babchenko not only as marked by death, but as a dealer of death himself. His descent into the Land of the Dead has made him a killer, and even though we never see him kill anyone, at that moment, we see what he has become: someone who is willing and able to kill another human being over an imaginary insult. Babchenko and the rest of the column pass safely out of Chechnya, but like Persephone, the fruit they have tasted—juicy, delicious fruit is a repeated motif in this cycle of stories—keeps them trapped down in the Underworld, and their escape is only partial and temporary.

Or maybe like Eurydice, they never escape Hades at all. Babchenko ends "The Summer of 1996," as he does "The Runway" and "Mozdok-7," with the idea of death, only this time, the soldiers are not just associated with death, but are actually dead, sometimes physically, sometimes psychologically:

> Every shell that hit us tore apart both the flesh and the soul. Our whole outlook on life crumbled and collapsed beneath this demonic fire, and there was nothing to fill the emptiness it left. The only thing we have left is ourselves and our brothers in arms. [. . .] We fought only for each other. Our entire generation may have died in Chechnya, a whole generation of Russians. Even those of us who stayed alive—can they really be those same eighteen-year-old laughing boys who once got seen off to the army by their loved ones? No, we died. We all died in that war.[103]

"The Runway," "Mozdok-7," and "The Summer of 1996" form a fairly continuous narrative of Babchenko's service in the North Caucasus during the first war. The most coherent and chronologically continuous and contiguous cycle of stories in the book, these three pieces, on the one hand, show "the face of war with all cosmetics off," as Philip Caputo is quoted as saying on the book's dust jacket. Every critic who discusses Babchenko's work mentions, some approvingly, some disapprovingly, the simplicity, the lack of literary pretention, and the focus on day-to-day life instead of the genre conventions and grand themes of war literature.

---

102 Ibid., 154.
103 Ibid., 155.

On the other hand, these three stories do in fact partake in grand themes of literature on a mythological/archetypal level. Each one is the story of the hero(ine)'s descent into the underworld; taken together, they form an epic story of a heroic journey into Hell. It just so happens that the heroic conventions in use here are not those typically associated with the male hero, but the female heroine. While Babchenko and his friends are all unequivocally male and experience no confusion about their sex, gender, and sexuality, the storyline that they follow is much closer to Persephone or Eurydice's than it is to that of, say, Ajax, Achilles, or Hercules. This unusual choice is a significant factor in both the shock factor and the emotional power of Babchenko's book: he flouts the conventions of the genre in which he is writing, while tapping into the archetypes behind the most popular and widely read of contemporary fiction genres: the romance novel. Like a romance heroine, Babchenko-the-character in these stories is both vulnerable and brave, causing the reader to fear for his physical and emotional safety; also like a romance heroine, he undergoes a profound transformation following his forced sojourn in the Land of the Dead. The difference—other than the complete absence of a romantic or sexual plotline here—is that, while a fictional romance heroine manages not only to climb out of the Land of the Dead, but to bring her hero back to the Land of the Living with her, Babchenko and the other young soldiers are, like Eurydice, betrayed by those who were supposed to save them, and trapped forever in Hell.

"The Runway," "Mozdok-7," and "The Summer of 1996" form a trilogy about Babchenko's experiences during the first war, but there is also a fourth story that tags on to the end of the cycle, filling out the story of his first term of service. In "Special Cargo," it is winter and Babchenko-the-character is back in Moscow. The story opens, however, not with him but with a general explanation of "what happens to soldiers who die in Chechnya."[104] Coming as it does on the heels of "The Summer of 1996," which closes with the words "We all died in that war,"[105] this anchors the action firmly in the Land of the Dead, driving home the fact that the soldiers are still in Hell, amongst the dead, even though they have survived the war and are finishing out their tour of duty during peacetime.

In keeping with the underworld theme, the first several paragraphs from Babchenko's point of view say nothing about what has happened to him and how he has jumped suddenly from summer in Chechnya to winter in Moscow, and why he is currently serving in a disciplinary battalion responsible for transporting dead bodies around the city. Instead, he drops us directly into his

104 Ibid., 156.
105 Ibid., 155.

thoughts and sensations as he rides around in the back of a truck with a coffin, growing colder and colder and angrier and angrier. It is only halfway through the story that the explanation comes: while on leave to attend the funeral of his father, he had been hospitalized with pneumonia and dysentery, and upon his recovery, he had been arrested for desertion and assigned to this disciplinary battalion as punishment for his alleged cowardice and dereliction of duty.

But that comes later. The first few pages of "Special Cargo" describe the transportation of yet another coffin through the frozen Moscow streets. As in the earlier stories, Babchenko emphasizes how ordinary death has become to the soldiers: they sit casually on the coffins, no longer bothered by the presence of death and certain that "these people had died and didn't give a damn where the kids moving them sat."[106] The soldiers are aware that the main thing separating those moving the coffins from those lying in the coffins is luck, and that, now back in Moscow as when they were in the combat zone in Chechnya, the line between the living and the dead is razor-thin, with the living already as good as dead inside:

> We're only nineteen but we're already dead. How are we supposed to live now? How are we to sleep with girls after these coffins, or drink beer, and rejoice in life? We're worse than senile, hundred-year-old men. At least they're afraid of death; we're not afraid of anything, and we don't want anything. We are already old, since what is old age anyway if it's not living with memories of a past life? And all we have left is our past. The war was the main thing we had to do in our life and we did it. The brightest, best thing in my life was the war and there won't be anything better. And the blackest, lousiest thing in my life was also the war, and there won't be anything worse. So my life has been lived.[107]

The Babchenko we see in "The Runway," "Mozdok-7," and "The Summer of 1996" is fearful, vulnerable, and naive. He is stunned by the cruelty and callousness of his seniors, finds actual combat to be like something out of a nightmare, too terrible for him to comprehend with his conscious mind, and is still capable of joking and playing, child-like, with his equally young and inexperienced friends. Faced with the imminent prospect of death, he and the

106 Ibid., 160.
107 Ibid.

other young soldiers are desperate to live, even as they become indifferent to the deaths of others.

The Babchenko of "Special Cargo" is only a few months older, but psychologically, he is almost unrecognizable. By dropping the reader directly into a particular day in his life in the disciplinary battalion with no explanation of how he got there, and allowing us to ride along in his mind as he goes about his miserable day, he deftly and economically shows us just how changed he is, heightening the shock effect. By this point the sympathetic reader will most likely have become emotionally invested in the health and safety of the young Babchenko, and formed a mental image of him as essentially sweet and child-like, in need of protection from others. To turn the page and find him exploding into outbursts of rage at his friends is a sharp reversal from the image he has carefully created of his younger self over the preceding 100+ pages.

Even more shocking is his response to women. Throughout the book, women occupy a small but significant space, largely as idealized, romantic figures who take the soldiers away from the war, representing physical comfort and cleanliness, emotional support, and moral goodness. As in the passage quoted above, sex with women is seen as desirable, but as a representation of wholesome, life-oriented behavior, not mindless debauchery or brutal conquest. The Babchenko of the first war is shy but respectful around women; the older and more experienced Babchenko of the second war is less shy but still enjoys the civilizing presence of the women who visit or serve in their regiment, and his thoughts and fantasies about his girlfriend make her a moral compass and a center of domesticity, not a sex object to be conquered and exploited. While he mentions in the earlier stories that he and his other teenage friends believed that in order to be a real soldier it was necessary to chase women, their actual attempts to do so are crowned in humorous failure, as they are too shy to do anything, and nowhere in the book is any sex actually depicted.

Furthermore, it is the sight and knowledge of female victims of the war violence that Babchenko finds particularly disturbing. His "first kill" of a man is not mentioned at all, possibly because he has no idea when it happened or who it was, and his conscience is not, at least consciously, particularly weighed down by the knowledge that he has killed: at this point in the psychological transformation that *One Soldier's War* chronicles, the fact of having killed is not so much a mortal sin as it is a marker of experience. The tragedy of all these young soldiers, most still in their teens, is not that other people are dead because of them, but that they are dead inside because of the deaths of other people. The only death that Babchenko agonizes over, during the second war, is that of a young girl. Elsewhere Babchenko has said that he considers violence and women incompatible, and that women should be kept away from war because it is their role to heal the wounds war causes, not deal them out.[108] Accordingly, Babchenko-as-protagonist does not as a general rule threaten, harass, or mistreat women.

In the first part of "Special Cargo," however, in distinct contrast to the rest of the book, one of his outbursts is directed at a woman. A well-dressed woman catches sight of him attempting to warm up his frozen feet while sitting at a stop light in central Moscow. Acutely conscious of the incongruity of his dirty, shabby appearance against the backdrop of the upscale casinos and hotels around him, he explodes: "'Stupid cow! What the hell are you staring at! I'd like to get you and your curls in the back of this truck, you fancy bitch!' I angrily looked into the blonde's eyes and then suddenly and to my own surprise I spat on the shiny red hood of the car."[109] Just a few months earlier Babchenko was fending off rape threats aimed at him, but now he is dealing them out himself, and, like his tormentors back in Mozdok and the war zone, over trivial or even imagined offenses.

It is this disturbing encounter with a woman that demonstrates just how out of control Babchenko has become. "Special Cargo" is the last story about his first term of service, and is near the halfway point in the book. In its placement and its subject matter, it forms the nadir of the overall arc of the book, the lowest point in the hero's journey, when, having been dragged down into Hell, he is given the illusion of escape, but in fact discovers that he is trapped there forever, responsible for ferrying other souls, Charon-like, into the underworld. While actually in the war zone, during both the first and second wars, Babchenko knows, although he finds it hard to envision, that there are places where war is not happening and people are leading normal, "alive" lives, amongst the land of the living. During this interlude, however, he has been returned to the land of the living—only to bring the land of the dead with him, corrupting the living world and proving how truly trapped he and his fellow soldiers are.

The second half of the story, though, begins the climb out of the absolute depths of the first half. This return to life and civilization is, like the descent into lowest, darkest depths of the protagonist's soul, triggered by a woman. The disciplinary battalion has just finished hauling an officer's coffin to the airport and are looking forward to warmth and food, when the order comes that they

---

108 As a side note, in my own first face-to-face meeting with Babchenko, he was vocal and explicit about his strict conceptions of gender roles, and said directly that it was his job as the only man in our group to act as the protector.

109 Ibid., 161.

have another delivery to make. This time the mother of the dead soldier rides in the truck with them, accompanying her son's coffin. Although she does not reproach the soldiers in the disciplinary battalion for their casual attitude towards the coffin, or even speak at all, her presence causes them to modify their behavior, and to realize that, dead inside as they may feel, they are still amongst the living, and that there are worse things than what they have gone through:

> Her presence broke down the defense shield that we threw up around ourselves with our swearing, spitting and profane joking. We felt guilty in front of her, the guilt any living person feels before the mother of a dead person. And although we had all been through the same experiences as her son, and every one of us had the same chances of being killed, and it wasn't our fault that we had stayed alive, still . . . We, the living, were now carrying her dead son back home, and not one of us could look into her empty eyes.[110]

While handling the coffins and being surrounded by constant reminders of the deadly side of war, a death that could just have easily happened to them, makes the soldiers feel as if they are also dead, encountering the living mother of a soldier who really is dead reminds them that they are, in fact, still alive, and brings to the fore the guilt that they feel over what has happened to them and what they have done, guilt that in general they are successful at suppressing. Although they count themselves as the walking dead, consumed with grief for their ruined lives, their grief is not as deadly and all-consuming as hers, their sensation of being dead an illusion.

It is also the mother's presence that breaks Babchenko out of his cycle of uncontrollable outbursts of rage. When the major in charge begins lecturing the soldiers moving the coffin that they are deserters and criminals who should be ashamed to stand in the presence of the mother of a soldier killed in action, Babchenko is about to burst into a verbal, or possibly physical, response to the major's words when he catches sight of the mother, who is staring, not at him, but, he fancies, "to a place where her son was still alive."[111] Babchenko's rage is suddenly replaced with shame, not because he believes he is a deserter, but because he realizes that he is part of the same army that is responsible for the

---

110 Ibid., 163.
111 Ibid., 164.

death of her son. He curbs his outburst at the major, wanting instead to explain himself to the woman.

It is then, nearly at the end of the story, that he gives the backstory of how he ended up in the disciplinary battalion: an unhappy story, but one that connects him to other people and to his own past and future nonetheless. The silent stare of the grieving mother snaps him out of his own self-absorption, breaking the death-like isolation that has had him in its grip for the first part of the story, enabling him to connect and empathize with others, a certain marker of life rather than death.

The thawing of the protagonist on the emotional level is paralleled with his literal thawing on the physical level: his feet, which are numb from cold throughout the story, finally warm up in the final passage, when he returns to the barracks and crawls into bed. His (temporary) physical and emotional warmth does not mean he has escaped from the underworld: he knows that tomorrow he will have to get up and spend the day hauling coffins in the cold again. Nor has he been completely cured of his anger: the story ends with him fantasizing about revenge against the major. But, in a major shift from the previous three stories, the focus of the final lines is not on death. While "The Runway," "Mozdok-7," and "The Summer of 1996" all end with direct references to death, and explicitly put the protagonist amongst the dead, even though he is technically still living, the end of "Special Cargo," although it does, just like the other stories, place the protagonist in the same space as the coffins he handles, shows him as an active, conscious subject, speaking out loud and making plans. He is still in Hell, still at the bottom of his journey, but now there is a faint suggestion that his face is turned towards the light of the overworld, instead of down towards the darkness of the underworld.

The four stories that describe Babchenko's first term of service, including his first tour of duty in Chechnya, are autobiographical and on the surface focus heavily on physical details, making them appear to be examples of journalistic realism, with little imaginative embellishment. In apparent support of this, Babchenko himself has said in a Facebook post that "I don't give a damn about made-up fantasy—reality burns more than any fantasy could ever dream of."[112] And indeed, the situations Babchenko describes and the characters that people his stories are overtly physical and grounded in the realia of the crude realities of war: blood, mud, sweat, and tears, with a side of diesel fumes and bad food. The protagonists undergo intense emotional experiences and psychological changes, but these are generally signaled in the text by physical signs: cold or warmth,

112 Babchenko, Facebook post, June 27, 2017.

hunger or satiety, danger or safety. The more emotionally intense the experience, the more laconic Babchenko's writing becomes, so that what presumably are the most traumatic things that happened to him—the rape attempt at Mozdok, for example, or the ride through the "field of fire" in Grozny—are covered in a couple of short, unemotional paragraphs. The effect is one of compression to the point of flatness, in which deadly battles pass by so quickly they barely register before they are over, leaving nothing behind but a list of the dead bodies and burned-out vehicles that the surviving soldiers have to haul back to the base.

While Babchenko sees little glory in combat, the effect of these super-compressed battle scenes is not so much to de-glorify combat as to express its psychological truth: the human mind is not capable of processing what is happening during combat, especially combat involving high-speed, high-powered weapons. Babchenko does not experience any kind of clarity and calm while fighting; despite the state of hyperarousal he achieves in the war zone, time does not slow down for him and allow him to act with the conscious purposefulness of a trained martial artist. Instead, he has little idea what is happening, and in retrospect cannot understand why he lived while others died. It is afterwards, in the long lulls between the battles, that the effects are felt and the battle is really fought.

Babchenko's focus on the quotidian, noncombat side of war is thus hyperrealistic from both the objective and subjective points of view: objectively, the soldiers in even the hottest zones spent more time not fighting than fighting, and subjectively, it was during these periods of inaction that they processed their combat experiences mentally and emotionally. Babchenko's almost obsessive focus on brief periods of time and a few telling details, with little attention given to things such as where the soldiers are and what is going on in the rest of the war, and his habit of jumping around in time, is thus, while in contravention of the conventions of linear, realist prose, conveys an inner realism built up of external details. It is also in line with Herman's description of traumatic memories, which "lack verbal narrative and context; rather, they are encoded in the form of vivid sensations and images."[113] Readers of these four stories may come away with very little idea of what actually happened during the First Chechen War, but they will have an excellent idea of what it felt like for the troops serving there on the ground.

At the same time, these four stories, while autobiographical and aggressively realistic, also sketch out a heroic journey based on myth and archetype, albeit myths and archetypes more commonly associated with vulnerable female

113 Herman, *Trauma and Recovery*, 38.

protagonists rather than bold male warriors. The combination of these two layers lends a richness and poignancy to the narrative, rendering it dramatically unexpected and emotionally affecting. While I reject Pustovaia's claim that female readers cannot as a rule appreciate or enjoy battle sequences as such,[114] it is noticeable that, when I teach *One Soldier's War*, it often elicits a strong positive reaction from female students, inspiring them to research the Chechen Wars and conditions in the Russian army in a way that more traditional war stories do not. Perhaps the crowning achievement of *One Soldier's War* is that it manages to convey the horror, brutality, and inhumanity of war in general and the Chechen Wars in particular while also being more than just a litany of abuses and atrocities, taking the protagonist's individual experience and elevating it to something universal. The heart of that achievement is these four stories, in which an innocent adolescent on the threshold of adulthood is sucked into an anti-heroic journey, plunging him into the depths of Hell.

The feminization of the narrator in the first part of section two is also characteristic of what Maya Eichler sees as the contradictory depictions of Chechen War veterans, with their emphasis on fragility and intense emotional states. As she writes, "The emotions some men experience in war such as anxiety, shame, and pain lay bare the contradictions and inherent fragility of militarized masculinity. Such emotions are usually associated with femininity and seen as contrary to the image of the tough, military man."[115] The reaction, as she points out, is for such men to turn to "practices that Tracey Xavia Karner has called 'toxic' masculinity: alcoholism, drug abuse, and aggressive behavior."[116] We see those reactions in Babchenko-as-narrator and his comrades in the second half of section two.

Section two of *One Soldier's War* is composed of nine stories, the first four about the first war and the last five about the second war. This is not, however, indicated by any special marks or breaks in the text. "Special Cargo" is followed directly by "New Year's Eve," in which the protagonist, who had originally hoped to spend January 1, 2000 in Paris, instead finds himself back in Chechnya. How and why is not explained: the overall narrative of the book jumps directly from the end of the first war to the beginning of the second, skipping over the intervening three years as if they have not happened—which, in a way, they have not. As Babchenko says in his preface, he and the other soldiers who re-enlisted for the second war never really returned from the first. The seamless transition

114 Pustovaia, "Guy with a Gun," 71.
115 Eichler, *Militarizing Men*, 121.
116 Ibid.

from the first war to the second, such that a reader who does not know the history of the Chechen Wars, or one who is merely inattentive, may not realize that several years have passed and the protagonist is now fighting in what is technically a different war, represents the internal sensations of the protagonist and the underlying reality that the second war led directly from the first, with hardly a break between them.

The Babchenko of "New Year's Eve" is already a different person than the protagonist of the first four stories, however. He is no longer the naive and vulnerable child of "The Runway," "Mozdok-7," and the beginning of "The Summer of 1996," nor is he the semi-feral creature prone to violent outbursts of the end of "The Summer of 1996" and "Special Cargo." He and his comrades in arms, now in their twenties rather than their teens, have picked up some survival skills and a tiny modicum of level-headedness, which allows them to scrounge together a New Year's "feast" and enjoy their canned food and cookies. They even put on an impromptu "fireworks" show with their weapons.

All is not fun and games, however: while Babchenko and his friends are no longer at the very bottom of the totem pole, they are still subject to abuse, and the relations between the officers and the enlisted soldiers are still strained: during the "fireworks" show, Babchenko is punched in the face by the HQ commander, who "is afraid that in the noise someone will deliberately shoot him or the battalion commander."[117] The contract soldiers, of whom Babchenko is now one, although this is not made clear until later stories in the cycle, are not subject to the same level of hazing as the new conscripts, but violence is still the default method for communication and dealing with problems. For all the liveliness of their New Year's celebrations, the soldiers are still in the land of the dead.

That the soldiers are trapped in the underworld, and have been transformed into subterranean, wraith-like (or mole-like) creatures is suggested by a passage describing the protagonist's sensations upon stepping out of the dugout in which the celebration is being held. Back in the dugout there is light, warmth, and food, and in a moment the soldiers will begin firing off tracer rounds, lighting up the outdoors as well in a joyous display of light and color, but at that moment of transition:

> The dark is impenetrable; you can't even see the hand in front of your face. It seems there is no sky, no ground, no life, no light, no joy, no love, and no heroism. Just night and death. Because

117 Babchenko, *One Soldier's War*, 171.

> night is the time of death. Every time the sun goes down life dies. We don't know if we will live to see the next day, and all we can do is freeze motionless in our trenches, press ourselves into the ground and wait for sunrise as we listen into the darkness. Our eyesight is useless but our hearing is razor sharp.[118]

In this short—"New Year's Eve" is only five pages—story, the protagonists and the reader are transitioned from the hell of the first war to the even deeper hell of the second war. "New Year's Eve," the introduction to the second war, is deceptively cheery and hopeful: there are no coffins; no rotting, dismembered corpses, a major feature of the previous stories; and no one is seriously injured or killed. But they are still in Hell, nonetheless, and death and darkness still surround them, waiting to take them if they let down their guard or are just unlucky.

"New Year's Eve" is followed, both in the book and in the chronology of the overall narrative, by "Alkhan-Yurt," which takes place just a few days later, during the first week of January 2000, when Russian forces have surrounded Grozny and are trying to prevent a breakout by Chechen fighters. (The Chechens would eventually attempt a breakout at the end of January, which Eldin recounts in *The Sky Wept Fire*).

"Alkhan-Yurt" starts off slowly, lulling the reader into a false sense of security. Babchenko's platoon is sent off into a swamp in order to stop up a gap in the Russian forces ringing Grozny. Much of the first half of the story is taken up with descriptions of the mud, cold, and hunger that the soldiers face: they think they are going into battle, but instead they end up spending the night inside a freezing troop transport vehicle with no food or decent water. At first Babchenko is terrified of the impending fighting, but then he, like the other soldiers, is worn down by the wait in the cold. As the night drags on and there is no sign of the enemy, the wraith-like soldiers abandon their precautions in favor of "the eternal preoccupations of the soldier: get something to eat, warm up and have a smoke."[119] They try to hunt ducks but fail to hit any of them, instead dining off of frozen hawthorn berries washed down with unfiltered, untreated marsh water.

It is then, as they are shivering and scrounging for food, that Babchenko explains how he re-enlisted for the second war and delivers a diatribe against Yeltsin, part of his increasing political awareness, intimating the political activism Babchenko the author would take up after the war. He goes on to tell

118 Ibid., 170.
119 Ibid., 192.

his friend and fellow Muscovite Igor, "'They've ruined my life, see? You don't know it yet, but they've ruined yours too. You are already dead—you won't have any more life. Yours ended here, in this marsh. How I waited for this war! I never really came back from the first; I went missing in action in the fields by Achkhoi-Martan."[120] Becoming increasingly agitated, he concludes "We can no longer do without human flesh. We're psychopaths."[121]

In the first half of "Alkhan-Yurt," as the soldiers are freezing in the swamp, Babchenko compares them to cannibals and dead men, even as he acknowledges that the war has given him a peculiar kind of freedom, or at least the illusion of it: "I can die or survive, as I wish. If I want, I can go home, or I can go missing in action. I live and die the way I want. I'll never be this free again."[122] War, as he understands it now, is both "a dream,"[123] one totally removed from his real life—"I have nothing to do with Chechnya, and I don't give a damn what it is, because it doesn't really exist,"[124] he thinks as he sits there freezing in the swamp—and the realest kind of real life compared with peace and life back home, where "Everyone is so petty there, so uninteresting."[125] Spending the night in the swamp waiting for a battle that never happens gives Babchenko plenty of time to philosophize and contemplate his woes, physical and spiritual.

As with the earlier stories, much of the weight of the narrative is given to the nonfighting side of the soldier's experience, since that is what is most acutely felt. While lacking in the drama of a fight scene, these scenes are painfully compelling for the simple misery that they depict: "My body kept going numb on the sharp corners. It was cold, my wet things wouldn't dry and I was shivering. And the whole time I was busting for a pee,"[126] Babchenko says about the night he spends inside a carrier in the frozen swamp. In this as in the other stories, Babchenko forcefully brings home the fact that battles are generally brief, but spending a January night in damp clothes in an unheated carrier with a full bladder can seem like an eternity.

The platoon passes the night with nothing worse than a nasty chill and, in Babchenko's case, a frozen bladder. When the attack finally comes, it surprises the soldiers, who have turned their attention from the possibility of an enemy attack to a quest for food. Luckily for them, the first attack is not from the

120 Ibid., 197.
121 Ibid., 198.
122 Ibid., 199.
123 Ibid., 200.
124 Ibid., 201.
125 Ibid., 199.
126 Ibid., 205.

Chechen side, but is conducted by the Russian forces, which are bombarding the village of Alkhan-Kala. The platoon watches the bombardment passively, and it is at moments like this, Babchenko tells the reader, "when houses whirl among tons of earth in the air, fly apart in fragments and leave behind craters the size of ponds, and the ground trembles for two miles around from the impact of the massive shells, that you are especially aware of the frailty of the human body, the softness of bones and flesh and their defenselessness against metal."[127] Having spent the night contemplating his own physical needs and weaknesses, which are brought home by the acute suffering caused by comparatively minor and short-term deprivation, Babchenko witnesses the physical destruction of a village at the hands of Russian weapons, driving home just how vulnerable everything and everyone is, and how thin the line between life and death is.

This exposure to such outsized violence is more likely to lead to extreme trauma reactions afterwards. As Herman notes:

> traumatic events generally involve threats to life or bodily integrity, or a close personal encounter with violence and death. They confront human beings with the extremities of helplessness and terror, and evoke the responses of catastrophe. According to the *Comprehensive Textbook of Psychiatry*, the common denominator of psychological trauma is a feeling of "intense fear, helplessness, loss of control, and threat of annihilation."
>
> The severity of traumatic events cannot be measured on any single dimension; simplistic efforts to quantify trauma ultimately lead to meaningless comparisons of horror. Nevertheless, certain identifiable experiences increase the likelihood of harm. These include being taken by surprise, trapped, or exposed to the point of exhaustion. The likelihood of harm is also increased when the traumatic events include physical violation or injury, exposure to extreme violence, or witnessing grotesque death.[128]

Babchenko's response to the high-caliber canons suggests that even being on the side using them can lead to trauma, perhaps exacerbating the trauma of then being under attack. Just as Eldin describes after seeing his first battle, simply witnessing buildings and other people being blown apart by high-powered

127 Ibid., 213-14.
128 Herman, *Trauma and Recovery*, 34.

weaponry primes the narrator of *One Soldier's War* for trauma, or even causes trauma in and of itself.

After witnessing the bombardment of the village, the platoon pulls out of the swamp and begins their return journey without ever actually taking part in any action. As they are on their way home, a tracer round is fired their way, interrupting Babchenko's musings on the nature of time and memory ("Damn, how long a day can be! We had spent just one day, a little over twenty-four hours, in this marsh and it seemed to last half a lifetime—so long and unbearably endless. I could hardly remember what it had been like before, back in civilian life").[129] At first they do not even realize what is happening, and think they have come under friendly fire. It's only when the second bullet passes much closer to them that they realize they are being targeted by an enemy sniper, and the long-expected and long-foreshadowed battle sequence actually begins.

At first it is more of a farce than anything: Babchenko is pinned down by his neighbor in an awkward position against the armor of the carrier, and can't take cover or even get to his rifle. Once they get themselves sorted out, they all fire like mad in the direction of the sniper, but fail to hit him, instead losing one of their own men, who falls off the carrier and is left behind (he is later recovered: it turns out that he wasn't hit at all, just brushed off the carrier by some branches). They take shelter in a barn, where Babchenko's first thought as he takes cover is "just don't land in a cow pattie."[130] They try to pin down the enemy shooters, but they cannot even see them, and fire indiscriminately into a hut with their rifles, before eventually opening fire on the village with the carriers' large-caliber cannons.

Witnessing the shelling provokes a "chilling sense of unease"[131] in Babchenko, something that isn't exactly fear but "something more animal, left over from the genetic code of our ancestors."[132] This leads him to qualify and justify the difference between what the carrier cannons are doing, and what he does:

> I had killed before, or at least tried to kill those people who shot at me, but my killing was different, on a lesser scale and under my control. The death I administered was not grotesque—just a small hole in the body and that was it. My kind of death was fair; it gave them a chance to hide from the bullet behind a

129 Babchenko, *One Soldier's War*, 218.
130 Ibid., 222.
131 Ibid., 230.
132 Ibid.

> wall, just as I had hidden from their bullets. But to hide from a large-caliber cannon was impossible. This caliber could reach you everywhere; it crushed walls and killed terribly, with a roar, tearing off heads, turning bodies inside out, blowing the flesh off a person and leaving bare bones inside their tunics.
>
> I did not feel any pity or twinges of conscience for the Chechens. We were enemies. They had to be killed to the last man, and in any way possible. And the faster and technically easier it was to do this, the better.
>
> There was just one thing . . . What if they had large-caliber cannons too?[133]

Earlier, while sitting in the swamp, Babchenko had told his friend Igor that war had given him a kind of freedom that civilian life never could. It was, he claimed, up to him whether to kill or be killed, whether to live or die. The actual battle sequence that follows puts the lie to those words: he and the other soldiers have little control over what they are doing and less understanding of what is going on. Furthermore, the destruction that their side's weapons are dealing out is not only beyond human strength, but beyond human comprehension. It shreds human flesh, leaving behind nothing but scraps, and it also shreds the human psyche, leaving behind nothing but the fearful instincts of the lizard hindbrain. In the passage quoted above, Babchenko tries to justify his own form of destruction, which is "fair," since those at whom he shoots can hide from his bullets. But as the scene immediately preceding these reflections shows, hiding from bullets is no easier than hiding from cannon shells: when the hidden sniper first begins firing, the Russian soldiers do not know where the shots are coming from, and are trapped on the carrier, unable to hide. In fact, no one in the combat zone is free and no one has a fair chance: so much of what happens to them is down to dumb luck.

This is as much true psychologically as it is physically, as the protagonists' thoughts and emotions careen wildly from point to point as their circumstances change. War is hell, war is the ultimate freedom; combat is unspeakably frightening, combat "makes you heady and arouses you; it draws a sweat of exhilaration."[134] One moment the soldiers are angry at their circumstances, the next they are terrified, and the next they are overjoyed at still being alive and can't stop talking and laughing. "Alkhan-Yurt," which, unlike the compressed

---

133 Ibid.
134 Ibid., 226.

laconicism of the earlier stories with their tight narrative arcs, is a more expansive, meandering piece, follows the vicissitudes of the soldiers' external and internal circumstances, wandering back and forth with them as they swing from black despair to on-top-of-the-world exuberance, as they alternately bless and curse the war.

The teenage Babchenko of "The Runway," "Mozdok-7," and "The Summer of 1996" spares almost no thought at all to morality of what he is doing. He is initially horrified at the sight of the dead bodies he handles, especially that of a teenage Chechen girl with part of her skull blown out, and he occasionally thinks about the fact the soldiers and pilots setting off from runway are going to kill people, but the fact that he himself could kill people barely registers. He is too consumed with his own suffering and survival to worry about the lives of distant people, some of whom are actively trying to kill him themselves. In "Special Cargo" he does experience a flash of shame at his complicity in the actions of the army—but that is over the death of a fellow Russian soldier, not that of a Chechen. The passage quoted above is the first time in the book that he as the protagonist speaks about the morality of killing human beings and his own personal actions in the war. Just as he did in "Sharik" from section one, when he argues that everything and everyone is free to do as they will, and the dog Sharik sought out the soldiers of his own free will, thus consenting to his death at their hands, here in "Alkhan-Yurt" he seeks to reassure himself that there is nothing wrong with what he is doing, that it is "clean" and "fair," thus placing the blame on those whom he kills: they could have gotten away if they had really tried, or if fate and justice had meant it to be. And whatever evils he and the other soldiers may have committed, "We have atoned for a hundred years of sin in that marsh."[135] The terrors they have suffered justify any terrors they happen to inflict on others.

That combat sequence is immediately followed by another: "Alkhan-Yurt" is one of the most action-heavy of the stories, with extended cinematic battle scenes that differ from what might be encountered in a Hollywood movie only their dryly humorous depictions of mistakes, miscommunications, and absurdities: Babchenko and a particularly incompetent officer are ordered to go retrieve a wrecked vehicle and find themselves right in the thick of a battle, which they ignore as they hook up the truck to their carrier and haul it out of the combat zone; a mortar crew almost starts shelling on fellow Russian forces. It is during the latter scene that the true bombshell of the story is dropped. Like the physical attacks, it arrives unexpectedly.

---

135 Ibid., 240.

After the aborted mortar shelling of the village that actually contains Russian, not Chechen, troops, one of the officers casually mentions that two civilians were killed during the firefight that Babchenko had participated in the day before: an old man and a little girl. As he hears the officer calmly telling the story, Babchenko realizes that he is complicit in their deaths: he had been the one to say that the shots being fired at them were coming from the village, and had pointed to what he thought was movement in the window of a hut. Because of his words, they had all opened fire on the hut, first with their rifles, and then with the cannons from the carriers. Although he did not kill the little girl and her grandfather directly, he still feels responsible, thinking:

> if I had not shouted out the Kombat would have given the order to fire on the village a minute later, and the girl and her grandfather would have managed to find shelter in the cellar.
>
> Yesterday I murdered a girl. I suddenly felt sick. And there was nothing I could do about it: there was nowhere to go and beg forgiveness. I had murdered them and it was irrevocable.
>
> Now I would be a child killer my whole life, and I'd have to live with this. Eat, drink, raise children, be happy and sad, laugh and cry, be ill, love.[136]

In direct contradiction of the bravado of his earlier words, when actually confronted with the consequences of his participation in the war, Babchenko does not believe that what he is doing is "clean" or "fair," or that by his suffering he has paid for all his sins and more besides. Instead, he is sickened by what has happened. For the first time in the book we see him grappling with the consequences of the special place of the soldier in the experience of trauma, as noted by Tal in *Worlds of Hurt:* he is not only the victim but also the victimizer, bearing the weapons of oppression as well as being targeted by them. He is convinced that his hands are literally and metaphorically dirty, and thinks of cutting them off. That night, as he keeps envisioning the girl's death, he puts the barrel of his gun in his mouth. Instead of explaining what it was that kept him from committing suicide, that section of the story finishes with the words "Another day ended."[137] Skipping right over the rest of his internal struggles, and why he chose not to kill himself, the action picks up after a break with the regiment pulling out of Alkhan-Yurt. It seems that life as usual has returned.

---

136 Ibid., 251.
137 Ibid., 253.

But it hasn't. As he rides away from Alkhan-Yurt, he says, "I had died here, or at least the person inside me had . . . And a different soldier had been born in my place, a good one—empty, devoid of thought, with a coldness inside of me and a hatred for the whole world. With no past and no future."[138] Although Babchenko and his friends survive the battle physically, psychologically he is changed forever, becoming one of the dead and the damned in truth.

In the earlier stories, from the first war, his descent into Hell is marked as largely physical and symbolic, signified by border crossings, close proximity with the dead, and visions of ghosts. In the first part of "Alkhan-Yurt," there is what appears to be another physical/symbolic descent into the Land of the Dead, when they occupy the swamp. But that is a narrative red herring, and they climb out of the swamp/underworld unscathed the next morning. It is on the climb back into the land of the living that the true descent into the underworld happens: they are fired upon unexpectedly, and in response to that, they kill two innocent civilians, one of them a child, something for which Babchenko-the-narrator feels personally responsible. This sense of personal responsibility, rather than pulling him out of his self-enclosed inner torment, as it does in "Special Cargo," encases him in it even more securely. Like almost everything else about the war as it is depicted in "Alkhan-Yurt," it triggers a contradictory reaction: he is horrified by what he is done and wants to repent, but instead becomes finally and completely dead inside. His escape from the underworld at the end of the story is only illusory, just like his belief in the freedom that war offers him: now he is trapped by a guilt he cannot escape, and by carrying it with him, he carries the world of the dead with him wherever he goes.

Not only that, but he is now eager to draw others down into the underworld with him. "The Runway," "Mozdok-7," and "The Summer of 1996" all end with suggestions of his death, either physical or psychological. "Alkhan-Yurt" does as well, but this time, he ends the passage in which he describes his own internal death (quoted above) with the words "May they all go to hell."[139] Before, during the first war, the protagonist was ushered across the border between the land of the living and the land of the dead by others, and he helped ferry already dead bodies from one part of the underworld to another, but now, after having his complicity in the deaths of others brought home to him, and feeling responsible for a death that he considers particularly unforgiveable—that of a little girl—he

---

138 Ibid., 254-55.

139 Ibid., 255, «Пошли они все к чёрту» (May they all go to the devil). The original version of the story is narrated not in the first person, but in the third person, about a character named Artyom (Arkadii Babchenko, "Alkhan-Iurt," LitMir, accessed May 3, 2022, https://www.litmir.me/br/?b=2336&p=1).

is not only dead inside, but actively acting as the ferryman into the underworld himself. Persephone has been transformed into Charon, a Charon who carries the souls of children into Hades.

Charon, though, is not a wholly negative character: sometimes he ferries people out of Hades as well as into it. In the final scene of the story, the protagonist helps to transport an unconscious boy who has been badly injured by a mine to a helicopter. The story ends without any obvious resolution: we never find out if the boy lives or dies. Quite possibly the protagonist never finds out either, but for his personal journey the important thing, although he never states it, is not so much the boy's survival but the fact that he tried to help him survive, tried to reverse the motion of souls across the Styx. "Alkhan-Yurt" ends, despite the protagonist's earlier contemplation of suicide, with just the faintest glimmer of hope: he pulls back at the last minute from sending himself into Hell, and perhaps helps someone else climb out as well.

"Alkhan-Yurt" describes a couple of days in great detail, days that were particularly momentous for the protagonist, and seems to foreshadow other momentous events: "I did not know what lay ahead: the storming operation in Grozny; the cross-shaped hospital; the mountains, Sharo-Argun; Igor's death . . . that Yakovlev would be found gutted in that awful cellar, and the hatred and madness and that damned hill."[140] Most of these events are only ever mentioned in passing, however. Yakovlev's death is not described at all in the later, longer stories, but only in "Yakovlev," from the first cycle of very short stories that opens the book, as is their time in the mountains. Igor's death is mentioned as something that has already happened in "Argun," the last story about Babchenko's active service in Chechnya, and what exactly goes down in the cross-shaped hospital and on "that damned hill" is never spelled out. Although "Alkhan-Yurt" is the longest of the stories included in *One Soldier's War*, just slightly edging out "Mozdok-7," and it forms part of the more-or-less chronological narrative of section two, it is still essentially a snapshot of a few crucial moments. The reader is left on their own to piece together, from flashbacks and casual references to previous and upcoming events, exactly what is going on and when and where the action of the story is taking place.

There are various possible reasons for this. As discussed earlier, Babchenko's stories are autobiographical, based on his own experiences and featuring a protagonist also called "Arkady Babchenko" or some similar variant thereof, and he originally wrote them as a form of therapy, with no overarching artistic plan. Writing about things such as the death of fellow Muscovite Igor, or whatever

140 Babchenko, *One Soldier's War*, 255.

unnamed but terrible events that happened in Sharo-Argun, may simply have been too painful on a personal level. The fragmented memories and vivid images that appear in nonlinear order are also a feature of traumatic memory, as Herman describes.[141]

However, it is also an artistically effective approach. Babchenko's chosen technique allows him to focus on a few telling moments in great depth, describing their sights, sounds, smells, tastes, and touch sensations, as well as what the protagonists were thinking and feeling, and the moral, political, and philosophical conclusions he draws from those moments. It is simply not possible to describe lengthy campaigns in such detail: the book would become awkwardly large, and the reader would become overwhelmed and bored. Telling the reader that such-and-such a company advanced on such-and-such a position at such-and-such a time would not serve Babchenko's purpose of conveying to the reader as viscerally as possible what it was like to *be* in that company, advancing on that position—or retreating, or hanging around doing nothing but feeling miserable. And dropping references to other important moments adds another layer of reality to the reader's experience: these sharply rendered moments do not exist in a vacuum, but are one of many such moments. The reader does not need to read about all of them to understand this, but knowing that they exist places the experiences of the soldiers in a greater context: as in Aleksandr Solzhenitsyn's *One Day in the Life of Ivan Denisovich,* we are given one day, with the understanding that this one day is every day, and that this nightmare existence is not just for a short period, but repeats over and over again for months or years. The protagonist is trapped mentally and physically by his external circumstances and by his memories of these traumatic moments.

The story of Babchenko's active service is completed by "The Storming Operation" and "Argun." "The Storming Operation," which describes the storming of Grozny, although it is not explicitly mentioned, in January 2000, as Russian forces slowly squeezed the Chechen resistance holed up in Grozny until they made their desperate breakout attempt over the last days of January and first days of February, is the most action-heavy of the stories. Considerably shorter than "Alkhan-Yurt" and "Argun," the story that comes after it chronologically and in the book, it is perhaps the most condensed and saturated expression of Babchenko's preoccupation with time, fear, and the connection between the two. Throughout this short story, he emphasizes two semi-contradictory conceptions of life in the war zone: that on the one hand it is just ordinary life under very tough conditions, as he said in "The Summer of 1996," and that on

---

141 Herman, *Trauma and Recovery*, 37-38.

the other hand, it is so abnormal, and so terrifying, that the psyche melts under the pressure and can no longer keep track of time in a linear fashion.

Like a number of the other stories, "The Storming Operation" starts with a deceptively peaceful picture, one that is shattered by the realities of war. In this case, the opening paragraph sets up the themes of time and its perception under combat that will intertwine and clash over the course of the story: "It's quiet. Day has broken but the sun still hasn't risen and the cloudless sky in the east is illuminated by pink reflections. That's bad—it'll be another bright day, perfect for snipers."[142] The protagonist, as he does in the earlier stories, is aware, perhaps even more acutely than another person might be because of his super-heightened senses, of the natural world. Unlike the younger Babchenko of "The Runway" and "The Summer of 1996," who feels the incongruity of the natural beauty and the man-made destruction around him, and who can't believe that people can be killing each other under such a beautiful sky, the older Babchenko of "The Storming Operation" now sees everything in terms of its effect on his combat readiness: rather than admiring the pink sunrise in the cloudless sky, he sees it only in terms of the cover or lack thereof it will give him from snipers.

Although the main indication that "The Storming Operation" takes place after the events of "Alkhan-Yurt" is its placement in the book, we see here that the colder, "dead inside" soldier that the protagonist became at the end of "Alkhan-Yurt" has taken over. The lyrical reflections on natural beauty that alternate with the dirty realities of daily life at the front in the earlier stories are notably absent in "The Storming Operation" and "Argun"; instead, the protagonist is entirely focused on survival and creature comforts, to the point that he and his friends routinely steal food from abandoned civilian buildings (here in "The Storming Operation") and from their own regiment's kitchen (in "Argun"). No longer an innocent, vulnerable child, the protagonist of "The Storming Operation" is the same one of "The Apartment," from the beginning of the book, who considers killing two people a good day at the office.

He is not, however, immune to fear, and the fear during the storming operation is so intense that it distorts all his perceptions. This begins before the actual operation, when he is still waiting to go into combat:

> We're a bit scared, jittery; it's as if we're suspended in weightlessness, just temporary life-forms. Everything is temporary here: the heat from the fire, breakfast, the silence, the dawn, our lives. In a couple of hours we will advance. It'll be a

---

142 Babchenko, *One Soldier's War*, 256.

> long, cold, hard slog, but still better than the uncertainty that we face now. When it starts, everything will be crystal clear, our fear will abate and yield completely to the strong nervous tension that is already starting to overtake us. My brain is lapsing into soporific apathy and the urge to sleep is strong. I just want it to start.[143]

When it does start, though, Babchenko does not experience crystalline clarity and courage, but is deafened by the Russian aerial bombardment and the Chechen antiaircraft guns. Once they get used to the noise, however, everything is back to normal: the protagonist, who is waiting to attack in the second wave, sees one soldier not currently participating in the advance "sitting on a rocking chair, smoking and looking out the window like he's watching TV."[144] The actual advance is nothing like the expectations Babchenko has from watching Soviet war films about World War II; instead, "it's all a lot simpler than that, ordinary even,"[145] with a handful of soldiers lugging their weapons and armor slowly over an embankment towards the enemy positions, "indifferent and accustomed to death."[146]

Once he does join the attack, the protagonist is also, as he had hoped beforehand, calm: between the firing, the platoon member who keeps setting off trip wires while remaining miraculously unharmed, and the fact that no one knows where they are or where any of the other platoons are, they have little mental space for fear. And once they stop for the night, their primary preoccupation is eating the food they've pilfered from the building they're occupying, and setting up a comfortable and not too dangerous watch post, something that takes up a significant portion of the story. The protagonist cannot even be bothered to make sure that the soldiers relieving him on watch are awake enough to stand guard. He and everyone else has become inured to danger and death to the point of being blasé.

A few hours of comparative peace change things, however. The next morning the protagonist is sent to find out what is going on with the 3rd platoon, which is quartered two streets away. It should be a short and relatively safe walk, but for the protagonist, it is anything but:

---

143 Ibid.
144 Ibid., 258.
145 Ibid., 259.
146 Ibid., 260.

> I have to run across the street but I can't force myself to leave the yard. After the peace of the early morning this seems far more terrifying than it did yesterday, when we were constantly showered with shrapnel. During this short peaceful morning I have managed to shed the continual readiness to die; I have relaxed and I am now loath to throw myself headfirst back into cold death.
>
> Finally, I steel myself, draw my lungs full of air, exhale sharply and run out of the open gates in sprints. The street seems to be very large, enormous, like it's thousands of miles wide, a whole continent covered in very fine smooth asphalt without a single rut that might afford protection. Slowly, like a slug, I am crawling into the sights of some sniper. That's probably what I look like through a telescopic sight—a small, helpless slug trying to escape death in the middle of a huge street.[147]

The protagonist does make it safely across the first, terrifying, street, and at the next block "I cross the second street more confidently. I've greeted death again and things have now settled into their usual rhythm."[148] On his way back from the 3rd platoon's command post, he is once again blasé about his surroundings, and it's back to business as usual: "A burst of fire echoes from the Chechen lines, then another. Our guys shoot back and a firefight ensues. Then a mortar joins the fray. The day has begun."[149]

The protagonist of "The Storming Operation" has been honed down to a deadly machine who sees everything in terms of fighting and killing. Although he is less prone to unprovoked outbursts of rage than the protagonist of "Special Cargo," he is even more deadly, something of which he is vaguely aware: at one point, while he is on guard duty and watching his surroundings through a night-vision sight, he sees the driver for the 3rd platoon, and his first thought is "in such visibility I could put a bullet in his ear."[150] Not yet quite a psychopath, he finds that thought disquieting and puts it out of his mind, but part of him has become completely detached and predatory, seeing everything and everyone around him in terms of their threat to him, and his possible (deadly) response.

---

147 Ibid., 271-72.
148 Ibid., 272.
149 Ibid.
150 Ibid., 269.

At the same time, his psyche is deeply split, more so than it was earlier in his story arc. He goes back and forth between the cool detachment of a killer, possibly demonstrating constriction, and a state of hyperarousal that causes him to experience terror on an almost cosmic scale, when time stretches a few seconds out into an eternity, and his imagination paints him as a tiny helpless creature against a vast, hostile background. The two sides of his psyche alternate control, depending on circumstances. When under direct fire, the detached, constricted side takes over. When he is in comparative safety, his imagination, in what is probably an example of intrusion, or the "indelible imprint of the traumatic moment,"[151] takes over, dredging up images and ideas from his subconscious and his reptilian hindbrain. In this life-and-death situation, the contrast between them is especially sharp, and the line between them especially thin: war has peeled away the civilized, "human" outer layer of his personality, revealing both the merciless predator, and the fearful prey, underneath. In a constant kill-or-be-killed situation, the protagonist is painfully aware that he could be either, but the knowledge is so disturbing that he cannot bring himself to face it head-on. Instead his psyche is forced to blunt the awareness by a retreat to a perception of normalcy in abnormal circumstances.

The split in the protagonist's psyche at this period is also seen in "The Apartment," from the first cycle of stories in the book. Also set, it now becomes apparent, during the storming of Grozny, when the Russian soldiers are camping out in abandoned residential apartments and looting everything they can get their hands on, something Babchenko records without judgment or justification, presenting it as a given under the circumstances, the protagonist sneaks into "his" apartment every night to engage in involved fantasies of domestic bliss. Earlier I described that first cycle of stories as a narrative of increasing violence, culminating in the protagonist's matter-of-fact acceptance of killing fellow human beings. Taken against the backdrop of the longer stories of the second half of section two, which describe the same time period and events in more detail, this early, extremely compressed cycle, in which a single moment or moments are sketched out in a few impressionistic, and yet highly detailed, paragraphs, can also be seen as the protagonist's growing psychic alienation from his surroundings and himself, peaking in his retreat into a solitary fantasy world.

The protagonist's body, and a good part of his mind as well, are trapped down in the underworld, forcing him to seek escape where he can by imagining himself back in the land of the living. The frequent references to death and

---

151 Herman, *Trauma and Recovery*, 35.

allusions to the land of the dead in the earlier stories from section two have been replaced by the protagonist's longing to live, and his intense fear of death, which, while logical under the circumstances, has grown to superhuman proportions, dwarfing the protagonist's human thoughts and actions. He is now the one at whom the large-caliber guns that he felt such instinctive fear for in "Alkhan-Yurt" are being aimed, along with the sniper rifles and knife attacks that have threatened him from the beginning. This almost mystical fear, which is neither a logical response to the real dangers that surround the protagonist, nor a short-term adrenaline response to immediate threats, appears in "The Storming Operation," but the protagonist is able to shake it off by exposing himself to more danger, which is what his body and mind now consider to be "normal." In "Argun," the next story in the cycle, the fear will become all-consuming.

"Argun" is the least action-intensive of the stories about the second war. The narrative jumps forward several months, skipping over the events at the cross-shaped hospital and Sharo-Argun, which are referred to once again but never described, other than to list the number of people lost there, people who appeared in the earlier stories but now are mentioned only as killed in action at various places the protagonist and his still-living friends are naming as they write down a list of all the places they've fought:

> [A]ll names of death. There's something shamanistic about them, strange names, strange villages. Some of my comrades died in each one and the earth is drenched in our blood. All we have left now are these odd, un-Russian words; we live within them, in the past, and these combinations of sounds that mean nothing to anyone else signify an entire lifetime to us . . . This land is steeped in our blood; they drove us to our deaths here.[152]

The most active part of the war is almost over and the protagonist's part in it is also almost over, although he cannot be sure of it yet. But for the moment his battalion is camped in a comparatively safe location, an abandoned canning/meatpacking plant, and the enforced inactivity and lack of danger—there is only one, insignificant attack on their position during the story—is making everyone antsy, driving the soldiers to lash out, attack each other, and experience mental breakdowns.

Hardened and made cynical by their previous experiences, not the least of which must have been looting Grozny, although that connection is never drawn,

152 Ibid., 278.

the protagonist and his friends are now the ones to sell weapons to the enemy in exchange for drugs and steal from the company's supplies, which they see as normal and justifiable behavior, part and parcel with the rest of the war:

> Thieving is both the foundation of the war and its reason for continuing. The soldiers sell cartridges; the drivers sell diesel; the cooks sell canned meat. Battalion commanders steal the soldiers' food by the crate—that's our canned meat on the table that they snack on now between shots of vodka. Regimental commanders truck away vehicle-loads of gear, while the generals steal the actual vehicles themselves. [. . .]
>
> And we've been sold too, guts and all, me, Arkasha, Pincha, the Kombat and these two guys he is beating now, sold and written off as battle losses. Our lives were traded long ago to pay for luxurious houses for generals that are springing up in the elite suburbs of Moscow.[153]

The Babchenko of the first war was outraged at the callous mistreatment he and his comrades experienced, and horrified at the disregard in which their lives were held by their superior officers. The Babchenko of the tail end of his tour of duty during the second war is still outraged, but his outrage has sharpened its focus and taken on political tones; instead of crying out against fate, he now sees what has happened to him and everyone else in the army as the result of a specific, dysfunctional system, in which violence, lawlessness, and self-centered grabbing for whatever you can get are fostered at the expense of everything else, including battle-readiness and the concept of not selling arms to the enemy, arms that might be used against you.

The most horrifyingly violent moment in "Argun" is not the minor firefight that breaks out when the hand grenades that the protagonist and his friends have sold to some Chechen children in exchange for marijuana are thrown back across at them, but when some other, newer soldiers are caught selling cartridges to the Chechens. This engenders outrage not because of the deed itself but because these particular soldiers have not yet earned the right to sell weapons to the enemy—"only we [the more experienced soldiers] are entitled to do that. We know death, we've heard it whistling over our heads and seen how it mangles bodies, and we have the right to bring it upon others. And these

153 Ibid., 296-97.

two haven't."[154] In punishment, the officers fashion a makeshift torture rack out of pipe, hang the two soldiers up from it by their arms, and proceed to beat them, shock them with electric current, and shoot into their body armor at close range. The rest of the battalion is marched out to witness this, but it leaves them largely unmoved, since "We have been beaten ourselves and it has long ceased to be of any interest,"[155] and "We understood long ago that any beating is better than a hole in the head. There have been too many deaths for us to care much about trivia like ruptured kidneys or a broken jaw."[156]

This casual attitude towards torture and even death, providing it is not your own, and the belief that only those who are brothers in arms deserve to be treated with consideration, is repeated towards the end of the story, when Shepel, one of their friends, is wounded by an accidental discharge and later bleeds out. Another friend, Oldie, rides with him to the hospital in Khankala and when their carrier is held up at the gate because the driver doesn't know the password, Oldie starts shooting into the air. He is arrested, but his treatment is unexpectedly humane, since Khankala is full of journalists who are on a crusade against the *zindan*[157] pits that captives were often held in.

That the *zindan* pits have drawn the journalists' attention and led to accusations of torture seems ridiculous to the protagonist, and he wishes a few journalists had been with them when they were fighting in the mountains, or when the two soldiers were being beaten and electrocuted on the rack in Argun. When Oldie announces his plans to kill the driver who accidentally shot Shepel, the others approve: in their opinion, "The value of a human life is not absolute and Shepel's life in our eyes is far more valuable than the life of some drunken driver who never had a single shot fired at him, was never pinned down by sniper fire, never used his hands to stanch flowing blood and never saved anyone's life."[158] Having grown used to dealing out death to the officially sanctioned enemy, the soldiers are now ready to deal it out to anyone they consider their enemies, with or without official sanction. Their experiences and shared suffering have made them a law unto themselves, incapable of obeying any other law, or connecting with anyone who has not undergone what they have.[159]

---

154 Ibid., 294-5.

155 Ibid., 294.

156 Ibid., 296.

157 *Zindan* pits were holes in the ground in which prisoners were forced to crouch. Politkovskaya describes them at length in *A Small Corner of Hell*.

158 Ibid., 331-32.

159 Years later, Babchenko continues to divide the world into an us/them dichotomy, and have an ambiguous relationship with the military and other institutions of forced comradeship. In a Facebook post he stated that the problem with the Russian political opposition, of

In *The Sky Wept Fire*, Eldin divides people into two groups: those who obey the code of the warrior, and those who do not. Babchenko also divides people into two groups, those who have experienced combat and those who have not. His division of "us" and "them" is based on shared physical experiences, rather than any kind of ideology or faith. This provides him and the other soldiers with strong bonds of brotherhood between each other—but cuts them off from anyone else. Because combat experience is not something that can be gained by just anyone, but only by those who happen to have the (mis)fortune to be members of the group that is expected to carry out combat operations—namely, healthy young men—and who happen to be doing their military service at a time when combat is called for, and happen to be deployed to a combat zone, and who happen to come under fire, membership in this group is largely a matter of (bad) luck. There are no honorary members, no allies, no way of joining the group except by falling prey to the same (bad) luck. As his part in the war is winding down, the protagonist is now completely unsuited to leave it. He has finally become the brutal, uncaring killing machine that was required all along and that he had such trouble becoming earlier on. His psyche is no longer split, or rather, the split has been so submerged that he is no longer aware of being psychologically torn. Instead, he is overcome with fear, which serves to cut him off from his brothers in arms, leaving him totally alone.

The fear first takes over him when his platoon is ordered to go deal with some rebels. At first he cannot understand what his happening to him: for some reason his fingers do not work properly as he attempts to mount his grenade launcher on the carrier. Then he suddenly thinks, "Today, near Mesker-Yurt, I will be killed."[160]

Instead, though, he is sent to go get more grenades and misses the column when it sets off. Watching them leave without him, "I sit uncomprehendingly, on the verge of vomiting. I haven't felt such terror in ages."[161] Despite sitting back at the base—and, he later discovers, his battalion not taking part in the

---

which he is nominally a part, is that most of them have never served in the military or done prison time, and therefore are "terribly far away from the people"—a people who are "raising cannon fodder and don't understand a damn thing about how their children are dying and getting captured [in Eastern Ukraine]" (Babchenko, Facebook post, July 1, 2017). In this post he does admit to the possibility of education taking the place of direct experience, in that people could choose to read the foreign press and learn about what is happening in the Donbass, but he is pessimistic about the chances of that, and believes that the liberal elite is incapable of understanding "the people," because they have no first-hand contact with them.

160 Babchenko, *One Soldier's War*, 321.

161 Ibid., 322.

fighting at all—he is so frightened he can't manage to light a cigarette. And the fear stays with him. He becomes more and more obsessed with the danger he believes he is in, to the point that he is unable to interact with others, distrusting the other sentries and lashing out at them with physical violence over minor offences, just like the older soldiers who abused him so badly when he was a new recruit during the first war. His only concern now is remain alive long enough to make it back home: "I stop talking to people altogether. I don't laugh or smile any more. I am afraid. The desire to go home has become an obsession. That's all I want and I can think of nothing else."[162] His premonition of death has made him aware that, although he is in the underworld, trapped in Hell, he is still alive and could potentially escape back up into the land of the living.

However, when his battalion is withdrawn and he and the others are about to be discharged, he feels an intense sense of closeness with his comrades, many of whom are no longer among the living. Now that his part in the war is over, the terror recedes, and he is able to reconnect with this comrades—except that many of them have crossed definitively over into the land of the dead, while he is being returned to the land of the living. As the battalion moves out under a rainstorm, the story ends:

> I remember all of my comrades; I remember their faces, their names. At last we have peace, boys—we waited for it for so long, didn't we? We so wanted to meet it together, to go home together and not part company until the whole platoon had been to everyone else's home. And even after that we would stay together, live as one community, always close, always there for each other.
>
> What will I do without you? You're my brothers, given to me by the war, and we shouldn't be separated. We'll always be together. We still have our whole lives ahead of us.
>
> Hey Kisel, Vovka! How's it going, Igor, Shepel?
>
> I stand up to my waist in the hatch. The runway is deserted. Warm rain falls. Large raindrops roll down my cheeks and mix with tears. I close my eyes and for the first time in the war I cry.[163]

In a story that is, even by the standards of the book, full of explicitly dirty and disgusting details, chosen for maximum shock value—the above-mentioned

162 Ibid., 324.
163 Ibid., 333.

torture on the rack, the bloody dysentery that all the soldiers get, the nasty water that they drink—this is an unexpectedly lyrical ending. In earlier stories, the protagonist had frequent flashes of awareness of the natural beauty that surrounded him in this hellish place, and contrasted them with the squalid mess that humans were making. By "Argun" that is almost entirely gone, stripped away by the war. The protagonist is largely indifferent to suffering and does not even see beauty. Occasionally—as during his rare interactions with women—he remembers something of his former self and is able to feel something other than rage and terror, but for the most part he is locked within himself, able to experience only his own instinctive fear of death, and a frequently uncontrollable rage at those who have not suffered exactly what he has.

In this last passage, though, the separation between the protagonist and the natural world, and between him and his friends, has been breached by the rain. At the same time, it is at this moment that the separation becomes actual: the protagonist is leaving the war zone, still alive, while the friends whom he lists have all died. By leaving the war zone—Hell—still alive, he cuts off his main point of communion with them. They will not in fact be "always close, always there for each other." Instead, those that have died will remain dead, and those who return will be caught halfway between the two worlds, unable to die—something the protagonist alternately desires and fears to do—but unable to live as an ordinary member of the land of the living.

The ending of "Argun" forms a full circle with "The Runway" and "Mozdok-7" on multiple levels. The protagonist has now become exactly the kind of person who so horrified his younger self when he first arrived in the Caucasus: constantly thieving, indifferent to death (at least the deaths of others), prone to outbursts of physical violence against those younger and weaker than him. This ending scene also takes place on a runway on a warm spring day. But instead of a bright blue sky and the sun shining down on the "silvery sacks" holding the bodies of dead Russian soldiers that greets him on his arrival, it is a warm rain that washes over him on his departure, melting away some of his internal barriers, so that he starts to cry—"rain"—as well. The two ends of his story are thus balanced, and show the protagonist falling out of harmony with the natural world in the beginning, and then returning to harmony with his surroundings in the final scene of the final story of his active service in Chechnya.

The two cycles of stories in section two thus form one large, overarching cycle of the protagonist's development into the very thing that he fears at the beginning, and the beginnings of his rehabilitation afterwards. The effect is created with deceptive artlessness—the stories are autobiographical, and they follow the outlines of Babchenko's actual experiences closely, so that it is, for example, a historical fact that he first arrived in the North Caucasus in the spring, and departed for the second time in the spring as well,[164] when the Northern Hemisphere is warming up and coming back to life, or that the encirclement and storming of Grozny took place in January and February, the coldest, darkest, and deadest months of the year. Rather than making the symbolic side of these facts overt, in most cases Babchenko instead focuses on their physical aspects: the soldiers are either hot or cold, either choking on dust or slogging through slush. Furthermore, the months that he spends in the North Caucasus are not depicted as passing in an even, linear fashion, but as moments that stretch out into eternity and take on universal significance, only for the narrative to skip forward or backwards by weeks or months, with the barest references to what happens in between.

Much of the book is presented as "slice of life" sketches, with little attempt to connect the dots or give the stories a coherent narrative arc—certain things happen in the stories, it is true, but the events are both heavily pruned, and seemingly chosen at random. From things the narrator says, it could be assumed that there are at least as many things he does *not* write about that would be just as interesting and just as representative of what the war was really like. The stories that make up *One Soldier's War* were not originally intended to form a book or any kind of a coherent project, but to be a method for Babchenko to "squeeze the war out of [his] system";[165] the writing process was, he says, "a form of madness."[166] And this is certainly the initial impression they give on the first read through: of intense emotions and brutal physical experiences set down almost willy-nilly on the page.

Still, once the stories and symbols are pieced together, what emerges is a mythic cycle of a young person's forced descent into Hell, and semi-successful struggle to emerge back into the Land of the Living. This is not a stereotypical heroic journey, in that there is little that is heroic about the hero's experiences or actions: he sets off only semi-voluntarily,[167] with no comprehension of what is going to happen to him, and acts largely out of fear rather than any desire to be heroic. Naive, vulnerable, and inexperienced, he is forced to fend off

---

164 Babchenko originally arrived in the North Caucasus in May of 1996, and was demobilized for the second time in April of 2000

165 Ibid., xi.

166 Ibid.

167 Babchenko did volunteer as a conscript to be sent to the Caucasus, but he notes that everyone else in his regiment was sent as well, even those who specifically requested not to be sent. His second tour of duty, as a contract soldier, was also ostensibly voluntary, but he considered it more of a sick compulsion than a rational decision made with free will.

attacks by his supposed comrades and navigate his way through these dangers largely alone. There are no scenes where he is congratulated by older soldiers on achieving some marker of maturity and heroism and then welcomed into the group; instead, he has to carve out his own group, in the process becoming the kind of predator who once preyed on him, making him one of the denizens of Hell in truth. And as with Persephone and Eurydice, others attempt to save him, and he attempts to escape, but can never return fully to the warm and sunny land of the living. The final stories in the book—"A Soldier's Dream," the last story in section two, and the short journalistic pieces that make up section three—show his attempts either to pull himself completely out of the war, or immerse himself back into it, with only limited success.

Section two is capped off by "A Soldier's Dream," a short piece that both pulls together all the preceding stories, and marks a sharp change in direction. Written while Babchenko was already working as a journalist, at the same time as the stories from section three, it starts off with the protagonist in a snowstorm in some unidentified, unrecognizable mountain in Chechnya. He is happy to have survived the night, since:

> Nighttime means loneliness. No lights around, no sounds, no movement. A huge, endless sky above you where you know a plane with lights and passengers inside will never fly. There is no one around, you are quite alone. And even if there are a hundred of you, you are still alone. All of you are alone.
>
> There is no life around either; you yourself are life and comprise your whole world. You are a little soldier in the middle of enormous Chechnya under the black southern sky, and everything is inside you.[168]

At this moment, despite all the previous claims to brotherhood with other combat veterans, the night peels away that pretense and reveals that each person is alone, just themselves and death, who stalks the soldiers at night.

But the protagonist survives the night, and as he is sitting there, enjoying the rays of the rising sun, his friend Igor appears to him and asks him to follow him to a battle that is taking place on the mountain. Now, long after it actually happened, we are given the death scene of the protagonist's close friend Igor, but distorted through the lens of nightmare:

168 Ibid., 335.

> There is a hole in his head, just above the left eyebrow, and frozen blood and snow have formed a flat crust on his face.
>
> "Let's go. You aren't home. We all stayed here, you know that, and there's no way out. Go on." He motions again with his hand.
>
> And I see myself. I am lying not far from Igor, also dead, the snow around me covered in blood, my blood, and all around me infantry are scrabbling and falling, slipping on my blood.
>
> Damn it, such a shame. I so wanted to be home and they went and killed me. And I have to go to the mountain—I can't be one of the living if I'm dead.
>
> Igor sets off in the direction of the mountain and I follow. I want him to let me go but I can't stay behind—how could I be alive while here's there, dead?[169]

The protagonist and Igor argue: Igor wants him to follow him to the mountain, but the protagonist remembers his wife and says he can't come with Igor, he can't leave Olga behind. At the end of their argument, Igor turns back into a corpse, while the protagonist says, "I return to the land of the living."[170] His connection with the land of the living is tenuous, however, as the final words of the story, echoing and also reversing the final words of the first three stories in the cycle, are "I want to die."[171]

In the beginning of his descent into Hell, the protagonist becomes aware for the first time in his young life of the presence and possibility of death, and fears it. He is repeatedly put in contact with the dead and made to shadow them: riding in the same truck as the body bags at the end of "The Runway," preparing his dog tags and wondering how many people have died already in the conflict in "Mozdok-7," and declaring "We all died in that war" in the final lines of "The Summer of 1996." But he does not, in fact, die in the war; instead he returns physically almost unharmed.[172] Mentally, however, he is trapped halfway between the two worlds, torn between his lost friends and the land of the dead that they inhabit, and the land of the living occupied by his wife and mother. This in-between state means he is truly alone: he is alienated from the land of

---

169 Ibid., 337.

170 Ibid.

171 Ibid., 338.

172 Babchenko was never seriously wounded while in the war, and remained remarkably healthy on a diet of stray dog meat, foraged berries, and unfiltered water, but says that he later, unsurprisingly, developed chronic health problems as a result of it.

the living and those who live there, even though they try to hold him there, and longs to rejoin his comrades in the land of the dead—but can't quite do it.

This trapped state of in-betweenness is suggestive both of Herman's intrusion and of what Dominick La Capra, in *Writing History, Writing Trauma* calls "traumatropism," a state in which trauma is transformed by its victims into "a limit experience or as stigmata demanding endless melancholy or grieving."[173] La Capra singles out recurring nightmares as a particularly strong kind of traumatropism, because they are experienced "not as symptoms to be worked through but as bonds or memorial practices linking them to the haunting presence of dead intimates."[174] As such, trauma victims may refuse or be unable to let go of these "bonds or memorial practices," because this would involve cutting off ties to others who have shared their experiences, as well as to their own "founding trauma as myth of origins."[175] We can see this struggle in the narrator of "A Soldier's Dream" played out in the tug-of-war between Igor and Olga, who try to drag the narrator into their own realms of death and founding trauma (Igor) or life and "working-through" (Olga).

Related to this tug-of-war, "A Soldier's Dream" brings together the literal and symbolic sides of the central cycle of stories in the book. Like the previous stories, it is saturated with concrete physical details: "Ash from my cigarette falls onto the bolt of my rifle,"[176] "At night [my boots] get wet, tighten and freeze to my puttees,"[177] "The sheet is soaking wet and I am shaking."[178] At the same time, it is, by virtue of being a dream, the most overtly symbolic of the works, as the protagonist's psyche is explicitly shown as caught between the land of the living and the land of the dead, and he is initially confused about which he is in, before flying away from the mountain of death as a disembodied spirit. His suicide wish that ends the story and the entire cycle seems to be as much about the profound loneliness that he suffers from as anything else: it is not guilt that haunts him, but the knowledge that he cannot rejoin his friends, but nor can he leave them behind. He is torn apart by his connection with these dead people, unable to form connections with the living, trapped halfway between the two states and the two worlds. The narrative arc the protagonist follows is cut off before it reaches its conclusion, leaving him dangling, his journey and his story unfinished. Incapable of separating himself from his brothers in death, he is desperate to return to the place that destroyed him.

---

173 La Capra, *Writing History, Writing Trauma*, preface to 2014 ed. (e-book version).
174 Ibid.
175 Ibid.
176 Babchenko, *One Soldier's War*, 336.
177 Ibid., 335.
178 Ibid., 337.

Section Three

And return he does, but with only partial success. Section three is made up of stories Babchenko wrote while working as a journalist in the early 2000s, when he went back once again to Chechnya, this time as one of those war correspondents whom he and his comrades found so laughably squeamish in "Argun. These pieces are, by and large, more obviously polished than some of the earlier stories, as well as more detached and less personal, with their focus on others who also served. They highlight the fragmentary, nonlinear, subjective nature of the earlier stories, referencing many of the same events but with occasional slight differences in timing or emphasis.

They also return to the same point Babchenko made repeatedly in the earlier stories, but from the other side: that the bond formed by comradeship under fire may be tight, but it is insular. As he seeks to relive his earlier experiences and connect with others who have also undergone them, Babchenko-the-journalist discovers that he cannot understand, and be understood and accepted in turn, by these others who in theory are the only people in the world who can truly grasp what he has been through.

In the earlier stories in section three, it seems to Babchenko that he can reconnect with his old, wartime life. Indeed, the opening passages of "Field Deception," the first story in the group, describe how the runway at Mozdok feels the same as it was all the other times he was there: "It seems that nothing has changed since then. And there's the same smell that was here two, three and seven years ago: diesel and dust tinged with sadness . . ."[179] Even so, the more he travels around Chechnya, the more it appears changed: buildings have been restored, towns repopulated, there are more civilians and fewer soldiers, and it appears that peace may really have come.

But appearances are deceptive. When Babchenko goes to see acquaintances from a recon battalion, they start telling him the hidden story of the still-ongoing war: that they are overwhelmed with work, running mission after mission without a break and suffering heavy casualties. Their anguish, like that of Babchenko and his comrades when they were in the same situation, isolates them from everyone, including those who should be able to understand them: as they recount their woes, they soon come to "hate everything, including me."[180] Babchenko himself, however, *is* able to overcome this barrier, so that, as he hears

179 Ibid., 341.
180 Ibid., 348.

their stories and witnesses their rage, says that "I see myself in them."[181] In the end of "Field Deception," while standing by the runway, Babchenko experiences a moment of transcendent union with all the other soldiers who stood on the same field:

> I shut my eyes and feel like an ant. There are hundreds of thousands of men like me who stood on this field. Hundreds of thousands of lives, so different and so similar, pass before my eyes. We were here, we lived and died, and the death notices flew to all corners of Russia. I am united with them; we are all one on this field. A piece of me died in every town that received these death notices. And a piece of this field remains forever in every pair of bottomless, war-charred eyes that had seen it.[182]

As in "Argun," in "Field Deception" the protagonist has a moment of connection with the natural world as he is on a runway, about to leave Chechnya, something that allows him to connect to his comrades in arms, even those who have been killed, as well. Here the literal and metaphorical deaths of the soldiers in Chechnya are once again conflated: even those who made it through the war unscathed physically were still killed inside by their contact with violence and the deaths of others.

And yet, here, for the first time, the protagonist, who is now a civilian but also still part of the war via his work as a war correspondent, is able to experience some amount of healing and union. Although he is still torn apart, scattered, and dead, he and his comrades, both the living and the dead, are united through this shared experience of this particular field, which haunts them but also provides them with a form of continuity, even immortality: the field keeps on being the same, no matter how many soldiers pass through it, and no matter what happens to them, and they all carry the field with them, even after they leave it behind forever. The field thus serves as a physical and mental focal point, and ensures the continuation of the soldiers' memories: those that died, and those that survived, are all linked by their contact with this field, which is the gateway between the land of the living and the land of the dead. By carrying it with them, the soldiers who have been on it all have access to that same gateway, and can pass through it in thought and memory even when they are far removed from it physically. This is not necessarily a happy thing, as the memories and experiences they are

181 Ibid., 349.
182 Ibid., 350.

carrying within themselves are often sad and even actively painful, but it helps cut through the barriers that the war has created inside of them, and serves as a point of connection with each other when their suffering is so great that it threatens to cut them off even from the only people who can understand them.

In the subsequent stories Babchenko makes an effort to extend that understanding to others who were touched by the war but whose experiences were different than his, some of whom he even dislikes on principle. He interviews the family and commanding officer of a soldier who was killed in combat ("Lais"), and writes about soldiers who chose to go over to the Chechens ("Traitors"), criminals who volunteered in order to escape prison sentences ("Chechen Penal Battalion"), and women who served on both sides of the conflict ("Hello Sister").

In all cases he makes an attempt, in a striking contrast from his writing about his own experiences, especially in the second war, when he is locked into his own misery, to see things from the other person's perspective. His attitude towards those who went over to the Chechens is clearly negative, but he puts himself in the mind of the deserters, recounting what he believes they must have been thinking and feeling when they made that decision, before abandoning all attempts at compassion (not something that marks Babchenko's writing especially strongly) concluding with the story of the legal wrigglings and misdealings that may make it possible for these people to escape prosecution.

He is slightly more sympathetic towards the soldiers in the penal battalions—after all, he ended up in a disciplinary battalion himself—but considers them to be an infectious cancer in the military, spreading their criminal behavior and rules of *dedovshchina* to everyone with whom they come into contact. This leads him to make an explicit critique of the military in its current form, with a pessimistic assessment of the chances of long-term improvement: "The army has been living according to prison-camp rules for a long time. A male collective in a confined space inevitably assumes a prison's model of existence."[183] At the end of "Chechen Penal Battalion," he does lay out a suggested program of reform, but concludes that "this is clearly a utopia";[184] his sympathy and trust towards others, which is extended very slightly in these stories, cannot at this point imagine a society capable of that level of reform.

Although Babchenko sees war as a primarily male activity and the army as a primarily male space, he treats this fact ambiguously: he does not believe war is a place for women, but, as seen above, he considers all-male spaces and activities

183 Ibid., 387.
184 Ibid.

to be inevitably morally corrupt and prone to horrific oppression and violence. In "Hello Sister," the women in his regiment serve as a disturbing element, but also pull the soldiers out of their self-focused misery, making them "fluff up our feathers and dig the earth with our hooves"[185] in an attempt to show off, but also acting as a civilizing, and at times literally healing, element: most of the few women there are nurses, and the other soldiers mainly come into contact with them when their injuries and illnesses are being treated.

They also act as a bridge between reality and fantasy, and the land of the living and the land of the dead. His stories of women have a dream-like quality, in contrast to the gritty reality of much of the rest of the text. His girlfriend/wife appears as a fantasy (of very ordinary, down-to-earth domestic bliss) during "The Apartment," and, in a scene highly reminiscent of Lermontov's poem "A Dream," he imagines her at her birthday party as he is in the mud of Alkhan-Yurt in "Alkhan-Yurt"; later in the same story he will think of her during his moment of psychosis after he find out about the death of the little girl, for which he feels responsible.

The only time his wife is physically present is in "A Soldier's Dream," when she is lying next to him in bed, asleep and subconsciously pulling him away from his dream-world of the dead, back into the land of the living. Like all the women who figure in the book, she has a physical, ordinary aspect—his living, breathing wife, sleeping a perfectly ordinary sleep next to him, which he makes a point not to interrupt—and also a spiritual, even supernatural, aspect: she is the one who can stand at the threshold between the worlds and pull him back from the land of the dead into which his friend Igor tries to drag him every night. "A Soldier's Dream" makes explicit the dichotomy, which underlies much of the symbolism of *One Soldier's War*, between maleness, which is associated with war and death, and femaleness, which is associated with peace and life. The protagonist's tragedy is that he is not only trapped between the two, but is torn between them, desiring them both and unable to reconcile them.

Returning to "Hello Sister," the theme of women as both physical creatures and liminal beings who not only straddle the line between the two worlds, but act as a conduit between them, is developed with increasing strength as the story progresses. Early on the piece, he describes how during the first war, he fantasizes about rescuing the female nurse—thereby depicting women as sources and subjects of fantasy—and having her cry sympathetic tears over him as she bandages him, and, in one of the most lyrical moments of a gritty, dirty book, tells of witnessing her walk with her lover across a minefield in

185 Ibid., 366.

the early-morning mist, appearing to float as they miraculously avoid all the trip wires. This (no doubt very ordinary) woman is able, in the protagonist's imagination, literally to float above all the dangers of war, passing unharmed through the field of death and carrying her male companion with her.

Later, in the second war, he and some friends, including the nurse Olga, decide to go fishing and end up in the valley where Basaev and his troops attempted to retreat from Grozny and ended up in a minefield. When Babchenko and his friends stumble into it, the valley is still full of dead bodies, including those of two Russian women who had fought as snipers on the Chechen side.[186] One of the two women was named Olga, just like the nurse (and, it should be noted, the protagonist's wife/girlfriend).

When the men see the dead women, they see them as sexual flesh and nothing more: they are "dead female bodies"[187] that are nonetheless "coquettish."[188] In contrast, the woman's contact with these "dead female bodies" takes on spiritual overtones, that affect not only the woman, but the men as well. In this literal valley of death, the living Olga, perhaps (the narrator thinks) guided by some kind of mystical intuition, goes straight over to the dead Olga, who not only bears the same name but resembles her physically as well, and stands over her, staring at her and, the narrator believes, experiencing some kind of nonverbal spiritual illumination, which the male observers witness but cannot fully partake in:

> She stood silently over her, not saying anything, just standing and looking, and at that moment her eyes acquired an incredible depth; all the secrets of the universe were mirrored in them, as if she had suddenly understood the meaning of life.
>
> I looked at these women, the living and the dead, and thought that they were very similar. Both were petite, both in camouflage, both had chestnut-colored hair, both sharing the same name. It was as if Olga were standing above herself, like in dreams when you see yourself from the outside. Then she silently turned and went back to the carrier without looking at

186 A significant number of women took up arms for the Chechen cause during the second war, primarily as snipers and suicide bombers, some voluntarily, but tragically, many not. For a detailed account of women's participation in the two wars, see Paul J. Murphy's *Allah's Angels: Chechen Women in War* (Annapolis, MD: US Naval Institute Press, 2010).

187 Babchenko, *One Soldier's War*, 373.

188 Ibid.

> anyone. We all just stood there by the dead women and watched the living one walk off, and none of us made a single sound.[189]

Like the narrator's girlfriend/wife Olga, who serves as his psychic connection back to civilian life/the world of the living while he is in the war, and who stands on the threshold of the two worlds and pulls him back into the land of the living once he returns physically from the war but is still trapped there mentally and emotionally, these two Olgas represent the dual nature of femaleness in *One Soldier's War*: women are both living and dead, real and ideal. True Persephones, they can pass between the two states and act as bridges between the two worlds in a way that the male characters cannot. A considerable portion of the mental suffering the male protagonist experiences is caused by his inability to act as that kind of bridge himself: instead, he is trapped by his physical circumstances and his mental scars, and passage between the worlds is only partial, achieved with great difficulty.

The last two stories of the book, "Operation 'Life' Continues" and "I Am a Reminder," deal explicitly with the difficulties of reintegrating back into society and civilian life, and the inability of returning veterans to bridge the gap between them and everyone else, even other veterans. The difficulties veterans face in reintegrating into civilian society have been discussed at length; for the purposes of this book, I will simply note Herman's descriptions of some of the key psychological problems for veterans: firstly, that they often feel themselves to possess a "special status as an initiate in the cult of war,"[190] and secondly, that:

> this view of the veteran as a man apart is shared by civilians, who are content to idealize or disparage his military service while avoiding detailed knowledge of what that service entailed. [. . .] Thus the fixation on the trauma—the sense of a moment frozen in time—may be perpetuated by social customs that foster the segregation of warriors from the rest of society.[191]

"Operation 'Life' Continues" begins with a direct discussion of the separation between the (male, death-dealing) veterans and (female, life-giving) civilian life:

---

189 Ibid.

190 Herman, *Trauma and Recovery*, 66.

191 Ibid., 67.

> Mothers get back a sad semblance of their sons—embittered, aggressive beasts, hardened against the whole world and believing in nothing except death. Yesterday's soldiers no longer belong to their parents. They belong to the war, and only their body returns from the war. Their soul stays there.[192]

The returning veterans are forced to live out a fake life, as they pretend to be normal, ordinary people, but feel utterly cut off from everyone around them, who cannot understand what the war was like, just as "a man can't know what it's like to give birth. They simply don't have the necessary sensory organs."[193] Writing about the war offers the promise of some sort of healing, but the result is that "you write and write and whine with helplessness and sorrow, and tears pour down your face and stick in your stubble. And you realize that you should not have returned from the war."[194] The written word, like everything else, is a weak vessel, unable to give the protagonist the healing he needs, or help him pull together the fractured shards of his life and his psyche. It cannot even really allow him to communicate his experiences to others, since they lack "the necessary sensory organs." The protagonist has been broken and can't be repaired, and neither can his relationships with others.

This is brought home in the final story of the book, "I Am a Reminder." In it Babchenko interviews a crippled veteran who now begs at a subway station near his apartment in Moscow. Babchenko goes to sit and talk with him, since "He is my brother, they all are, brothers given to me by the war. The whole of Moscow is full of such brothers; there's at least one in each subway."[195] Babchenko is able to establish a connection with this other soldier, at least on his end. But, as with the recon unit he interviews when he goes back to Chechnya as a journalist, his interviewee is so caught up in his own rage and pain that he is unable to reciprocate this understanding. The crippled veteran is furious at what has happened to him, and even more furious that no one back home spoke up against it, considering those who did not serve in the war to be:

> Pointless people. A whole world full of pointless people. A lost generation. It's not we who are the lost generation, it's them, those who didn't fight, they are. If their deaths could bring back

---

192 Babchenko, *One Soldier's War*, 388.
193 Ibid., 389.
194 Ibid., 391.
195 Ibid., 393.

> just one of those boys then I'd kill all of them without hesitating. Every single one of them is my personal enemy.[196]

This echoes the feelings of Babchenko and his friends at the end of "Argun," when they want to take revenge over the death of their friend Shepel, killed in an accidental weapons discharge. Like the nameless veteran here, they considered the value of a human life to depend on whose life it was, and the lives of those who had seen combat and served with them to be worth more than that of someone who had not been under fire. Now, though, Babchenko is seeing this from the outside; he is now one of the people who cannot understand, and his attempts at understanding and telling the truth will always only be partially successful. The super-senses the soldiers gained in the war, allowing them to sense danger and react to it instinctively, and to feel that they were tied together with inseparable bonds of brotherhood, no longer function in civilian life, and not only can they not forge connections with civilians, but they cannot forge connections with each other.

Furthermore, they are cut off from the truth as well. *One Soldier's War* is an attempt to convey the truth of the soldiers' experiences in Chechnya to those who lack the knowledge and the physical senses to understand what war is truly like. Like all the authors profiled here, Babchenko tries to engage in the cathartic "telling and retelling" that Tal defines as fundamental to the literature of trauma, as he bears witness to his own and his comrades' experiences. He is also the author who most clearly engages in the back-and-forth between reaching out to and withdrawing from others as he seeks to share his story.

As in *The Sky Wept* Fire, although to a lesser extent, *One Soldier's War* takes personal experience and generalizes it to include all those who underwent similar experiences. It is "one soldier's war," but, with its mythological underpinnings and its connection to eternity as well as specific moments in time, it is "every soldier's war" as well. Those who participated in the war received, in return for all that they gave up, the true knowledge of war and of themselves. The war stripped them of the trappings of civilization, gifting them in return with strength, speed, supersensory perception, and moments of overwhelming terror and intense euphoria. Their true natures, good or bad, were revealed to themselves, and those with any gift for self-reflection at all were forced to come face-to-face with their inner natures, the heights they were capable of achieving, and the depths to which they could sink.

---

196 Ibid., 394.

But that, it turns out, was all temporary and conditional. Once they were removed from the war, they not only had to pass as ordinary civilians, they became ordinary civilians themselves, but civilians with serious psychological problems and sometimes debilitating physical injuries as well. They are permanently cut off from each other and from the taste of truth and eternity that they bought with their pain in the war. The story, and the entire book, ends on a melancholy note, admitting defeat in its main aim of sharing the story of the war:

> "Half-truths everywhere, half-sincerity, half-friendship. I can't accept that. Here in civilian life they have only half-truths. And the small measure of truth we had in war was a big lie. So many boys died and I survived. The whole time I used to wonder what for. They were better than I was, but I survived. Surely this not pure chance. Maybe I lived so that others remember us? I am a reminder," he says with another evil-sounding laugh.
>
> I get up silently and leave him cigarettes, matches and vodka. There's nothing else I can give him apart from money. I walk away without saying anything and he doesn't even look at me. For him I am also "one of them." Which means whatever I say is a half-truth.[197]

Confronted with death, the death of her namesake and doppelganger, Olga in "Hello Sister" is reduced to silence, but she also sees, and reflects, all the secrets of the universe. Confronted with this living reminder of his own destruction, the narrator is also reduced to silence, a silence that is not pregnant with meaning, but impotent and helpless. He cannot reflect all the secrets of the universe; he cannot even reflect the simple truth of his own lived experiences. He and his brothers in arms have, through some astounding piece of good fortune, escaped from Hell, but they are now doomed to wander the earth as maimed shades, incapable even of communicating with each other, the people closest to them in the world. The trauma that initially brought them together now isolates them more than ever, and their society has fragmented under the pressure of the return to civilian life, just as their psyches did under the pressure of war.

One Soldier's War is, without question, a profoundly pessimistic book. It depicts war as a destructive, addictive force, causing people to commit hideous atrocities for no good reason, and then, instead of freeing themselves when they

---

197 Ibid., 395.

get the chance, returning to do so again and again, caught up in a codependent, self-perpetuating cycle of violence and hatred. Duty, honor, and patriotism are slogans used to bamboozle the naive into signing up for something that will not only destroy them, but cause them to destroy others in turn.

Babchenko sees possible treatments for some of these ailments—for example, moving to a professional, all-volunteer army; providing soldiers with proper equipment, provisions, and training; and cracking down on hazing—but sees little hope of these measures being taken and enforced in a meaningful fashion. He sees all-male organizations as inherently exploitative, oppressive, and violent, but does not, in general, support the integration of women into the military,[198] preferring instead to idealize his female characters as providers of comfort, cleanliness, domesticity, and spiritual insight. The one good thing that came out of the war, his sense of brotherhood with his fellow soldiers, turns out to be a flimsy half-truth, as the soldiers all go their separate ways after demobilization and are unable to reconnect in civilian life, often treating each other as one of "them" instead of "us" once they are no longer serving together.

The historical moment of the Chechen Wars is depicted as one in which these soldiers' Motherland betrayed them, sending them off to die by the thousands for no good reason, and then abandoning the ones who made it back alive to poverty and debilitating psychological distress. Babchenko depicts his generation as one that has been chewed up—sent into the meatgrinder—and spit out, cut off from the preceding, proudly patriotic, Soviet generations, and unable to join the new, consumeristic and materialistic, generation that expects good food, nice cars, pretty clothes, and trips to the theater as its right. Both perspectives are, to those who have been broken in Chechnya, a silly, or possibly sick, lie, and the people who believe in them are not just lightminded sheep, but actively dangerous to those who do know the truth: after all, these lightminded

---

198 It should be noted that the objections of Babchenko and other Russian war writers to women serving in the military is not, as it often is in the United States, couched in terms of physical fitness. Women frequently proved themselves to be highly effective fighters, especially in partisan or guerrilla forces, in the Soviet Civil War, World War II, and, on the Chechen side, in the Chechen Wars, and there are several women in the pantheon of Soviet war heroes. Their objections are based rather on the conception of maleness as associated with violence and death, and femaleness as associated with nurturing and life. From a practical point of view, it is felt that women should be protected from the psychological damage of war themselves in order to be able to heal the trauma of the men sent off to fight. Like Politkovskaya, Babchenko and other male war writers seem to be espousing a feminine "ethics of care"—providing it is practiced by women, in the service of men. Women in these works are both figures of immense power, and tied tightly to gender-specific roles.

sheep are the ones who, when the soldiers themselves are serving on the front and unable to get to a ballot box, vote.

At the same time, *One Soldier's War* exists on another plane, one that transcends its rather grubby, nasty historical moment and its pessimistic conclusions that everyone is alienated from everyone else and there is no possibility of telling the whole truth or forming a real connection. Babchenko-as-character and his comrades in arms are shown as living out mythological cycles, touched, for all their dirtiness and coarse language and preoccupation with the grossly material matters of life—food, water, excretion, and shelter—with the same divine spark that touched the creators and characters of ancient myths and legends that still exist within the human psyche today. The soldiers and former soldiers in *One Soldier's War* feel profoundly alone, but they are not: instead, they are tied to all the generations before them and all the generations to come through these shared human experiences. *One Soldier's War* has its boots firmly in the muck, but, as it shows, muddy boots cannot prevent their wearers from reaching out and touching the stars and the whole human and natural world, at least in their minds.

6

Zakhar Prilepin: The Warrior-Bard of Russian Patriotism

> People like you save yourselves by devouring Russia, and people like me—by devouring our own souls. Russia is nourished on the souls of her sons—she thrives on them. Not by the righteous ones, but by the cursed. I am her son, even if I'm cursed.
>
> —Zakhar Prilepin, *Sankya*

"The Russian person—now there's a paradox,"[1] Prilepin writes in response to a recent poll in which Stalin was voted the most significant figure in Russian history. The same could be said about Prilepin himself. Educated, articulate, and socially active, a critically acclaimed and commercially successful writer who uses his success to support the arts and carry out humanitarian missions, Prilepin seems like he should be yet another pro-Western member of the liberal intelligentsia, criticizing the Putin regime and bemoaning the current moribund state of Russian civil society. But the truth is something quite different.

Born in 1975 in the Ryazan Oblast as Evgeny Nikolaevich Prilepin, and subsequently moving to the Nizhny Novgorod Oblast, Prilepin depicts a Russia that is different from that of the Caucasian Eldin or the cosmopolitan, urban Muscovites Politkovskaya and Babchenko. His Russia is the village heartland, where even now people live in wooden huts and are known to travel by horse-drawn sleigh rather than motorized vehicle.

His works are considered to be representative of the "new realism" style in Russian prose. This "new realism" is opposed to both modern liberalism and *pochvennichestvo,* literally "soilness," "groundedness," or "earthiness," a literary

1 Zakhar Prilepin, "Russkii chelovek primirilsia sam s soboi," *Svobodnaia pressa,* July 5, 2017, http://svpressa.ru/society/article/176116/?rss=1.

movement beginning in the nineteenth century celebrating native Russian culture and related to Slavophilism. Instead, it focuses on "charisma, bravado, the red-brown nonconformism of A. Prokhanov, Iu. Mamleev, and E. Limonov; the main thing is fatigue of 'postmodernist ridicule' and the image of 'bestial Russians.'"[2]

Prilepin as a literary personality has been called "the Gorky of our time"[3] and "a phenomenon, one of the first in the literature of the new century and one of the most colorful."[4] Prilepin's works are described as marked by a "strong life instinct,"[5] full of "brutal machismo and rebellion,"[6] but also metaphysical themes.[7] His main artistic approach is "not to explain, but to give a tremendous opportunity to feel, to guess."[8] His works often contain "a narrator who possesses the gift of narrating his emotions, emotions that are positive and even in some ways not entirely masculine, [. . .] a personality that has not been encountered in Russian literature for a long time."[9] His fictional characters tend to be autobiographical (a hallmark of the "new realism"), down to the shaven scalp and stubbly cheeks that Prilepin himself often sports.

Prilepin has a degree in philology and is widely read, something that comes across in his interviews, in which he holds forth on the development of Russian literature and the meaning of the Russian state. He completed that degree, however, in between service first in the regular army in 1994, and then in the OMON, including in Chechnya in 1996 and Dagestan in 1999. His close connection to the military comes across both in his writing—*Pathologies*,[10] his first novel, is set during the First Chechen War, and his characters in other books are often marked by military service and war—and his interviews, which during 2016-2018 were often conducted in camouflage fatigues from Eastern Ukraine.

---

2 Natal'ia Tsvetova, "Zakhar Prilepin: 'Nochi net,'" *Opera Slavica* 26, no. 1 (2016): 7.

3 Irina Bulkina, "Proza 'nulevykh,'" *Znamia: Literaturno-Khudozhestvennyi i Obshchestvenno-Politicheskii Zhurnal* 9 (2010): 205.

4 Kirill Glikman, "Novyi, talantlivyi, no . . . Zakhar Prilepin," *Voprosy literatury* no. 2 (2011): 185.

5 Ewa Pankowska, "Mir umiraiushchei derevni v tvorchestve 'novykh realistov,'" *Studia Wschodniosłowiańskie* 15 (2015): 112.

6 Natal'ia Igrunova, "Zakhar Prilepin: 'Ia liubliu mir, gde "Iliada" i "Odisseia,"'" *Druzhba narodov* 3 (March 2010): 198.

7 Karen Stepanian, "Metaphysics and Physics," *Metaphysics and Physics, Russian Studies in Literature* 52, no. 1 (2016): 67-9.

8 Tsvetova, "Zakhar Prilepin," 8.

9 Halina Waszkielewicz, "*Patsanskie rasskazy* Zakhara Prilepina. Novyi avtor, novyi geroi," *Slavica Wratislaviensia* 153 (2011): 446.

10 *Патологии: Роман* in the original Russian. (*Patologii: Roman* [Moscow: Ad Marginem Press, 2009].)

In 1999 he began work as a journalist, and also began writing *Pathologies*, his debut novel. He published under multiple pseudonyms, his most well known being that of Zakhar Prilepin for his fiction, and Evgenii Lavlinskii for his journalism. *Pathologies* came out in 2005 and was short-listed for the "National Bestseller" prize; it was followed by *Sankya*[11] in 2006 and then a whole stream of later works. Although he has not garnered as much attention in the West as similarly popular Russian authors such as Pelevin, Sorokin, and Ulitskaya, he has received considerable critical acclaim and scholarly attention by Russian scholars, and by the 2010s he was one of the most-read authors in contemporary Russian literature. His novel *The Monastery*[12] was declared the most-read book in Moscow libraries in 2015,[13] while Prilepin himself was the author most mentioned on Russian social media in 2016.[14] Along with his prose writing activities, he is also active in the spheres of acting (he starred in the movie *Gailer*[15] in 2017, and the award-winning short film *Phone Duty*[16] in 2018), rap music, and television, hosting several talk shows.

He is also a political activist, although his political activities have undergone a sharp change. For a number of years a member of the National Bolshevik party and its successor Another Russia, he was an outspoken critic of the Putin regime. The foreword for the English edition of *Sankya,* about a nationalist opposition group, was written by opposition leader Alexei Navalny, who states that "Prilepin has not merely turned inside out the consciousness of the entire post-Perestroika generation of politicized young Russians and laid it bare, but he also, in large part, predicted the patterns of development of radical political groups and the government's strategy in combatting them,"[17] and "If you want to feel the real raw nerve of modern Russian life, what you need isn't *Anna Karenina*—what you need is *Sankya.*"[18]

---

11 *Санькя* in the original Russian. (*Sankya*, trans. Mariya Gusev and Jeff Parker, with Alina Ryabovolova [Ann Arbor, MI: Dzanc Books, 2014].)

12 *Обитель* in the original Russian. (*Obitel'* [Moscow: AST, 2014].)

13 "Samoi populiarnoi knigoi v bibliotekakh Mosvky stal roman Prilepina," *Gazeta.ru*, December 16, 2015, https://www.gazeta.ru/culture/news/2015/12/16/n_8020739.shtml.

14 Svetlana Bobrova, "Dar'ia Dontsova nazvana pisatelem goda," *Life.ru*, December 26, 2016, https://life.ru/t/%D0%BA%D1%83%D0%BB%D1%8C%D1%82%D1%83%D1%80%D0%B0/952414/daria_dontsova_nazvana_pisatieliem_ghoda.

15 *Гайлер* in the original Russian. (*Gailer*, directed by Pyotr Dikarev and Mikhail Men'shikh [Russia: OOO "Prodiuserskii tsentr '1 fevralia,'" 2017].)

16 *Дежурство* in the original Russian. (*Dezhurstvo*, directed by Lenar Kamalov [Russia: n.p., 2018].)

17 Quoted in Zakhar Prilepin, *Sankya*, trans. Mariya Gusev and Jeff Parker, with Alina Ryabovolova (Ann Arbor, MI: Dzanc Books, 2014), v.

18 Ibid., vi.

The events in the Donbass region changed all that. Following the separatist uprising there, Prilepin turned away from criticizing the Putin regime and began collecting and transporting humanitarian aid to the region, eventually joining the armed resistance movement and becoming a major in the army of the DNR (Donetsk People's Republic). In 2018 he was also expelled from Another Russia for his membership in the pro-Putin All-Russia People's Front.[19]

Although from the outside this may seem like a sharp, one might even say hypocritical, about-face, Prilepin himself does not see it that way. In response to my question of whether he was a "writer of position" or a "writer of development," he explained that, "as an author I don't have any kind of position. The truth, and nothing but the truth. A position is harmful. A writer has no opinion. But they do have a Motherland."[20]

In the same interview he also disavowed nationalism, instead praising Russia's heritage as a multiethnic empire, something echoed in some of his Twitter posts from the same time. What exactly he meant by that is open to interpretation, especially in light of his most recent political activities. Although a person of conviction, Prilepin's convictions have changed over time, or, it might be more accurate to say, his commitment to Russian patriotism has changed its outer forms in response to external circumstances. Indeed, in the article "Donbass as the Nightmare of the Bourgeois," he declared that "We [Russian patriots] were always in the position we now occupy,"[21] and explicitly stated that it was not his convictions that had changed, but the current regime's commitment to Russia's territorial integrity.

Thus, while he was still attending literary events in Moscow and conducting the TV show *Tea with Zakhar*,[22] in which he, dressed in an elegant, old-fashioned suit and drinking from a delicate tea service, interviewed cultural scholars about the history and future of Russia and Russian culture, he began spending a significant portion of his time in the Donbass.

From there, dressed in combat fatigues, in 2017 he cohosted the pro-DNR talk show *Donetsk Format*[23] with Aleksandr Kazakov, and posted cheerful pictures of smiling DNR volunteers on his Twitter feed. Judging by an opinion piece

---

19 Общероссийский народный фронт in Russian. For details of the expulsion see "Eduard Limonov iskliuchil Zakhara Prilepina iz partii 'Drugaia Rossiia,'" *Radio Svoboda*, December 29, 2018. https://www.svoboda.org/a/29682822.html.

20 Prilepin, email interview, July 20, 2017.

21 Zakhar Prilepin, "Donbass kak strashnyi son burzhua," APN.com, accessed September 12, 2017, http://apn-nn.com/145136-donbass-kak-strashnyj-son-burzhua.html. This website has been shut down.

22 *Чай с Захаром* in the original Russian. A play on the phrase "Tea with sugar."

23 *Донецкий формат* in the original Russian.

posted in *Svobodnaia pressa,* a news site of which Prilepin is the chief editor, and Navalny's own remarks during his debate with Igor Strelkov,[24] Prilepin fell out with Alexei Navalny over the issue of the Donbass;[25] as of 2020 the feud was still going strong, with Prilepin devoting an episode of his talk show *Russian Lessons*[26] to suggesting that Navalny's August 2020 poisoning by Novichok was a Western plot, and that Navalny and his supporters are shallow, infantile conspiracy theorists.[27]

The events in the Donbass caused him to largely turn his back on the Russian opposition, focusing instead on the struggle in Eastern Ukraine, in which he took active part during most of 2017 and 2018. In 2019 he announced the formation of a new political party, For Truth,[28] which was officially brought into being in early 2020, before merging with the parties A Just Russia and Patriots of Russia in February 2021.[29] In a speech from winter 2020 outlining For Truth's positions, Prilepin calls for Russian politics to "move to the left economically and to the right socially," declares that the current Russian opposition needs to separate itself from the West and the pro-Western liberal elite, makes what to many outside observers would seem like alarming calls for "diplomatic, cultural, political, linguistic, and in extreme cases—military" expansion, and suggests that if Russia had had a proper militia in 2014, the conflict in the Donbass would have turned out very differently.[30] So although he no longer appears to be spending most of his time in the war zone in Eastern Ukraine, he continues to support the cause, quite literally putting his money and his body where his mouth is.

How active a part he took and is taking in the conflict is a topic of some interest, and one that he refuses to discuss directly; in an interview with Dozhd TV, for example, his response to the direct question "Have you killed people in this war?" was to look away and mutter hoarsely, "Next question, please."[31] This,

---

24 Навальный LIVE, "Debaty Live. Navalny vs. Strelkov," YouTube video, 1:22:16, July 20, 2017, https://www.youtube.com/watch?v=cjbQdbJUibc.

25 Zakhar Prilepin, "Artist Alyosha, aktyor Oleksii," *Svobodnaia pressa,* July 4, 2017, http://svpressa.ru/war21/article/176184/.

26 *Уроки русского* in the original Russian.

27 Zakhar Prilepin, "Naval'nyi ili bunt sytykh detei," *Uroki russkogo,* no. 117, October 28, 2020, https://youtube/9sXnI9XoYq0—this video has been taken down.

28 За правду in the original Russian.

29 "'Spravedlivaia Rossiia ofitsial'no ob"edinilas' s dvumia partiiami," *Interfaks,* February 22, 2021, https://www.interfax.ru/russia/752106.

30 Zakhar Prilepin, "My—luchshe, chem vlast'," *Komsomol'skaia Pravda,* February 1, 2020, https://www.kp.ru/daily/27086.5/4158233/.

31 Zakhar Prilepin, "Zakhar Prilepin: 'Liudi prosto ottachivaiut umenie ubivat'', eto vkhodit i v zadanie nashego batal'ona," interview, *Telekanal Dozhd',* July 12, 2017, video 3:30,

unsurprisingly, led to an explosion on social media and a furious rebuttal from Prilepin himself of both the claims that he has never killed anyone, and that he is a "serial killer."[32] The reader may make of that what they will. What is certain is that during the period of 2016-18 he spent a considerable amount of time in the Donbass and was the second-in-command of a battalion, for which he provided financial support.

Unsurprisingly, this move drew both rapturous applause and harsh criticism, and led to the banning of various works associated with him—for example, the 2013 Aleksey Uchitel film *Break Loose*,[33] based on a short story by Prilepin, and in which Prilepin himself appears in a minor role, was banned in Ukraine. Busy with his new military responsibilities, Prilepin declared that he had taken a break from writing, although he did still occasionally find time to read and interact with other writers, expressing, for example, his admiration for the Chechen/Russian writer German Sadulaev, who also wrote about the Chechen Wars.[34]

Prilepin's ready courting of controversy and his outspoken anti-Western, anti-liberalism stance may explain why a surprisingly small amount of his work is available in English translation. *Pathologies*, unfortunately, has yet to be translated. Those wishing to read his work in English can choose between *Sin*, a cycle of short stories and poems that form a semi-coherent narrative culminating in a tragic battle in Chechnya; *Sankya*, about a member of a violent political opposition group; and *The Monastery*, a historical novel about the Solovki prison camp, which was only released in English in July 2020. For those wishing to teach Prilepin in English translation, *Sin* is the most flexible work, since individual stories and poems can be assigned. *Sin* is what I myself have assigned to my own classes, and I have found it a useful introduction to Prilepin's work. *Sankya* is a deeply insightful look into the mindset and milieu of the modern Russian "red-brown" opposition, who disavow both the current regime and Western liberalism. *The Monastery* is an epic historical novel that may be Prilepin's best work to date, but will require a major commitment of reading and classroom time, as the English edition weighs in at a solid 998 pages,

---

https://tvrain.ru/teleshow/interview/zahar_prilepin_v_donetske_i_krymu_proizoshla_antiburzhuaznaja_revoljutsija_i_eto_spaslo_rossiju-439279/.

32 Zakhar Prilepin, "Krovososy," *RenTV*, July 18, 2017, http://ren.tv/blog/211112.

33 Original title *Восьмёрка. Vos'myorka*, directed by Aleksey Uchitel (Russia: Kinokompaniia "Rok," 2013).

34 Комсомольская Правда, "Zakhar Prilepin: My ne khotim byt' terpil'nymi voiskami" (interview), YouTube video, 45:01, July 12, 2017, https://www.youtube.com/watch?v=HW--GRDspkI.

and the story requires extensive background knowledge of the early Soviet prison camp system.

Prilepin and his works also have a considerable screen presence, which can be incorporated into the classroom in a variety of ways. The movie *Break Loose* mentioned above, based on Prilepin's short story *Восьмёрка* (literally *Number Eight*, referring to the make of car driven by the main characters) and directed by Aleksey Uchitel, is a brilliantly done, if disturbing, look at the life of members of a provincial OMON unit in 1999. As of the time of writing, it is available with English subtitles exclusively on Amazon Prime. For Western students, *Break Loose* can be a rewarding, if challenging, glimpse into the culture of the Russian military and police forces, and of the transition from the Yeltsin era to the Putin era. *Phone Duty*, an eight-minute film directed by Lenar Kamalov about a member of the DNR militia who answers the calls coming into the mobile phones of Ukrainian soldiers killed in action, is a much shorter and more readily available piece that encapsulates both the contradictions inherent in Prilepin's work, and the contradictions in the war in the Donbass in general. While the Russian in it is fairly difficult to follow, making it challenging for all but the most advanced students, it is subtitled in English and could be used for an English-language class on a variety of contemporary topics.

Prilepin's YouTube channel, which as of the time of writing had 173,000 subscribers, contains an extensive collection of videos, including the series *Tea with Zakhar*, *Russian Lessons*, and *Donetsk Format*, as well as *Phone Duty*. Watching these videos, along with the numerous interviews Prilepin has given over the years,[35] can give Russian speakers the opportunity to understand Prilepin on a personal and political level as well as an artistic one. As Prilepin tends to speak quickly, with a slight mumble, videos of him are best suited for very advanced language students, but those willing to make the effort may find much that is enlightening about Prilepin himself as well as contemporary Russian society and politics. Like everything to do with Prilepin, his on-screen self-representation is complex and seemingly full of contradictions—contradictions that resolve only by taking the wide view of Prilepin's career, which shows someone deeply committed to Russian patriotism, even as his outer expression of that changes, Proteus-like, with the changing political winds.

And while he is the least friendly of the authors profiled here to Westerners and Western ideologies, he may be the most important for Westerners to study,

---

35 For a rare interview with Prilepin with English-language subtitles, see the 2013 documentary *Russia's Open Book: Writing in the Age of Putin* (hosted by Stephen Fry), YouTube video, 55:04, https://www.youtube.com/watch?v=vRPDM7OTMrI.

as a necessary counterweight to the strong pro-liberalism, pro-West tendency in most works that are translated into English and most scholars and activists who are given voice on English-language media. In fact, his strong sense of patriotism and nationalism is something he shares with other major opposition figures; even Alexei Navalny, who is often depicted in the West as the pro-Western savior of Russia, has expressed numerous nationalist beliefs. In the current climate in Russia, it seems that any political movement must have a strong nationalist strain to have any chance of success. Prilepin's deep patriotism and nationalism is, I believe, sincere. It also represents the *zeitgeist* of the moment in Russia. Prilepin, whether intentionally or not, has become the bearer and figurehead of a very significant trend in Russian culture.

In all his political and cultural activities, Prilepin represents himself as a serious and well-intentioned actor, and in fact he has, by all accounts, arranged for and in some cases personally transported considerable humanitarian aid to the Donbass, which he gathered via his website. In *Donetsk Format* he was, despite uttering phrases and opinions that many Western liberal intellectuals and pro-Ukrainian thinkers will find hard to swallow, thoughtful, articulate, and well informed. He challenges stereotypes about Russian nationalists, especially members of the forces of the DNR, who are easy to dismiss as uneducated skinheads, a label that Prilepin and his comrades both court and defy with their scruffy, shaven-headed appearance.

At the same time that he carries some of the signs of a member of the intelligentsia, he also presents himself as a man of the people and a son of the countryside. In a similar vein, his literary works are infused with an earthy sensuality that is entirely at odds with the works of the other authors surveyed here. He also possesses a stinging sense of humor, more than any of the other authors here (although Babchenko is also not lacking in a certain dry, sardonic wit) which bursts out in his literary and journalistic writings, sometimes in a deliberately provocative and overtly sexual fashion. The overall impression Prilepin produces, both as a political actor and an author, is as someone who is both self-aware and sincere, someone who is self-promoting and self-sacrificing, someone who is and is not what he appears to be.

His (heavily autobiographical) characters are also a strange, and strangely attractive and repugnant, mix of idealism, tenderness, and physical violence that frequently explodes out of control. His first character, Egor Tashevsky, the protagonist of *Pathologies,* is particularly violent, and particularly unthinking: not that he has no feelings, but he acts out of instinct, something that the war unleashes in full measure.

Pathologies

Pathologies, Prilepin's debut novel, has in general received less critical attention in the West than his later works and has not, unfortunately, been translated yet into English. Although *Pathologies* is less accessible to Western readers than *Sin, Sankya,* and *The Monastery,* I am concentrating on it here as the most direct example of Prilepin's war writing. Both formally and linguistically, it is a challenging read, with a nonlinear structure and extensive use of military jargon and slang. Advanced students of Russian may wish to try it out as a "stretch" assignment, and graduate students and scholars of contemporary Russian literature will find it of considerable interest as a premier example of the current trends in Russian fiction and especially Russian war writing.

Of the authors of Chechen War prose, Prilepin is generally accepted as the most "literary." Valeriia Pustovaia and Andrei Rudalyov both agree that *Pathologies* is clearly a literary work, not just a piece of journalism or journaling, as other war writers are accused of producing. On the other hand, Aleksandr Bushkovskii, who served in a SOBR[36] unit, considers the book to be full of inaccuracies about the military side of things.[37]

It certainly true that the special forces unit in which the protagonist, Egor Tashevsky, serves is not a shining example of professionalism and honor, and Tashevsky himself is hardly an exemplary soldier, consumed as he is with his own problems, including his terror of the war. In fact, he is often fearful and lazy, and is happy to sneak off whenever he can and leave his men—he is a squad leader, much to his horror—to do the heavy lifting whenever he can. He is the exemplar par excellence, not of the war hero, but of the hero of the new war prose as Pustovaia sees it, who "is frequently not a war hero at all. The protagonist is weak, cowardly, indecisive."[38] Rather than believing unequivocally in his mission and the righteousness of his cause, Tashevsky, like the protagonists of the new war prose in general, is full of doubts, fears, and random thoughts. *Pathologies* is fictional, but it is similar to the nonfictional works included here in its slice-of-life grittiness and its focus on the experiences of ordinary people.

---

36 SOBR: Специальный Отряд Быстрого Реагирования, or Special Rapid Response Team, was a special forces unit under the command of the MVD, similar to OMON, and, like OMON, was supposedly merged into the new National Guard of the Russian Federation.

37 Aleksandr Bushkovskii, "Izuchaia *Patologii*: Nelepitsy i strannosti v rasskazakh o voine," *Voprosy literatury*, no. 2 (2011): 195-209.

38 Pustovaia, "Guy with a Gun," 65.

Tashevsky's anti-heroic qualities in some ways bring him in line with a significant trend in contemporary war literature in both Russia and the West: that of the veteran-victim, one who has suffered trauma and lacks, or has lost, typical macho manliness. According to Caleb Cage, in his recent book on war narratives, "America's understanding of veterans in recent times can be reduced to two basic narratives: the hero narrative and the victim narrative."[39] Meanwhile, Maya Eichler writes in her study of gender roles and Chechen War veterans:

> Russian soldiers fighting in the Chechen Wars have been portrayed as questionable warriors and as men who upon their return do not sufficiently conform to hegemonic notions of masculinity. Multiple representations of the men who fought in Chechnya emerged as a result of soldiers' experiences and actions, societal perceptions, and state policy. The ideal of the heroic warrior was contested by four representations of the Russian serviceman: unwilling warrior, excessive warrior, fragile warrior, and unrecognized warrior.[40] (109)

As will be seen in the analysis of *Pathologies*, Tashevsky fits in with all those categories outlined by Eichler. However, he also rebels against the categories imposed on him by others. As Cage points out in his discussion of the simple hero/victim dichotomy applied to veterans, "These narratives accommodate various social and political needs: they serve as shorthand, they affirm political preconceptions, but they often fail to match the same when described by those who experienced them."[41] Prilepin, through his protagonist Tashevsky, subverts both the hero and the victim narratives surrounding modern veterans, whether Russian or Western, of the global War on Terror, and insists on speaking his own truth and denying the right of others to judge him or impose their narratives on him.

By writing fiction rather than memoir or autobiography, Prilepin is able to explore and express the truths he wishes to tell about war in a more symbolic, and perhaps more accessible, fashion than nonfiction authors. This is also an emerging trend in contemporary Western war literature, especially about the wars in Iraq and Afghanistan. As Cage notes, "Fiction does not only allow

---

39 Caleb Cage, *War Narratives: Shaping Beliefs, Blurring Truths in the Middle East* (College Station, TX: Texas A&M University Press, e-book, 2019), chapter 6.

40 Eichler, *Militarizing Men*, 105.

41 Cage, *War Narratives*, chapter 6.

readers and writers to go beyond the basic narratives of the current politics, and it not only allows more people access to the important conversations that need to be had. Fiction also allows them to access and explore truths in different ways."[42] Cage discusses how American author Phil Klay uses fiction to "access the intricacies of life-altering events, not just for himself as a writer, but for his audience as well."[43] Prilepin takes similar advantage of the flexibility and power of fiction to tell his own story and make his own points about the Chechen War experience.

Although fiction can make an experience more accessible to its reader, *Pathologies* is not designed to be easy reading. Structurally, it is complex and a challenging read. When asked about his construction of the novel, Prilepin explained, "I was acting intuitively. Three mini-chapters within each chapter—the first and third military, with a civilian one in the middle. It seemed to me that there was a certain rhythm to that, a certain melody." [44] Thus, while the initial impression it gives is of a work that is fragmented and in places hard to follow, it does in fact have an overall narrative and symbolic arc that both come together in the ending.

The action in *Pathologies* takes place on three temporal planes—four if you count the afterword. This afterword depicts a day some unnamed amount of time after the events of the central story of the novel, but is the opening chapter.

In it, the main character, who has not yet introduced himself to the reader, is out on the town of Holy Savior[45] with his three-year-old adopted son. Why he has an adopted son, or even what the son's name is, is not explained. Instead, we are plunged into the protagonist's fears for his son.

The novel opens with the line "Driving across the bridge, I am often tormented by the same vision."[46] What that vision is, though, is not explained for several more paragraphs, as the protagonist describes eating ice cream with his son and watching the movement of the river. The boy asks, "When will it [the water] run out?"[47] causing the protagonist to think, and then to utter out loud, "When it runs out, we'll die."[48] This does not upset the boy, who wants to wait for the water to run out instead of going home. The protagonist convinces him to get

42 Ibid., chapter 8.
43 Ibid.
44 Prilepin, email interview, July 20, 2017.
45 Святой Спас in the original Russian.
46 Zakhar Prilepin, *Patologii: Roman* (Moscow: Ad Marginem Press, 2009), 5. All translations of *Pathologies* my own.
47 Ibid., 5.
48 Ibid.

on their route taxi[49] instead, but then is visited by his recurring vision of the bus going off the bridge and plunging into the water.

This vision takes up the majority of the afterword, as the protagonist describes how he is sitting next to the driver, where he always sits when he is with the boy, how he manages to protect the boy's body with his own as the bus rears up and then plunges off the bridge, somersaulting into the river and filling with water, how he strips himself of his clothes and swims, holding the boy by the scruff of his neck in his teeth, to the surface.

As he claws his way to the surface, he is (re)born: "I moved in complete darkness, and around me was no longer liquid, but flesh—bloody, warm, bleeding, so comfortable, squeezing my head, breaking the bones of my skull, deforming my incompletely developed, slippery head . . . I could hear the unending scream of a woman giving birth."[50] He is dragged down under the water several times, until he and the boy are finally rescued. The child is taken by a woman in a white lab coat, and "Sobbing, I watched the woman. Once again she gave the child life. After several minutes water gushed out of his nose and mouth."[51] What happens after that is never explained, nor is the relationship between the protagonist and his adoptive son, or between him and the woman in the white lab coat: is she the child's mother? The doctor who attended his delivery? Or is she Everywoman, the feminine force that, for Prilepin, drowns and gives life in equal measure?

The afterword and its story of a vision that is more real and more developed than the "actual" events of the chapter, serve to set up, not the action of the novel, but the symbolism that will guide it. Egor (still not named at that point) will undergo a similar catastrophic near-drowning and rebirth. Like the two memoirs covered here, *Pathologies* is a story of transformation caused by war, but it is a very different kind of transformation. Egor does not change as Eldin and Babchenko do, turned from naive youth to hardened soldier by the brutalities of war. Instead he plunges into himself, pulling together the threads of his memories in an attempt to understand himself—although he does not qualify his actions as such—into a story that explains how he has come to be who he is. The opening afterword suggests, not forward process, but a cycle of death and rebirth, as both Egor and his unnamed son are dragged out of the deadly but lifegiving feminine water and brought back to life, expelling water as they return to the world of the living.

---

49 Маршрутка in the original Russian.
50 Ibid., 12.
51 Ibid., 14.

In keeping with the structural plan of pulling together separate strands into a single whole, *Pathologies* is in some ways the most fragmented and confusing of the works discussed here, even though the individual scenes have a strong narrative impetus, more so than the other, nonfiction, works. The main action takes place in Grozny, but indications of when, exactly, are unclear. The most likely period would be the 1996 Battle of Grozny, when Chechen forces infiltrated Grozny and drove out the Russian forces, which is what happens in the final battle scene. The characters repeatedly refer to GUOSh,[52] the MVD headquarters in Grozny in 1995-6, which strengthens the supposition that this is during the first war.

However, the 1996 Battle of Grozny took place in August, and the final battle in *Pathologies* seems to take place in September, since, upon returning from an earlier operation, Egor mentions baring his "forehead to the September Chechen wind."[53] Furthermore, during the climactic battle one of the characters says, "we've got some Chechens wasted in the crapper,"[54] which sounds like an allusion to Putin's infamous phrase, uttered in 1999, that "we'll waste them in the crapper." Is the character deliberately quoting Putin, or is Prilepin having fun with the reader? Either way, there are few specific markers of time or place. Grozny is named, but the streets and neighborhoods the protagonists travel through are not, and it is unclear exactly how long the protagonists spend there: although the Grozny plotline is more or less linear, it is not defined by specific dates other than the occasional mention of September. According to Prilepin, the novel is based on "general impressions," with no reference to specific events,[55] and indeed, Egor's war story is an Everywar story. The intent is to evoke emotions, not to recount historical details.

The main, Grozny plotline is intersected by two other plotlines: Egor's memories of his recent relationship with his girlfriend Dasha, and his memories of his childhood and how he lost his parents and his dog, Daisy. These two storylines, unlike the "Grozny" plot, are presented in nonchronological order. Their fragmented, nonlinear form, and their tendency to force themselves upon Egor in moments of stress in what appears to be intrusion, suggest that they are the true traumatic memories that he is trying to process. Sometimes they depict specific events and hint at events that have already happened but will only be revealed later in the novel, as in the first "childhood" scene when Egor says of his

52 ГУОШ in the original Russian.
53 Prilepin, *Patologii*, 193.
54 Ibid., 252.
55 Prilepin, email interview, July 20, 2017.

dog Daisy that "She climbed down from the bed and crawled under it—she was already mad at me,"[56] but does not explain why Daisy was mad at him till a later chapter. Sometimes they depict habitual actions, as in the first "Dasha" scene, when Egor recounts his typical, idyllic, mornings with Dasha:

> Mornings Dasha slept restlessly, like a nursing infant before being fed. She'd make a few random movements, turning over funnily, hitting my face with her hair, leaving the light sensation on my skin of being touched by the wing of a passing swallow, and then she'd settle down for a few minutes.
>
> Trolleybuses went down the street with the sound of water being poured on hot iron, even though the night before it had seemed that they had died off forever, like dinosaurs.[57]

Egor lives, as this passage suggests, in a world that is both physical and sensual, and highly symbolic. He is always acutely aware of physical sensations, as well as sights, sounds, and smells, and he perceives them "as they are" but also as representative of an imaginative, symbolic world, with porous borders between the two, just as there are porous, undefined borders between the three storylines: in one paragraph Egor might be reminiscing about his childhood or lying at Dasha's side in bed, and in the next riding through Grozny.

The "Grozny" plotline begins with Egor arriving in Chechnya in the opening scene of the first chapter—or rather, at Mozdok, on the other side of the border, which comes as a surprise to the soldiers on the plane: "Mags in, someone crossed himself. We disembarked—turned out we were in Mozdok, still far away from the war."[58]

This confusion over where they actually are is not the temporary result of flying into a war zone, but a permanent state of Egor's being. Acutely aware of the sensations of his skin and the symbolic or archetypal ideas behind his feelings and sensations, he is often confused about basic things such as where he is or what is actually happening around him. Existing in what appears to be a permanent state of hyperarousal that precedes his arrival in the war zone, he lives in a world in which dreams and memories are at least as real as current events, his thoughts and fantasies only occasionally punctured by the horrifying realization of where he is and what is really happening around him.

---

56 Prilepin, *Patologii*, 42.
57 Ibid., 17.
58 Ibid., 16.

Connected as he is with his own internal world and the larger archetypal/ symbolic world, Egor tries to connect with the outer world as well, believing he can "read" it and use it to predict the future. When he arrives first in Mozdok, and then in Grozny, he expects to come under fire immediately, and, in one of the many examples of hyperarousal in the text, is constantly searching for omens that he will or will not be killed. As he is riding through Grozny from the airport, he thinks "Every second it seems like they're about to start shooting. From everywhere, from every window, from the roofs, from the bushes, from the ditches, from the children's playsets . . . And they'll kill all of us. They'll kill me. [. . .] I sense that the guys next to me share my premonitions."[59]

Trying to counter these premonitions, he tells himself that the smile of an OMON officer leaving Grozny means "they're not killing people on every street corner."[60] When a little boy waves his fist and shouts at them, Egor tries to catch his gaze, since "it seemed to me that he knew what would happen to us, to me."[61] Later, once the soldiers have settled into the abandoned school that is serving as their barracks, he watches Anvar Amaliev, the platoon clerk, write down the names of everyone in the platoon, and tries to guess who from the list will be killed. He decides it will be every third soldier, and counts down the list, until he comes to his name. "'I'm the third,' I conclude to myself with the tone a doctor would use to tell me I have brain cancer."[62] Living in a highly symbolic world, one in which he is closely connected both to its physical, material side and its abstract, supernatural side, Egor is convinced that he can foretell the future, if he can just figure out which of all the myriad objects, actions, and sensations assaulting him are the significant ones.

As in the afterword, he engages in lengthy and detailed doomsday fantasies about terrible things that could happen to him, starting right from the beginning of his tour of Grozny. Unlike the protagonists in *The Sky Wept Fire* and *One Soldier's War*, Egor is not naive to the dangers facing him at the beginning of his war experience, and he is not blasé about them at the end. In some ways, despite being a macho special forces soldier, Egor is an example of Eichler's "unwilling warrior," who doesn't want to be part of this or any war. Right from the start he knows he can be killed, and that being killed would be an irreversible tragedy. As he sets off on his first sweep (the infamous *zachistki* of which Politkovskaya wrote so critically), he thinks: "It's really scary. I really want to live. I really like

59 Ibid., 22.
60 Ibid., 21.
61 Ibid., 23.
62 Ibid., 79.

living. Living is so great. Dasha . . ."[63] As they jog down the streets in their heavy gear, he finds himself imagining how:

> Any minute something's going to go bang, and right at my head. Even if it doesn't go through my helmet, it will break my neck, and that'll be it . . . And why, after all, should it hit you? Or will it hit my chest? An SVD[64] can go right through body armor, it can go right through your body. The bullet will come out somewhere under your shoulder blade, it won't be able to go through the second half of the body armor, so it'll ricochet back, make a nasty zigzag in your internal organs and end up, for example, in your spleen. And that'll be it, curtains.[65]

Always on the lookout for omens, and frequently fantasizing about what terrible things might come to pass, Egor is, however, often blind to the actual warning signs of disaster that are sprinkled throughout the early part of the novel, and the ways in which the three separate parts of his life—his early childhood, his relationship with Dasha, and his current situation in Grozny—are all interconnected. It takes the entire novel for him even to begin to understand how his childhood actions and what he sees and does in Grozny all tie back to the central tragedy of his life thus far: his failure to save his relationship with Dasha, the first woman in his life, and the main focus of his emotional center. As he attempts to pull together the different parts of his life into one narrative, he presents all the pieces to the reader, but often cannot see them himself, either at the time or in retrospect.

And in fact, Egor can be an unreliable narrator, something he admits in the second scene in which he describes his idyllic mornings with Dasha. While in the first scene he describes how they would cuddle together in bed, and he could not bear to tear himself away from her in order to go smoke, in the second scene he says, "I lied when I said I didn't go smoke. I went all the time,"[66] and describes how she would steal the blankets and he would admit defeat and go smoke in the cold kitchen until she woke up. When she does wake up, he thinks to himself,

63 Ibid., 59.

64 A type of sniper rifle, literally Снайперская винтовка системы Драгунова, or "Dragunov Sniper Rifle," widely in use in the USSR and former USSR.

65 Prilepin, *Patologii*, 60.

66 Ibid., 27.

"What kind of a child was she, dear Lord, what kind of a girl did I have, a little puppy-dog, a sweet little paw."[67]

Although his reference to her as "a little puppy-dog, a sweet little paw" is affectionate, it also signals the problems ahead: a couple of chapters later, during one of his childhood reminisces, Egor recalls how he once saw his beloved dog Daisy mating with a male dog, and is outraged that she is not ashamed of her actions and does not feel the need to seek forgiveness from him. He responds by shouting at her, chasing her, and throwing rocks and dirt at her until she loses patience with him, growling at him and running off for the rest of the day. When she returns, she "looked at me with disgust. From that point on that was the only way she looked at me, with disgust."[68] Later Egor will recount how, just as with Daisy, he is wildly jealous of Dasha and hounds her about her past boyfriends, descending to the point of stalking both her and them, until one day she, like Daisy, snaps and runs off.

Even more ominously, for the soldiers and for Egor's desperate love for Dasha, on that first ride through Grozny the column encounters a sick dog who vomits and then collapses into her own vomit, before "jumping up, as if she can tell that she had lain down in that very place where she would meet her death."[69] And she is right: one of the soldiers shoots her in the head. Although, desperately ill as she is, this is more an act of mercy than an act of violence, it also suggests how Egor will ruin/already has ruined his relationships with the two most important people in his life: Daisy and Dasha.

Hints of the bloodbath that will engulf the soldiers in the denouement of the novel are also given right from the start. "Uncle Iura," the medic, is described at the beginning as looking like "a penguin who's lost a little weight."[70] Later, when the barracks are assaulted by enemy forces, Uncle Iura will be captured and his arms chopped off, making him look like "a penguin who had been dropped on the ground."[71] And the death of the sick stray dog is also ominous: she senses "that she had lain down in that very place where she would meet death," and a number of the soldiers are later killed in in their "bedchamber," the room in the school turned into their dormitory. Even the bunks themselves hint at death: they are arranged "in a large letter C,"[72] the first letter of the word "death" (смерть) in Russian. It is not the OMON officer or the little boy who know the

67 Ibid., 27.
68 Ibid., 77.
69 Ibid., 21.
70 Ibid., 44.
71 Ibid., 245.
72 Ibid., 24.

outcome of the soldiers' assignment to Grozny: it is the sick dog whom they shoot down upon arrival who predicts the future events in the book, both those that actually are in the narrative future, and those that are in the narrative past but are only revealed later.

The early chapters of the novel also introduce a theme that will become an important motif as the action develops: religion. Egor himself is never shown attending a service, wearing a cross, or demonstrating other signs of Christian faith, but religion keeps intruding on his consciousness in the Grozny storyline, and even before—his hometown is "Holy Savior," and their platoon is made up of locals from Holy Savior. Once they leave for the war, someone crosses himself as they land in Mozdok, and later Egor discovers that one of his soldiers wears a cross, while Anvar is the subject of a certain amount of semi-good-natured joshing over his Muslim faith.

The most important representative of the "religion" theme, though, is the soldier nicknamed "Monk," a former seminary student who failed his exams and somehow ended up in a special forces unit instead, despite being a declared pacifist. Monk irritates the other soldiers with his unattractive appearance, his unpleasant voice, and his clumsiness, and they are openly scornful (unsurprisingly) of his pacifism. An argument breaks out in the "bedchamber" over the interpretation of the commandment "Thou shalt not kill," with Monk claiming that it applies without exception to humans but not to nonhuman animals, although God is one and the same for all living creatures.

Egor, not normally prone to philosophy and not overtly religious, bursts out in a furious denial of all that, outlining his own religious and moral beliefs:

> "How does faith come into being?" I say, turning in his direction. "Those who believe are those who are able to doubt, whose doubts are insoluble. Those who cannot resolve their doubts begin to believe. Animals can't doubt, which is why they have no reason to believe. But humans have elevated their doubt into an absolute."[73]

When Monk counters that God is not doubt, but love, they fall into a fierce argument, mixing up the Ten Commandments and the Sermon on the Mount—it is never explained how Egor, who was raised in the atheist Soviet Union and attended, presumably, atheist Soviet schools, knows these scriptural quotations with which he sprinkles his speech, or if he simply channeling them

---

73 Ibid., 51.

without being aware of what they are—over whether or not it is ever acceptable, according to Scripture, to kill. Monk upholds the position that it is pointless to combat evil, since it is all God's will. Egor defends the idea that is acceptable to kill under certain circumstances, since people must actively work to fulfill God's will and "my anger is not without a cause."[74] They only stop when one of the other men shouts at them, and each of them continues the argument under their breath afterwards.

This is one of the few times when Egor is shown as exhibiting outward emotion; despite his (over)active imagination, he rarely shares his thoughts and feelings with others, and there are few signs that other people are aware of what is going through his head. But the religion issue and the question of whether or not it is ever acceptable to kill or commit violence brings something out in him that the actual violence he encounters does not, while also, like the other events in the first chapters, foreshadowing the bloody ending to the novel.

Highly attuned as he is, or thinks he is, to the real and symbolic/imaginary worlds, Egor is surprisingly clueless about what is going on around him and what other people are thinking and feeling, something he himself does not realize, but that is particularly evident when he goes on sweeps with his squad. This is partly just how Egor is, but it may also be part of the cognitive dissonance that Egor and the other soldiers experience over the atrocities they not only witness, but, unlike the other characters in the works featured here, commit.

Like Politkovskaya, but unlike Eldin and Babchenko, Prilepin, who participated in sweeps himself as an OMON officer,[75] makes his fictional but still autobiographical war very up close and personal, as the soldiers in *Pathologies* are largely responsible for conducting sweeps and arresting suspected rebels, rather than engaging in large-scale battles with long-range weapons. Prilepin's characters in *Pathologies* do not watch from afar as aerial and artillery bombardments soften up the enemy positions before firing in the direction of unseen enemies. Instead, they go house-to-house and interact with both civilians and rebels directly, often with no clear idea of which is which. This leads to frequent abuse by the Russian soldiers, something we know from eyewitness

---

74 Ibid., 52. This appears to be an allusion to MT 5:22.

75 A homemade video of/by Prilepin participating in sweeps in 1996 is sometimes available on YouTube under the title "Zakhar Prilepin v sostave Nizhegorodskogo Omon" (Zakhar Prilepin with the Nizhegorodsky OMON): https://www.youtube.com/watch?v=r9kwlmziczg&t=374s. As of the time of writing it has been taken down and replaced with a heavily redacted, much slicker version under the title "Chechnia": Захар Прилепин, "Chechnia," YouTube video, 1:23, March 2, 2021, https://www.youtube.com/watch?v=adn3l2d0IN0.

accounts of actual sweep operations is all too realistic. Several of the soldiers in Egor's platoon very definitely fit in with Eichler's categorization of the "excessive warrior," shooting civilians and engaging in extrajudicial executions of unarmed prisoners. Egor himself, who is largely concerned with saving his own skin, does not commit many abuses, but he stands by while other members of his platoon do, and his internal dialogue, otherwise extremely chatty, tends to fall silent in the presence of these abuses, as if he cannot process what is happening. In Herman's classification of the different responses to trauma, Egor appears to be experiencing constriction in the face of violence, even violence inflicted by his own side.

The first sweep takes place after the soldiers have managed to settle in and feel that maybe things are not so bad. And the first sweep is fairly non-disastrous—for them. They are sweeping a burned-out, abandoned neighborhood, and the first person they come across turns out to be a dead Chechen. This is the first dead body that Egor encounters, and he says nothing about his emotional reaction to the sight, instead describing it in terms that suggest his confused horror at what he sees: "In the corner of the house there is a scorched corpse. Completely naked. An open mouth, no lips, a thrown-back head, Adam's apple split in two. Burned, black, raised up, like an erect penis."[76]

Egor is not the only one who sees the corpse in sexual terms: one of the other soldiers jokes about giving it mouth-to-mouth. And then they move on without further comment, but the corpse and its description suggest Egor's inherently sexual filter through which he perceives the world, and the castration anxiety that he cannot bring himself to name directly but that keeps reappearing in the text: earlier, at the school, one of the soldiers sets off a tripwire in one of the classrooms and is wounded by shrapnel in the groin; Egor suffers terrible jealousy over Dasha and fantasizes about castrating her other lovers; and so on. Sex and death are inextricably linked for him, so that he "kills" his sexual relationship and sees the death around him in sexual terms. But this, like much of the rest of his other issues, is hidden from him, even as he spends much of his time ruminating and reminiscing, trying to figure himself and his life out.

Their encounter with the enemy only takes place at the end of the first sweep, when they are taking a food break and see six Chechens walking down the road towards the building they are currently in. They take cover and listen to the Chechens, and as he listens, Egor is forced to feel their shared humanity:

---

76 Prilepin, *Patologii*, 59.

> I hear how one them, and for some reason I think it's definitely the one in sneakers, slips in the dirt and, in Russian but with an accent, swears vigorously under his breath. I feel kind of sick from his words. Probably the sound of him saying out loud the uncensored designations for sexual organs makes me aware on a physiological level that he is a living person. Soft, white, hairy, sweaty, alive . . .[77]

When he saw the dead body earlier, Egor could not bring himself to identify with it, even though he does see it in physical, even sexual, terms. Hearing someone swear—something Egor considers himself particularly good at, and a skill he uses to arouse Dasha during their trysts—brings home to him how much he and the Chechens he is supposed to be rounding up and killing have in common.

This does not, however, cause him to try to defend them when the platoon first kills two other Chechens who happen to drive by, and then line up the remaining six against the wall and execute them on a vague suspicion of being rebels. It is not until they set the bodies on fire that they discover that they were carrying ammunition, and that they had, in fact, executed rebels and not random civilians.

Throughout the sweep Egor remains largely passive, not participating in the short, one-sided fight between the soldiers and the Chechens. The main thing he does is to ask for volunteers from his squad to carry out the execution, but he does not show himself actually asking the question. He merely says that "about five people volunteer,"[78] but does not name who they are, nor does he participate in the burning of the corpses.

Afterwards, when they are celebrating with vodka, he and Sania Starling, the soldier who wears a cross under his tunic and who was unable to shoot one of the injured Chechens at point-blank range, leave the festivities and sit together in silence on the stairs, and Egor thinks "There's no need to talk about it. Today we took the lives of eight people,"[79] although neither he nor Sania were directly responsible for the deaths. At that moment, however, Egor is able to connect with others on a mental and emotional level, and admit to the gravity of what had happened. When he saw the burned corpse at the beginning of the sweep, he could not, for all his interest in omens, consciously process what it

---

77 Ibid., 65.
78 Ibid., 68.
79 Ibid., 71.

foreshadowed, which was the eight burned corpses that the Russian soldiers would themselves would create. Only afterwards is he able to look back and put together some of the pieces, just as he can with his life as a whole.

On the second sweep operation he is just as cut off from the people he encounters as on the first. This time they are sweeping occupied houses, and they have to go into individual dwellings and search and question the inhabitants. Once again Egor is afraid and looks for omens of salvation or disaster, seeing more of the latter than the former. As he's smoking in the lavatory beforehand he thinks that "we got lucky on the first sweep, so we certainly won't on the second"[80]—which does not prevent him from taking off his helmet and body armor when given the chance, as opposed to Anvar, who is openly afraid of participating in the sweeps and wears not one, but two flak jackets.

Although on the inside Egor is terrified, just like Anvar, it is Anvar who can't hide his fear and receives the mockery of the rest of the platoon, while Egor can pass as a fearless special forces soldier by faking his courage. This may be why he is quick to believe, for example, that one of the women whose apartment they go into is not frightened but "pretending to be frightened,"[81] even though by objective accounts she has ample reason to fear the Russian soldiers, telling them how "soldiers had been killing everyone, they'd raped her neighbor in the entranceway, and shot her grandfather and thrown him out the window, and something else as well—those mean soldiers had committed total outrages."[82] We can see most clearly with Egor the dichotomy that Tal notes in *Worlds of Hurt*: Egor clearly experiences violence and trauma, but as a soldier he, unlike other types of victims, also brings violence and trauma to others. However, at this point in the narrative he is only able to recognize his own fear and trauma, and discounts it in those around him, especially in the victims of violence committed by Russian Federal troops.

In the case of the woman in the apartment, Egor treats her account with mockery, and, although he does not attack her himself, he does nothing to stop her mistreatment by the others. When the platoon leader drags her sister off to the bathroom for unnamed, but almost certainly bad, reasons—like the other male authors here, Prilepin is coy about rape, admitting to its existence but not depicting its victims or even taking them seriously—and she tries to go after them, the other soldiers hit her in the face. One of them argues for taking away her sister in order to "convince her to talk on the topic of the location of

---

80 Ibid., 81.
81 Ibid., 85.
82 Ibid., 86.

her spouse [. . .]. I saw some pincers there. And an iron. Everything you need for a serious conversation."[83] The soldiers who find themselves trembling uncontrollably from terror before a sweep have no compunction about planning terrible atrocities when faced with those even more vulnerable than themselves.

They do not carry out their plan to torture the woman, but they do take away her father, who ends up dead when they run into enemy fire on their way back to the base. But, while Egor is repulsed by the sight of more corpses, and has to turn away and light up to keep from vomiting, he cannot bring himself to empathize with the Chechens, even—maybe especially—the women. He does not seem to care what others think of him, but he instinctively falls into the role of tough guy, no matter how inappropriate it is for his internal world, and he sees the others around him as playing roles too, which further isolates him.

This is particularly apparent in his relationships with women. The scene described above is not the only one in which Egor has ambiguous or negative interactions with women or females in general. For all his overt sexuality, throughout the book Egor is cut off from what we might call "the feminine principle," and his attempts to connect with it end in failure. He is abandoned by his mother as an infant, and after the death of his father ends up living in a boarding school before entering the military and joining an all-male special forces unit. If he were a real person psychologists could nod their heads meaningfully over this and murmur things about abandonment issues and early childhood trauma; as a fictional character this background is highly symbolic of a person who has been rejected by femininity and is cut off from the forces of generation and reproduction, causing him to scramble and clutch at them desperately with one hand, even as he pushes them away with the other.

Halfway through the novel he does have a brief flash of insight about his relationships with women, saying:

> Having grown up apart from women, I saw any of them as a rare, shiny New Year's decoration, and would hold her anxiously in my hands. And I couldn't even think—as happens with spoiled children, who thoughtlessly smash their toys out of stupid curiosity—about the internal arrangement of this decoration, seeing her as a whole and complete blessing that had been given just to me.[84]

83 Ibid., 87.
84 Ibid., 111.

This flash of insight explains much of Egor's attitude towards women and females, but does little for him personally: even when he has these moments of self-understanding, he does not strive to change anything about himself and his behavior. An essentially static personality for much of the novel, he strives to catch the signs of the universe and force the world and all the creatures and objects in it to bend to his will and serve his purposes, something he has particularly little success in when it comes to female sexuality. As a child he was unable to stop Daisy from going into heat and mating with male dogs, and as a man he is unable to undo the fact that Dasha had already taken other lovers. In the afterword he is trapped and almost drowns in the feminine water of the river, which he specifically compares to female reproductive organs, and when he breaks free, like a child being born, he is dependent on a woman to resuscitate his son. Femaleness and female reproduction surround him throughout the book, while also rejecting him, either for their own reasons or because he rejects them in his desperate struggles to assert his independence and gain control.

The primary feminine object he is able to simultaneously love and control is his Kalashnikov rifle, which is both inanimate and highly phallic. Despite the masculine imagery normally associated with guns, Egor sees his gun in androgynous or even explicitly female terms. When he cleans it, the emotions and images that accompany the action are highly suggestive of both a sexual encounter with a woman, and of (male) masturbation; in either case, Egor treats his rifle with an unambiguous loving tenderness, and receives from it sexual pleasure that he cannot experience with the actual women in his life.

The multipage and extremely sensual gun-cleaning scene begins with the phrase "I'm cleaning my rifle. I like cleaning my rifle. There's no activity more relaxing."[85] He spends a paragraph explaining the care he takes in making sure there's no round in the chamber, before describing how, piece by piece, he strips down the weapon until it "becomes light, naked, and defenseless."[86] He speaks to the rifle "affectionately,"[87] handling the spring "like foreskin,"[88] before rubbing the rifle down with oil "The way you'd wash yourself. Your elegant woman."[89] He concludes by forcefully thrusting the cleaning rod all the way through the barrel and ending the paragraph with an ellipsis—the closest we come in the novel, despite its numerous explicit sexual encounters, to seeing Egor achieve orgasm.

---

85 Ibid., 96.
86 Ibid., 96.
87 Ibid., 96.
88 Ibid., 97.
89 Ibid., 97.

When he is actually with Dasha, the narratives focuses on the appearance of her body and the initial foreplay, but either coitus is interrupted, or the text cuts off before the actual sexual act takes place. With his rifle, however, Egor is able to go "all the way," and when he meets an obstruction, he is able to break through it by slamming the cleaning rod against the floor in order to drive it deeper into the barrel. The rifle's resistance to his advances are only feigned and can be overcome, for the rifle's own good, with physical force.

When he treats the actual females in his life the same way, though, the result is not conquest and victory, but defeat. Dasha leaves him and Daisy treats him "with disgust," as do the various Chechen women he comes across, who accuse him and the other Russian soldiers of committing heinous acts of violence. Unable to face the truth about his behavior, or even the very existence of other, physically alien, living beings as both separate from him and yet equally conscious and aware, Egor—and the other men—accuse the women (and dogs) in their lives of dishonesty and mercenary motives.

This is most clearly stated in a long conversation Egor has with Sania Starling as they are drinking (in another recurring motif that turns out to be an evil omen that no one picks up on, the whole platoon is constantly sneaking contraband vodka and beer into the base and getting stinking drunk, even while on duty). Sania, the one member of Egor's squad who wears a cross, and who wanted to comfort the women the others assaulted while on the sweep, suddenly blurts out to Egor, "I want a girl," followed immediately by "it's horrible that there are girls on this earth . . . slender, tender . . ."[90] When Egor asks him why it's so horrible, he breaks into a lengthy monologue:

> "Egor, just understand, all these creatures are walking around, they've got their panties on, all kinds of cute little clothes . . . girls are carrying around their breasts . . . their cute little asses . . . and every one of them, just think, every single one of them—there's not a single exception—has between her legs that pink . . . gray . . . hidden—" Sasha swallowed back some saliva. "That they have this is a gift from God. It's not a gift from God for all of them, of course . . . For many of them—it's just a thing, just an organ . . . but for some of them it's a gift from God. But girls, Egor, all girls sell it. They play with it—this gift. They don't sell it in order to whore around, but they just trade it . . . like Papuans . . . for all kinds of trinkets."[91]

90 Ibid., 126.
91 Ibid., 126.

Sania then goes on to describe how he worked out a number of strategies to get the women at his former place of employment to have casual sex with him, often through a combination of trickery and force. But even though he has done so in the past and wants to do so again right now, Sania is horrified that women are willing to have sex with men, including giving oral sex, which "I won't ever believe some random person could find pleasant!"[92] He is unable to make peace with the fact that he cannot walk up to a strange woman on public transport and begin touching her without causing a scandal, but if he acts strategically and chooses the right time and place, women will agree to have sex with him, even though these are one and the same women with one and the same sexual organs. For this "foolishness" and "shamelessness" he believes that "God is punishing them."[93]

Furthermore, he believes that women control sexual desire and sexuality. That women can be sexually attractive to men, and yet make decisions about when and with whom to have sex, and even enjoy the sexual act, including voluntarily coming into contact with male sexual organs, which he considers unattractive and base ("A dick is a dick. It just hangs there. What kind of gift from God is that?"),[94] is incomprehensible and disgusting to Sania.

His words confuse Egor, who is unable to respond to them—probably because Sania's words reflect Egor's own thoughts and feelings. Like Sania, Egor is thrown into a state of uncontrollable outrage when he witnesses the casualness with which Daisy mates with a male dog, and later with which Dasha tells him about her past lovers.

Just how disturbed Egor's feelings are about Dasha and about women in general is first clearly demonstrated in the next scenes. After their conversation about women, Egor and Sania go to the market to buy vodka. Sania tries to flirt with one of the women at the market, a half-Chechen, half-Russian woman who has attracted the admiration of all the men at the base, but who does not return their affection. This time, Egor hears her say to Sania, echoing and reversing Sania's earlier words about women, "'Why are you here? [. . .] Who called for you? You killed my children. Your children will be punished for this.'"[95] A few moments later, the market comes under fire, and the first Russian casualty of the novel happens: a paratrooper who was at the market is shot in the head just as everyone thinks they have made it to safety. It later turns out that he had just

92 Ibid., 128.
93 Ibid., 129.
94 Ibid., 128.
95 Ibid., 129.

become a father the day before, when his daughter, whom he had not yet seen, was born.

The two events—the confrontation with the market woman and the death of the new father—suggest that the men do not have control over themselves, their lives, or their generative and sexual powers, and not only that, but that they are the villains in the story. Sania thinks that God must be punishing women for being sexual creatures, but the firefight and subsequent casualty at the market suggest that it is the "masculine principle" that is truly dangerous and self-destructive: not only were the Chechen woman's children killed by Russian soldiers, but a Russian soldier and new father is killed in the fight before he can ever come into contact with his (female) child. These men are literally destroying the forces of sexuality and generation with their violence, and cutting off the generations from each other, so that mothers lose their children and daughters lose their fathers.

It is in the scene immediately following that one when Egor remembers the first real cracks in his relationship with Dasha. As they are lying in bed, he tells her, "I love you pathologically. I love you hysterically,"[96] which she takes as a joke, but that turns out not to be the case. At that time, Egor says, he could no longer bring himself to ring her doorbell when he would visit her. He would instead loiter at her door and then run away, muttering to himself, "My God, I can't! Give me something that's mine! Just mine!"[97]

He would have to go through this process, which may have happened just once or may have happened many times, before he was able to summon up the courage to be with Dasha. That this is his fault he is aware. "I had cultivated these spirits [of Dasha's past lovers] myself, like slovenly housekeepers cultivate flies [. . .]. I had summoned them with my constant ruminations on her, my Dasha's, past."[98] And yet he cannot take responsibility, or at least, he considers himself unable to combat what is happening to him: "The spirits had landed on the body of my darling, and by doing so were tormenting me, while I was completely defenseless."[99] Once again, Egor sees himself as passive and helpless, acted upon by others instead of acting upon them, even though the reverse is often true.

Although Egor is particularly cut off from women and femininity, and sees femaleness as a sham or deception, he also has moments of being cut off from his own comrades, and is unable to comprehend that they may be going through

96 Ibid., 135.
97 Ibid., 137.
98 Ibid., 138.
99 Ibid., 138.

the same emotions and internal experiences as he is. This is especially true in times of stress, as when they are setting off to carry out a dangerous assignment. When Egor is chosen to be part of a hand-picked group to arrest a known rebel, he is terrified beforehand, thinking, "Why am I too embarrassed to hide under the bed and say that my stomach hurts?"[100] Egor could thus be taken as an example of Eichler's category of "fragile warrior," suffering psychological trauma from the terror of (incipient) battle.

However, he hides his fear and fragility under a tough outer posture. But as with his encounters with Chechen women, he is unable to generalize his experiences to those around him. Before the sweep, he cannot believe that the other soldiers are also hiding their fears under a calm exterior, just as he is. When he sees his platoon leader using the time before they have to set off to darn a sock, he thinks "contemptuously" that "Apparently he's planning to come back."[101] He calms down a little when one of his squad mates tells him, "I just took a shit for the last time,"[102] since that means "at least there's one normal person here. While some darn socks. Jesus Christ."[103]

When they are lying in wait, Egor is terrified to the point of trembling uncontrollably, but he nevertheless forces himself to remain still despite the discomfort of his position, waiting until the others have started shifting position before he does as well. In fact, most of the other soldiers are as fidgety and uncomfortable as he is, making jokes to hide their fear, but he does not perceive that as such: when his friend Kizia suggests that they just hide in the bushes and then say back at the base that their target never showed up, Egor says, "I can hear by his voice that Kizia's joking around. If it had occurred to me to say the same thing, it would have sounded too sincere. Kizia's brave. Probably braver than me, I decide with chagrin."[104]

When Neck (so called because of his muscular neck), the platoon leader, speaks to the other soldiers after knocking out the rebel, Egor is struck by his calmness. Highly attentive to external reality, and trying to match it to an internal or symbolic reality, Egor in his moments of stress is incapable of seeing the other soldiers as having complex inner lives and as feeling one thing while expressing another, as he does himself.

Egor's own inner life, mental and physical, is split between the way he perceives himself and the way others perceive him, something that comes across

100 Ibid., 145.
101 Ibid.
102 Ibid.
103 Ibid.
104 Ibid., 146.

in the text, although he himself is largely unaware of this. While he often fears for his life, and has numerous incidents in which he feels, or is, clumsy—he almost chokes on a piece of shish kebab, he accidentally flicks a lit cigarette into his own eye, before setting off on an operation he has trouble lacing up his boots, and even struggles to chew and swallow his food—he is in fact strong, imposing, and in many cases physically dexterous and brave.

When he goes on a mission to capture rebels in a village outside of Grozny, he is terrified beforehand, to the point that he cannot squeeze toothpaste onto his toothbrush, squeezing it onto the floor instead. But once the operation begins, his training and his physical well-being take over. As he jumps into the back of the truck that will carry him to the village where the capture operation will take place, he thinks "what strong, hard muscles I have,"[105] although the thought is accompanied not with joy but with "bitterness."[106] When they arrive at the village and he and the rest of the platoon are running up a hill towards it, though, "my legs are already running; it's easy to run, and it seems like I'm about to push off and take flight [. . .]. There's not a single thought in my head. A hat on my head and a rifle in my hands. Everything's in place."[107]

Once the village is surrounded, he does not kill anyone, but he does lead the way when his squad is commanded to capture a house, and when they encounter a drunken Russian warrant officer who starts firing at them, he makes "an excellent balletic leap, because the burst [from the warrant officer's gun] passes right under my feet," and then "with a practiced mechanical motion, stepping out of the line of fire ahead of time, I kick the warrant officer under the knee, simultaneously grabbing his gun with my right hand and pulling it slightly towards myself,"[108] saving himself and the others in his squad from being hit by friendly fire.

Egor's body is in fact a highly developed and trained weapon, and when he is able to let his body take over from his mind, he becomes what he has been trained to be, and does not suffer any of the mental agonies that he does when he is not fighting. While the passages describing his downtime at the base are full of his thoughts, hopes, fears, and fantasies, good and bad, the passages describing the actual operations in which he participates are full of descriptions of the physical actions of Egor and the other soldiers, with no reflections whatsoever. In another example of constriction, Egor's mind, so busy during periods of

---

105 Ibid., 170.
106 Ibid., 170.
107 Ibid., 177.
108 Ibid., 191.

inaction, becomes curiously blank during the operations themselves, as if Egor is no longer describing something that is happening to him personally, but is watching and narrating the action from the outside. The readers are never told what Egor thinks and feels about the shooting of unarmed captives or any of the other brutalities committed by the other soldiers, or even whether he was afraid when the drunken warrant officer fired at him. At these moments, Egor is either able to achieve a complete unification of his body and mind, or his mind completely shuts off in a refusal to accept what is going on, turning total control over to his body; it is left for the reader to decide which it is.

Although Egor is less reflexively brutal than his platoon commander Neck or his squad mates Andrei Horse (so named for his large build) and Kizia, all of whom by this point in the story have made multiple kills, he is able to fulfill his assignments adequately and without revealing to his comrades just how frightened he is. Anvar Amaliev is a target of constant mockery for his unhideable fear and active avoidance of sweeps and capture operations, and Monk for his pacifism, but Egor is never mocked for fear or cowardice. On the contrary, the other soldiers treat him with trust and respect, in that they joke in front of him about their own fears, as if he can sympathize with them (unlike Neck or Andrei Horse) but is not afraid himself. He is chosen to carry out especially tricky operations, such as the capture of the known rebel in Grozny. In the bathroom before they set off on the operation in the village, when he is so frightened he cannot manage to get his toothpaste onto his toothbrush, he still manages "to stroll to the sink with the step of a young man who's calm, even able to hum something."[109] Egor is thus an example of the kind of fakery and the split between inner and outer worlds that he suspects in others.

The war also brings home to Egor a split that he cannot reconcile: the fact that living beings, including ultra-alive beings such as himself, who is so energetic and strong, can be killed in an instant, and not only that, but their ultra-alive bodies carry the seeds of death within them, in that their skeletons and internal organs, which are often revealed when people are killed by the weapons of modern warfare, are always there, peeking out and showing themselves at inopportune moments. Egor is never able to escape the presence of death, because he carries its promise inside of him, something of which the war makes him increasingly aware as he sees more and more dead bodies.

Death greets him on his entrance to Grozny, when Neck shoots the sick dog, revealing the inside of her head. Egor's first encounter with a dead human body, when they find the burned corpse in the abandoned building during their first

---

109 Ibid., 164.

sweep, confuses him: it is both horrifying and strangely sexual. The reality of death is fully brought home to him slightly later, when he is accompanying his captain on a run to the airport. Near the airport they come across the bodies of eighty-six demobilized soldiers, who were ambushed and killed by rebels as they were making their way, already disarmed, to the airport to go home. Egor's subordinate Sania is unable to make himself leave their jeep and come over to the line of dead bodies, but Egor, despite being in a state of such horror that he doesn't know how he will manage to get out of the jeep and go investigate what is going on, still finds the strength to do so.

When he tries to look at the first corpse in the line, "I can't see the dead man as a single whole; I see his ear, full of dirt, his fingers with their nails standing on end, his ragged sleeve, his hair standing on end, his unzipped fly, one boot is missing, his white toes with clumps of dirt between. My eyes are afraid to grasp him as a single whole, they vainly slip around."[110] When he goes to the next corpse, he sees "A wide-open mouth, and greedy equine teeth bared like an animal's, as if the dead man is asking for a lump of sugar, ready to take it in his lips."[111] He goes on down the line, describing the dead soldiers, until a colonel comes along and orders that the dead bodies be removed from the side of the road.

Back in the jeep, Sania asks the driver to turn the car around; when the driver tells him to close his eyes instead, Sania tell him, "They won't close."[112] Having seen these dead soldiers, the living soldiers cannot unsee them, and furthermore, Egor starts seeing them in himself. As he tries and fails to brush his teeth before leaving for the operation in the village, he looks in the mirror and sees:

> the teeth of that guy, one of the dead ones that I saw by the airport—lips drawn back, dead, white teeth, sticking out of his torn-up mouth like a palisade fence. I squeeze my brush, looking at myself in the mirror. I'm afraid to even open my mouth, to bare my teeth, because on my face, it seems, the bony cheeks and dead chin of that guy will immediately show through.[113]

Constantly searching for signs as he is, Egor cannot ignore this sign, nor the certain knowledge that living beings such as himself can be turned into dead

110 Ibid., 119.
111 Ibid., 120.
112 Ibid., 123.
113 Ibid., 164.

bodies in the blink of an eye, and that he is (semi)voluntarily putting himself into harm's way, courting exactly the same type of death that he has seen strike others.

And yet, he is not killed in the operation, nor are any of the other soldiers in the platoon. From their point of view, the operation is a success, and all the fears and the evil harbingers that Egor feels and sees beforehand herald, not his physical death, but the death of his relationship with Dasha. As they leave the village, after Egor has saved them from the drunken warrant officer, he thinks, "seems like we've gotten lucky again"[114]—and falls into reminisces about Dasha and his descent into insanity with her.

Although the Dasha storyline is not simultaneous with the Grozny storyline, it is presented almost as such, with descriptions of the idyllic early days cut in with Egor's first days in Grozny, when things seem to be going well, and scenes of Egor's growing jealousy and attacks of insanity alternating with his increasingly violent experiences in Grozny. Egor's development in the novel is not that of the naive young soldier who comes to know the truth of war and become a hardened, embittered veteran—instead, that character development arc takes place during the Dasha storyline.

It is after their first, successful, operation outside of Grozny that Egor remembers how Dasha told him about her former lovers. It is unclear if these memories are of a time before or after the previously recounted memories of the Dasha storyline—probably before it, as they narrate how Egor first finds out about her former lovers. One day she says to him, casually, that she'd just counted up all the men she had been with, and if he has an equal number of women, that means that he and she are embarking on a new phase in their life together. Although Egor does not take it this way, it seems likely that Dasha meant for this to bring them closer together. Instead, it separates them, as Dasha admits to having been with twenty-six men already, while Egor tells her "You're my first,"[115] although he can't "decide what to tell her—the truth, or a lie?"[116] Dasha promptly accuses him of lying, which he does not deny, but she is certainly the only woman he ever thinks about. His reliability as a narrator, which the earlier Dasha episodes had already cast into doubt, is further put under question here, but at the same time, he is certainly telling *a* truth—the truth of his inner experiences.

114 Ibid., 193.
115 Ibid., 196.
116 Ibid.

Egor responds to Dasha's revelation by pressuring her to tell him about her previous lovers, which she does "with surprising readiness,"[117] although it is likely that she is unaware of how Egor is truly feeling. He himself is surprised at how well he is able to speak and ask questions, and while talking to her about this "I demonstrated a rare composure."[118]

But this is all feigned, as Egor's outer behavior often is. He promptly tracks down one of the men, a teacher at their institute, and, finding him in the restroom, manages to open his stall and sneak a peek at his genitals. What Egor thinks of the man's "small, plump, mouse-colored"[119] genitals is never stated: the operation is carried out with the same lack of emotion and internal monologue as the fight scenes, and the scene cuts off at that moment, the action jumping back to Grozny.

After that, though, as if he had won some kind of significant victory or exorcised the evil spirits that had been haunting him, Egor's attitude towards Grozny changes. The next Grozny scene shows him hanging out and joking with his platoon mates on the base, before they are called on to go find three "little soldiers" (солдатики [soldatiki]), or ordinary conscripts, who have gone missing while on a vodka run. Rather than falling into a panic, as he has before all the other operations, Egor, already slightly drunk, is in "an excellent mood,"[120] and looking at the burned-out houses they ride past makes him feel "soft and warm, like the belly of a bitch who's just given birth."[121]

And indeed, the rescue operation turns out extremely well for the squad: the three missing "little soldiers" turn up on their own at their base, and while they are being beaten up and shouted at by their commanding officer, Egor and his squad manage to steal a roast chicken and all the vodka out of their truck. They make it safely back to their own base despite drinking heavily on the road, and drink so much afterwards that Egor blacks out and doesn't remember that part of the evening when he wakes up the next morning.

When he does wake up, his fear of death continues to be absent. Still too hungover to get out of bed, he thinks, "Why didn't they shoot us yesterday? [. . .] Right now I'd be happy to be lying in a coffin. Maybe I'd fly home quicker that way."[122] And when he drags himself out of bed and discovers that they are leaving

117 Ibid., 197.
118 Ibid., 198.
119 Ibid., 200.
120 Ibid., 207.
121 Ibid., 208.
122 Ibid., 217.

in fifteen minutes for "unpleasant and unwelcoming places,"[123] instead of feeling frightened and worrying about death, he jokes about it with his bunkmates, and says nothing about being afraid on the ride to the village where they are supposed to capture potential rebels.

Unlike the descriptions of the previous operations, in which the run-up to the actual action is described at length, with Egor dwelling on the terrible things that could happen to him and his terror of death, filling up page after page with bad omens and doomsday scenarios, the ride over to the village and the encirclement of the house holding the suspected rebels is described in a scant few paragraphs, and everyone in the platoon is either too caught up in their hangover to be afraid, or in a good mood. Particularly cheerful are Neck, the platoon leader, and Slava Telman, who was in disgrace after unintentionally abandoning their commander, Major Kutsy, aka Semyonych, when they came under fire at the market, but who is now back in his good graces and is chosen to go into the house second, behind Neck.

The operation is thus missing all the bad omens of the previous ones—or rather, Egor fails to apprehend them. Neck and Slava, who were so particularly happy at the start of the operation, are killed instantly upon entering the house. They are the first casualties in Egor's platoon, which has been lucky thus far, despite all his fears. But when he lets down his guard and stops being afraid, two members of his platoon—the particularly fearless ones—are killed. The death that he believes has been stalking them from the beginning has finally taken her first victims, just when he least expected it.

The deaths of the two platoon members is followed by a deluge, soaking everyone on the ride back to Grozny, wetting their guns and extinguishing their cigarettes. The rain continues for the rest of the Grozny storyline, flooding their base during the final, climactic, multipart battle sequence in which most of the platoon is killed and the survivors are forced to abandon the base and escape through a ravine behind it.

The novel thus ends as it begins, with Egor's near-death and rebirth in the deadly, feminine forces of water and hidden depths. The fight scenes are intercut with the final stories of his failures with Daisy and Dasha, in which he tries to "plumb their depths" psychologically, to understand and control what they are thinking and feeling, and is rejected. Instead, he is thrust into the turbid waters of the flooded ravine.

After their return to the base, the surviving platoon members drink to their fallen comrades, whom Semyonych is transporting to headquarters, leaving

123 Ibid., 218.

Kostia Joiner, the leader of the other platoon, in charge. Everyone drinks late into the night, including those on watch: the city seems quiet and the only thing attacking the base is the rain, which is threating to "wash us off the roof."[124]

Egor, who is not on duty, goes to bed, "Infinitely tired, more tired than I've ever been in my life [. . .]. Probably I was just as flabbergasted by what had happened, just as tired, and felt myself to be just as happy, when I was born." As he sinks into sleep, the story cuts to the Dasha storyline and Egor's deepening insanity.

This time the focus is not on Dasha's beautiful and sexually attractive body, but on the bloody revenge that Egor would like to wreak on her former lovers, and his imaginary conversations with her:

> *You've maimed me. You've turned me into a monster. You've touched me to the depths of my soul. Their faces swim before me, their hands crucify you every day in my head. I want to have something that's mine! At boarding school everything I had was shared! I want my own!*
>
> I looked at her with crazy eyes and stayed silent.
>
> *I dream of going, with a cutlass clutched to my breast, to every single one of the men who have been with you. I dream of gathering all these men's organs that you've classified* [in an earlier scene, Dasha explains to Egor that men's bodies, including their sexual organs, are all different] *into a single bag. A large clear plastic bag, filled with something like squashed tomatoes. I can see myself walking down the street; the bag is dripping, and ambulances race past me to those houses I was just at. I want to bring this bag to you and say: "Here you go! This is yours!"*[125]

Egor's possessiveness and need to control those around him, his quest for something "his own," is extended to Dasha: not only does he want to control and own her, but he wants to present her with the sexual organs of the other men she has been with, thus emasculating them and turning them into objects of possession in one fell swoop.

Egor's fear/fantasy of castration reaches its apotheosis at this moment: all the hints of castration and its links with death—the first corpse they find in Grozny, the dead Russian soldiers by the airport who have been shot in the groin—come

124 Ibid., 237.

125 Ibid., 240. Italics in the original.

out in full flower here, as Egor makes explicit his desire to castrate other men in order to have total possession of Dasha.

The final line—"Here you go! This is yours!"—echoes his own, frequently repeated, desire to have "something of my own," especially since in the original Russian, the possessive pronouns are all in the neuter singular. When Egor thinks "I want my own!" he is not thinking of Dasha, or of any woman at all, which would be grammatically feminine, and when he mentally offers her the bag full of severed penises he is not offering her either the bag (пакет) or the penises, both of which are grammatically masculine, but the abstract concept of possession, which is filled out on the physical plane with sex and/or food.

Egor, who was rejected by both his mother and his dog, and who lost his father to heart disease at an early age and was subsequently raised, apparently (the details, as is often the case in the novel, are sketchy) by neighbors and/or a boarding school, has never had anything that was truly his. Even his rifle, the object for which he feels the most affection and with which he has the closest thing to a satisfying sexual relationship, is not his, but standard-issue; at the end of the cleaning scene the men are warned not to mark their kills on their rifles, since they do not own them and are not supposed to damage or deface them.

Egor does indeed not seem to have anything that is truly his: during the Grozny storyline he wears only his uniform, carries only standard-issue weapons and gear, sleeps in an army-issued bunk under army-issued blankets, and eats food provided by the platoon cook. The few things that are personally his are alcohol and cigarettes, and occasionally snacks, normally either stolen or bought on the sly, and always consumed and discarded. Egor has never had anything of his own that he has been taught how to preserve and take care of, and, just as he says himself, he treats the living beings around him just as he does his cigarettes, to be smoked up, stubbed out, and tossed away.

This may explain some of the horror that he (and the other men) have at the idea of women not being able to know the father of their children. Both Sania, in the long passage quoted earlier about the shamelessness of women, and Egor, in the same section as the passage just quoted, are driven into a state of madness by the thought of women having sex with multiple men in the same month and potentially conceiving a child of unknown paternity—in such cases it is impossible for a man to know if the child is "his own." It does not occur to Egor or Sania that a woman's child is "her own" regardless of paternity, and thus the problem of having something "just mine" is less pressing for women, and easier to solve, rendering the issue less important from the female point of view.

Of course, the men also have something that is "just theirs": their sexual organs. But, obsessed as they are with them, and as much as the words "penis" and "dick" appear in the text, they do not actually love or admire them, considering them to be base, coarse, and easily damaged or even cut off entirely, and with them, their possessors' ability to procreate and thus live on.

And Egor's androgynous/hermaphroditic rifle, which he treats both as a beloved woman and as male genitalia, produces neither life-giving semen, nor actual live children, but death-dealing bullets. Nothing, not even his sexuality or reproductive capabilities, truly belongs to Egor. Not even the son that he saves from drowning in the visions of disaster in the opening afterword is his flesh and blood: he is consistently referred to not as "my son" (мой сын [moi syn]) but "my adopted son" (мой приёмыш [moi priyomysh]). Which is not to say that Egor loves him any less—indeed, he demonstrates towards him the same all-consuming, semi-pathological, love that he feels for Dasha (is she the mother? Does she in fact conceive a child with another man, just as Egor fears she might, and then get back together with Egor once he returns from Chechnya? The text never says)—but that on a physical, genetic, and perhaps legal, level, he is not "his own," but must be shared, just like everything else in Egor's life.

Taken together, however, the above-quoted scene and the afterword do suggest that Egor does achieve some small amount of personal growth over the course of the story, although it is all revealed at the beginning, not the end, even if the beginning is actually the end, chronologically speaking. While in the scene from which the above-quoted passage is taken Egor is so overcome with possessiveness that he wants to castrate his imagined rivals, by the events in the afterword, he is able to accept the son of another man as his own.

The above-quoted passage also foreshadows the events in the next scene, although once again, Egor is no longer on the lookout for omens and does not experience it as such. The reminisces about Dasha are portrayed as happening while Egor is sleeping off the vodka that he and the others consumed. He is awakened in the middle of the night by the need to urinate, but can't wake up enough to get out of bed and take care of the problem. Towards morning, though, the need forces him awake. He gets up, noticing that everyone in the "bedchamber" is asleep but no one is snoring, making Egor wonder if "Maybe we're angels?"[126] He thinks he can hear a "guttural cry"[127] from outside; he assumes he's imagined it but takes his rifle with him in any case.

On his way to the bathroom he discovers that all the sentries have come inside to take cover from the rain, and then fallen asleep at their posts. He wakes them up, and, desperate to urinate, undoes his fly as he's hurrying to

126 Ibid., 242.
127 Ibid., 243.

the bathroom—only to see "bearded people dragging a half-naked man out of the bathroom."[128] Chechen forces have invaded the school while everyone was asleep and captured Uncle Iura, who had gone into the bathroom slightly ahead of Egor. Egor is unable to save Uncle Iura in time and loses sight of him; the next time he sees him, both his arms have been cut off at the elbow, making him look like a penguin, just as Egor had previously imagined him. Egor participates in the ensuing firefight with his fly undone.

Egor's thoughts and dreams are in fact prophetic, even though he fails to heed their prophecies. He fears being replaced or pushed aside by other men—and other men invade his territory, driving out him and his comrades. He thinks of cutting off other men's extremities—and other men cut off his comrade's extremities. He is obsessed with the power and fragility of male genitalia—and his urogenital system almost, but not quite, wakes him up in time to warn the others of the attack. Afterwards, he engages in a lengthy fight with the intruders with his genitals literally vulnerable and unguarded, as he cannot even manage to do up his fly. He thinks of the other men, sleeping in their beds drawn up in the shape of the letter C (the first letter of the word "death" in Russian), that they are angels—and many of them die before the night is out. He even sees one of his early dreams, from when he first arrived in Grozny, threaten to come true before his eyes: on one of his first nights at the base, he dreams of "Bad Boy [the platoon cook], who was peeling the head of a dead Chechen like a potato. He was carefully stripping away the skin, under which a white skull was revealed, with a knife."[129] Later, once the attack begins, Bad Boy pulls out a knife and suggests that they "saw off their heads."[130] Egor *is* able to predict events and see into the hearts of others, just as he wishes he could, he just cannot read the signs that come his way.

The final battle lasts for at least twenty-four hours, and takes place in multiple phases, each one intercut with a scene of Egor's past. At first, despite losing Uncle Iura and a couple of other members of the platoon, the soldiers are able to push back the attackers and hold the school as they wait for reinforcements, which do eventually arrive: Semyonych, who had gone to headquarters with the bodies of Neck and Slava, is, after much wrangling, able to commandeer a SOBR unit and three BTRs.[131] But after dropping off Semyonych and extra weaponry and ammunition, the SOBR unit departs, leaving the soldiers in the school

128 Ibid., 243.
129 Ibid., 78.
130 Ibid., 252.
131 Armored personnel carriers, normally wheeled and frequently armed.

behind, since they cannot all fit into three BTRs. The two platoons—now more like one and a half platoons, and one leaderless—are left to save themselves as best they can.

During breaks in the action Egor recalls how he became obsessed with Dasha's diary, which she let him read excerpts of but never the whole thing, finally throwing it away when he pesters her about it too much, causing him to go dig through the dumpster behind their apartment complex and then go to the city dump in search of it. His search is in vain, and he torments himself with the thought that "How horrible, oh God, what a pity that now I'll never get to know that Dasha—her thoughts, what she was thinking, everything that I was trying for so long and so unattractively to guess."[132]

His memories are broken up by more fighting; when he returns to them later, after being knocked out by a flying brick, it is remember how he went to visit his father's grave with Daisy, and how she refused to return his affection and even ran away from him when he tried to chase after her. He finally catches her, but as he pets her, she "looks at me with distrust, fearfully glancing at my hands, cringing, ready at any moment to run away from me."[133] This is the last Daisy scene, and it ends unresolved: Daisy does not run away, and even allows Egor to pull burrs from her coat, but she does not return his affection either. The scene closes with Egor sitting with his dog, whom he loves so much but whom he has alienated, at his father's unkempt gravesite.

This is arguably the nadir, or at least the closest to death, of Egor's childhood memories, as it is at this moment that the full force of his irretrievable losses are brought home: his father is gone forever, and no one can be bothered to keep up his gravesite, while Daisy is not going to forgive Egor for what he did to her, and can barely manage to tolerate his presence. These memories come when Egor is actually unconscious and are broken off by his slow and painful return to consciousness, which is accompanied by memories of how his neighbor's chicks had gotten into fresh tar and died despite all their attempts to save them. As he rises higher into consciousness, Egor finds himself thinking, "I'm going to die, and I'm not scared."[134] When he does fully come to, he discovers that not only is he lying next to the dead body of one of his comrades, but he is lying in a pool of the other man's blood. He has actually brushed with death in this scene, on both the physical and spiritual planes, unconsciously foreshadowing, once again, what will happen next.

---

132 Prilepin, *Patologii*, 271.
133 Ibid., 294.
134 Ibid., 296.

Meanwhile, the lower floors of the school have been flooded with water and captured by enemy forces. The decision is made to escape from the school by jumping out the window into the flooded ravine. Egor, accompanied by Sania, his favorite member of his squad, goes to round up the soldiers who are still holding distant points of the school. They are almost back to safety when Sania falls through a hole in the floor down into the flooded, occupied first floor, and is shot and killed before Egor can pull him to safety. From the occupied floor below come laughter, heartrending screams, smoke, and the smell of burning. Shortly afterwards, Egor's squad mate Andrei Horse refuses to jump out the window into the ravine, and "descends down the stairs, shooting somewhere into the smoky darkness, where you can hear hideous shouting and guttural laughter."[135] Andrei does not make it out of the school alive. The bottom floor of the school has been transformed into Hell, with all the trimmings and trappings thereof.

When he is knocked unconscious by a blow to the head and falls into reminisces about his visit to his father's grave, Egor is, on a symbolic level, thrown down into Hell. Up until this point, the "war is hell" metaphor has not been developed at any great length—although Egor is afraid and wishes he were not there, much of the time he is neither in danger nor suffering any serious physical discomfort or deprivations, and his conscience does not seem to be overly bothered by the abuses committed by his platoon mates and, by extension, him.

Unlike Eldin and Babchenko, the other two writers surveyed here who experienced active fighting, Prilepin does not dwell on the day-to-day physical suffering that many of the fighters on both sides of the conflict experienced. Egor's suffering is mainly mental, even when he does participate in fights: at those moments he is mainly aware of how strong and fit his body is, in contrast to (he thinks) his weak, fearful mind. But at this point in the narrative, Egor does make a journey down into the underworld, as he loses consciousness and remembers visiting his father's grave and seeing a clutch of helpless chicks die after being covered in tar. And then, upon awakening, he watches his squad mates descend, or in Sania's case, get literally dragged down into the flooded, smoke-filled, underworld, where human devils laugh at the screams and suffering of Egor's men.

Egor himself manages to escape the Hell that the school is becoming, as the water rises and enemy forces capture more and more rooms. When he jumps out the window into the flooded ravine, he does plunge into Death, landing in

135 Ibid., 313.

a pile of dead bodies and then almost drowning as he desperately tries to swim away from the school, losing his assault vest and his boots in the struggle.

He is pulled to safety by Monk, the member of his squad that no one liked because of his pacifism, religiosity, and generally annoying character and personal habits. Once again, this is something that is predicted by Egor himself early in the text, but which he subsequently ignores: while setting off on a mission Egor finds himself staring at Monk in distaste and thinking, "Why the fuck did he come on the mission?"[136] but then tells himself "Maybe he . . . maybe he'll be the one who saves me from death. Well, what else can I come up with."[137]

Egor does not take his momentary premonition that Monk will save him from death seriously, and continues to dislike and disagree with him—until Monk is in fact the one who saves him, first by pulling him out of the waters of the ravine, and then, shortly afterwards, by breaking his commitment to pacifism in order to stab an enemy who is about to attack Egor. Monk, the former seminarian, acts as a literal savior, midwife, and godfather to Egor, dragging him from the life-and-death-giving waters of the ravine by the scruff of his neck, guiding him towards warmth and safety, and killing his attacker. While the soldiers whom Egor liked and relied on, such as Sania Starling and Andrei Horse, are sucked straight down into Hell, the soldier whom he discounts is the one who saves him from Hell and who helps him on his journey to rebirth.

Monk helps Egor not only by saving him physically, but by pushing him to resolve his questions about religion and the meaning of life and death. During a lull in the attack on the school, Egor asks Monk once again about the existence of God and the meaning of faith. Monk tells him that God exists "So that people don't lose their way,"[138] an answer that Egor finds unsatisfying, telling him, "That's for the living. What about the dead?"[139] When Monk asks him what he thinks, Egor starts a debate with him:

> "I don't know . . . God endows the birth of a human being with divine meaning—the appearance of a creature in the image and likeness of God. While humans have to endow their deaths with divine meaning themselves," I say.
>
> *Then they will be repaid*, I want to add, but I don't. *Otherwise what are our guys dying here for . . . ?* I also want to say, but I don't.

---

136 Ibid., 103.
137 Ibid, 103.
138 Ibid., 280.
139 Ibid., 281.

> "So is that the meaning?" he asks, nodding at the window.
>
> A corpse is lying there, I remember.
>
> "Divine meaning," Monk repeats quietly after me. "You talk a lot about things you aren't capable of sensing."
>
> Several hours later I go to bed in the "bedchamber." I wander and struggle in my sleep, as if I'm walking among blown-down trees.
>
> I dream words. These, it seems: *God holds the earth the way a thirsty child holds a cup of milk—with tenderness, with agitation . . . But he could drop it . . .*
>
> I wake up.
>
> "He could drop it," I say clearly.
>
> "Wha . . ?" someone asks angrily.
>
> "He could drop it," I answer.[140]

The disagreement, and Egor's subsequent dream, highlights the differences between Monk's and Egor's worldviews and beliefs. Both of them are believers, although in different ways: Monk has been formally educated in the Orthodox tradition and has a strict, rule-based concept of religion and faith. Egor, although he does not say so explicitly, must also be familiar with Christianity and religious texts, as in his arguments with Monk he is able to quote fragments of Scripture. He is also inclined to ponder questions of religion, morality, and faith in a way that he shares only with Monk: Egor is the only member of the squad who discusses these things with him.

Although Egor dislikes Monk and disagrees with most of his positions, he takes him seriously, unlike the other soldiers, who only make fun of him. More than that, Monk's arguments push him to consider and develop his beliefs, pulling him out of his preoccupations with food, alcohol, sex, and terror of death, and forcing him to attempt to understand his life and give it meaning. For the most part Egor does not question the morality of what he is doing: he is afraid of being killed, but he does not question the point or morality of war as such. After their first mission he is struck by the fact that they have ended eight human lives, but that does not prevent him from going out on the next mission—his main concern is always his own life, and possibly those of his immediate comrades, but death and war as abstract concepts do not, for the most part, trouble him.

However, at this moment, when a number of his comrades have been killed, and he himself has killed for the first time, he seeks to create some kind of

140 Ibid., 295.

meaning out of what is happening. Just as in his first debate with Monk, when he claims that "my anger is not without a cause," here in this second debate he believes that their deaths are not meaningless, and that what is happening must be something more than just pointless, random violence. And it must be something more precisely because they themselves will make it so.

That is the fundamental disagreement between Monk and Egor: Monk believes that everything is in God's hands, and humans must simply heed and obey. Resistance, so to speak, is futile: what will be, will be. Egor strenuously disagrees with that position, something he expresses during their first argument.

He expresses it again, more abstractly, in this second argument, when he says that humans must create meaning for their deaths themselves, thereby taking control and responsibility for their lives. This could be seen as just another side of Egor's tendency towards possessive, controlling behavior, but it also gives a hint of personal growth that Egor could, possibly, experience at the end of the novel. As he digs through his past like he dug through the dumpster to try to find Dasha's journal, he turns up the underlying pathologies of his personality. At the time he thought they were out of his control, just as, in the war zone he believes that his death is out of his control, but this conversation with Monk suggests that, perhaps, he could exert some level of control over both his life and his death, or at least give it some kind of meaning, instead of bouncing from situation to situation, always dependent on others for his physical and mental well-being. And it is Monk, the person he likes and respects least in the platoon, who pushes him towards this understanding.

Monk's statement that "You talk a lot about things you're not capable of sensing," is, like Egor's own attempts at foreseeing, mistaken: Egor proves that he *is* capable of sensing, even if not understanding, the divine or supernatural side of things, not only with his arguments, but with his dream. Like all his dreams, it is prophetic, although not in a direct fashion. The image of God as holding the world like a thirsty child holds a cup of milk—with love, but also clumsily—emphasizes Egor's just-stated believe that it is up to humans to take care of themselves: Egor's God is not an all-loving, all-seeing father, but a somewhat careless, distant father, like Egor's own father, who took care of him as best he could when he wasn't drinking, but then abandoned him, even if unintentionally, by his death. And Egor's own little world is about to be "dropped": no one will come to rescue the soldiers besieged in the school, and many of them will be killed and the rest will have to abandon their position and flee through the ravine.[141]

The descent into the ravine is not only a descent into the underworld and the land of the dead ("So many corpses!"[142] Egor thinks as he lands in the water after jumping out the window), but also a rebirth for Egor, which is suggested by multiple motifs and images.

When he is scrambling through the water in the ravine, he is "like a crippled mammal that has decided to become a fish"[143] and becomes a blind, unhuman creature flopping in the water—like an ancient fish, but also like a fetus. He is forcibly yanked out of the water by Monk, and vomits and sobs uncontrollably, covered in water and saliva—like a newborn infant.

His mind then jumps to memories of his last day with Dasha, when he walks down the sidewalk with all the new mothers taking their babies out for an airing, and discovers that the female collie who lives near Dasha's apartment has given birth and is now caring for three newborn puppies. Egor congratulates the male collie, who is beside himself with excitement, admires the puppies, and goes up to Dasha's apartment, only to discover that she is not there. Whether this is a temporary or permanent absence is not indicated and Egor himself may not know: two days later he arrives in Mozdok. In any case, it is a sign of a break in their relationship, since Dasha was not waiting for him as she always had before, and there is never any suggestion that they correspond or communicate in any way while he is in Chechnya.

The juxtaposition of these two events in the text suggests a birth for Egor, in which he is cast out by his "mother"—Dasha—into the harsh world of war, then pushed out again from the school into the flooded ravine, and then yanked out of the ravine into a state of life, but helpless life: he is unable to undo his fly and wets himself, and loses the power of speech and even rational thought, even as he loses his assault vest and his boots, leaving him half-naked, further stripping him of the signs and status of a self-sufficient adult human.

He only returns to his status as an adult human when he gets into a fight to the death with an enemy soldier, whom he kills with his bare hands, while Monk

141 The religious theme makes frequent appearances throughout Prilepin's works, and seems to be of growing important both in his writing—for example, with the publication of *The Monastery*—and in his personal life. On a YouTube video from July 10, 2017 ("Boets Kuban' i Zakhar Prilepin o vazhnosti very") he can be seen discussing the importance of faith for people participating in a war, suggesting that his own views have evolved since the creation of Egor, but that the basic idea is still the same: soldiers need some kind of faith in order to justify and strengthen their actions.

142 Prilepin, *Patologii*, 313.

143 Ibid., 313.

kills the second enemy soldier with a knife. Both men were originally repulsed by the idea of killing, Monk explicitly and for moral/religious reasons, and Egor implicitly, because he is horrified by the thought of death. But in this life-and-death situation, they both instinctively kill their attackers, an action that warms them up and quite literally returns them to life, as well as allowing Egor to dress himself again. This gives them the strength to keep walking, and they soon find a number of their surviving comrades who had also made it out of the school and have gathered together on a sort of "island" in the flooded ravine.

The next morning the surviving soldiers are picked up by the relief forces that have finally arrived and driven the attackers out of the school by shelling it from tanks. As he is walking down the road back towards the school, Egor is touched on the face by a swallow flying by, something he takes as a sign that there will be peace, but that also hints, possibly, at the return of Dasha into his life, since when they were lying together in bed, her hair would touch him like the wing of a swallow.

Later, as he showers at HQ, he washes off the dirt of the ravine and, he thinks, cleans the skin of his friend Sania and the man he killed out from under his fingernails, before dressing in new, clean clothing and returning to the school, where the bodies of his comrades as well as his enemies have already been cleared away. He is thus cleansed of his sins and failures, and remade as a "new man," one who has survived this terrible ordeal and been baptized and reborn.

In the final scene in the book both the circularity of the plot, and the possibility of an escape for Egor from his hopeless circling and perhaps fix the problems and internal flaws that have been tormenting him, are signified by the flight home from Mozdok. When the soldiers board their plane, a "fearful, dirty little dog"[144] follows them on board, and refuses to be shooed away, eventually settling down next to Egor. Khasan, the other squad leader in the platoon, gets out a pack of cards, the same cards that he and Egor used on the flight over to win money off of everyone, only now damaged by water. As the plane takes off, Egor finds himself having a series of thoughts/quasi-hallucinations:

> I thought sluggishly that there was some kind of meaning in this: cards . . . we played with them . . . with these cards . . . as we were flying here . . . But there wasn't any kind of meaning in this at all.
>
> I looked at the ceiling of the plane taking off into the sky and with a weak-willed hand stroked the little dog, who was still afraid of us. Her sides, skinny and dirty, were trembling.

---

144 Ibid., 350.

> *For we know that the whole creation groaneth and travaileth in pain together until now*—this phrase, huge as a cloud, floated out into my head.
>
> It seemed to me that I was crying and hugging the dog. That I was whispering: "My little puppy-dog, forgive me, my little puppy-dog . . . may everyone forgive me . . . and you too, my little puppy-dog . . ."
>
> That what it seemed like to me. But I wasn't crying; instead I was looking with dry eyes up at the ceiling. I was not asking anyone forgiveness for anything.[145]

In this final passage, as in the rest of the book, Egor seems to be contemplating the possibility of being an "unrecognized warrior," in Eichler's classification, as well as being seen as an "excessive warrior." He is perhaps also flirting with the two different narratives about veterans of the Global War on Terror as defined by Cage: that of the veteran-hero and the veteran-victim. But he rejects these classifications, insisting instead on the righteousness of his own actions and his autonomy from the judgment of others. Having passed through Hell and come out the other side, Egor seems to consider himself above judgment. Instead, he once again channels Scripture, with Romans 8:22 appearing "huge as a cloud" in his head.

In this final passage Egor also recognizes the circularity of the situation: he and Khasan were playing cards as they flew into Mozdok, and now Khasan wants to play with these same cards as they fly out. Always on the hunt for signs and greater meaning, Egor immediately thinks that there must be some kind of meaning in this, but then promptly rejects the idea. The reader, though, may be less quick to reject the possibility.

The cards, however, are less significant than the plane itself. In the opening scene of the Grozny storyline, Egor and the other soldiers descend through the sky to Mozdok. They are, in essence, carried in the womb of this machine out of the sky (heaven) to the war zone (hell), where they are "birthed" as they disembark from the plane. Now, at the end of the novel and the Grozny storyline, they are loaded back into the "womb" of the plane and carried back up into the sky, a sky at which they had looked "for so long and so attentively, like they, probably, never had before in their lives. Except maybe in childhood . . ."[146]

---

145 Ibid., 332.
146 Ibid., 331-2.

This return to the sky is both an escape from the Hellish underworld of Chechnya and Grozny, and a return to childhood, even infancy or their unborn state. The surviving soldiers who are loaded back into the plane and sent home experience both a second death—they are sent up into the sky, like the "angels" that Egor thought they might be, in the moment before he sees the enemy forces invading the school—and a second birth, as they return to their flying, metallic "womb" and carried up into the sky of their childhood.

The female dog that sneaks onto the plane with them strengthens the overall "rebirth" motif, and in particular Egor's return to childhood. Like his childhood companion Daisy, the unnamed female dog is afraid of him, but nonetheless she does not leave him—in fact, she stays by his side despite her fear of him and the other soldiers, hinting at the hope that perhaps this time, Egor will not be rejected and abandoned by the women in his life.

His perception that he is crying and begging her forgiveness suggests that, for the first time, he has fully grasped his own part and his guilt in everything that has happened. The recognition is entirely internal—the final lines of the novel, describing his external state, contradict his internal perceptions—but it is there even so.

Whether or not Egor will act on it, or whether he will continue to be the two-faced personality he has been since the beginning of the novel and which he still is here in its concluding lines, where he thinks and feels one thing, and presents something entirely different to the outside world, is up in the air. Does the afterword that begins the novel promise that he will become a different, more consistent, honest, and connected person, one who is capable of loving and properly caring for another living being, or does it tell us that he is still split between his inner and outer worlds? And in that case, what does the rebirth there herald? Is Egor ever to escape this Buddhist-like *samsara*, the suffering-filled wheel of death and rebirth, and achieve nirvana or a Christian ascent into Heaven, or is he trapped for several more cycles of death and reincarnation? The novel leaves that open to interpretation.

Egor's inadvertent quotation of Romans 8:22 in the final internal monologue may, though, be a sign of hope. The exact verse that he quotes implies mutual suffering, something that Egor struggled to believe in, as he convinced himself that neither Dasha nor his platoon mates could understand what he himself was going through, both in his torments of jealousy and his terror of death. This is in keeping with the experience of many sufferers of PTSD, especially combat veterans, who are "isolated not only by the images of horror that [they have] witnessed and perpetrated but also by [their] special status as an initiate in the cult of war."[147] This "special status," and therefore isolation of the veteran from the rest of society, can also be strengthened by the current popular conceptions of veterans in recent wars in both Russia and the West as outlined by Eichler and Cage.

But Romans 8:22 states that everyone, "the whole Creation," suffers together (совокупно in the original Russian text of *Pathologies*), and that, consequently, Egor's individual suffering does not cut him off from those around him, as he feels it does, but unites him with them: suffering is something they all share, rather than something that separates them. Although Egor does not consciously think this, there is a hint, just as there have been hints all throughout the text of future events, that he *could* come to this understanding, just as he came to the understanding that he was incapable of relating to women as separate, sentient beings, and thus, perhaps, learning to see them as the separate, sentient beings that they are.

Romans 8:22 also implies the theme of (re)birth that is so significant for the novel, something that is suggested in the Russian text and the King James version I have used in the English translation, but is more explicit both in the original Greek[148] and in the more modern English versions. The travail that all of creation is experiencing is the travail of childbirth, as the world struggles to be reborn "from the bondage of corruption into the glorious liberty of the Children of God"[149] and shed its sinful, carnal form for its spiritual form.

Earlier, when arguing with Monk, Egor declared that humans may receive meaning for their lives from God at birth, but they have to give meanings to their deaths themselves. Romans 8 says the meaning of suffering and death is to be united with Christ, something that humans can hope for without necessarily seeing the physical proof of it, "for what a man seeth, why doth he yet hope for?"[150] By thinking of this section of Romans, Egor seems to be giving himself an answer to some of the questions that have been tormenting him: he is *not* alone, even in his suffering; the deaths of his comrades *do* have meaning; he *is* right to look to the unseen as well as the seen, even as he is immured in his own, extremely carnal, body; and most importantly of all, he *can* and *should* hope for the future, even if the future does not seem hopeful right now.

Pathologies is not an uplifting novel, and, despite the commonly accepted critical opinion that Prilepin produces works with positive, macho protagonists

---

147 Herman, *Trauma and Recovery*, 66.
148 My sincere thanks to Rawley Grau for enlightening me on this point.
149 Rom 8:21, KJV.
150 Ibid.

and heroic storylines, it is a not very heroic storyline about a not particularly positive or heroic hero. Egor's occasional flashes of physical bravery are easy to overlook amidst all his internal terrors and weaknesses, which occupy the bulk of his ruminations and internal monologues. Although he does not desert or let down his comrades, he participates in a number of heinous actions, including attacking unarmed women and executing prisoners without trial. In the final battle, his platoon is driven out of the school by superior enemy forces, and they end up leaving Grozny entirely shortly afterwards; if that really was part of the third Battle of Grozny in 1996, then all the Russian forces soon followed suit.

Egor is thus not a particularly shining example of the square-jawed (although he probably does have a square jaw to go along with his apparently impressively muscled physique) hero of Soviet war films, who either triumphs through sheer force of (good) will, or sacrifices himself willingly for the good of the cause. Egor does not seem to believe in his cause very much, even if he says that his anger is not without a cause, and he certainly isn't interested in sacrificing himself, willingly or otherwise. Like the other works surveyed here, the war story in *Pathologies* is dirtied and crumpled by its subject matter, and the war hero is splintered and torn apart by his experiences. In *Pathologies,* however, the war also has, if not a redeeming feature, then the opportunity for the hero to face and recognize his inner demons, and attempt to stitch himself up back together afterwards.

Pathologies may be, therefore, the most hopeful of the works discussed here, even as it is also in some ways the most disturbing. Egor's evolution as a hero is in the opposite direction from that of the other protagonists in these works: rather than only being pulled apart by the widening gyre of war, he is remade by it, with the promise of redemption and rebirth upon his return to civilian life. Egor's fundamental traumas, that of losing his family and the woman he loves, is in some ways healed by his participation in war and the confrontation with his fragmented, traumatic memories that combat forces upon him. It is tempting, and possibly even in part correct, to see this as an early example of the aggressive, militaristic Russian nationalism Prilepin now expresses.

One of the benefits of fiction, however, is its complexity and unwillingness to be easily categorized. *Pathologies* is a psychological, rather than political, work, even if the psychology depicted in it can also be enlightening in the political sphere. Either way, it can give the reader cause for hope. While earlier I called Egor a static personality, he does in fact experience change and growth. He spends most of the book unable to find any kind of connection with those around him, and engaging in pathological patterns of clinging and rejection with the two most important females in his life, Daisy and Dasha. At the end, though, he finds himself meditating on the interconnection of all things. Despite the somewhat ominous claim that "I was not asking anyone forgiveness for anything" that ends the novel, Egor shows the possibility of both contrition and connection in his rescue of the stray dog in the final scene. By bearing witness to and telling the story of his earlier traumas, Egor does achieve catharsis, at least in his own mind. The other works featured here end with motifs of destruction, defeat, and the impossibility of telling the whole truth. *Pathologies,* though, ends with the promise of (re)birth, not just for the protagonist but for the whole of creation.

Conclusion

For all four of the writers surveyed here, the wars in Chechnya were Hell. Their perception and treatment of it was very different, however. For Politkovskaya, the Chechen Wars were the epitome, culmination, apogee, and defining symptom of the sickness of the Soviet and post-Soviet system, which treated its citizens as disposable objects, to be exploited for gain and then tossed away. For Eldin, war was Hell—but it was also a cleansing hellfire, which stripped away his civilized pretenses and allowed him to come into contact with the divine. For Prilepin, war was Hell, but it was also an opportunity to experience death, life, and (re)birth. For Babchenko, war was perhaps the most Hellish of all, as his autobiographical protagonist is dragged down into it and can never fully escape, becoming instead one of its gatekeepers.

This ambiguous relationship with war, particularly these especially unpleasant wars, and the extreme trauma they inflicted on everyone who experienced them, is reflected not just in the subject matter of the literature about them, but in its form. None of the authors featured here, all of whom were chosen as being important and representative of the writing about the Chechen Wars, have produced coherent, straightforward narratives. Instead, their writing is marked by its fragmentariness, as they struggle to pull together their impressions into something that the reader can understand, when the main thing they want the reader to understand is just how impossible it is to understand the Hellish madness that is the prime hallmark of war, especially these wars.

Each author has depicted the fragmentation caused by the trauma of war in a different way. Politkovskaya's works are collections of articles and essays, all featuring different people and differing viewpoints. The Russia she depicts is a nation that is splintering apart into apathy, corruption, and violent nationalism. Rather than tell a single coherent story, she tells the story of this splintering through brief slice-of-life vignettes from the different actors involved. This polyphony, I argue, represents the trauma of the nation as a whole, as she attempts to tell the story of post-Soviet Russia and the Chechen Wars by presenting opposing sides and unwelcome truths, even as she binds the whole thing together with her own commitment to the truth as she sees it and her rock-hard conviction in the righteousness of her cause. She also counters the rights-based masculine ethics of the current Russian regime and of modern democratic and semi-democratic nations with a feminine ethics of care, while basing much of her own moral authority on her status as a woman and a mother. Gender and specifically femininity is thus central to her writing and her overall stance, even though she is writing on the most masculine of all topics, war. Part of the Hellishness of the wars and of current Russian society, in her formulation, is that it criminalizes the maternal instinct and fails to provide for its sons as a good Motherland should.

Eldin's experiences of the wars are marked by the brain damage and severe psychological trauma he sustained while being tortured by Russian forces. This is represented in the text through nonlinear, stream-of-consciousness passages, which often jump from the first person singular to the second person or the first person plural. This literal disassociation from himself is, he explicitly acknowledges, his way of dealing with these traumatic memories, allowing him to tell his story without reliving it directly. At the same time, he shows his own personal experience as being representative of Chechnya's national experience, paralleling his own suffering and eventual personal victory with that of the moral victory he sees Chechnya as having won. Although his work is much less focused on gender than Politkovskaya, he does depict Chechnya as both feminine (a sacrifice to a dragon) and masculine (Christ and St. George), and emphasizes positive masculine (the honorable warrior) and feminine (the brave and pure woman supporting her warrior) roles as examples of Chechen spirit. Of the works featured here, his memoir is perhaps the most consciously aware of the effects of his personal trauma on his memory and psyche, while also being more than just one person's experience of PTSD. Instead, he turns his initial individual trauma and eventual triumph into a story of national trauma and triumph. Like Politkovskaya, his narrative is the narrative of an entire nation, one that was offered up by the world as a sacrifice to the dragon of Russia's long-time colonial ambitions and current post-Soviet anxieties.

Babchenko's book is also both personal and collective, although in his case the collective is that of combat veterans, not the nation as a whole. He tells the story of One Soldier's War, which he turns into Every Soldier's War, through short narratives that jump back and forth in time and leave out as much as they include. Rather than writing yet another "kill memoir," Babchenko has given us a kind of "anti-kill memoir," where combat and killing are given little weight, while the protagonist's psychic experiences are given center stage, and the person who is killed in the story is, metaphorically at least, himself. At the same time, even as he shows himself and his fellow veterans as trapped in Hell and cut off from the world of the living by their trauma, he also shows them as being connected to each other and to countless generations of other soldiers and trauma victims through the mythic cycles they are all enacting. Although Babchenko shows no conscious intent to play with or subvert gender roles, the mythic cycles he depicts are often feminine in nature, with a strong presence of the myth of Persephone in section two of the book. It is only women, however, who can actually live out the entirety of the Persephone and Demeter story in Babchenko's formulation; men are unable to pull themselves out of the underworld and back into the land of the living. *One Soldier's War*, with its desperate desire to share the story of the wars and its closing insistence on the impossibility of telling their whole truth, may be the clearest example of the oscillation between clinging and isolation, and the sense of special apartness, that Herman describes as typical of trauma victims, particularly combatants.

Finally, Prilepin's semi-autobiographical fictional protagonist Egor Tashevsky also undergoes a descent into the Hell of war. In his case, however, this does not tear him apart into fragments as it does for Eldin and Babchenko, but pushes him into rebirth and the potential for wholeness. Tashevsky displays many of the characteristics of trauma and of the different popular conceptions of veterans of the current Global War on Terror, whether Russian or Western, but he refuses to accept others' labels of him. And while war was Hellish for him, the trauma it inflicts on him is also a reflection of his primal trauma of the dissolution of his family and rejection by the females, canine and human, whom he loves. Deeply sexual, and yet cut off from others and especially females and the generative forces of femininity, Egor struggles with gender and sex throughout the book. His near-death and rebirth in the deadly, life-giving, feminine waters of the river and the ravine at the beginning and end of the book, though, followed by his rescue of the stray female dog in the final scene, signal some kind of acceptance of and by femaleness, suggesting the possibility of reconciliation and healing. By descending into the Hell of war and the underworld of his own memories, Tashevsky is eventually able to reconstruct himself as a whole individual, thus making *Pathologies* perhaps the most disturbing and yet hopeful of the works featured here.

For all of these authors, war was not just a gateway to Hell, but the portal to Truth, even if their truths were all different. Politkovskaya and Eldin both wanted to tell an objective truth: Eldin the truth of the Chechen side of the war, and Politkovskaya the truth of all sides. Eldin also describes coming into contact, through his suffering, with a higher truth, a spiritual truth that anyone, presumably, can access under the right circumstances. Prilepin and Babchenko's goals were different, with both of them in their own ways setting out to tell the truth of their experiences in the war. Theirs is an internal truth, rather than the external truth of Politkovskaya and Eldin, although their internal truths are by necessity different. For Babchenko's autobiographical protagonist, the truth is what he, personally, experienced, on both an extremely physical level—the mud, the hunger, the cold—and on an emotional level, as his protagonist struggles to keep his equilibrium amidst alternating states of terror and exhilaration. For Prilepin's fictional Egor, the truth is something that must be pulled together from different threads of untruths and old memories, and the war is the catalyst that allows him to do that.

For all of these writers, whatever their truths might have been, the truth was something they had an intense compulsion to share with others, baring their souls in a very public manner and risking social ostracism and political backlash, and even, in the case of Politkovskaya, paying for it with her life. This intense need to share the truth, as both a form of bearing witness and a way of achieving catharsis, unites all these works as being the "literature of trauma." Not all of the truths these authors have chosen to share are palatable, but the fact that they were willing to risk so much to share them argues that we should pay close attention.

And what do these works herald for the future? Can we use them, like Prilepin's Egor, as crystal balls, trying to divine what will be for Russia and the rest of the world within its sphere of influence? Divination is a risky business, but perhaps we can give it a shot, or at least draw a few useful conclusions.

First of all, Russia itself seems deeply fragmented and divided. This is not surprising in a huge, multiethnic country that has been through so many traumatic events in the past three decades, but it does the rest of us well to remember that "Russia" is not a monolithic entity, and neither are "the Russians." All the authors featured here are on one level "Russian," in that they were all citizens of the Russian Federation and spoke Russian, and on another, not wholly Russian. Eldin is Chechen and Politkovskaya, Prilepin, and Babchenko all have at least some Ukrainian roots, something that became increasingly important as the situation in the Donbass dragged on and Prilepin and Babchenko very publicly took opposite positions on it, both of them alluding to their Ukrainian heritage as they did so. The multiethnicity of so many of Russia's citizens, and the shared heritage of so many Russians and Ukrainians, could serve as a cause for hope for some kind of a mutually agreeable settlement in Eastern Ukraine, and for greater ethnic tolerance in Russia in general, but so far the opposite is the case. Indeed, the conflict in the Donbass has, at the time of writing, descended into full-scale war following Russia's invasion of Ukraine in February 2022. As part of this tragedy, nationalism has been separating Russians from Ukrainians, and Ukrainians from Russians, serving as a rallying cry for conflict rather than as a call for cooperation. As I suggest in the chapter on Prilepin, there may be some slight cause for hope for a change in the attitudes of the uber-nationalistic, at least on the Russian side—but as of yet, that hope is very faint.

Second of all, one can conceptualize the collective subconscious of Russia as deeply traumatized. As Herman notes, all of Eastern Europe is experiencing a kind of communal, national PTSD, since:

> In the aftermath of systematic political violence, entire communities can display symptoms of PTSD, trapped in alternating cycles of numbing and intrusion, silence and reenactment. [. . .] Like traumatized individuals, traumatized countries need to remember, grieve, and atone for their wrongs in order to avoid reliving them.[151]

This may the most important thing for outside observers to understand: that Russia as a country is much like the individual Russian veterans who appear so tough on the outside, but who are constantly on the edge of an internal implosion, refighting the war over and over again inside their own heads, always on edge, always on the lookout for danger. This should not be taken as simple weakness, however: such people are in fact in many cases quite ready to make more war under the right circumstances (and how often the right circumstances seem to crop up!), since war is what they know, war is where they feel at home, war is where they feel safest and freest. Russia is full of such people, and they vote, engage in political demonstrations, and hold political office. This is not

151 Herman, *Trauma and Recovery*, 242.

to point the finger at veterans in particular: those who were never within a thousand kilometers of any of the many front lines that have run through the former USSR within living memory are still affected by the collective trauma of World War II, the collapse of the Soviet Union, the civil war in Tajikistan, the Chechen Wars, and the current conflicts in Nagorno-Karabakh and Ukraine. These books on the Chechen Wars are as much emblematic of this overall trauma as they are about the specific trauma of these small, if dirty and Hellish, wars, and the wars and their aftermath can be seen as a microcosm of the entire post-Soviet experience. One could argue that all of Russia is suffering from a shared PTSD, and (re)acts accordingly to threats and encroachments on her personal space—as we are currently seeing played out in Ukraine.

At the same time, all the authors provide faint glimmers of hope. All of them suggest the possibility of empathy for others and a kinder, more connected society, even as they reject it as a current reality. Politkovskaya describes numerous examples of person-to-person connections that provide help for those in need, and argues forcefully for a shared sense of values and an emphasis on the personal and human over the impersonal and inhumane. Eldin depicts both a connection with the divine, and a shared code of the warrior that enables fighters on opposing sides to understand and even empathize with each other. Babchenko struggles to connect with civilians and even other soldiers, but ultimately shows himself and everyone else touched by the war as part of the same mythic cycles, finally achieving a moment of transcendent union as he stands on the same runway where so many other soldiers have stood before. Prilepin's semi-autobiographical protagonist Egor consistently denies his connection to others, while also discovering himself through combat and, in the end, connecting with others through shared suffering and travail, as expressed in Romans 8:22. All of these works are as fragmented in form as the individual and national psyches they represent. But they all also depict a yearning for wholeness, and potential paths towards achieving it. While each path is different, they all suggest that, ultimately, breaking through the isolation and oscillating dance of outreach and withdrawal that marks trauma and its aftermath is possible, if only those on both sides of the divide can summon up the courage to do so.

So, if we wish to engage in this thought-exercise and see these individual works as representative of the post-Soviet experience as a whole, what does that mean? How can those on the outside best relate to individuals and nations in this situation? Especially when that nation is Russia? Nation-wide interventions and forced therapy, even if they were not unacceptable attacks on another person's and another nation's sovereignty, which some would certainly consider them to be, are not possible in the case of Russia, a nuclear superpower. Even in the case of smaller, less militarily aggressive nations, such actions do not have a great history of success. Understanding may be the only option left. It is my sincere belief and my sincere hope that literature, which is the closest one can come to sharing thoughts directly with another person and achieving immediate, mind-to-mind empathy, is one of our best tools for achieving this. We cannot prevent what has already happened in Chechnya. But perhaps there are those who, if they can summon up the wisdom and the compassion, can prevent similar tragedies in the future. The knowledge is there if we would be willing to heed it.

Bibliography

Ackerman, Elliot. "My Veteran Problem." *New York Times,* February 12, 2021. https://www.nytimes.com/2021/02/12/opinion/veterans-Capitol-Cherry-film.html.

Akbar, Arifa. "The Sky Wept Fire: My Life as a Chechen Freedom Fighter by Mikail Eldin, trans. Anna Gunin—Book Review." *New Yorker,* December 12, 2013. http://www.independent.co.uk/arts-entertainment/books/reviews/the-sky-wept-fire-my-life-as-a-chechen-freedom-fighter-by-mikail-eldin-trans-by-anna-gunin-book-8998790.html.

Allison, Juliann Emmons. "Peace Among Friends: A Feministic Interpretation of the 'Democratic Peace.'" *Peace & Change* 26, no. 2 (April 2001): 204-22.

Babchenko, Arkadii. "Alkhan-Iurt." https://www.litmir.me/br/?b=2336&p=1. Accessed June 28, 2017.

———. Blog Arkadii Babchenko. *Ekho Moskvy,* accessed June 20, 2017. http://echo.msk.ru/blog/ababchenko/. *Ekho Moskvy* has been shut down.

———. "Bolotnaia. 5 let." *Ekho Moskvy,* May 7, 2017. http://echo.msk.ru/blog/ababchenko/1976598-echo/. *Ekho Moskvy* has been shut down.

———. "Desiat' serii o voine." *Zhurnal'nyi zal.* Accessed June 2017. https://magazines.gorky.media/october/2001/12/desyat-serij-o-vojne.html. Accessed February 11, 2021. Originally published in *Oktiabr',* no. 12, 2001.

———. Kasparov.ru. Blog posts by Arkadii Babchenko. http://www.kasparov.ru/author.php?id=5118F91FEC073 Accessed June 20, 2017.

———. LiveJournal site. http://starshinazapasa.livejournal.com/. Accessed June 20, 2017.

——— [Arkady Babchenko]. *One Soldier's War*. Translated by Nick Allen. New York: Grove Press, 2007.

———. "Rezhim Putina proderzhitsia dolgo, no postepenno stanet zagnivat'" [interview]. KUB prm.global, July 12, 2017. YouTube Video, 56:31. https://www.youtube.com/watch?v=GYCe-cx3ShE.

——— [Arkady Babchenko]. "The 'Unpatriotic' Post on Facebook that Meant I Finally Had to Flee Russia." *Guardian*, February 24, 2017. https://www.theguardian.com/world/2017/feb/24/unpatriotic-post-facebook-finally-flee-russia. Accessed June 20, 2017.

———. "Voina ot pervogo litsa. Interv'iu v 'Trude.'" LiveJournal post, May 11, 2012. http://starshinazapasa.livejournal.com/396147.html. Accessed June 26, 2017.

Bering, Henrik. "Fightin' and Writing." *Policy Review* 163 (October/November 2010): 71-84.

Bobrova, Svetlana. "Dar'ia Dontsova nazvana pisatelem goda." *Life.ru*, December 26, 2016. https://life.ru/t/%D0%BA%D1%83%D0%BB%D1%8C%D1%82%D1%83%D1%80%D0%B0/952414/daria_dontsova_nazvana_pisatieliem_ghoda. Accessed July 5, 2017.

Bodrov, Sergei. *Sviaznoi*. N.p: Amphora, 2007. https://www.e-reading.club/chapter.php/7067/154/Bodrov_-_Svyaznoii.html. Accessed August 12, 2017.

Braithwaite, Rodric. "Dedovshchina: Bullying in the Russian Army." *Open Democracy*, March 9, 2010. https://www.opendemocracy.net/od-russia/rodric-braithwaite/dedovshchina-bullying-in-russian-army. Accessed June 24, 2017.

Buchanan, David A. *Going Scapegoat: Post-9/11 War Literature, Language and Culture*. Jefferson, North Carolina: McFarland & Company, 2016.

Bulkina, Irina. "Proza 'nulevykh.'" *Znamia: Literaturno-Khudozhestvennyi i Obshchestvenno-Politicheskii Zhurnal* 9 (2010): 202-8.

Bushkovskii, Aleksandr. "Izuchaia *Patologii*: Nelepitsy i strannosti v rasskazakh o voine." *Voprosy literatury*, no. 2 (2011): 195-209.

Cage, Caleb S. *War Narratives: Shaping Beliefs, Blurring Truths in the Middle East*. College Station, TX: Texas A&M University Press, 2019. E-book.

Campbell, Charlie. "Czech Republic Forced to Remind the Internet that Chechnya Is in Different Country After Boston Bombing." *Time,* April 23, 2013. http://newsfeed.time.com/2013/04/23/czech-republic-forced-to-remind-the-internet-that-chechnya-is-a-different-country-after-boston-bombing/.

Campbell, James. "Combat Gnosticism: The Ideology of First World War Poetry Criticism." *New Literary History* 30, no. 1 (1999): 203-15.

Carriger, Gail. *The Heroine's Journey: For Writers, Readers, and Fans of Pop Culture.* N.p: Gail Carriger LLC, 2020. E-book.

Chelysheva, Oksana. "Anna Politkovskaya. One Voice Amid Silence." *Problems of Post-Communism* 54, no. 5 (September/October 2007): 40–46.

Clothier, Meg. "No Quiet on the Chechen Front." *Guardian,* November 21, 2007. https://www.theguardian.com/books/2007/nov/21/biography.

Coughlin, Con. "Wretched Russian Conscripts." *Telegraph,* November 15, 2007. http://www.telegraph.co.uk/culture/books/non_fictionreviews/3669261/Wretched-Russian-conscripts.html.

Dikarev, Pyotr and Mikhail Men'shikh, dir. *Gailer.* Russia: OOO "Prodiuserskii tsentr '1 fevralia,'" 2017.

Doucette, Fred. "In Any Language and In Any Place, War Is Hell." *Globe and Mail,* March 15, 2008. https://www.theglobeandmail.com/arts/books-and-media/in-any-language-and-in-any-place-war-is-hell/article1201584/.

Earle, Harriet E. H. *Comics, Trauma, and the New Art of War.* Jackson, Mississippi: University Press of Mississippi. 2017. E-book.

"Eduard Limonov iskliuchil Zakhara Prilepina iz partii 'Drugaia Rossiia.'" *Radio Svoboda,* 29 December, 2018. https://www.svoboda.org/a/29682822.html.

Eichler, Maya. *Militarizing Men: Gender, Conscription, and War in Post-Soviet Russia.* Stanford: Stanford University Press. 2012. E-book.

Eldin, Mikail. "Ia real'no khotel umeret'" [interview]. *NEP Prague,* January 29, 2021. YouTube video, 40:59. https://youtu.be/D2bLQCws60g.

———. "Russkie ne dolzhny molchat'" [interview]. *NEP Prague,* January 30, 2021. YouTube video, 4:42. https://youtu.be/-88FM2DjwWw.

———. "The Second Night is Ending" *Granta.* https://granta.com/the-second-night-is-ending/. Accessed June 5, 2017.

———. *The Sky Wept Fire: My Life as a Chechen Freedom Fighter.* Translated by Anna Gunin. London: Portobello Books, 2013.

Evangelista, Matthew. *The Chechen Wars: Will Russia Go the Way of the Soviet Union?* Washington, DC: Brookings Institute Press, 2002.

Gall, Carlotta and Thomas de Waal. *Chechnya: Calamity in the Caucasus.* New York: New York University Press, 1998.

Glanville, Jo. "Books of the Year 2007." *New Stateman,* November 22, 2007. http://www.newstatesman.com/books/2007/11/faber-novel-review-press.

Glikman, Kirill. "Novyi, talantlivyi, no . . . Zakhar Prilepin." *Voprosy literatury,* no. 2 (2011): 184-94.

Goldovskaya, Marina. *A Bitter Taste of Freedom* (*Gor'kii vkus svobody*). Russia/Sweden/USA: GoldFilms, 2011.

Gould, Rebecca. *Writers and Rebels: The Literature of Insurgency in the Caucasus.* New Haven: Yale University Press, 2016.

Heberle, Mark A. *A Trauma Artist: Tim O'Brien and the Fiction of Vietnam.* Iowa City: University of Iowa Press. 2001. E-book.

Herman, Judith, M. D. *Trauma and Recovery: The Aftermath of Violence—From Domestic Abuse to Political Terror.* New York: Basic Books, 2015. E-book.

Holy Bible, King James Version.

Human Rights Watch. "Russia. New Anti-Gay Crackdown in Chechnya." May 8, 2019. https://www.hrw.org/news/2019/05/08/russia-new-anti-gay-crackdown-chechnya.

———. "Russia: The Wrongs of Passage." https://www.hrw.org/reports/2004/russia1004/6.htm. Accessed June 24, 2017.

Igrunova, Natal'ia. "Zakhar Prilepin: 'Ia liubliu mir, gde "Iliada" i "Odisseia."'" *Druzhba narodov* 3 (March 2010): 198-206.

Izmailov, Viacheslav. "V Genshtabe strashnaia dedovshchina." *Novaya gazeta,* July 10, 2006. http://2006.novayagazeta.ru/nomer/2006/51n/n51n-s11.shtml.

Kamalov, Lenar, dir. *Dezhurstvo.* 2018. YouTube video, 8:30. https://www.youtube.com/watch?v=7L2gR-wQ--E.

Katzarova, Mariana. "Ten Years with Politkovskaya. Lessons in Truth, Courage and Humanity." *Problems of Post-Communism* 54, no. 5 (September/October 2007): 47–51.

Kolesnikov, Andrei. "Vladimir Putin and Angela Merkel Work Together." *Kommersantъ,* October 11, 2006. https://web.archive.org/web/20070930184736/http://www.kommersant.com/p712110/r_527/Putin_visit_Germany/.

Kozlova, Ekaterina. "O literaturnoi storone boevoi medali." *NG Ex Libris*, October 23, 2003. http://www.ng.ru/ng_exlibris/2003-10-23/5_babchenko.html.

Krentz, Jayne Ann, ed. *Dangerous Men and Adventurous Women*. Philadelphia: University of Pennsylvania Press, 1992.

Kyle, Chris with Scott McEwen and Jim DeFelice. *American Sniper: The Autobiography of the Most Lethal Sniper in U.S. Military History*. New York: William Morrow, 2012.

La Capra, Dominick. *Writing History, Writing Trauma*. Baltimore: Johns Hopkins University Press. 2001, 2014. E-book.

Lib.ru. *Chechenskaia voina*. http://www.lib.ru/MEMUARY/CHECHNYA/. Accessed February 18, 2021.

MacFarquhar, Neil. "For Russia, Links between Caucasus and ISIS Provoke Anxiety." *New York Times*, November 20, 2015. https://www.nytimes.com/2015/11/21/world/europe/for-russia-links-between-caucasus-and-isis-provoke-anxiety.html.

Mills, Dan. *Sniper One: On Scope and Under Siege with a Sniper Team in Iraq*. New York: St. Martin's Press, 2007.

Muratov, Dmitry. "The Chechen Wars Murdered Russian Democracy in Its Cradle." *Guardian*, December 12, 2014. https://www.theguardian.com/world/2014/dec/12/-sp-chechnya-russia-war-anniversary.

Murphy, Paul J. *Allah's Angels: Chechen Women in War*. Annapolis, MD: US Naval Institute Press, 2010.

Myers, Steven Lee. "Hazing Trial Bares a Dark Side of Russia's Military." *New York Times*, August 13, 2006. https://query.nytimes.com/gst/fullpage.html?res=9E06E7DF173EF930A2575BC0A9609C8B63&pagewanted=1.

Navalny Live. "Debaty Live. Navalny vs. Strelkov." YouTube Video, 1:22:24. July 20, 2017. https://www.youtube.com/watch?v=cjbQdbJUibc.

Nemzer, Andrei. "Fleita v rasstroennom orkestre." http://www.ruthenia.ru/nemzer/jurnaly12_02.html. Accessed June 20, 2017.

Pankowska, Ewa. "Mir umiraiushchei derevni v tvorchestve 'novykh realistov.'" *Studia Wschodniosłowiańskie* 15 (2015):109-132.

Politkovskaya, Anna. *A Dirty War: A Russian Reporter in Chechnya*. Translated by John Crowfoot. London: The Harvill Press, 2001.

———. *Is Journalism Worth Dying For? Final Dispatches*. Translated by Arch Tait. Brooklyn, NY: Melville House, 2011.

———. "Anna Politkovskaya Raw in War Interview." RAWinWAR. YouTube Video, 3:38. https://www.youtube.com/watch?v=HHfu5vXSbzk. Accessed February 2, 2021.

———. *A Russian Diary*. Translated by Arch Tait. New York: Random House, 2007.

———. *A Small Corner of Hell: Dispatches from Chechnya.* Translated by Alexander Burry and Tatiana Tulchinsky. Chicago: The University of Chicago Press, 2003.

———-. "Tsentrovoi iz Tsentoroia. Interv'iu s Ramzanom Kadyrovym." *Novaya gazeta,* June 21, 2004. http://politkovskaya.novayagazeta.ru/pub/2004/2004-051.shtml.

Prilepin, Zakhar. "Artist Alyosha, aktyor Oleksii." *Svobodnaya pressa,* July 4, 2017. http://svpressa.ru/war21/article/176184/.

———. "Boets Kuban' i Zakhar Prilepin o vazhnosti very." ФОМА ТВ Live. YouTube video, 4:36. https://www.youtube.com/watch?v=EmKcGSp8B-8. Accessed May 4, 2022.

———. *Chai s Zakharom.* Царьград ТВ. YouTube video. https://www.youtube.com/watch?v=XBBykBfz8c8. Accessed May 4, 2022.

———. "Chechnia." Захар Прилепин. YouTube video, 1:23. https://www.youtube.com/watch?v=adn3l2d0IN0. Accessed May 4, 2022.

———. "Donbass kak strashnyi son burzhua." APN.com. http://apn-nn.com/145136-donbass-kak-strashnyj-son-burzhua.html. Accessed September 12, 2017. This site has been shut down.

———. *Donetskii format.* YouTube playlist. https://youtube.com/playlist?list=PLWcMfv8vMRNlC8xgRKWNLJ9ID7DDIfPx5. Accessed May 4, 2022.

———. "Krovososy." *RenTV,* July 18, 2017. http://ren.tv/blog/211112.

———. "My—luchshe, chem vlast'." *Komsomol'skaia pravda,* February 1, 2020. https://www.kp.ru/daily/27086.5/4158233/.

———. "Naval'nyi ili bunt sytykh detei." *Uroki russkogo,* no. 117. October 28, 2020. YouTube video. https://youtu.be/9sXnI9XoYq0. This video has been set to "private."

———. *Obitel'.* Moscow: AST, 2014.

———. *Patologii: Roman.* Moscow: Ad Marginem Press, 2009.

———. "Russkii chelovek primirilsya sam s soboi." *Svobodnaia pressa,* July 5, 2017. http://svpressa.ru/society/article/176116/?rss=1.

———. *Sankya*. Translated by Mariya Gusev and Jeff Parker, with Alina Ryabovolova. Ann Arbor: MI: Dzanc Books, 2014.

———. Twitter feed. https://twitter.com/ZaharPrilepin. Accessed October 15, 2019.

———. *Uroki russkogo*. https://youtube.com/playlist?list=PLSgy-gJ-dkS9QmKvn-FoHK9EwSNTIBofF. Accessed May 4, 2022.

———. http://zaharprilepin.ru/. Website. Accessed July 6, 2017.

———, YouTube channel. https://www.youtube.com/c/PUSHKAOFFICIAL/featured. Accessed May 12, 2022.

———. "Zakhar Prilepin: 'Liudi prosto ottachivaiut umenie ubivat', eto vkhodit i v zadanie nashego batal'ona." *Telekanal Dozhd'*, July 12, 2017. https://tvrain.ru/teleshow/interview/zahar_prilepin_v_donetske_i_krymu_proizoshla_antiburzhuaznaja_revoljutsija_i_eto_spaslo_rossiju-439279/.

———. "Zakhar Prilepin: My ne khotim byt' terpil'nymi voiskami." *Komsomokaya Pravda*, July 12, 2017. https://www.youtube.com/watch?v=HW--GRDspkI.

———. "Zakhar Prilepin v sostave Nizhegorodskogo Omona, Chechnya, 1996." https://www.youtube.com/watch?v=r9kwlmziczg&t=374s. Accessed May 4, 2022.

Pustovaia, Valeriia. "Guy with a Gun—Condemned Man, Rebel, Writer: 'War' Prose by Young Authors." *Russian Studies in Literature* 42, no. 2 (Spring 2006): 61–93.

Roudakova, Natalia. "Journalism as 'Prostitution': Understanding Russia's Reactions to Anna Politkovskaya's Murder." *Political Communication* 26, no. 4 (2009): 412-29.

Rounding, Virginia, quoted in "Power and the Proper Soldier." *Guardian*, November 17, 2007. https://www.theguardian.com/books/2007/nov/17/featuresreviews.guardianreview.

Rudalyov, Andrei. "Obyknovennaia voina: Proza o chechenskoi kampanii." *Zhurnalnyi zal*. http://magazines.russ.ru/druzhba/2006/5/ru14.html. Accessed May 15, 2022. Originally published in *Druzhba narodov* 5 (2006): n.p.

Russia's Open Book: Writing in the Age of Putin [documentary hosted by Stephen Fry, narrated by Juliet Stephenson]. Intelligent Channel. https://www.youtube.com/watch?v=vRPDM7OTMrI. Accessed April 14, 2021.

"Samoi populiarnoi knigoi v bibliotekakh Mosvky stal roman Prilepina." *Gazeta.ru*, December 16, 2015. https://www.gazeta.ru/culture/news/2015/12/16/n_8020739.shtml.

Sokolov, Sergei. "Nesmeite govorit', chto ubiistvo raskryto." *Novaya gazeta*, October 7, 2016. https://www.novayagazeta.ru/articles/2016/10/06/70089-ne-smeyte-govorit-chto-ubiystvo-raskryto-video.

"'Spravedlivaia Rossiia' ofitsial'no ob"edinilas' s dvumia partiiami." *Interfaks*, February 22, 2021. https://www.interfax.ru/russia/752106.

Stepanian, Karen. "Metaphysics and Physics." *Russian Studies in Literature* 52, no. 1 (2016): 67-90.

Tal, Kalí. *Worlds of Hurt: Reading the Literatures of Trauma*. Cambridge: Cambridge University Press, 1996.

Taylor, Alan. "Photos: A Second Weekend of Protests in Russia." *The Atlantic*, February 1, 2021. https://www.theatlantic.com/photo/2021/02/photos-second-weekend-protests-russia/617888/.

Tsvetova, Natal'ia. "Zakhar Prilepin: 'Nochi net.'" *Opera Slavica* 26, no. 1 (2016): 5-15.

"Ubiitsu Politkovskoi podvela pechen'." *Novaya gazeta*, June 13, 2017. https://www.gazeta.ru/social/2017/06/13/10719695.shtml.

Uchitel, Aleksey, dir. *Vos'myorka*. Russia: Kinokompaniia "Rok," 2013.

Van Reet, Brian. "A Problematic Genre, the 'Kill Memoir.'" *New York Times*, July 16, 2013. https://atwar.blogs.nytimes.com/2013/07/16/a-problematic-genre-the-war-on-terror-kill-memoir/.

Waszkielewicz, Halina. "*Patsanskie rasskazy* Zakhara Prilepina. Novyi avtor, novyi geroi." *Slavica Wratislaviensia* 153 (2011): 443-51.

Index

www.ingramcontent.com/pod-product-compliance
Ingram Content Group UK Ltd.
Pitfield, Milton Keynes, MK11 3LW, UK
UKHW021646250226
468387UK00007B/91